M000113470

Try Anything Twice

Try Anything Twice

Josh Jango

CyberActive Media®
www.cyberactivemedia.com

Copyright © 2011 by Josh Jango.

All rights reserved.
No part of this book may be reproduced or transmitted
in any form or by any electronic or mechanical means,
including photocopying, recording, or information
storage or retrieval system, without permission
in writing from the publisher, except by a reviewer
who may quote brief passages in a review.

This is a work of fiction. Names, characters, business
organizations, places, events, and incidents either are the
product of the author's imagination or are used fictitiously.
Any resemblance to actual persons living or dead,
events, or locales is entirely coincidental.

Cover design: Al Teter.
Cover photographs copyright © iStockPhoto®.
Cover photos used for illustrative purposes only
and any person depicted in the cover art is a model.

Published in the United States by
CyberActive Media, PO Box 698, Edmonds, Washington 98020

ISBN 978-0-9834526-6-9

4 3 2

www.joshjango.com

for Mark VonWald

spirit brother

You made it all possible.

Special thanks to Rick, Maura, Brock, Bill, Lynn, and Doyle

Chapter 1

AWAKENING

OUR LITTLE GROUP was already sloshed, but my boyfriend wanted another drink, so I was elected to fight the crowd. I told him I got the last round, but he said, "Shut up, Josh. Just get the fucking drinks."

So I circled around the dance floor and made my way through the noisy crowd, the pounding music, and the smell of fresh sweat and cologne.

I liked the look of the club. It had a carnival-like décor, classy and clean, with a big dance floor and a flashy light show. And plenty of people.

This nightclub, and the city itself, was new territory for all of us. My friends and I had just driven up to St. Louis for the weekend.

As soon as I got in line for drinks, I noticed the guy at the bar. He was sitting on a stool, looking out over the crowd.

Intriguing.

And more fascinating the longer I watched him. There was just something extraordinary about him. He was handsome, but in a unique way, his way. His own look. I could see right off he was at peace with himself. He radiated warmth, tranquility.

I liked his attitude, too: self-confident, but not arrogant. He was relaxed, casually dressed, fit looking, and sexy as hell. He just drew me in, everything about him. Even his baseball cap.

A totally straight-looking guy, in a gay bar. Well, by that time of night it was an after-hours bar; half the people there were straight. So he probably was, too, but I just couldn't keep my eyes off him.

He saw me looking and smiled. Smiled so warmly, so openly, I smiled right back at him before I had time to get embarrassed.

Then I realized; he must have mistaken me for someone else. Or maybe not? Maybe I knew him from somewhere. It was strange. No, I was sure we'd never met.

He was so hot. Way out of my league. I'd embarrass myself if I tried to speak, but he was very nice to look at.

The line for drinks kept moving up, and I got closer and closer to him. Finally I was at the head of the line, standing right next to him. I didn't want to make an ass of myself, so I tried not to stare.

I heard him say, "Hi."

I knew he wasn't talking to me, but I turned around and looked at him anyway. He was smiling, looking at me.

My face started burning; I knew I was blushing. I said, "Hey." Where in the hell did I know him from? Nowhere. I'd never met this guy before, but it was like I was meeting the brother I never knew I had.

Crazy. And he looked at me the same way, like he knew me.

The bartender came, I ordered my drinks, and I looked at him again. He was still smiling. Was he waiting for me to say something?

His eyes were beautiful. He looked directly into mine, shamelessly. It felt like he was looking beyond my eyes, deeper. Like he could see me better than I saw myself, and he approved.

I didn't know what to say. Hell, I'm shy to begin with, but he was so perfect I couldn't talk. I tried to, but my mouth wouldn't work right.

"Having a good time?" he said.

"I guess." I glanced over at my friends to see if they were watching, but they were looking the other way.

"Could be better, huh? I know how that goes."

"No, I'm okay. Uh . . . ."

"Just okay?" He had a questioning look on his face, as if he really wanted to know.

I said, "Listen, I know this sounds stupid, but do I know you from somewhere?"

"Naw. Not yet. But we can change that, dude, no problem." He grinned. "Anything's possible."

I thought, *Damn. Where were you two years ago?*

Or maybe I said it out loud. He said, "What?"

"Uh, sorry, just talking to myself. Wished I met you two years ago, is what I said."

"Oh." He smiled. "Dude, no. You're thinking of some other alternative universe. In this one, we don't meet until now." He grinned. "No time like the present, right?"

The bartender came back and set down my drinks. I paid him, picked them up, and faced the guy again. I couldn't go, not now. Not yet.

He said something to me, but I didn't hear it because the music was so loud. I said, "What?"

He leaned closer. "I said you look a little bit out of place here, dude."

"Oh, jeez." I looked at my friends again. Now my boyfriend, Fred, was watching me, and he didn't look too happy, but that wasn't anything new. "You're the one who looks like you don't belong here," I said.

The guy laughed and said something, but I didn't hear it.

"What'd you say?"

He got close to my ear and said, "This isn't the greatest place to talk, is it?"

"No," I said. "The music's too loud for that."

"We could go outside," he said. "Wanna hang out for a while?"

This was getting more unreal by the minute. I started to look behind me to see if he was talking to somebody else.

He gently touched my arm. "You're a shy one, aren't you?"

Yes, I thought, *and I can't believe you're hitting on me.*

"You don't have any reason to be shy," he said. "You're on fire, dude."

It was so hopeless. "I'd better get back to my friends."

"Come on," he said. "I'll bet we have a lot to talk about."

"My boyfriend's over there, probably wondering what happened to me."

"Fuck." The guy looked that way and then he turned back to me. "Well, maybe next time?"

I nearly choked on that. "I'm not from around here."

"Yeah, I know."

"You come here a lot?"

"Nah. Once in a while on a Friday, that's about it," he said. "You sure you don't want to hang out? Might be our only chance."

I looked at my friends again. My boyfriend looked angry now. "I'm sorry, but I can't."

"Okay. That sucks, but okay."

"Thanks, though."

"Can't say I didn't try."

I wanted to shake his hand, but my hands were full. Kissing him was out of the question, but I wanted to. I said, "Um, take it easy."

"Always." He grinned.

I turned my back on a miracle. It was just incredible.

—

I CARRIED THE DRINKS to my friends, feeling like I just closed the door on the only sunshine I'd seen in years.

My boyfriend wanted to know what took me so goddamn long, and who the hell I'd been talking to. Beyond that, nobody seemed to care if I was there or not, except Tony. He asked what was wrong.

How could I tell him? I barely knew, myself. I was stunned. I felt like I'd been slapped in the face. Or woken from a coma. Tony watched me, worried.

Now I knew what I'd been missing for the last two years. Friendship. Love.

Hell, I was lonely. Love-starved lonely. That's not supposed to happen when you have a boyfriend, is it? Fred wasn't happy with me; I already knew that, but now I realized I wasn't getting much out of this relationship either. Abuse, that was about it.

He seemed nice, at first. We met in '83, two years back, after I moved to Memphis. I thought I'd found the partner I'd been longing for. My first boyfriend. Then he asked me to move in with him.

I don't know why, because after I moved in, nothing I did was good enough for him. People actually asked if he ever hit me. I told them no, but I knew he wanted to. Sometimes it *felt* like he was hitting me. He could project that.

Nobody ever came right out and asked me, does Fred even care about you? I couldn't have said. And that was nuts; I should know. There shouldn't be any doubt.

When I was standing there that night, in that bar in St. Louis, that's when I finally realized the truth. I *would* know if he cared. It wouldn't be a mystery; I'd know.

Tony asked me again what was wrong. As soon as I could, I explained it to him, but I don't think I did a very good job of it.

Our group left the nightclub soon after that. Without me seeing my new friend again. I wish I'd been the one driving that night, I would have stayed there longer. I would have found that guy and thanked him for giving me a reality check. Maybe I could have talked to him some more.

Meeting him changed everything.

The next day my boyfriend left me.

And this time, by god, I made up my mind we were going to stay that way. He didn't know it yet, but the partner from hell was history.

5

Chapter 2
NIGHTCLUB ACROSS THE RIVER

THE REST OF FRIDAY NIGHT went smoothly enough, but Saturday morning Fred had one of his blowups, angry at me for something he'd done himself hundreds of times.

Fred had pulled this trick before. He'd get furious over something stupid and tell me we're through; then after I'd been properly abused, he'd consent to take me back.

This time he left me behind in St. Louis. Fred and the other guys drove back to Memphis Saturday morning without me.

That nailed it. I'd rather be single. I wasn't going to play that meek little suck-up role again. I got along without him before I met him; I could do it again.

I went back to the club that night.

I knew it was probably hopeless, seeing that guy again; he wouldn't come back for another rejection. The previous night had been my only chance, and I missed it. But I went anyway. It was my last night in St. Louis, and I probably wouldn't be coming back. Memphis was three hundred miles away.

This time I stayed completely sober. I looked at everyone in that place that night, at least a half-dozen times, looking for that guy. No luck. If only I'd gotten his phone number.

It was really packed that night. Everyone was having a grand old time, ready to party all night long, but I was feeling more lost and lonely and frustrated by the hour. I finally gave up. I hadn't found him, and I hadn't connected with anyone else. I went outside to get some fresh air.

A couple dozen people were out there, gathered in groups in the parking lot. I wandered around a bit.

I ended up next to a couple of guys talking to each other who ignored me earlier, inside the club. But I wasn't trying to pick them up. Not at first. I just wanted someone to talk to.

I knew I didn't measure up; either one of these guys could probably get anybody he wanted. But hell, you never know unless you try, especially when it's that late at night.

The one named Chris was doing most of the talking. He was saying how horny he was, how much he'd really like to smoke some bud and let somebody suck his dick for hours. He said he was so damned horny, he didn't even care if it was a girl or a guy, just as long as the dude took plenty of time to really worship his dick and then take his load.

He looked my way when he said that, so I asked him if he was talking to me. He looked me over like he hadn't noticed me before. Then he went back to talking to Mark, the other guy.

Chris said he already knew where he could get some good weed; now all he had to do was find a cocksucker who had a little money to pay for the weed, since he already spent all his money in the bar.

I was about to say something, but then a third guy stepped up out of nowhere and joined in. He was kind of a goofy-looking guy, but I mean that only in a good way. That's the type I like best. Very attractive, in his own unique way. And sexy, too. He wore glasses, but that only added to his charm.

Tall, lean, and solid, and he moved like an athlete. The same age as the rest of us: early twenties, maybe younger. He looked familiar; I thought for a minute that I knew him from somewhere. But then I realized he looked like an actor in a movie I'd seen recently. He was hotter than the other two guys; the kind I figured probably wouldn't bother to look at me twice.

He jumped right into the conversation, and I was out of my league again. People like that, who find it easy to talk and who know what to say and stuff, just make me nervous, and then I can hardly think of anything good to say.

7

But I wanted to be part of this group anyway, even if they didn't think much of me. Hell, sometimes people surprise you. One of the guys, the third who joined in, gave me a chance to talk a few times. And he stood right next to me, too. So I felt like part of the conversation, even though I didn't say much. Let's face it, I'm kind of shy. Especially around strangers.

They were saying the night was still young and they wanted to go somewhere and party some more, smoke some weed and hang out and maybe see where that would go. At least that was my impression. Sometimes when nobody listens to what I have to say anyway, my mind wanders. I miss some of the conversation.

I was paying more attention to the guy standing next to me. His hair was dark brown, just like his eyes, with a light growth of hair on his arms. He was just a little taller than me, like about six foot one or six two. His feet were a little smaller than mine.

I wished I could look at his bare feet. I would have loved to see him naked. He stood there talking to the other two guys, relaxed and alert, while I looked him over.

Then I heard Chris say, "Well, fuck it. You driving? You following me, or what?"

Now, people say I'm pretty smart. Book smart, maybe, but I'm not street smart. Sometimes I miss stuff that's obvious to other people, and then I feel really stupid. I wanted to be part of what these guys planned, so I said, "My car's parked right over there, what are you driving?"

Chris looked at me like I was dirt. He said, "Who the fuck are you?"

That sure busted my bubble. All of a sudden I felt like I was two inches tall, and even that wasn't small enough. I wished I could flat-out disappear. I almost got teary-eyed.

Then the guy standing next to me, the third guy, said, "He's with me." He looked me over, and then he said, "Dude, you're my ride, okay?"

That made me feel better. At least one of them wanted me there. I said, "Sure."

He told the guys, "We're cool. The more the merrier, right?"

"Fuck merry," Chris said. "But as long as you've got some cash, I guess it's okay."

I wondered if I missed something. But hell, it all seemed pretty innocent. Chris wanted to get high, and he didn't have any money. Or maybe they were going to play poker. Whatever they had planned, I was up for it, even if it didn't include sex. Hell, I was lonely.

Chris pointed to his car and said, "That's me, the red Cadillac." He started walking for it, with Mark following right behind him.

My new buddy said to me, "Let's go, Professor. Lead the way."

—

WE WALKED A COUPLE OF ROWS OVER and I pointed at my car, a yellow '73 Mustang. "That's mine," I said.

"Dude! Nice. How's it run?"

"Needs a tune-up, but it got me here from Memphis just fine."

"Yeah, I knew you were from the South," he said. "From Memphis, huh?"

"Well, not originally, but, yeah, I moved there two years ago, in '83. I just came up here for the weekend, with my friends." I unlocked the doors and we got in. I started the engine.

"Go ahead," he said. "Drive around. He'll be waiting for us. You okay to drive?"

"Huh? Oh, sure. I didn't drink tonight."

When the guys in the raggedy old Cadillac saw us, they pulled out. Chris rolled down his window. "We're headed out near the airport. Try to keep up," he said.

We left the parking lot, and in a couple of minutes my new friend and I crossed over the river into Missouri and followed them north on I-70.

The two of us didn't talk at first. He was staring out the window.

His hair was short, and he had that soft, unshaved facial hair like a young kid just reaching manhood. It looked so sexy. I wanted to run my fingers through it. Or, better yet, rub my face in it. Ha! Fat chance of that.

He turned to me and said, "Where are your friends? I didn't see you with anybody tonight."

"They're probably back in Memphis by now. Long story. We had a falling out this morning. For the last time, too, as far as I'm concerned. Over something stupid."

"Bummer."

"Yeah, but hell," I said, "it's probably for the best. Actually, it's a big relief. Except now I'm out on the street when I go back. I'll have to find some other place to live."

"That sucks."

"Yeah. It's really bad timing, too."

"Now listen," he said. "Chris said we're going over to his place, right?"

"Yeah, okay."

"He said he could sell us some weed, you caught that, right?"

"Not exactly, but yeah, that's cool. We're gonna get stoned and hang out and stuff, right?"

"Yeah, bro, I'm definitely up for that. Not with them, though. Or is that what you wanted? To be with them?"

"Well, yeah, whatever. I mean, I want to hang out with you guys. Whatever you do is fine with me."

"Really?"

"Yeah, sure."

"What if we decide to rob a bank, you want in on that?"

I laughed. "No, definitely not."

"Um, how about if we shoot up some heroin? You wanna join in?"

"Hell, no. I'm not that stupid."

"Okay," he said, smiling. "Just testing you."

"Did I pass?"

"Yeah, so far. It's not over yet, though." He looked out the window. "I still haven't figured out what those guys are up to."

"What do you mean?"

"Oh, nothing. Look, this might sound weird, but if they pull off the road, like, somewhere away from other houses, a dark road or someplace isolated, where nobody else can see us, then we're not gonna stop. Okay? They drive into some woods or something, we don't stop, we don't follow, we stay on the road and drive right on by and keep on going. Okay?"

"Jeez, what do you think they might do?"

"Nothing, probably. I don't know. It's just good to be careful, alright?"

"My god, I thought you knew those guys! What am I getting myself into?"

"Dude," he said. "Don't you think you should have thought of that earlier?"

I just looked at him.

"Hey," he said, "just teasing, bro. Don't worry. We'll be all right. Just stay on your toes, and do what I tell you, okay?"

"Okay."

"I'm just a cautious guy. Probably worrying for nothing. They said they're driving up to the north end of town. We'll be all right. If anything looks shady we'll take off and forget it."

"Works for me."

"They're gonna sell us some herb. Let me handle it, okay?"

"Alright."

"Do you want to go halves? How much money do you have?"

"Um, eighty or ninety dollars. Maybe more."

"Christ, don't let them see it. Don't let them know you've got more than, say, twenty-five. Put the rest in your shoe or something. How much did you want to spend on weed?"

"Depends on how good it is."

"The good stuff's going for forty, forty-five dollars, unless you just want a dime bag or something."

"That's cool."

"Tell you what; let me hold all but twenty-five of your money. They see you've got lots of cash, it'll just be something else for us to worry about."

"Okay. I'm glad you're gonna handle it. I'm no good at haggling with prices."

"No problem. Then, if it costs more than that, I'll throw in the difference, and let them think it's out of my own pocket."

"Okay."

"So, anyway, dude, where'd you live before Memphis?"

"Washington, D.C. is where I grew up. Maryland, actually. The D.C. suburbs."

"I've been there," he said. "In eighth grade, on a field trip. We went to the museums, down on the mall. We saw all sorts of stuff. A dinosaur, T-Rex. And an old locomotive, and a model-T Ford that looked brand new. It was awesome. Lindbergh's plane was there, too, the Spirit of St. Louis."

"The Smithsonian. Yeah, I've been there lots of times. I love that place."

"You grew up there?"

"Yeah."

"You miss it?"

"Yeah. I do. Memphis isn't like I thought it would be."

"Oh, yeah? How's that?"

"I thought it would be all friendliness and southern hospitality, you know, and upbeat and real, but it's not upbeat. Not Memphis. People are nice enough, I guess, but I never expected there'd be so many rules."

"Look, they're getting off at this exit."

"Yeah, I see them."

"So, what do you mean, rules?"

"Well, like, customs, I guess. Stuff you're supposed to do, and say, and think. And stuff you're not supposed to do. And they think you're weird if you don't act the way they do. I don't know, it's hard to explain."

"I know what you mean. Tradition. Some places, that's all they have."

"Sometimes I feel like a prisoner there. No matter what it is, there's only one way to do it, and if you don't do it their way, then it must be 'cause your momma didn't raise you right, and if your momma didn't raise you right, then you must be trash. Or a Yankee."

"Oh, hey," he said, "we're into the neighborhoods now. I guess they're not gonna take us into the woods and kill us after all."

"Yay, we get to live another day, huh?"

"Don't get cocky. The night's not over yet."

"Look," I said. "They're parking."

"Christ, the street is crammed full of cars. They took the only spot. No, wait, there might be one at the end of the block. Yeah."

So we parked, locked up the car, and walked back to where the other guys parked.

They were standing next to the Cadillac, waiting. We followed them into some ugly apartments that reeked of ancient food smells. Decades of corned beef and cabbage, maybe, or sausage and sauerkraut.

We walked upstairs to the second floor, to a door at the end of the hall.

—

HALF AN HOUR LATER, we walked out again.

13

My friend put his finger to his lips; we silently walked down the stairs and outside. I didn't say a word. We walked to the car, me in the lead and him watching out behind us. Neither one of us said anything until I pulled out.

"Sweet," he said. "We did it."

"Did we?"

"Hell yes. We got out of there alive, which is always good, and not only that, we scored some good shit. Here, smell this stuff." He opened the bag and held it up to my nose.

"Wow."

He sealed it up again and stuffed it into his pants pocket. "You've smoked bud before, haven't you?"

"Yeah. Sinse, you're talking about, right? Seems like they just keep finding ways to make weed better." I smiled.

"Nothing like progress. Hey, get on route 170 up here, okay? It'll be quicker. It's the next right." He showed me the way and then we were headed south.

"You really knew what you were doing in there," I said.

"What do you mean?"

"That grey stuff he tried to sell us. I thought he was gonna pull a gun on us when you told him it was bug-sprayed oregano."

"Nah. He knew it was crap. He just acted angry so we wouldn't see how shamed he was."

"Is that why he sold us the good bud so cheap?"

"It wasn't cheap. He still made a profit. Assholes like him take as much as they can, but they'll settle for less if they have to."

"Well, anyway, we got some good weed, for sure."

"Yeah," he said.

"We grew some pot in our garden, one year."

"Really? Outside of your house? Damn, bro!"

"Yup. We had a whole row of huge, healthy, dark green plants," I said. "We had to cut them back a few times, just to keep them from growing taller than the corn."

"You had more balls than I do. That was risky."

14

"We didn't even know the difference between male and female plants. But that pot was as good as anything else we'd ever smoked. It got you high as a kite."

"Yeah, that's the cool thing about weed. You don't have to grow it like a pro to get a good high."

"I lost my job because of that pot, though."

"Really?"

"Yeah. I was stupid and mentioned it to a guy at work; told him I could give him a little sample of our crop if he wanted it. Give, not sell. We didn't grow it to sell it. He turned around and told my boss I was growing pot. Next thing I knew, I was fired."

"Damn."

"That was back in Maryland, a couple years ago. But I just lost my job again, a week ago in Memphis."

"No way," he said. "What happened?"

"Well, I didn't get fired this time, just laid off. Same result, though. No paycheck coming in."

"What are you gonna do?"

"Oh, I'll find something else. Might take me a couple weeks," I said, "but I'll find something, no problem."

"Damn."

My stomach was growling. "I'm hungry. You want to stop somewhere and get something to eat? Is there any place open this late?"

"I'm starving," he said. "There's an all-night diner up here; I'll show you. Take route 40 going east, and then it's four exits over."

We made it to the restaurant and sat down in a booth. Then we were drinking coffee and looking at each other across the table, waiting on our bacon and eggs and pancakes.

—

"SO, REALLY," I said, "you never met those guys before today?"

"I've seen them around, but no, I never talked to either one of them. Never wanted to."

"I thought you knew them."

"Why'd you think that?"

"The way y'all talked together," I said.

"What do you mean?"

"You know, relaxed, informal. Up front."

"Same way I talk to everyone, bro."

"Oh. Well, that's good. That you didn't know them. They seem like trouble."

"They're dicks, is what they are. I won't be messing with either one of them again, trust me."

"I thought you must have known them. They weren't gonna let me come along if you hadn't spoken up."

"Uh, actually, that's not true," he said. "You were the one they wanted from the start, dude. It was me who finagled my way along."

"What? No way!"

"It's true. They were checking you out, earlier. I heard them talking."

"I didn't think they even noticed me. What'd they say?"

"Mark pointed you out to Chris and said you tried to pick him up. Chris said you hit on him, too, and he was thinking about going for it. Then Mark said maybe you'd like the idea of both of them together."

"That's so weird. I did try to talk to them, both of them, inside the club. But they acted like I wasn't worthy."

"Yeah, they think they're hot shit. But you did get their attention."

"Why didn't they talk to me, then? Inside? I don't get it."

"Maybe you weren't their only, uh, possibility."

"Oh."

"Or maybe they were playing hard to get."

16

"Oh, jeez. I've never understood that hard-to-get stuff. Why do people do that?"

"Well, it's not complicated. People generally tend to want whatever they can't get. It's human nature, I guess. The sly ones in this world know that, and take advantage of it. It's just one of their tricks."

"Oh." I pondered that for a minute. "But isn't that kind of pointless? If I want them only because I can't have them, then once I have them, I wouldn't want them anymore, right? Not unless I wanted them anyway, in which case they didn't need to play hard to get in the first place."

"Well," he said, "that makes sense, as far as it goes. But there's another part of it, too. People tend to put a lower value on something if they get it too easy. If some stranger comes up to you and says, 'here, take this, I want you to have it,' then you're probably gonna wonder what's wrong with it. Or what's the catch. Either way, you'll probably think it's not worth much, because if it was, the person wouldn't have given it to you so cheap."

"Okay," I said. "I get it. So you're saying it works the same way with people. If somebody's too easy, you might get the wrong idea and think he's cheap."

"You got it. Except it wouldn't be the wrong idea. If somebody's too easy, then by definition he *is* cheap."

He put it so simply, and it made such plain sense, and it applied to me so intimately, it was like a revelation. My god, I'd been cheap for as long as I could remember. Maybe my entire life.

We sipped our coffee.

"Have you been to St. Louis before?"

"No," I said, "this is my first time here."

"How'd you find out about Faces?"

"Oh, it was on a list of bars in a gay travel magazine. A 'must-see.' That's what sold my friends on it. I liked the fact that it was a mixed bar, straight and gay."

Josh Jango

"Yeah, me, too," he said. "Those jock and frat bars, with all the uptight guys acting macho and the women trying to look like bimbos, those get old really fast."

"Most gay bars are the same way," I said. "Too many clones, trying to fit in and look like everybody else."

"I like a more relaxed atmosphere," he said. "That bar we were at tonight, the women who go there are more down to earth. And more fun, too."

"I believe it. That place is like a small town gay bar. All sorts of different people go to the same place and mix together. There's such a big variety, nobody tries to fit in. Everybody relaxes and has a great time, just being themselves."

"Yeah," he said, "it's better that way."

"The only difference is, the gay bars in small towns don't have straight people. In a small town, straight people wouldn't set foot in a place like that. They'd be afraid of ruining their reputations."

"Nobody has to worry about his reputation where we were at tonight," he said. "That place is hip enough, anyone could survive being seen there."

We drank our coffee.

"So you were inside the club, tonight? What time did you get there?"

"Oh, I don't know," he said, "about one, I guess."

"I was in there, too. We didn't talk to each other, did we? No, of course not. I'd remember."

He looked at me kind of funny. "No, we didn't talk, not to-night."

Then the waitress brought our food, and not a minute too soon. I was famished.

18

Chapter 3
A PLACE TO STAY

WE SAT THERE IN THE BOOTH and chowed down on our food, too busy to talk. After we took the edge off our hunger, he took a sip from his coffee and said, "Where are you staying? At a hotel?"

"Yeah. It's already paid for, might as well use it. It'll give me a chance to figure out what I'm gonna do when I get back to Memphis."

We were silent again, eating our food.

Then I said, "You think they were planning to rip me off?"

"Yeah, it looks that way," he said. "But with those two, who knows? They might have thought they could fuck you over in more ways than one."

"Jeez! I guess it's a good thing you were there."

"You're damn right it was! God, I hate it when people take advantage of somebody like you. The bastards."

"Somebody like me? What do you mean?"

"Aw, man, you know."

"No, really, what do you mean, someone like me?"

"You know," he said.

"No, tell me."

"Innocent."

"Innocent? Me?"

"Yeah, you. And naive. But that's not necessarily a bad thing. Hell, dude, all you need is someone to look out for you. Teach you something once in a while. Look, you don't know it, I can tell you don't know it, but you're special, okay? You are. Guys like you don't know how special you are."

"Uhh . . . I'm special 'cause I'm stupid?"

"You're not stupid. You're smart. You just haven't learned all there is to know about how things work, that's all. There's no shame in that. And you're humble, too. You're handsome as hell, dude, and I'll bet you don't even know it, do you?"

"Oh, jeez. I'm not handsome."

"Yeah you are. Good-looking, and kindhearted, too. Hell, you must have figured out by now that I like you. Haven't you? Fuck, no way was I gonna let those guys take advantage of you."

"How'd you know they even wanted to?"

"Oh, uh, well, you know. It was kind of obvious."

"Not to me, it wasn't. How'd you know?"

"Dude, I don't want to hurt your feelings."

"Just tell me, okay? How am I gonna learn anything, if nobody tells me the truth?"

"Alright, but don't get mad, okay? Those kinds of guys, when they look at you, that's what they see: a person to victimize."

"But why? Why me?"

"Okay, well, see, you're this innocent, trusting guy, and lonely, right? And you're in a gay bar, and you're not looking at the ladies, so it's a dude you want. Maybe you just want to fuck some dude's brains out, or maybe you want to fall in love. Not a damn thing wrong with that, either way, but those guys, when they see someone like you, they see an opportunity.

"They've done jail time. Both of them. Probably not big time, just the local lockup, piddley-shit stuff, but it never fails. After spending a year with the other inmates, they come out of there with a different outlook. Before they went in they were harmless jackasses. Now it's a game to see who they can rip off. Maybe they think they won't get caught, or maybe they don't care if they do.

"When they see you, they see an opportunity. They'll be who-ever you want them to be, and then they'll take whatever they want. They're smart enough to know how to snag you, and they know how to keep from scaring you off. And they're dumb enough to think it won't all come back in their faces one of these days."

I just stared at him. I didn't know what to say.

"Alright," he said, "so, tell me I didn't hurt your feelings, okay? I don't want you mad at me."

"Nah, you didn't." But it did hurt. I felt so stupid.

"Yeah," he said, "I did. I'm sorry. Just telling it like it is. You know, telling you how guys like that think."

"You didn't hurt me. It's knowing people like that are out there, that's what hurts. I really want to believe the world is a good place. But guys like that make it seem so evil."

"Oh, there's good out there, believe me. Look at us, right? We're good, aren't we? But there's bad out there, too. You just have to learn how to tell one from the other."

"I've never been good at that."

"Takes practice. And it helps to have a good teacher along the way, too."

"You knew those guys were bad, way before I did. How did you know? How could you tell?"

"Oh, you pick up on things."

"What kinds of things?"

"Little things. How people treat the waiter or the bartender; that's a sure sign. See if people are honest when they don't have to be; that's a good one. I learned something about you that way, bro."

"About me?"

"Sure. If you observe somebody and pay attention, you learn. For instance, look at what the guy thinks is funny and what's not. That'll tell you something. And you can watch how he looks at people, how he looks at you. Whether he looks people in the eye. Little things."

"You can tell just from stuff like that."

"Sure. The basics, anyway. It's like a big equation. One thing might not tell you much, but when you add things together, you start coming up with an answer. And like I said, practice helps. I've had lots of practice. I didn't have much choice about that," he said.

"Much choice about what?"

"I got an early start in the real world. My mother gave me up for adoption when I was four years old. Let me tell you, nobody wants to adopt a four-year-old. They want little babies. So, yeah, I got plenty of practice, early on, telling the good from the bad in this world."

I stared at him, but I couldn't think of anything to say. That *anyone* could be abandoned like that was awful, but especially this nice guy sitting in front of me. I pictured him, four years old, going for a ride to some place he'd never been before, and the look he must have had on his face when his mother left him there and walked out of his life—my eyes started to water.

"It wasn't all bad," he said. "You hear horror stories about orphanages, but I wasn't completely deprived. Hell, I guess I got my share of love from one place or another. There are plenty of kids worse off. My mother probably did me a favor. Think about it. Would you want to be raised by someone who could give you away like that and never want to see you again?"

I thought about it. "No, I guess not."

"Anyway," he said, "your turn. What were your folks like?"

"I hardly knew my dad, even though he was right there the whole time I was growing up. We never did anything together. We never talked about stuff. He'd come home from work, read the paper, eat dinner, and then go up to his room. He never showed any affection, not to us kids, and not to my mother, either. I guess we were supposed to think paying the bills was the way he showed his love, but it sure didn't seem like love to me."

"Did he ever beat you?"

"No. I guess I'm lucky for that," I said. "He never even spanked us, except for when my mother made him do it. Usually it was my mom who did the spanking."

22

"What's she like?"

"She was nice, most of the time, but it was kind of insincere. She had this idea that God was watching her every minute, so she had to be nice."

"I've heard of people like that," he said. "They claim to believe in an all-knowing god, and yet they think they can easily fool him with superficial lies."

"She had a lot of gall, for sure. If you asked her, she'd tell you God talked to her on a regular basis. She and God had a very special relationship. God *confided* in her. My mother knew exactly what God thought about everything."

"Jesus. No wonder your dad was so withdrawn."

"I grew up thinking my family was normal. I didn't figure out how weird they were until after I left home."

"You have any brothers or sisters?"

"Three older brothers and one younger sister," I said.

"Wow. Big family."

"I guess."

We ate our food in silence.

"Did you and your brothers sleep together?"

"Yeah, sure," I said. "Always. I shared a bed with one brother or another the whole time I was growing up."

"Were you okay with that?"

"Oh, sure. I liked sleeping together. Hell, it was about the only time we touched each other. I miss that. I looked up to my brothers. It was nice, sleeping with one of them every night."

My friend nodded his head.

The waitress came by and topped off our coffee.

"The orphanage was my family," he said, "but it all seems so long ago. I've been through a lot of shit since then." He finished his food and took another sip of his coffee. "What the hell, it's all character building, right? You've heard that cliché: What doesn't kill you makes you stronger. It's true."

That sounded odd coming from somebody who was probably younger than me. He didn't look more than nineteen or twenty years old. I couldn't think of anything to say about it, so I didn't say anything. I just kept looking at him.

He kept looking at me, too.

Then he said, "My name's Ziggy, what's yours?"

"Josh." We reached across the table and shook hands.

"Good to meet you, Josh." We laughed.

He was quiet for a while.

Then he said, "You need a really small place to stay?"

—

IT WAS AN ODD QUESTION. I didn't understand for sure what he meant. Stay in St. Louis?

"I thought maybe you could use a place to stay," Ziggy said.

"I was planning on going back to Memphis."

"Yeah, I know. But do you really want to? You're looking forward to it?"

"Hell, no. I'm dreading it. I don't know what I'll do when I get there. I don't have any place to live, and no job. It's definitely fucked up."

"But other than that, you like living in Memphis?" He looked at me with those brown eyes. He already knew the answer.

"No. I don't. I hate it."

He just nodded his head.

I sighed. "Memphis is okay, I guess. Some people like it just fine. Some people think it's great. Not me. I don't care if I ever go back."

"Well, maybe St. Louis would suit you better, dude. If you give it a chance. Hell, I love it here."

"Maybe. I don't know. Either way, I'd still have to find a job."

"That's what I'm saying, bro. You have to find work, either way, so why not find it here?"

"But I don't even know anybody here, Ziggy."

"You do know somebody here. You know me."

"Well, yeah, but—"

"And my place is small, but it's big enough. You can stay with me, bro. If you want to."

I was speechless. I just stared at him.

"You need a place to stay, right?"

"Sure," I said.

"We could split the rent."

"Jeez, you're serious." Suddenly it all seemed so right, it almost scared me.

"Come on over and take a look, at least. We can sleep on it, if you want," he said. "You're dropping me off anyway, aren't you? Stop in and check it out."

I was too tired to think straight. "Okay," I said. Why not?

—

SO WE DROVE OVER to his place.

"It doesn't look like much from the outside," he said, "but it's a pretty decent place. Suits me just fine." Ziggy was right; it was just an old brown-brick building shaped like a box, nothing fancy.

I parked the car and we went in. They kept the entry door locked, so that was a good thing, and the entrance hall was clean. At least somebody was taking good care of the place. And there were some nice touches here and there.

No elevator, but a little exercise never hurt anybody. We walked up two flights of stairs to the top floor. His apartment was the back one on the left. He unlocked the door and we went inside. Hardwood floors. Nice. He wasn't kidding about it being small. It was just a one-room studio apartment.

It wasn't crowded, though. He kept it neat and uncluttered, and the only pieces of furniture he had were an armchair, a little coffee table, a twin-size bed, a dresser, and a bookcase crammed full of books. That was it.

"Have you read all those?"

"Nah, not yet," he said. "Well, some of them." He sat down on the bed and took off his shoes and socks. "When I finish a book, I don't keep it unless I think I might read it again. Otherwise I trade it in at the second-hand bookstore. So, yeah, most of those, I haven't read yet. Except for my favorites, down there on the bottom shelf. Do you read much?"

"Sure. All the time."

"Way better than TV."

"Yeah, I don't watch TV much." I looked around. "Wow, you don't even have one, do you?"

"Nah. And I don't want one, either. It's better this way."

"I won't argue with that."

"Hang on," he said, "I have to piss like a race horse. Go ahead, sit down if you want." He padded into the bathroom in his bare feet, leaving the door wide open. He stood at the toilet and let out a long, noisy stream of piss.

There wasn't anything much to see from where I was, except for his butt, because he faced directly away from me. I watched him anyway. I liked the casual informality, and I was glad he wasn't concerned about privacy. It was intimate and familiar. Got my imagination going, too. And I liked the way his baggy jeans hung on his ass.

He peed for a long time. Finally he let the last few drops fall, shook it a couple times, and stuffed it back into his briefs. He turned around as he zipped up, and fastened his belt as he walked out. "So," he said, "what do you think? I told you this place is small."

"I like it. It's definitely small, but it isn't crowded."

"We'll get another armchair if you move in," he said. "There's room for it."

I looked around, trying to figure out where the hell we'd put another bed. It just didn't seem possible, no matter how we rearranged things. Unless maybe we could put the bookcase and the dresser in the closet. "Are you sure you want me in here? It'll be pretty crowded," I said, "with another chair, and another bed."

"Another bed?"

"Well, yeah. I'll need a bed."

"What for? We can share mine."

I looked at him in astonishment.

"Sure," he said. "When I was in the orphanage we used to double up all the time. In beds smaller than this. I'm used to it. You slept with your brothers, right?"

I got an instant hard on. I was amazed at what he was suggesting. It was just a twin-size bed. If we tried to sleep in it together, we'd be all over each other. My god . . . .

"I don't mind," he said.

Yes, absolutely, I liked the idea of sleeping with him. Jeez, the guy was so incredibly sexy, and he didn't even try to be. But as far as I could tell, he was straight. That could be a problem. "Uh, I don't know," I said. "Are you sure? What if I move around in my sleep, wouldn't I wake you up?"

"Nah. I sleep like a rock. You won't wake me. But if I do wake up it's no big deal; I'd just go right back to sleep again, no problem."

He was serious! I tried to figure out how this could possibly work. Picturing him and me together in that bed was making my dick harder than it ever had been, and it was telling me in no uncertain terms, *Go for it!* But, fuck, I didn't even know of any married couples who slept in such a small space together. Not on a daily basis.

A straight man and a gay man trying to share a tiny bed like that, it seemed certain to be a disaster. Or at the very least, outright torture. My dick said, *Yes!* but my brain told me there was no way in the world I could even fall asleep with the constant hard-on I'd have.

There wasn't a snowball's chance in hell of it working. I knew that without a doubt. The smartest thing to do would be to tell him so, but when I went to say it, the words that came out instead were, "Well, hell. I guess I'm a pretty sound sleeper, too." I almost slapped my hand over my mouth.

"There you go," he said. "It might take you a day or two to get used to, but you'll see. You'll like it better than sleeping alone. I know I always did."

I looked around the apartment, wondering if I could really make this place my home. Assuming, that is, I could survive the sleepless nights.

It was tempting. Ziggy seemed to be living such a simple, un-complicated life. I could find a job, come home to a cozy little place, eat dinner, talk with my roommate about life, and read, read, read to my heart's content. And then, in bed, I'd have a warm, friendly body to cuddle up to. Well, maybe not cuddle. No, I was dreaming, there. A straight guy wouldn't want to cuddle, but even just sleeping next to him would be nice.

A simple life. It was what I'd been wanting, since day one. Not a lonely life, not a complicated life, just simplicity, and a friend. "I do like this place," I told him. "And we seem to get along with each other. We'd probably make good roommates."

"I think so," he said. "I have a good feeling about you, dude. Believe me, I wouldn't invite just anybody in here. Most of the time I'm kind of a loner. Not on purpose, it's just worked out that way so far, I don't know why."

"Being alone has its advantages," I said. "You seem like you're really at peace, living here."

"Well, I definitely don't mind living alone. I'm fine with that. A person's got to be his own best friend. And I do some of my best thinking when I'm alone. But I don't think you would mess that up. Hell, it would be cool to have someone to talk to. I can always go for a walk in the park if I want to be alone. I do that a lot already."

I didn't know what to say. He seemed so sure we would get along. I wished I could be that certain.

"It's no biggie, though, either way," he said. "I just thought maybe you needed a place to stay."

"I do. Somewhere. It's just so unexpected. St. Louis? My god, it's like picking out some random place on a map, blindfolded."

"Dude! St. Louis is not random. It's where you're standing right now, in case you hadn't noticed."

"Yeah, but until a few days ago, I never even thought of *visiting* St. Louis, let alone living here."

"And it's not just 'some place on a map,' either. It's a good place to be. And dude, you have friends here."

"I do?"

"Yeah, of course. At least one, anyway. Me." He looked at me, smiling. Waiting for an answer. As if people make snap decisions about moving from one city to another all the time.

"My god, Ziggy." He was so sure of this. "I'll tell you one thing; I've never met anybody like you before. And probably never will again. Fuck! I just don't know."

"Suddenly you miss Memphis, huh?"

"No, I hate Memphis. Okay, look, I know I'd be stupid to pass this up. Maybe I'm afraid, uh, afraid something might come up later to change your mind. After I move in."

"Okay, dude, well, I know what we could do. How about if we try it out for a week? You stay here for a week, and we'll see how it goes. That ought to give us plenty of time to see if it's gonna work. At the end of the week, either one of us can back out of the deal, no explanation needed, no hard feelings. What do you say to that?"

"That sounds a little more realistic. But, um, look, Ziggy, there's one thing I want to make sure you know, okay?"

"What's that?"

"You know I'm gay, right?"

"We already talked about that, bro. Yeah, I know. So what?"

"Well, I just wanted to make sure you remembered. Since we'd be sleeping together and all."

"I'm not worried about it if you're not. You're not gonna try and fuck me in my sleep, are you?"

"No! Of course not. I would never do that!"

"Okay. I didn't think you would."

"Alright. Just making sure you knew. I mean, most straight guys would be worried about their reputation, if nothing else."

"Dude. We might as well get one thing clear right now. I don't *care* what other people think. What matters is, I like you. The hell with what people think. I thought it would be cool to share this place with you. If *you* want to."

"How about if I let you know tomorrow?"

He just looked at me.

"Ziggy, let me think about it, okay?"

"Yeah, yeah," he said. "Okay. Sure, think it over."

"I'll let you know tomorrow."

"But you know what'll happen."

"What?"

"You'll think of all the reasons why you shouldn't."

He was right. Knowing me, I'd probably talk myself out of it.

"Ziggy, I want to say yes. I really do. It's just that I hadn't even thought about living anywhere but Memphis until now. My god, I'm so tired right now, I can't even think. I need to get some rest before I decide something important like that."

"Okay, that's cool, bro. I understand. It was just a thought."

"I'll think it over. I promise. I'll come back tomorrow and give you an answer."

"Cool," he said. "Hey, we had a little adventure tonight, didn't we? It's hard to believe we only just met this weekend."

"Yeah, I know. It almost feels like we're old friends."

Try Anything Twice

"You never know," he said. "Maybe we are. Maybe we were friends in a past life. If you believe that kind of stuff." He laughed.

"Yeah, maybe," I said.

He looked out the window. "Damn, Josh, look outside. It's getting light out already. It's time we put it to bed, I guess."

"Yeah, I'm keeping you up. Sorry. I should have left a long time ago."

"No, man, it's been good."

"I hope I don't fall asleep driving."

"Where's your hotel?"

"Down near Six Flags, off I-44."

"No!"

"It was the cheapest place, when we were making reservations. And it was near the amusement park."

"Do you even know how to get there from here?"

"Yeah, I think so. If I can find the interstate I think I'll be alright."

"We're pretty close to I-44, but . . . fuck! That's a long drive, dude. Even if you don't get lost. Hell, why don't you sleep here?"

"Oh, man, are you serious? I don't know, all my stuff is at the hotel. Clean clothes, my toothbrush, all that stuff."

"You can use mine, no big deal. I just did my laundry; I've got plenty of clean clothes you can wear. We're about the same size. I might even have a new toothbrush around here somewhere."

"Well, uh, I don't want to put you out." Damn, my boner was back in full force, stiffer than ever.

"Hell no, it's no trouble. Don't worry about your car, either, nobody'll bother it. Unless you left a camera in the backseat or something. It's locked, isn't it?"

"Yeah, it's locked."

"Cool! Hey, you want to do a couple of bong hits before we go to bed? I just remembered, we've got weed."

"Um, sure. If I can stay awake that long."

31

"Take your shoes off, bro. Get comfortable." He reached into his pants pocket. "I owe you some money, too. Here, take the weed. My bong's up in the last cupboard, top shelf, behind the cereal. You get it ready while I find you some fresh underwear and stuff. In case you want to shower."

"Do I need one?"

"Yeah, dude, you stink! Just kidding. No, you don't need one, Josh. I just thought you might want one."

"I'd love a shower. I'll sleep a lot better." *That is,* I thought, *if I can sleep at all.*

I went into the kitchen and found the bong in the cupboard. When I came out, Ziggy was at the dresser, taking out some white briefs and a black t-shirt.

"Here's your new suit, Jackson," he said, grinning. "Now I'll see if I have a toothbrush for you."

He went into the bathroom, while I went back and put some water in the bong. It was a nice one; a small, short, ceramic bong, with random colors. It looked like it was dropped and glued back together a couple times, but I guessed it would do the trick, or else he would have replaced it. I set it on the counter and loaded it up.

He came out of the bathroom waving a red toothbrush. "We're in luck, Josh. Brand new, just took it out of the package. Too bad; I know you had your hopes set on using mine."

I laughed. "Yuck."

"Just kidding. You probably aren't kinky at all."

"Oh, I don't know about that," I said. "I guess it depends on what you call kinky."

"Oh, really? Hmmm. Well, uh, let's see, are you into gerbils? Now, that I would definitely call kinky." He laughed. "Not that there's anything wrong with that. Except for the gerbil, that is."

"No, nothing like that," I said. "By the way, you know that's just a made-up story, right? Nobody ever did that."

"Yeah, I kind of figured as much."

"I think I've got this bong ready. Wanna go first?"

"Yeah, sure. Hang on a sec. I'm gonna put your toothbrush in here next to mine, okay? Mine's the blue one." He poked his head into the bathroom; then he came back out to the kitchen.

"Nice bong," I said.

"Yeah, I really like it. Thank god for superglue, huh?" He picked up the lighter and fired it up. He cleared the whole bowl, with breath to spare. He handed it back to me and I refilled it while he got a couple of sodas out of the refrigerator. "Want some cola?"

"Sure."

"It's my greatest weakness. I must drink at least four of these a day."

I looked at the label on the can. "RC Cola? Don't see that around much."

"Yeah, I know. Most people like Pepsi or Coke, but RC is my favorite, call me weird."

"You're kinky, that's what you are."

He laughed. "Yeah, I guess I am, why deny it? Makes life interesting, though."

"You have any other kinky secrets I need to know about?"

"Nothing, really. I guess I'm actually pretty tame. No surprises."

"Damn," I said. "I'm disappointed."

"But hell, I'll try anything twice."

"For real?"

"Sure, why not? Life's too short as it is," he said. "No need to make it boring, too."

It was my turn to take a hit on the bong. I fired it up and burned all of what was in there. I blew out my smoke and handed it to him. "Here you go. I want to see how you like to load it."

"Thanks. Don't mind if I do." He pulled apart a bud and packed it into the bowl. He put in more than I did.

"Just letting you know," I said, "it doesn't take much to get me stoned. Two hits does it. Three good hits of stuff like this and I might get dizzy on you."

"I get stoned easy, too," he said. "I've gotten stoned plenty of times on just two hits. Three does it better, though, for me, or even four. No more than that, though. I'd much rather be zonked and trippin', than zonked and wiped out."

Ziggy flicked the lighter and started drawing smoke from the bong. He'd filled it deeper than I had, but he kept drawing until the bowl was clear. Smooth.

"Damn, a real pro," I said.

He blew out the smoke and said, "Nah, just lots of practice. You, too, bro, I can tell."

"Yeah. Four years, anyway."

"Is that all? I had you figured for a regular stoner. You started later than me, then."

"Well, nobody I knew in high school smoked. The summer after graduation, though, me and my friends turned on. It opened new worlds, let me tell you."

"I'll bet."

"So, when did you start?"

"Oh, hell," he said, "when I was ten or eleven years old."

"No way!"

"It wasn't with the kids at school. It was this one boy at the orphanage. He got me stoned sometimes."

"Okay."

"I liked it, too. All it took was two hits on one of those thin little joints him and those other guys smoked, and I was buzzed. Then he would take advantage of me."

"What?"

Ziggy laughed. "That's just what he called it."

This was getting interesting. "What did you call it?"

"Oh, well, I don't know. Not that. He was always so gentle. I'll always remember that. Gentle. Careful. He was always careful not to hurt me. I didn't mind."

"You didn't mind?"

"Nah. Hell, I wanted him to. It felt good. He made sure it felt good. Maybe he was using me, but he was teaching me, too. He was teaching me how to fuck. And I was paying attention, bro."

I just stared at him.

"I use his tricks on every girl I meet, if I can. It works. I might not go out much, and maybe I don't always find what I'm looking for, but when I do, I can throw a righteous fuck into a girl. First I make sure she wants it, and then I make sure she enjoys it. That's the way I was taught. They remember it afterwards, I guarantee." He laughed.

"Damn!" was all I could think of to say.

"You learn a lot, in an orphanage," he said.

"I didn't know," I said.

"So, yeah, I learned to appreciate the sacred cannabis plant at an early age. It's your hit," he said. "Did I fill it up too much?"

"No, this is good. I can handle this."

"Famous last words."

It was a bigger hit, but I finished it like an expert. "That ought to do me. I'm feeling stoned already."

"You sure? We've got plenty," he said.

"Yeah, I'm sure."

"I'm gonna take a couple more hits; then I'm gonna take a shower."

"Yeah, I want one, too," I said.

"Then take your shower now, Josh. You go first. Take a long one, I don't care. I'll go after you're done."

"Uh, okay, sure."

"Help yourself to ever what you see in there. Holler if you need anything."

"Okay. Thanks." I took off my shirt and my undershirt, and looked around for someplace to put them. I lay them across the back of the chair. I stripped off my socks and my jeans while Ziggy watched. Then I stood there in just my underwear.

"You work out, huh?"

"Yeah," I said. "For the last year or so. You can tell?"

"You kidding? You have some nice muscle tone, dude. It shows." He was looking at me, all over.

"Thanks." I felt myself start to blush, and my cock began to rise, in what I knew was the start of irreversible and highly exponential growth. "Okay, shower time," I said, and I dashed into the bathroom.

I shut the door before I had time to think about whether I should leave it open. Damn. What if he had to use the bathroom while I was in the shower? Was I rude to shut the door, in his apartment, when it was just us guys anyway? Earlier, when he peed, he left it open. Was I being rude?

I figured it would be a bit weird to open the door now, after closing it. And anyway, my cock was rock hard, pretty much out of control. There was no way to miss the gigantic rod pushing out in my shorts. Once I dropped them, it would be sticking out like a batter at the plate. I didn't know who would be more embarrassed, him or me, if he saw me like this.

So I left the door closed, stripped off my briefs, and stood buck naked at the toilet, trying to pee. Hard thing to do, in the state I was in.

All of a sudden he opened the door and said, "I forgot to tell you, the hot water is really, really hot, so be careful, okay?"

"Okay," I said. I stood there with my back to him, naked as a jaybird, looking down at my hard dick, trying to act natural, wishing I could pee, picturing him standing there behind me.

Half a minute later I still hadn't heard the door close, so I looked back over my shoulder to see if he'd left. He was still standing there, looking at my naked butt. He saw me looking at him and smiled. Then he went back out the door. He left it open a little, like about three inches.

Okaaay, I thought, *I'll just slide sideways over to the shower, get in, and close the curtain.* Jeez, the shower curtain was transparent plastic. I'd be on full display if he peeked through the door.

Then I thought, *Fuck it. Damn it to hell anyway, he knows I'm gay. If he has a problem with seeing me with a hard on, then that's his problem, not mine.*

So I turned the water on, made sure I wasn't going to get second-degree burns, and stepped in.

It felt so very, very good. I was tired, and the hot water relaxed me so much I could have fallen asleep on the spot.

If I wasn't so horny.

I decided to jack off right then and there, and the sooner the better. If I didn't beat off, I'd never be able to sleep.

My dick was already leaking pre-cum, so I closed my eyes, pictured a blurry scene of him and me, one of us inside the other, who cares which was which, fucking like rabbits gone wild, and it only took a couple of strokes before my body started jerking and my cum started splashing against the shower wall.

Right then he pushed the door open wide again and walked right in, stripped down to just his briefs and a t-shirt. He said, "I'm gonna lie down for a couple of minutes while you finish in here, okay?" He saw my stiff cock standing straight out, still dripping, and said, "Nice one, dude." He paused a few seconds, looking at it, and then he said, "Anyway, I might be asleep by the time you get out, okay? I think I'm gonna skip the shower. I'm nodding out, big time."

"Okay," I said.

"Don't worry about waking me up. And if I hog the bed too much, just push me over to one side or the other, okay? It won't bother me."

"Okay."

"Goodnight," he said.

"Night," I said.

Then he was gone out of the bathroom, and I was left standing under the wonderful, soothing hot water, wondering if all of this was really real.

I stayed under the shower another five or six minutes, but I got so relaxed and drowsy, I almost fell asleep standing up. That was all I needed, to fall over and knock my brains out. So I turned off the water and opened the curtain.

I dried myself off, wrapped the towel around me, and brushed my teeth. I could see him, his full length stretched out in the bed, halfway under the covers. I turned out the bathroom light and went out there.

He was still wearing his t-shirt. Probably his underwear, too, because I didn't see them lying around anywhere. His jeans were crumpled up on the floor next to the bed.

He wasn't snoring or anything, but the regular rhythm and the long breaths told me he was asleep. At least for the moment.

I let the towel fall to the floor, and put on the briefs and t-shirt he left out for me.

I turned out the kitchen light, pulled back the covers, carefully climbed over him, and slid in beside him.

Chapter 4
NUTS

THERE WAS JUST BARELY ENOUGH ROOM. Ziggy was lying on his side; I squeezed in next to him, like one spoon behind another. There wasn't any other way to fit.

This was nuts. The bed was designed to sleep one person, not two. I was wedged between him and the wall. I didn't have any choice; I had to lie up against him. My cock was pressed up against his butt.

I didn't exactly mind that, of course. It was fine with me, except I was worried about what he would think when he woke up and felt my marble-hard dick pressing against the crack of his ass. Didn't I just shoot off ten or fifteen minutes ago? My cock was already stiff and hard again.

I didn't want to spoil this. There was already a trust between us. We had connected somehow, and I didn't want to mess that up. I'd never met anyone like him before. He talked about me being innocent, but he had his own kind of innocence. Or at least a willingness to remain optimistic, even in the face of all that he had been through.

I figured it would be best to keep the touching to a minimum, especially when a boner was involved. After all, he was straight. Wasn't he?

Hell, it didn't mean anything, that he let some guy fuck him when they were both just kids. Guys will try just about anything they can think of, at that age. Then they grow out of it, no big deal.

Not only that, I had it on the best authority some straight guys like butt sex. Some straight guys like having their wives strap on a dildo and give it to them that way. Adults. So it wouldn't make a guy gay, to like that.

No, Ziggy was straight, I was sure of that. And no matter how gay-friendly he was, he wouldn't like waking up to some creepy pervert who couldn't keep his hands — or his dick — to himself long enough to let a guy sleep.

The bed was close to the wall, so at least I didn't have to worry about falling off. But I had to do something about my wood. Not only for his sake, but for mine. At this rate, pressing up against him like this, pretty soon we'd have a gummy mess down there, and it would only get worse as the night went on.

So I managed to turn onto my back, to free up the hard rod in my briefs. This wedged me even tighter between him and the wall, but he didn't show any sign of waking up.

My movement was restricted, but I loved the contact. The only thing between his bare flesh and mine was the thin cotton fabric of our t-shirts and briefs, and that just made it more sensual. This was almost as good as us wrapping our arms around each other. Very erotic.

With him so sound asleep, I was briefly tempted to explore a little and get even more intimate, but no, I couldn't do that. No telling what he would think if he woke up with my hands all over him, but one thing for sure, if we were going to be roommates, we had to trust each other. And that included trusting each other not to take any liberties.

So I lay there on my back, still buzzing a little from the weed, listening to Ziggy slowly breathe in and out, wondering if my dick would ever go down, wondering if I could ever fall asleep, wondering whether I deserved to have such a friend as him. Time would tell.

My gut feeling was, what was really required of me was a pure heart, and to trust my instincts. In other words, just be myself, and hope that I was right for him. If we were meant to be friends, then we would be.

The only thing that bothered me was the wall. I didn't think I'd be able to sleep, wedged in that way. I needed a little more room.

He said if he hogged the bed I should push him to one side or the other. *It's okay to put my hands on him,* I thought. *And push on him. He told me that's what I should do.* So I tried.

First I nudged him, thinking he might move over a bit on his own, but no, that didn't work. He wasn't going to wake up, so I pushed harder, trying to move him myself. But he was heavy, at least 180 pounds. Solid, lean, strong. I could move him a little, but when I let go, he'd just fall back to where he was to start with.

So I lay there. Thinking.

What I was supposed to do? I really didn't think I could sleep this way. It was like being crammed inside a shoebox.

Couldn't budge him. And even if I *was* able to move him, it couldn't be far, or else he'd fall right off the bed.

He said in the orphanage they doubled up in bed like this all the time. So, how the hell did they do it? There had to be some key element I was missing.

They were younger then, and smaller, maybe that was it. Even a few inches in size would have made a big difference.

But no, he said their beds were smaller, too.

My balls hurt from my cock being hard so long. I reached down and squeezed my stiff rod. Felt good to feel it, but damn, I needed to get off again, bad.

He was sound asleep, and I was wide awake. I thought about what he said. Don't worry about waking him up; that's what he said.

Jeez, if pushing him didn't wake him up, nothing would.

What the hell, I thought. *I'm taking it out.*

I pushed my briefs halfway down to my knees and let my big boy out, standing straight up and throbbing. It felt good to let it free. I pushed the briefs down farther and managed to kick them all the way off. I pulled my t-shirt up all the way past my nipples.

It wouldn't take much to get me off, so knew I'd have to go easy. I wanted to prolong this. I wanted this to last at least, say, two or three minutes. So I held the shaft gently. I squeezed it just a bit, but not near the head.

Oh, it felt so good. I was lying on my back, and I closed my eyes. Gently, slowly, I stroked. I knew I couldn't last long; I needed this too much, and I was right on the edge.

But then I felt the bed move, so I let loose of my dick and pretended to be sleeping, thinking maybe Ziggy was waking up.

What was he doing? Slowly, I opened my eyes and looked over at him.

He was dreaming! His feet twitched a little, in rhythm. Maybe he was dreaming he was running. Then his feet slowed down, and his hands started twitching.

I had a brief, wicked idea of putting my cock in his twitching hand, but I gave that up immediately. It was just a momentary fantasy. I continued to watch him.

His hands stopped moving, and then the only sign of him dreaming was the movement of his eyes underneath his closed eyelids.

And soon enough, even that stopped, so I thought maybe his dream was over. I was about to grab my stiff cock and resume my own rhythm when he sighed and moved his arm. It was one of those moments when a person changes his position in his sleep without waking up.

He had been on his side, facing away from me, but then he rolled my way, to lie on his back, and he landed right on top of me!

He didn't wake up. He was still asleep. He had most of my body pinned underneath him, including a few stiff inches of the base of my dick. Forget about moving my left arm; it was completely immobilized under his back. His right arm was stretched out across me and the weight of it held down my own right arm. The top half of my hard cock was sticking out from underneath the underwear-covered cheek of his ass.

I was in a panic. I could hardly move.

At least my balls weren't being crushed. The panic gradually subsided, and I started to enjoy it.

It was an impossible situation, but not without its perks. I was thrilled to have the weight of him on top of me. Lying next to him was exquisite; lying under him was heavenly. His head was on my shoulder, his back and shoulder lay across my chest, his ass was on my dick, and one of his legs was draped over mine. Even our feet were touching. He had one of his soft, smooth bare feet resting snugly in the curve of one of mine.

Yes, he was lying right on top of me, and so what if he was asleep? It didn't keep me from loving it. And my dick felt like it was about to explode, not so much from his weight but from the ecstatic pleasure of his ass pressing against it.

I was okay with lying there like that all night. I was savoring the incredible intimacy, which was so totally unexpected and so unlikely to happen again. But surely he would soon move off of me, back onto his side again, because this couldn't be comfortable for him. Could it?

Meanwhile, the juices were now flowing non-stop out of my dick, which was still pinned down by the cheek of his ass. I was incredibly aroused. Pre-cum leaked in a steady flow out of my cock, dripping onto my belly.

We lay there like that, neither one of us moving, for at least five incredibly long minutes. I didn't want this to ever end.

The slick pool of clear fluid on my belly started overflowing and dripped down into the crevice between us. It created a growing wet spot in his t-shirt, but I couldn't do anything about that. If I tried to move, he might wake up, and I didn't want him to wake up.

Another minute or two went by. I was so very close to shooting off. This was almost like torture, but I was in heaven. Never in my adventures with ejaculation had I ever managed to prolong this state of ecstasy for more than half a minute, but here I had been close to the edge for something like ten minutes, and hard as a rock for even longer than that.

Suddenly he lifted his arm and scratched at the wet spot in his t-shirt. His wrist brushed up against the slippery underside of my dick head, inadvertently stroking the most sensitive part of my cock, and I gasped at his touch. That did it. My pre-come ecstasy instantly became a full-blown eruption. I groaned as rapid-fire spurts of cum shot out of my cock. Most of them landed on my face; one hit my forehead, the next one landed on my mouth. I moaned as my face and neck got covered with cream.

Maybe it was my loud groans that woke him up. Or maybe it was my hips jerking while I shot my load. He lifted his head, groggy from sleep, and murmured, "What happened?"

I hadn't even finished coming yet. I groaned as my cock spat out one last shot.

Then he realized he was on top of me. He rolled off of me and stood up, beside the bed. "I didn't hurt you, did I?"

"No," My body jerked one last time. Then I raised myself up on one elbow. "You didn't hurt me."

He rubbed his eyes, and then he reached down and felt the slick, wet spot in his shirt. He raised his hand up to his face and looked at the sticky stuff on his fingers.

I was so embarrassed. "You were lying right on top of me," I said. I got up and sat on the side of the bed.

He sat down next to me. "Sure," he said. He was still waking up. He rubbed the slippery tips of his fingers together. "That's part of sleeping together."

"I didn't know."

"Well, of course it is. Not usually like that, though. Most of the time it's side by side. You know, up against each other."

"Okay." I looked around for something to wipe off my face with.

He said, "I must have been out of it, huh?"

"Yeah, you were definitely dead to the world." I pulled my t-shirt off and wiped my face. My underwear was still somewhere under the covers. My cock hadn't gone down yet, and a few drops of cum were still oozing out. I was naked and covered with jizz, but I didn't even think about it until Ziggy said something.

He pointed and said, "What's that on your chin, dude?" Then he looked down lower and focused on my hard cock.

I looked down, and there was a long strand of cum stretching almost to the floor.

"I guess I got some on my face," I said. I was so embarrassed.

His puzzled look turned into a grin, and then he laughed. "Dude! You just shot your load?"

"Yeah." Damn. I dreaded this moment. Now he would think I was a sex-crazed pervert and he wouldn't want to have anything to do with me. Chalk one friendship down the drain. "I couldn't help it, Ziggy!"

"Hey. No problem, Josh. Don't even worry about it." He reached over and picked up the wet towel I left on the floor. "Here you go, dude. Clean yourself up and we'll go back to sleep, okay?"

I took the towel from him and said, "I'm sorry." I finished wiping the cum off my face and neck, and cleaned off the end of my dick.

"Sorry for what?"

"Getting out of control. You must think I'm a pervert or something. Jacking off in bed."

"No, man. No. Look, Josh, what, you think I've never jacked off in bed before? There's nothing perverted about that. Don't worry about it."

"You sure?"

"I'm sure."

"You're not just saying that?"

"Josh. Look. You're a dude, right?"

"Sure.

"That's what guys do. We get horny, we get hard. It's a guy thing. When we get hard, we wanna come. It's pretty basic."

"I guess."

"You guess?"

"Well, okay, I know you're right, but still, I feel like I was out of line. I didn't mean to be doing it in front of you."

"Why, you think I've never seen a guy shoot off before?"

"No, I don't think that, but . . . ."

"Josh, you're worrying too much about this. We're gonna be roommates, dude. You can jack off anytime you want. It won't bother me."

"For real?"

"For real."

"You won't think I'm, like, a sex-crazy faggot or something?"

He frowned. "Josh, don't call yourself that. Anyway, hell, it's a *guy* thing, not a gay thing. All of us guys are sex-crazy, when it comes right down to it."

"You think so?"

"I know so." He laughed. "So, listen, don't be surprised if it works the other way, too, okay? If we're gonna be roommates, you're gonna see me with a hard dick sometimes, too. I'm not gonna cover up, just because you're around. I don't believe in that shame stuff. That's fucked up, people being ashamed of their own bodies."

"Damn," I said. "You sure are open-minded, for a straight guy."

"Who says I'm straight?"

"Oh, jeez, Zig. You like women. Duh."

"Well, yeah, that much is true. But anyway, I've thought about it a lot. And it doesn't make sense, any other way. Hard cocks and bare skin are part of life. Why be ashamed of something so natural?"

"Well, I'm glad you see it like that," I said. "I was wondering if I was gonna have to sneak around here, pretending like I don't ever get horny around you."

"Nah. Just be yourself, Josh. That's all I expect. And hell, I guess I ought to warn you, if you're gonna be running around here jacking off all the time, it'll probably make me horny, too. I'm not gonna be ashamed of that, either. You're not gonna have a problem with that, are you?"

"No!" This was too much. "Of course not. You can jack off in front of me anytime you want."

Ziggy laughed. "Now why am I not surprised to hear you say that?"

"And," I said, "if you want to bring a girl home, just let me know, okay? I'll disappear for a while, no problem."

"I appreciate that, Josh. I might take you up on that sometime. You're a gentleman and a scholar."

"I don't know about that," I said. "But I'm tired, I know that much. I feel like I haven't slept for a week. Yeah, let's go back to bed."

"Excellent idea."

"And this time, I want you to show me how we're supposed to get a good night's sleep in that tiny little bed, without somebody falling off the edge."

"Aw, hell, it's easy, dude. As long as you don't mind cuddling up together."

—

I REACHED AROUND under the bedcovers, feeling for my underwear. I had to put something on, for god's sake, if I was to retain any sanity while snuggling up with this lovable, handsome, sexy, straight boy.

I found the briefs and put them on. Then I picked up the t-shirt I'd used to wipe off my face, but it was still wet with cum.

So I decided what the hell, I don't need a shirt; I'll be warm enough.

Ziggy said, "Which side you want, inside or out?"

"Umm, inside, I guess. If it's okay with you. I'm afraid I'll fall off, if I sleep on the outside."

"Sure, either side is fine with me. You wouldn't fall out of bed, though, Josh. I wouldn't let you, bro."

I pulled the covers down and got into the narrow little bed. "This is gonna take some getting used to."

"Piece of cake," he said, smiling. "You'll get the hang of it." He slipped in beside me and pulled the covers up over us.

A minute later he sat up again. "Hold on, I'm taking this wet shirt off." He slipped the t-shirt over his head, tossed it on the floor, and lay back down again, wearing nothing but his briefs.

It was crowded, but that was fine with me. This was his show. If he wanted to sleep with us snuggled up against each other, I wasn't going to complain. We were touching each other. It was intimate.

I asked, "Um, am I doing this right?" My hand was on his bare shoulder, and my back rested on the wall.

He was facing the same direction, with his back to me. "I've got plenty of room, Josh." He turned his head and looked back at me. "Dude, are you touching the wall?"

"Yeah."

"Bring yourself up closer. Lie up against me, Josh, not the wall."

I scooted up a little, and my body fit snuggly up against his. Like spoons. Nice. "Like this?"

"Yeah, that's better."

My cock pressed right up against the crack of his ass, with only our thin cotton underwear in between. My bare chest and abs were pressed right up against his naked back. My cock was getting hard again. "Are you sure?"

"Yeah." He wiggled his butt slightly, just enough to tell me he felt my cock back there and he didn't have a problem with it. "Now put your arm around me."

I moved my hand from his shoulder and reached my arm all the way over in front of him. He took my hand into his hand, held my arm to his chest, and let out a sigh. "Yeah," he said. "Hold me up close, Josh. Like I'm your teddy bear. Did you ever have a teddy bear?"

"Yeah, I did. My mother made clothes for it and everything. I loved that bear."

"Did the bear sleep with you?"

"Sure. Always."

Ziggy sighed again, and held my arm closer.

I asked him, "Did you have a teddy bear? In the orphanage?"

"No. I didn't bring him with me. My mother didn't tell me to. I don't know what ever happened to him."

"Ziggy," I said. "That's so sad."

"Yeah."

Neither one of us talked for a couple of minutes. The more I thought about it, the crueler it seemed. I wondered if he was crying, because I was fighting back tears. The thought of him like that, abandoned and utterly alone, it was awful. I hugged him closer to me.

He moved his hands to change his grip, but continued to hold my arm close. "It wasn't so bad," he said. "At the orphanage, we had each other. They let us double up. Especially the little ones. We had each other."

The two of us lay there, awake, without talking, holding each other.

I had so many questions for him, but all of that could wait.

After a while, his breathing became deep and steady, and I remember thinking how good it was, to have him sleeping so peacefully in my arms.

THEN IT WAS SUNDAY AFTERNOON, and we slept in, in a major way.

It was a very restful sleep, for me. Sometimes I feel tired when I wake up, but that day I felt great. I could have leapt out of bed, but I didn't. I was happy to stay right there, with my arm around Ziggy.

I had some pleasant dreams, but I couldn't recall the details. What seemed special was that it was the best night's sleep I'd had in a long time. I was so relaxed. Like I had let everything go, everything that had been piling up for the last five years.

I felt Ziggy stir a little. He adjusted his grip on my hand, and then, with a sigh, he settled back into sleep.

There were so many unknowns, so many undecided things in my life at that moment. And I wasn't worried about any of them.

I remembered once walking through the Japanese Garden in Memphis. This here felt somewhat like that. I was in a peaceful, beautiful, quiet place where I could relax, where the noises and concerns of city life were out of sight and only slightly heard in the distance.

I was falling back to sleep when I felt Ziggy start waking up. We lay there for a few more minutes, without saying anything. Then he gently slipped out from under my arm and sat up.

"'Morning," he said, stretching.

I rolled over onto my back, smiling, with my hands behind my head. "Good morning."

"We almost slept right into tomorrow," he said. "Did you sleep okay?"

"Yeah. I'm surprised. That's the best night's sleep I've had in a long time."

He grinned. "I told you."

"Yeah, you did. And now I believe it."

He smelled his armpit and scrunched up his face. "I'm gonna shower." He stood up. "You want to pee, first?"

"Yeah." I pushed back the covers and got out of bed.

"Sorry I didn't shower last night," he said. "I was tired."

"No problem. You were fine." I walked into the bathroom, this time leaving the door open, and let it flow.

I could hear him in the kitchen. I flushed the toilet and then Ziggy took my place in the bathroom.

"I'll fix some breakfast when I get out of the shower," he said. "And coffee. You can shower while I'm getting breakfast ready, okay?"

He turned on the shower and pulled off his underwear. He tossed them on the bathroom floor and stepped in.

Oh my god, I thought, *wouldn't I love to be in there with him.* But it wasn't going to happen, and the sooner I gave up that idea the better. No harm in fantasizing, but it wouldn't be fair to either one of us for me to think he could get off on that, not the way I would.

I took another quick look at him standing naked under the shower, and then I sat down in the armchair.

I had to keep a grip on reality. Maybe Ziggy and I would become the best of friends, but we were never going to be lovers. If I could accept that, truly accept it, then the two of us could share in an honest, open friendship, without any secret yearnings on my part, no hidden hopes to spoil it.

He was straight. When he desired a romantic partner, it would be a woman; that was part of his nature. He surely took that for granted, but I might have to remind myself of it once in a while.

There were going to be some challenges, I could see that, but I felt like I was up to it. He believed in me. It felt so good, to have someone believe in me.

I heard him shut off the shower. Then a couple minutes later he walked out, his wet hair all mussed up, wearing nothing but a wet towel loosely wrapped around his waist.

"Much better," he said, grinning. "Sometimes I don't know how I'd survive without hot showers."

The wet towel clung to his round ass, and of course there was the bulge of his cock in front. I imagined the towel coming loose and falling to the floor, and then I was well on my way to another erection.

"I'll put the coffee on," he said. He walked into the kitchen, still wearing the towel, and started getting things together.

I realized then that keeping a lid on my desire was not going to be such a simple matter. I could put romance out of my mind; the problem would be lust. I wanted his body. Even if I knew I couldn't have it, there was still going to be the looking.

Was it possible to change that? No, and I didn't want to. How could it be healthy to deny such a natural, normal reaction to the sight of a sexy, naked man?

He got the coffee brewing and then he went to the dresser and pulled out a fresh t-shirt and some briefs. He took them over to the bed and, facing away from me, pulled off the towel and dried his hair. It gave me a great opportunity to look at his beautiful butt. Nice and full, not flabby at all, meaty and solid.

He definitely had a beautiful body. Well-developed muscles, very little fat. Not exactly a swimmer's build; he looked more like he played a lot of basketball. He had that strong, solid but agile kind of body. Nice, smooth skin. Soft, furry brown hair in just the right places, especially on his legs.

He slipped the shirt on over his head, and then he picked up his briefs. He turned around to face me and stepped into them, giving me a great view of his soft, full cock for a few seconds before he stuffed it into the front of his underwear.

He looked at me while he pulled them on and said, "How do you like your coffee?"

"Um. Do you have any milk?" I was sitting there in the arm-chair in my underwear, watching him, my hands clasped together in front of me.

"Sure," he said, "I never run out of milk."

I wasn't trying to hide my erection, but I didn't want to make it obvious, either. Hell, he couldn't miss it, though. It was so stiff it was pulling the waistband of my underwear away from my belly, leaving a gap you could look through. Good thing my dick wasn't aimed upward; it would have been poking out a couple inches above my briefs.

I was determined not to be embarrassed.

He walked toward the kitchen, looking at me, and then he stopped. "Dude. Another boner, huh? You're one horny guy, you know that?" He laughed. "You've got a big one, too. I wish mine was as big as yours."

I looked down at my dick, and then I looked up at him. How do you reply to a remark like that?

"I'll bet yours is just as big," I said.

"Nah, not as big as that monster. You must be eight inches, at least."

"No, seven inches, max. I measured it."

"Well, you've got me beat by an inch, at least," he said, walking into the kitchen.

I felt funny just sitting there with a stiffy, now moist and making a wet spot in my briefs, but I would have felt just as awkward getting up and walking around with it.

I heard him, still in the kitchen, say, "I'll bet you've seen your share of hard dicks over the years. Being gay and all."

"I guess I've seen a few," I said.

He came to the doorway. "What's the longest dick you've ever seen? For real, I mean, not in a magazine or a movie?"

He was standing there, leaning against the doorway with his arms crossed, looking at me. I knew he could see the stiff rod in my underwear. It looked like he might be getting a hard on, too. "Um, like, ten inches." I held up my hands to show him how long. "It might have been more. It was at least ten inches."

"Really? Holy shit! That's incredible."

"I know. I was truly amazed."

53

He turned toward the kitchen, facing away from me, and looked down, like he was adjusting his cock.

"It was the very first hard dick I ever saw, too," I said. "Besides my own."

"Wow."

"Yeah."

All this talk about hard dicks sure wasn't helping mine go down any. I was getting to the point where I might have to do something about it; otherwise my balls would be aching.

He looked my way again. "How many cocks have you seen that were bigger than yours?"

"A few. But that was the only one I ever saw that big. Other than that one, the longest I've seen was probably eight inches. Usually they're more like five or six inches. Sometimes shorter than that, sometimes longer."

He disappeared into the kitchen again. I heard him open a cupboard, and close it.

Then I heard him say, "Are you gonna jack off?"

"Huh?" I certainly hadn't been expecting that.

He came back to the doorway and stood there, facing me. Now he definitely had a hard on. "Well, your cock is so hard, I was wondering if you were gonna jack off."

"Um, well, now that you mention it, I guess I'll have to, here in a little bit, if it doesn't go down."

"Really? That's cool," he said. "Mine's hard, too."

"Yeah?"

He looked down at his cock. The bulge in his briefs was bigger than ever. And very stiff. He looked up at me again and said, "Yeah."

I started feeling delusional. I thought I knew where this was going, but I could hardly dare to believe it.

I stammered, "Yours, uh, is hard, too?" I said this, even though my eyes had pretty much been locked on his dick for the last 60 seconds and I knew damn well how hard it was.

"Yeah," he said. We were in agreement, then. He definitely had a very stiff cock inside those briefs.

I figured he wanted me to look, so I kept gazing at it. Long enough to firmly establish it in my memory forever. Then I looked up. "Really, Zig." What could I say? "I'll bet yours is just as big as mine."

"Nah," he said. "It's little."

"Well, you could have fooled me. It sure looks pretty big from here."

"You wanna see it?"

"Sure," I said. "Show me."

He walked over in front of me with the biggest, hardest bulge pushing out the white fabric of his cotton briefs. He pulled down the front of his underwear and there it was. His hard dick stuck straight out, curving upward, throbbing. So close I could have reached out and touched it. Caressed it.

"Damn, Zig! That's a beauty."

"You think so?"

"Hell yeah. Magnificent." It truly was.

"Let's jack off," he said. "You want to?"

I said, "Hell yes."

Chapter 5
LET IT BE

I WAS SITTING IN THE ARMCHAIR in just my briefs and Ziggy was right in front of me, showing off his stiff, hard cock to me. As soon as we decided to jack off, he started stroking. Letting me see his hard dick was surprising enough, but stroking that thing in my face really startled me.

If it was anyone else, I surely would have wondered if he was offering it to me to suck. But not Ziggy. I was thrilled to see his hard cock, and excited about jacking off together, but I couldn't conceive of us having physical, sexual contact.

I wanted to pull my underwear down so I could join him, but I couldn't do it with him standing there so close, not without bumping into him. "Zig," I said, "let's go sit next to each other on the bed."

"Okay," he said, "sure." He turned around, and I stood up. He pulled off his t-shirt and then he sat down on the bed with his hand wrapped around his hard shaft. His underwear was halfway down his hips.

When he saw me pull off my briefs he stripped his off, too. I sat down next to him, with my hard dick arching out into the air, throbbing.

We didn't talk; we just sat there next to each other, raw naked, watching each other gently stroke our cocks. He really did have a nice one. Not much shorter than mine, and thicker. The head was even wider than the rest of it. His dick wasn't cut, which was fine with me. You could hardly tell, though, when it was hard like that. I wanted to lick it. Taste it.

He spat in his hand and stroked it into his cock.

I could have come right then, I was so turned on, but I wanted to wait for him. So I was gentle with my stroking. I looked at his face; he was really enjoying this. He looked right back at me and smiled.

He looked more at my cock than he did his own. No surprise, there. What guy doesn't have a curiosity about other guys' dicks? And jacking off together is a chance to see how other guys do it. Not that either one of us was analyzing things. When you're horny and your dick is stiff, your thought processes take a vacation. Your brain focuses on sensation.

We kept stroking, looking from one cock to the other, and watching each other's facial expressions. Hell, I gazed at every part of his naked body. How could I resist? I would have gladly licked every inch of him, too, if he ever said the word.

He took his hand off his cock for a minute, and just stared at it standing up straight and stiff. He saw me watching and grinned. Then he looked at my cock, and I did the same thing, took my hand off and let it stand out on its own, throbbing.

"I like the way your dick curves up," I told him. "I wish mine did. That's so sexy. Like a horn on a rhinoceros."

He looked at his dick and then looked at mine. "Yours is longer, though. And anyway, who cares which way it curves, as long as it gets hard, right?" He smiled. "I like the way yours moves up and down with your pulse, like it's trying to break free from gravity. It's not just stiff and hard, it's alive!"

I laughed. "Damn right it's alive." We stroked for a few minutes in silence, except for the sound of hands sliding back and forth over cocks.

Pretty soon he didn't have to use spit anymore. He was leaking pre-cum, steady. He brought his fingers across the head to scoop it up, then he'd lubricate the entire length of his rod with it. There is no sound quite like a hand moving up and down a slippery cock.

"I'm kinda close to coming," he said, breathing fast and heavy. "How 'bout you, bro?"

"Hell yeah," I said. "I've been close the whole time. I'm just getting off on watching you."

He grinned. "You like watching, huh?"

"Yeah, I do."

"Me, too," he said, looking at my cock. He opened his legs more, pushed his crotch forward to give me a better view, and pointed his dick in my direction.

I figured he was pretty darn close, the way his dickhead was bigger now and almost purple. His body twitched a couple of times. I told him, "I could come anytime, Zig."

"You come first, Josh. I wanna see you spurt, dude." He watched my dick.

"Okay," I said. "You asked for it."

With just a few more strokes, the feeling got more intense. Oozing more pre-cum, and then I was there. I let out a groan. I aimed my dick upward, the head expanded, and suddenly a big shot of white cum streaked out onto my neck, followed by another on my chest, and then another.

Ziggy watched the whole thing, stroking faster. "Ahh, yeah, shoot it, Josh. Aw, dude, I'm coming, too. Ahhhhh!" I watched his dick as his hips jerked and his cock started launching sperm in my direction. He closed his eyes and his head fell back in ecstasy.

Both of us kept on stroking and groaning, with cum flying everywhere. Mine landed mostly on my chest and belly, and I felt his cum hit my arm and my leg. Some of his jizz landed right on my dick. And on my hand.

Our gasps and moans and groans eventually slacked off, as our spasms eased up. Then we relaxed and went limp against the wall behind us.

He looked at me and grinned. "Dude."

"That was great," I said. I had cum all over me. His and mine. I licked it off my fingers, scooped up more, and licked that up, too. He saw me eating cum and looked at me kind of funny, smiling.

"Old habit," I told him.

"No problem, it's cool." He reached for his wet towel and wiped a glob of cum off his cock.

—

I LICKED MY HANDS CLEAN, and I used his towel to clean up what was left. "What a blast," I said.

"Yeah. That was horny, Josh. We ought to do that again some-time."

"Well, you know me. You won't have to twist my arm."

"Want some coffee?" He stood up.

"Sure."

He walked into the kitchen, naked.

"I'm gonna take a shower, Zig."

"Go ahead. I'll get started on breakfast. Eggs and sausage okay?"

"Yup, sounds great."

"How do you like your eggs?"

"Just about any way you can think of. Same as you're having yours." This time I left the door open. Why close it? I was feeling comfortable here with Ziggy, like there was nothing for me to hide.

I stood under the hot streaming water, completely relaxed. Being here was so incredible, it was almost like a dream. But it felt so right. No matter how unexpected it was, and even though it was all so new, everything about being here with Ziggy felt right. Somehow, I had stumbled into the place where I really belonged. That's what it felt like.

Should I give it a try, living here for a week? Why the hell not?

Sure, there were plenty of people who would probably tell me, don't do it. "Stick with what you know. Be afraid of strangers." And yet people like that were part of the pointless existence I was so sick of. To turn down Ziggy and go back to the unrewarding life I just left, seemed absurd. Impossible.

I wished I could pop down the street and ask old Mrs. Rainey what she thought I should do. My neighbor back in Memphis, my unofficial spiritual guide. Really, though, it wasn't hard to guess what she would say.

Her advice, always, was to get your heart connected to your brain and go from there. And if you still couldn't make up your mind? She'd say, "Honey, intelligence and common sense are essential, but when all is said and done, you have to follow your heart."

Follow my heart. Well, that made it an easy decision.

When I was done showering I walked out wrapped in a towel. Ziggy was in the kitchen. He had put some clothes on.

"Here's your coffee," he said. He poured a big cup, with lots of cream, and set it down in front of me. "I put some fresh clothes out for you. My jeans ought to fit you okay. We're about the same size."

"I don't want to put you out too much," I said. "The ones I had on yesterday are okay."

"Well, whatever you want. But all that stuff we had on last night really stinks. Cigarette smoke, from the club. We can wash clothes later; there's a laundry room in the basement."

I put on the pair of his briefs. It was erotic, wearing Ziggy's underwear, knowing that my dick and balls were resting right where his had been. His jeans fit me fine. A tad too long, but they'd do the trick.

"Go ahead and sit down," he said. "Breakfast's almost ready."

I sat down in the armchair, and he brought out the food. "Here you go," he said. I held the plate in my lap. Sausage, scrambled eggs, buttered toast and jam. "There's more where that came from, so speak up, okay? Don't want my buddy to go hungry."

"Thanks," I said. "This looks great."

He got his plate from the kitchen, sat down on the floor, and we dug in. Ziggy was a great cook. "Have you thought anymore, you know, about going back to Memphis?"

"Yeah," I said. "I don't want to go."

"Cool! You gonna give it a try, then, living here with me?"

"Yeah, I'd really like that. If you're sure you don't mind."

"Hell no I don't mind! Dude! That is so cool! I was hoping you would."

"How could I resist, man? I feel like I belong here."

"You do," he said, grinning.

"I just hope I don't wear out my welcome, with us being in each other's faces all the time. You're used to having your solitude. It'll be a big change for you."

"We'll give it a week," he said, "and see what happens. But I'm not worried about it. You're so easy to get along with, Josh. I don't know, dude, for some reason you just kind of fit right into my life. Don't ask me why."

"Oh, jeez. You're the one who's easy to get along with, Zig."

"Anyway," he said, "I can always find solitude when I want it. You won't mind that, will you? When I go off by myself somewhere to think?"

"No, hell no, of course not. Everybody needs to be alone sometimes. Me included. I can think better when I'm by myself."

"Yeah. Exactly." He grinned. "Oh, man, this is gonna be so great!"

Now I was totally thrilled with the idea. It could be the start of a new life.

—

I WAS DOING THE DISHES when I remembered my things. "I oughta call the hotel," I said. "We were supposed to check out today. They're probably wondering why my stuff is still there."

"There's a payphone at the market," Ziggy said. "I'll walk over with you. I need some stuff from the store, anyway."

It was my first look at the neighborhood in daylight. It was mostly residential: apartments and houses. Peaceful. The weather was nice. Warm, but not as hot as what I was used to.

The market was just a couple blocks down Clayton Avenue. I called the hotel while Ziggy went into the store.

He came back out with two sacks full of stuff. "Was the hotel still there?"

"Let me carry one of those," I said. "Yeah, no problem, but they were glad I called. They've been getting calls from my boyfriend. My ex-boyfriend, that is. Fred."

"From Memphis?"

"Yeah. They wouldn't tell me what he said, though."

"The dude who pissed you off?"

"More like the dude who I pissed off, but yeah."

Ziggy just looked at me.

"Well, he's kind of an asshole. Anyway, I need to swing by the hotel and get my stuff. Bring it over to your place."

"*Our* place, dude. For the next week, at least, it's *our* place."

"Okay," I said, grinning. "Bring it over to *our* place."

"You want I should go with you?"

"Sure, if you want to."

"Okay."

We went home, put away the groceries, and headed out in my car. Ziggy showed me the way to the interstate.

I asked him, "Did you grew up here? In St. Louis?"

"Yep. Born and raised. Far as I can remember, anyway."

"Your mother lived here?"

"Yeah, I believe so. Don't really know for sure."

We didn't say anything for a couple minutes.

Then I asked, "How does that work, when you're in an orphanage? I mean, do you get to leave the grounds on your own, or what?"

"Well, to go to school, sure. Then you have to report back after school. After that, it depends on your age. The little ones get watched over pretty carefully. As you get older, you get more freedom."

The hotel turnoff was coming up soon. Ziggy seemed to know the way. "There it is," he said. I took the exit and in another minute or two we were there.

—

I LET US INTO THE HOTEL ROOM. "Sorry the place is such a mess."

He looked around the room. "Jesus. How many nights did you guys stay here?"

"Just one. Thursday night. Friday night we stayed with some guys Fred knows, after we left the baths."

"The baths?"

"Yeah. Those guys, their favorite thing to do when they go out of town is go to the baths. There aren't any in Memphis."

"You mean like, public baths? Like they had in the frontier days?"

"Well, it's a little bit like that. But the baths I'm talking about involve more, uh, social interaction. You've never heard of the baths?"

"No, I guess not."

"Well, you're not missing anything. Anyway, Saturday morning, after Fred's blowup, they came back here to get their stuff, and then they left. He tore up the place in the process. I forgot what a mess it was."

"Lots of drama, huh?"

"Yeah, I guess you could say that." The light on the phone was blinking. "I'm gonna check the messages."

"Sure."

I picked up the receiver and punched in the code and listened. And listened. And listened some more. Feeling sicker each minute. Finally I put down the phone and looked at Ziggy. I didn't know what to say.

"Josh. Dude. That was a lot of messages."

"Yeah. Well. One from the hotel desk, and three from Fred. Cheery little messages from the psycho beastmaster. God, he's such a bastard."

"Your ex-boyfriend."

"Yeah."

"He sure did have a lot to say."

"The usual rant and rave. I should be used to it by now, but I'm not."

"Josh, you look sick, dude. No kidding, bro, you look ill. You oughta sit down."

"He's not a psycho, Zig, but he sure does a good imitation of one." Tears were in my eyes. "When he gets angry, he always fucks with my head like this."

"So, he's still angry with you?"

It took me half a minute before I could talk without my voice breaking up. "The first message, he told me I'm lower than dirt and he's through with me for good and as far as he's concerned I should stay in St. Louis, or even better, I can go to hell; he doesn't ever want to see me again. Said he was gonna put everything I own out on the street."

"Jesus."

"Well, it's basically the same thing he told me Saturday morning. I guess he just wanted to make sure I was listening."

"What the hell did you do, rape his mother?"

"Next message, he tells me how lucky I am to have a boyfriend like him, says I'm a first-class jerk, I don't deserve him, but he might take me back if I'm sorry enough. But only if I tell our friends what an asshole I was."

"Christ. Nice guy."

"Then, the last message, he says he's worried about me, says he's gonna call the police and report me as a missing person if I don't call and tell him I'm coming back."

"Jesus, Josh."

"Yeah." I looked at him and he looked at me.

"That's some heavy shit, dude."

"He finds a way to fuck with my head, every time."

"So, let me get this straight," Ziggy said. "You did something that pissed him off?"

"Yeah, but I didn't know he'd get mad about it. I can tell you what happened if you want. You'll think it's crazy, too."

"Going back to Memphis early, whose idea was that?"

"His."

"So, the two of you came up here with some other friends, right?"

"Yeah, there were six of us in all. We were gonna spend all day at Six Flags today, but he talked the rest of them into going back early. He said the weekend was ruined, anyway. They all rode back to Memphis in the other car."

"So it wasn't enough for him to be mad; he had to ruin it for everyone else. The guy sounds like a real jerk."

"He is. Not all the time, but when something pisses him off, that's when he makes me feel like a worthless piece of shit. It's always about something really stupid, too."

"Look," Ziggy said, "I don't know this guy from Adam, but I know you, Josh. Enough to know that you don't deserve that kind of abuse."

"Thanks, Zig."

"I don't think he even wants a boyfriend. He just wants someone he can manipulate."

"Yeah. That sounds about right. Sometimes I feel more like a puppet than a partner."

"Does he actually care about you? Like, does he get you something for your birthday, stuff like that?"

"I don't think he even knows when my birthday is."

"No way!"

"I've been with him two years, Zig, but he doesn't even know who I am. Never asks me about *me*. You probably know me better than he does."

"I *want* to know you," Ziggy said.

"And there's something else about you, too, Zig. You believe in me. He's my boyfriend; he's the one who's supposed to believe in me even when nobody else does. But the only thing he believes is that I'm gonna fuck up."

"Of course I believe in you, dude. Where would we be if we didn't believe in each other?"

Here was Ziggy, so kind, so nice, telling me I was somebody good, someone worth knowing. And then there's Fred, doing his psycho routine, pouring on criticism of every kind, making me feel bad and guilty.

I didn't want to cry, I really didn't. Ziggy was being so nice. But sometimes that makes me want to cry even more—when someone actually cares.

"I'm sorry, Zig." I could barely get the words out. "I didn't mean to throw all this on you."

"Hey, I want you to put it on me. You can't keep stuff like that to yourself; you'll go crazy. The guy sounds to me like a real asshole."

"He is."

I was looking at the floor because I thought if I looked at Ziggy I'd break into tears. At the same time, though, more than anything, I really needed to look at him. So I looked up and there he was, looking at me so compassionately. Tears started flowing; I couldn't help it.

"Hey," he said. "Hey, hey. Come here." He pulled me over, hugged me up close, and I held onto him. "Don't you worry, Josh. Everything is gonna be alright."

That's when I really let loose, the whole nine yards, crying and sniffling, snot running out of my nose, bawling like a baby. And the whole time, he's holding me close, saying, "That's right, Josh, let it out. Let it out." Stroking my back, holding me.

After a few minutes I finally stopped crying. I wiped my eyes with my shirt. I must have looked a real mess. "Thanks, Zig."

"Hey, no problem, Josh. One of these days I'll need a shoulder to cry on, too; wait and see."

"I'll be here for you, Zig." I looked around for something to blow my nose with.

"How often does he pull this kind of shit?"

"Oh, every month or two. Ever since we met."

"How long ago was that? Two years?"

"Yeah."

"That's crazy. I can see somebody going off like that one time, maybe, but only if it was some sort of earth-shattering betrayal. That's pretty sick if it happens on a regular basis. The guy sounds wacko, dude. Has he ever hit you?"

"No. I know he wants to sometimes, but he's chickenshit that way."

"Josh, listen to me. You don't deserve that kind of shit. You know that, don't you? Look, it's not about you, dude. I don't know what's wrong with that prick but he's completely out of line, making you out to be the bad guy. He's the one who's got problems, serious problems. But they're *his* problems, Josh. Not yours. You don't have to let them be yours."

"I think you're right, Zig. It's him, not me. But that just makes it hurt more. It wouldn't be so bad if I deserved it, but I don't. It's sick, him doing that to me."

"You're damn right it is."

"You don't know how many times I've wished he would do what he always threatens to do. Get out of my life for good. But he keeps me around. Or he always has, until now. This time will be different. I'm leaving."

"That's the spirit."

"I'm getting out of *his* life. I knew it yesterday. Even before I met you, Zig, I knew this time it was gonna be different. He's not gonna do this to me again."

"Right on. It's good to hear you stand up for yourself."

"I'd rather be alone than be with him. I'm giving up that bastard for good, Zig."

"You won't be alone, Josh. You've got a friend, bro. I'll be here."

"I know, Zig. I appreciate that. I'm just saying, I'd be giving him up, anyway. Alone or not. I have to."

Ziggy put his arm around my shoulder. "Breaking up's not always easy, Josh. But who knows. It might just be the best thing that's ever happened to you."

—

THE ROOM was still a mess. I didn't want to leave it that way, so I started straightening things up. Ziggy joined in. When we were done I said, "Well, I hate to do it, but I guess I better call him. Before I get listed on a missing person report."

"You want me to wait outside?"

"No! Please. Stay here, Zig. Okay? If you don't mind. I don't want to be alone when I talk to him."

"Sure."

I picked up the telephone and almost dropped it. "Don't know why I'm so nervous. I ought to be angry, not nervous."

"Damn right," Ziggy said.

"I'm not gonna let him fuck me over again."

"Now you're talking."

68

"He's the one who can go to hell."

"Damn straight, Josh."

I dialed our number. No, *his* number.

He answered on the second ring. "Hello?"

"Hello, Fred."

"Where the hell are you?" he said.

"At the hotel."

"Why didn't you call?"

"You didn't ever want to see me again, remember?"

"That's right, I didn't. I almost called the police on your ass."

"For what?"

"I would have thought of something."

"You said a missing person."

"I was worried about you. So sue me."

"I like it here."

"What are you talking about?"

"St. Louis. I like it here."

"Don't talk stupid. Are you gonna drive back tonight?"

"What for?"

"You have to work tomorrow."

"No, I don't. I don't have a job, remember?"

"Oh, yeah. I forgot."

"And I don't have a place to live, either. Remember?"

"What the hell are you talking about? I was just kidding."

"No, you weren't."

"Yes I was; you know I was."

"No, you meant it."

"Of course I meant it, but I changed my mind. Give me a break."

"And you know what? I'm not sorry, either."

"Of course you're sorry. What are you talking about?"

"You wanted me to say I'm sorry."

"Yeah, yeah. We'll talk about that when you get home."

"I don't have a home anymore, remember? All my stuff is out on the street."

"No it's not. You know it's not."

"Well, it better not be."

"Oh, yeah? And what if it was?"

"Stop changing the subject."

"When are you coming back?"

"Hold on." I put my hand over the mouthpiece of the phone. "He wants me to come back home."

"Tell him you have to think about it," Ziggy said.

I took my hand off the mouthpiece and told Fred, "I don't know."

"Who are you talking to?"

"A friend of mine."

"You don't have any friends in St. Louis!"

"Yeah, I do. I have a really good friend in St. Louis." I looked at Ziggy and smiled. Ziggy held both thumbs up. "And I need to go, Fred. Anything else you wanted to tell me?"

"Yeah, get your ass home right now, god damn it!"

"I'll think about it, Fred. Good bye." I could hear him yelling as I hung up.

I looked at Ziggy.

"Heavy duty," he said.

"Did I do good?"

"Damn straight. I couldn't have done any better."

"He wants me back."

"Of course he does. Who wouldn't?"

I looked down at the phone. So. Fred wanted me back. Well, that wasn't anything new. What was new was how I felt about it.

"So," Ziggy said, "are you gonna go back?"

"Hell no."

"Good. That bastard doesn't deserve anybody half as good as you."

"You really think so?"

"I know so. You kidding? He's got to be one ignorant, self-centered son of a bitch. The day he met you was his lucky day, but he's too stupid to know it. He pissed on his luck. He pissed on you. Over and over. He'll piss on you again, Josh, if he gets a chance."

"Yeah, you're right about that. He would. But he's not going to."

Ziggy held up his palm. High five! I slapped his hand. Things were going to be different from now on.

—

WE LEFT THE HOTEL ROOM as neat as possible. I packed up my things, dropped off the room key, and then we were driving back to the apartment.

"Do you have a lot of stuff back in Memphis? Furniture and stuff?"

"No furniture. I gave it all up when I moved in with Fred. All I have is my clothes and some boxes; that's about it."

"I'll help you get your things out of there if you want."

"There isn't much, really. Three cardboard boxes that I lug around every time I move. One is my memory box, for things like my high school yearbook, a photo album, letters from friends, letters from my girlfriend, just a whole bunch of sentimental stuff."

"You have a girlfriend?"

"I used to. Then there's another box I keep my tools in, like my piano tuning kit, a dictionary, my journals, that kind of stuff."

"You tune pianos?"

"Well, I try. Also there's the books. My favorites. The rest of my stuff is mostly just clothes I got from thrift stores, no big loss. It's just those three boxes; I'd like to have those. But hell, even that stuff is just sentimental. I can live without it."

"We oughta go get 'em," he said.

71

"Drive all the way down to Memphis?"

"Sure. Why not?"

"You serious?"

"Damn right, bro. It's your stuff."

"Well, okay. Yeah. If you really want to. Sure."

"I have to work all week, though. Can it wait until Saturday?"

"Oh, sure. Knowing him, he's taking it for granted I'll be back. He knows better than to mess with my stuff. That would be the last straw."

We drove north, into St. Louis. I watched the road while Ziggy looked at the scenery.

"Anyway," I said, "if he's gonna pitch my stuff, he's already done it. So waiting a few more days won't change anything."

"Okay. We'll take off early Saturday morning, then. Unless you want to leave Friday when I get off work."

"It's a five-hour drive, Zig. We should get a good night's sleep before we go."

"Saturday it is, then. Cool! We'll have us a little road trip."

"Do you have a driver's license?"

"Oh, sure. We can take turns driving if you want."

"Yeah, I'd like that. So, uh, where do you work?"

"I'm an auto mechanic. At a dealership."

"Oh, okay. That's a good trade. You like it?"

"Sure. Went to school for it and everything. I'm good at it, too."

"Nice."

"Hey, how about if I get your engine tuned up before we go? I can do it at work."

"Uh, sure. Cool."

"I'll drive it in to work on Friday, then, is that okay?"

"Yeah, great! Thanks."

"How about you, Josh, what kind of work do you do? No, wait. Let me take a wild guess."

I waited, smiling.

"Don't tell me," he said. "I'm still thinking."

"Okay."

"Um, you'd be a good teacher, I'll bet. Or maybe you're some kind of artist. Or both. Yeah, you're a painter. Or a writer. That's it, you're halfway through writing your first novel!" He grinned. "Am I anywhere close?"

"Not bad, Zig. I've thought about teaching. And I'd like to write a novel, too, but jeez, wouldn't everybody?"

"Nope. Not me. I couldn't do it."

"I believe I could, if I could think up a good idea for one. I've written short stories, but I haven't tried a novel, yet. Except for an X-rated one. Does that count?"

"Of course it counts!"

"You were right about it being halfway done. How'd you know that?"

"Just a lucky guess. Can I read it?"

"Of course you can. Uh, the sex is between two guys, though, just so you know."

"That's okay. I still want to read it. I'll probably even get turned on by it." He smiled. "Sex is sex."

"Sure, you can read it. I don't mind. If Fred hasn't thrown it out. It's down in Memphis with my other stuff."

"In that case, we *have* to drive down there and get your things. We can't let your novel get trashed, dude, no way."

"Okay. This weekend, right?"

"Yep." We were close to home again. Ziggy told me where to exit. "What kind of work do you do to pay the bills, Josh?"

"Uh, different stuff. I drove a school bus. That was one of my favorites. I was a grocery clerk for a while. And a telephone installer. And a couple of clerical jobs. So I guess I'll be looking through the want ads from A to Z, seeing what's out there." I parked the car.

"You shouldn't have trouble finding something. A smart guy like you."

Then we walked up to his apartment. *Our* apartment. We got inside and then we realized we needed another chair, so we went back out again. Ziggy led me on a tour of the second-hand stores.

—

WE VISITED FOUR THRIFT STORES and we still didn't find a decent chair, but one store had an awesome little two-person couch that was very comfortable. Ziggy said we could make room for it if I wanted it. So I bought it. We tied it on the roof of my car and carried it back.

We got it home and carried it upstairs, but things were pretty crowded. Ziggy said we didn't need his armchair, now that we had the couch, so we carried his chair down and dropped it off at one of the thrift stores.

When we got back he said, "Man, I need a shower."

"Me, too," I said. "We really worked up a sweat, moving that stuff."

"Go ahead, Josh, you go first."

I stripped off my clothes and got in. I lathered up and shampooed my hair; then I stood under the hot water to relax for a couple minutes.

Five minutes later I was still in there. Ziggy came in, wearing just his underwear, and stood at the toilet. "You don't mind if I pee, do you?" He'd already pushed his underwear down and was holding his cock out.

"No, course not. Sorry I'm taking so long."

"No problem, take your time." He watched the steady flow of piss stream out of his dick into the bowl. I watched, too.

I had never thought of peeing as an erotic thing until then. It was sexy, watching Ziggy pee. He finally finished, shook it a few times, and put it back into his briefs. He looked over and saw me watching. He grinned and said, "Leave me some hot water, okay?"

"I'm done." I shut the water off and Ziggy handed me a towel. "I was just thinking about the buttons I used to wear in high school. You know, with slogans? I had one that said, 'If it feels good, do it.' And another one said, 'Save water, shower with a friend.' I used to hope my best friend would take the hint and get in the shower with me, but he never did."

"You would have liked that, huh?" Ziggy stripped off his briefs.

"Oh, hell yeah." I dried myself with the towel. "You kidding? I love the idea of showering with another guy. And I really had the hots for him. I was afraid to let him know, though. I was afraid he wouldn't want anything to do with me if he ever found out."

"Did you ever wonder if maybe he wanted you the same way, but he just couldn't bring himself to say it?"

"For real, you mean? No, I didn't think it was possible. I used my imagination a lot about the two of us doing horny stuff together, but I never believed it could really happen. He was just so totally straight, "

"You were sure of that."

"Well, from what I could tell, it seemed very likely."

"Josh, you never know. Stranger things have happened."

Chapter 6
In It Together

ZIGGY STEPPED INTO THE SHOWER and I went into the living room. I unpacked a few things from my backpack, then I put on some jeans and sat down on the couch.

I heard the shower stop. Then Ziggy was there, right in front of me, naked, drying his hair. "I'll clear out some drawers in the dresser," he said, "for your underwear and stuff. There's plenty of room in the closet, too."

"Okay."

He sat on the bed and dried his toes. "Let's go for a walk," he said. "You want to?"

"Sure."

—

"THIS WEATHER REMINDS ME of Maryland," I said. "I love this time of year. Warm days and cool nights."

"Yeah, me too," he said. "There's something about fall and cool weather coming on that makes me feel cozy. That sounds weird, doesn't it?"

"No, I know just what you mean."

We walked on past the market and decided to eat while we were out. I got my first taste of "St. Louis-style pizza." The cheese was strange, but I liked the thin crust.

We picked up a Sunday paper on the way back. Ziggy said I'd have plenty of time to look at the want ads tomorrow, while he was at work.

"Circle all the ones that look any good," he said. He took off his shoes and socks. "When I get home tomorrow I'll look them over and give you some input. Since you don't know one part of the city from another."

He unbuttoned his jeans and pulled them off. "Are you okay with staying home all day tomorrow? You won't have keys to lock up, if you leave."

"Oh. Uh, sure, no problem." I sat down and took off my shoes and socks, too. I hate wearing shoes at home.

"It'll just be for one day. I'll get some keys made for you while I'm on my lunch break."

"Okay. Listen, Zig, I appreciate you sharing your place with me."

"No problem. You'd do the same for me."

"Sure, now that I know you. But I would have been afraid to invite a stranger into my home the way you did. I appreciate you taking a chance on me."

"You weren't a stranger, bro."

"We hadn't known each other more than a few hours!"

"Well, sometimes you learn a lot in a few hours. I knew that I liked you, dude. And also I knew I could trust you. But hell, the thing is, sometimes when everything is telling you something is right, you just have to go for it. While you can."

"Yeah, I guess so."

"You took a chance on me, too, Josh; don't forget that. Give yourself some credit. Most people would have turned me down, afraid I was some kind of loony."

"Oh, jeez, I knew better than that. You're one of the nicest guys I've met. The only thing I wonder is what I did to deserve you being a friend. Right when I needed one, too."

"You deserve it because of who you are, Josh. And, hell, I deserve a good friend, too. Nothing but the best for us, dude." He grinned and held up his palm. High five! I slapped his hand.

"Okay then. We're in this together," I said.

"Damn right, bro."

"Or at least, we will be, after we try this out for a week."

"Oh, hell, dude, nothing's gonna mess this up, I already know that." He put his arm around me and gave me a hug, and our bare feet touched. It gave me a thrill.

I wasn't used to getting hugs. My family never did that, but something in me had always yearned for that kind of physical contact. Now I had a buddy who thought it was natural to hug and touch. Even when he was stripped down to just his underwear.

"Okay, my friend," he said, letting loose of me. Then he looked me over. He said, "Fuck, why don't you get more comfortable, Josh? There's nobody here but us guys." He smiled.

"Yeah, you're right, we're home now." I unfastened my jeans and took them off. "Might as well be comfy."

"Hell yeah. This is our little nest, here. We can run around in our undies if we want to. Why not?"

"You're the best, Zig. I love your attitude about things."

"I like those colored briefs," he said. "They look good on you."

I was wearing my blue ones, with white trim. I looked down at them and then at Ziggy. "Thanks."

"All of mine are white. Boring, huh?"

"Zig, don't worry. Believe me; you look great in white briefs."

"Anyway," he said, "what do you want to do now?"

"Um, I don't know. Want to play a game or something?"

"Sure. What kind of game?"

"Oh, it was just an idea. You have any playing cards? We could play Rummy or Hearts or Spades or something."

"Nope," he said, "sorry. Hell, there hasn't been anyone to play cards with since I left the orphanage. I used to enjoy card games. They're fun."

"What did y'all play?"

"Oh, different stuff. Everything from Go Fish to Spades to strip poker."

"Really? You guys played strip poker?"

He shrugged his shoulders. "Sure."

"Wow. I always did want to do that, but I never got up the nerve to suggest it to my buddies. I was afraid they might think I was queer."

"Josh. Dude. That doesn't make sense. You *are* queer."

"Yeah, I know that, now. Okay, I knew it then, too. I just didn't want anybody else to know."

"That still doesn't make sense, Josh. How are you gonna hook up with other gay dudes, if you don't let people know you're gay?"

I just looked at him. It was another revelation. How could I have missed such a simple truth, for so long? "Zig, I feel so stupid. God, I wish I'd had somebody like you around back then."

"Yeah, that would have been cool, us being friends back then. Who knows, we might have even been best buddies."

"I guess I didn't want to be a freak. Look, I know this sounds crazy, but I hoped if I did meet another gay guy, he'd be able to read my mind. Don't laugh, it's true. That's what I was hoping."

Ziggy had this look on his face, like "Dude!" He kept his mouth shut, though. He didn't say anything.

"Okay," I said. "You can laugh. I know it's ridiculous."

He smiled. "No, it's not ridiculous. People do read each other, all the time. I'll bet you had your admirers, even though you tried to hide it."

"Maybe."

"Dude," he said, "you couldn't *not* have had admirers. You couldn't be who you are today, without being special back then. People noticed, I guarantee."

I didn't say anything else about it. I had to think about that.

Ziggy walked into the bathroom to pee, and I sat down on the couch. I listened to his piss hitting the water. Eventually it slowed, and stopped. Then the toilet flushed and he came back out and sat down next to me.

"Yeah," he said, "we played strip poker. It started out as a fun way to gamble. The game would end when the first guy lost his last piece of clothing. He was the loser. Then he had to do something crazy like run outside, completely naked, and run back in."

"Really? Actually run outside stark naked?"

"Sure."

"Oh, my god!" I grinned.

"That's nothing. If it was raining out, we made the guy run all the way around the building."

"No way!"

"For real. I had to do it twice, myself. It felt . . . daring. Exciting. Hell, it was fun."

"You never got caught?"

"Nope. Just lucky, I guess."

"And that was it? That was the end of the game?"

"At first, yeah. But then we realized, nobody wanted it to end that soon. So we thought up some more rules, to make it last longer and get more people naked. We worked it out so that everyone lost his clothes before it was all over."

"Yeah, I would have liked that much better," I said.

"We all did. It was more fun that way. Sometimes it got pretty horny, too. We played that the loser had to do whatever the winner told him to do. Of course, nobody knew who the winner would be until everybody else was naked first. The last guy with any clothes left was the winner. Sometimes we kept playing until he was naked, too."

"And he got to make the loser do whatever he wanted?"

"Yeah. Anything he wanted. It got pretty interesting. By the time it was over, everybody had boners, big stiff boners. We all wanted to see what the winner would make the loser do."

"Wow." I was getting a hard on.

"Yeah."

"We ought to get some cards," I said.

Ziggy laughed. "Why, you want to play strip poker?" He looked down at the bulge in my briefs and grinned.

"Oh, I don't know. Maybe not. It wouldn't be the same, would it? We already go around here in our underwear. Or less."

"Yeah, true enough. But it was fun to play. We could try it sometime if you want. Half the fun was knowing you'd be doing something horny if you were the loser."

"I guess I missed out on stuff like that when I was a kid."

"It's not too late, Josh. It's never too late to be a kid at heart. I'll get some cards and we'll play strip poker sometime, okay?" He smiled.

"Okay." I laughed. Ziggy sure did know how to make me feel good.

He looked at the bookshelf. "I was thinking about doing some reading, before we go to bed."

"Yeah," I said. "Great idea." He walked to the bookcase, and I walked into the bathroom to pee.

When I came back out, he was sitting on the couch with a book.

I sat down next to him. "What are you reading?"

"It's a book by Samuel Delaney, called *Dhalgren*. You ever heard of it?"

"No, I don't think so. Delaney writes science fiction, right?"

"Some of his books are science fiction, but this one is different. Takes place right here on earth, without any kind of science fiction angle at all. Well, nothing like space ships or aliens, at least. It's a really cool book. One of my all-time favorites."

"So, you've read it before, then?"

"Yeah, this is my third time."

"Wow. It must be good, then."

"It is. The best. Not everybody agrees, of course. Some people have a hard time following it, but it makes perfect sense to me. Anyway, you can read it when I'm done, if you want."

"I'll give it a look, for sure."

Ziggy went back to reading his book, with a contented look on his face.

"I'm ready to start one, myself," I said. "Got any favorites to recommend?"

"Oh, sure." He walked to the bookcase and looked at the bottom shelf.

Within a minute or two he pulled out four books and handed them to me. "Here you go. You might have already read them, though. That whole bottom shelf is my favorites, so any one of them has my recommendation."

The first one of the books was *The Wind in the Willows*, by Kenneth Grahame. Next was *As I Lay Dying* by William Faulkner, *Neuromancer* by William Gibson, and *Stranger in a Strange Land* by Robert A. Heinlein.

"*Neuromancer*? Never heard of that one," I said. "What's it like?"

"That's a new one, really wild. You've got to read it. Dude plugs into the computer network, literally plugs his brain into his computer, and then he's in a different world. Cyberspace, they call it. Takes place in the future, of course. They can do that. He's a cyberspace cowboy."

"Sounds pretty wild. Who knows, though. They're already selling home computers. Commodore, and Atari. I thought about getting one."

"Me, too," he said, "but then I thought, what the hell would I do with it? Anyway, *Neuromancer* is a cool book, dude. You ought to read it."

"Okay."

He sat back down on the couch. I decided to read *The Wind in the Willows* first. I was in the mood for fantasy.

I thought Zig would go to bed early, since he had to work tomorrow, but after we sat there reading a while I started getting drowsy. "Zig, I'm nodding out. I think I'm gonna go to bed."

"Sure, go ahead. I'm gonna finish this chapter at least, and then I'll join you."

"Alright." I put the book up, brushed my teeth, and went over to the bed.

My usual habit is to sleep naked; I've always been more comfortable like that. But I thought it might create problems, sleeping naked with Zig, so I left my briefs on, like last night, and slipped under the covers. I knew he didn't mind me getting a hard on, but a stiff boner flopping around loose would keep *me* awake.

Maybe it wouldn't be a problem. All I wanted was some peaceful, restful, uneventful sleep. If the night before was any indication, snuggling up with my new straight friend was going to be all I needed to sleep.

I probably fell asleep as soon as I closed my eyes.

I remember hearing the toilet flush, though. Then Ziggy was behind me, whispering, "Scoot over a little, Josh." I moved a bit closer to the edge, and then he fit snug up behind me. He wrapped his arm around me, holding us close together. Then, back to sleep.

Monday

I GOT UP DURING THE NIGHT to pee, half asleep, and stumbled back to bed. I lifted Ziggy's arm to snuggle in next to him. He stirred a little, then we went back to sleep.

Then I was waking up to daylight. I sat up and looked around; I didn't see any sign of Ziggy. The place was very quiet.

I found a note in the kitchen: "Josh — Help yourself to anything. I'll be home around 3:30 or 4. I hope you don't get bored. You'll have keys tomorrow. Enjoy your day off. — Ziggy"

He was right; it would be like a day off. I could be lazy all day. I made some coffee, went through the want ads, made a list of things to do tomorrow, and took a shower. Then I sat around in the buff, reading and taking it easy. When it was time for Ziggy to come home, I put on some clothes.

HE CAME IN FROM WORK about 3:30. His face and arms were dirty and greasy. No surprise, I guess, for a mechanic. "I got your keys, Josh, ol' buddy." He held out a key ring with two keys. "This one here is for our apartment. The other one is to the door of the building."

He had a big hard on. My dick got hard as soon as I saw it. He looked down at his crotch, then he looked up at me and grinned. "You noticed, huh? God, I've been horny all day."

I laughed. "Nothing wrong with that, Zig." I adjusted myself in my jeans.

"Naw. Nothing at all. Still, it's unusual for me." He took off his belt. "Usually I don't think about sex at work. But today it seemed like everyone I talked to wanted some."

"Sex?"

"Yeah, or if they didn't want it, they wanted to talk about it. Weird." He unbuttoned his jeans and pulled down the zipper, exposing the big, stiff bulge in his briefs.

"Maybe it's a full moon."

"Yeah, maybe." He sat down and took his shoes and socks off. "Even the stuck-up girl in the cashier booth was flirting with me. She's never done that before. And Eleanor, the receptionist, asked me out to dinner Thursday! I think she wants me to fuck her, Josh."

"Maybe it was you who was different today."

"Nah. I was just the same old me." He stepped out of his jeans, which left him in just his t-shirt and white briefs, with his dick still as hard as it could be.

"Different day, same Ziggy, huh?"

"Okay, well, I was in a great mood today, for sure. It's so cool to have a roommate." He pulled his t-shirt off. "A *good* roommate, too. I've been feeling really great about that. Maybe that's what they wanted, was some of my good mood." He tossed his shirt on the bed.

"Sure, that would explain it. Happiness is contagious."

"Must be, because everybody at work was having fun with me." He stripped out of his underwear and stood there completely naked, with his cock standing up big and stiff.

"Not only that," he said, "my boss gave me two tickets to a Cardinals game. Can you believe it? Just handed them to me and said, 'Here, Z, give your new buddy a taste of St. Louis baseball.'"

"They call you Z?"

"Yeah, most of the time. Anyway, you wanna go? It'll be fun!"

"Yeah, sure. Definitely!"

"Excellent."

"When is it?"

"A week from Friday. They'll be playing the Atlanta Braves. Dude, I can't wait."

I couldn't take my eyes off him. He took off all his clothes while standing right there in front of me, as if being naked with a hard dick was the most natural thing in the world. Which it is, of course, but, god, did it give me a hard on.

He must have noticed me staring, but it didn't seem to bother him. He just stood there and let me look. "Well, what do you think? Awesome, huh?"

"You got that right," I said. Then I figured out he was talking about baseball. "Um, I hope I don't have to work that day."

"No problem. I think it's a night game." He turned toward the bathroom, and now I had a great side view of his stiff, erect cock. "So, Josh," he said, "are you a baseball fan?"

"Um, I don't keep up with the different teams much," I said. Staring at him. "But hell, I love going to a game in person. It's exciting when you're actually there."

"Yeah, you know it. That's the best, when you can be there. The Cardinals are a great team, too, bro. St. Louis is big on baseball, you'll find that out."

"Cool."

"Well," he said, "I'm gonna get in the shower. It never fails, I always get grease all over me at work."

He went into the bathroom, leaving the door open as usual. Which was okay by me. He didn't seem to mind at all, letting me see him naked, even when he had a rigid, hard cock. I guess he figured I wouldn't mind. He was absolutely right.

He finished his shower and came out of the bathroom drying his hair with a towel. He put one foot up on the bed, then the other, drying his crotch and his ass and his legs. Then he took the towel to the bathroom. He came out and walked into the kitchen, naked.

I sat on our couch with the classified section spread out on the coffee table. I heard the fridge open. He said, "Did you find any good jobs?"

"Yeah, a whole bunch. Some of these sound pretty good. You want to look them over?"

"Yeah." He came into the living room and sat down next to me, still naked. I loved how he was so relaxed and casual about it. He saw me looking him over and said, "I like to dry out for a while, before I put any clothes on."

"That's cool," I said. "I used to stay naked all the time, when I lived by myself. It's more comfortable."

"Did you really? Same here, bro. I'm really a nudist at heart."

"Me, too. I'd go naked all the time if I could. Only trouble is, I'd probably have a hard on most of the time."

"Nah. Maybe you would at first, but you'd be surprised. You'd get used to it after a while."

"I don't know if I ever would. Not if I was around somebody as sexy as you, Zig. Jeez, I'm stiff right now, even with my clothes on."

"You'd get used to it, trust me. It might take a while, but hell, you can't think about sex all the time." He picked up the newspaper and looked at the ads I circled. Meanwhile, I looked at him.

"Some of these are way on the other side of town," he said. "You could drive to work, but the rush hour here is a hassle. Or you could take a bus. But you'll have more free time if you work close to home."

"Yeah, that's what I was thinking, too."

"I've got a map somewhere. If I can find it I'll show you where each of these jobs are."

I pointed out the listings that sounded especially good. Sitting there with him nude like that, though, I couldn't help but stay boned up. His cock wasn't hard, but it was filled out and big. I thought about how good it had looked when it was rigid and standing straight up. My dick got so stiff, I had to reach down in my jeans and change position.

He looked down at my bulge. "Dude." He looked up at me, smiling. "I thought I was the horny one. You're horny, too, huh?"

"Yeah."

"Go ahead. It's just us guys here. Get out of those clothes, Josh, let your hard dick stand up proud and free, bro."

"Um, I don't know."

"Oh, go on. You know you want to. Go ahead, dude. Get naked. I want you to."

"Are you sure?"

"Yes! Haven't you ever wanted to show off your cock to some-body when it's really hard?"

"Well, yeah." I was getting embarrassed. "How'd you know? But I feel like such a pervert, wanting to do something like that. Like, um, you know, one of those flashers or something."

"Dude, now's your chance. Show me that thing. Really, I wanna see it, Josh. Show me how proud you are of your body."

"Well, okay. If you're sure."

"Damn right," he said, grinning.

I stood up and took off my shirt, and then I stepped out of my jeans. I stood there in just my briefs, with Ziggy looking at the outline of my big boner. He looked up, smiling. "Go ahead, Josh. Take 'em off. Let me see that monster of yours."

He watched as I peeled off my underwear and my stiff cock stood straight out, throbbing. We both looked at it for five or ten seconds, and then I sat down again. He said, "Feel better now?"

"Yeah. Feels good to let it out."

I showed him the rest of the ads while the two of us sat there naked next to each other. My cock didn't go down at all. It was still throbbing, but we pretended to ignore it.

His dick was filling out more, too. It was halfway hard when he stood up and said, "I'll go find that map." He went into the kitchen and started looking through drawers. Then I heard him say, "I found it." He came back and sat down next to me on the couch again, and now his cock was fully hard.

He opened the map and spread it out. "This is where we live, Josh." He pointed. "See how close we are to the park? Over here is the river, and downtown. And see, here's East St. Louis, where that club is, where we met."

I sat there next to him with my dick throbbing, listening and watching his stiff cock.

"St. Louis has a good bus system, so you don't even need a car, unless you work out in the boonies or something." He saw me looking at his cock and he smiled. "Dude. Are you paying attention?"

"Hell yeah," I said.

"Yeah," he said, grinning, "I know what you're paying attention to." He looked at his hard dick. Then he looked at my stiff cock and said, "We're two horny-ass motherfuckers, aren't we?"

"Nothing wrong with that, right?"

"That's right," he said. "A hard dick is never anything to be ashamed of." He leaned back in the couch, and then he grabbed his cock, wagging it side to side. "I've been horny all day, Josh."

"Well then," I said, "let's do something about it."

"Yeah." He spit in his hand, started stroking his cock, and looked over at me.

I put down the newspaper, leaned back, and started stroking my dick, too. We watched each other work our cocks, taking our time, enjoying each stroke. Every so often he put more spit on his, to keep it slippery.

"I love this," I said.

"Yeah?"

"Yeah. Just jacking off like this with you is better than any sex I had with Fred."

"Really?"

"Yeah." We kept jacking.

After a while he said, "What kind of stuff did you two do together?"

"Oh, you know," I said, "the usual stuff."

"Okay." We kept stroking, watching each other. "I wish mine was longer, like yours," he said.

"Oh, jeez, Zig. What does it matter? I wish mine was thicker, like yours. So we're even. Hell, you've got a beautiful dick, don't you know that?"

"You think so?"

"Hell, yes." We stroked some more.

He looked down at my cock again. "I always wonder, though, what it'd be like to have a longer dick to jack."

I thought about that for a minute. Then I said, "You want to find out?"

"What do you mean?"

"Well, you know. What it's like to jack a longer dick." I took my hand off my cock and let it stand out on its own.

He looked at my cock, and looked at me, and looked back at my cock. "Uh, that's not what I meant," he said. "But . . . ." He continued to look at my hard cock, throbbing on its own in mid-air.

Then he reached out and held it.

Chapter 7
NATURE'S WAY

ZIGGY WAS HOLDING MY COCK! Oh, my god, I almost shot my load right then. If he stroked it even once, I know I would have come.

He just held it like that, for about five seconds, then he let go of it.

His face was a little red, from blushing. "Thanks," he said.

"I should thank you, Zig. Your hand felt good."

We went on jacking our own cocks some more.

"Sometimes," I said, "I wonder what it'd be like to jack a beautiful, fat dick like yours."

Ziggy looked at me and blushed again. Then he said, "Fair's fair." He took his hand off it and let it stand erect, the same way I did mine for him.

I looked at him to be sure; he nodded his head, so I reached over and wrapped my hand gently around his stiff cock. I had been yearning to touch him like this.

He let out an "ahhhhh" as my fingers wrapped around it. Then when I stroked it once, he moaned. I would have loved to stroke him off, make him come, but I didn't know if he'd be okay with that, and I didn't want to push it. So I only stroked him once, and then I reluctantly let go.

"Thanks, Zig."

"No problem."

"I love your dick."

"That's cool."

We kept jacking ourselves. Watching each other. I could have watched Ziggy stroke his rigid cock for hours. I wanted to memorize everything about it. He was watching me, too, watching me handling my stiff cock. Both of our dicks were oozing pre-cum now.

After another couple of minutes he said, "I'm getting close, Josh, what about you?"

"I've been close since we started."

"Okay." He stroked another couple of times, then he said, "Let's see if we can come together, want to?"

"Sure. Just tell me when, Zig." We had our cocks aimed up so the cum would shoot on ourselves.

He continued stroking, gently, drawing things out a little longer. His dick was leaking pre-cum like crazy. The head was big and looked ready to explode. He stroked a few more times, and then he moaned. "Ahhhh! I'm gonna come. This is it, Josh, I'm coming."

I stroked faster. "Me too, Zig," I gasped. My cockhead got bigger and suddenly it spat out a big shot of cum, and then another, all the way up to my shoulder and my neck. I looked over at him and saw his hips jerk and then a big spurt of cum shot out from his cock. He moaned as one shot after another flew out of his dick. I moaned, too. His sperm was shooting all over the place, while mine was hitting mostly on my chest and my belly. A couple of squirts of his cum landed on me.

Finally we slowed, and then we were finished. We collapsed against the back of the couch. Ziggy had his eyes closed, and I looked at him all over. This time more of his cum landed on him than on me. His dick was still hard. He opened his eyes and smiled.

"That was good," he said. "That was really good."

"Yeah," I said. "I needed that." I licked the cum off my fingers.

He looked around for something to wipe himself off with, but he left his towel in the bathroom.

"Here," I said. I reached over and scooped the cum off his belly and ate it.

"Dude!" He laughed. "You really like that stuff, huh?"

"Sure. When it's from a good buddy like you, and it's fresh? Hell, yeah."

He laughed again. "That's cool; I don't have a problem with that. Here, there's more up here, if you want it." He pointed at a couple of places on his chest where his cum had splattered and was starting to drip.

He thought I would use my fingers again, but on an impulse I leaned over and licked it all up with my tongue.

"Josh! Dude! Jesus."

I sat up again. "Just seemed easier that way, to get it all." I smacked my lips. "Sorry."

"No problem. Christ, I don't even need a towel, with you around."

"At your service, Zig." I smiled.

He was still holding his dick, which hadn't gone down much. He looked at it and said, "You missed some."

I looked at his cock and sure enough, there was Ziggy cum smeared all over the head. Without thinking I leaned over and put my mouth on it. He jumped a little and said, "Josh! Oh, fuck, dude! I was just kidding!"

In just a few seconds I slurped his cock clean, swirling with my tongue and then getting the rest of it with my lips as I pulled off.

He looked at me, astonished. "Dude!"

I thought, *Damn, that was stupid. I took it too far. I really screwed up now.* "I'm sorry, Zig. I should have asked you first. I'm sorry."

He was looking at his dick like he couldn't believe I did that. "That's okay," he said. "Don't worry about it." But he didn't sound so sure.

"No, really, I'm sorry. I got carried away."

"It's okay, Josh. It took me by surprise, that's all. I never had a guy do that to me before."

"Never?"

"Never. Hell, I've never even had a woman do that before. Not lick up my cum like that."

"For real?"

"Well, sure."

"No way."

"Way. See, for one thing, when I'm fucking a woman, I usually come inside a condom, inside her. First I get her to reach her orgasm, and then, in I go."

"Yeah, okay. Makes sense. But what about blow jobs, don't they ever suck you off?"

"I've never come inside anyone's mouth."

"What? No, I can't believe that!"

"It's not that I didn't want to. It's just never happened. I guess I've never been with a woman who was cock crazy. The only ones I could talk into trying it, didn't like it. Or else they didn't know what they were doing, didn't know how to make it feel good. But hell, it's never been a big deal anyway, because I like to fuck, and they like to get fucked."

"Wow."

"Yeah."

I leaned back in the couch and we sat there for a few minutes, recovering.

After a while he said, "You hungry?"

I put on my underwear, just out of habit, I guess. Ziggy hesitated, but then he put on some briefs, too. He walked to the kitchen to cook something up, and I went with him.

"How about sandwiches? We've got sliced turkey and plenty of cheese. I could put some spinach leaves on there, too."

"Sure. That sounds good."

"Josh, you mind if I ask you something? Personal?"

"Ask me anything you want, Zig. I can't think of anything I'd wanna keep secret from you."

"Well, it's kind of a medical question, I guess. No, let's eat first; it can wait."

He made sandwiches and put them on plates with chips. We each carried a plate and a can of soda into the living room and sat on the couch.

"This is so different from living with Fred in Memphis," I said. "Right now we'd be watching 'Scooby Doo' or the 'A-Team.' Or else he'd be channel surfing, which is even worse. Endless TV, until we went to bed. Sometimes he fell asleep with the TV on and slept all night in the living room. If I turned it off, he'd wake up and bitch at me and turn it back on again."

Ziggy said, "You miss it?"

"Hell, no," I said. He laughed.

We finished eating, carried the plates into the kitchen, and sat down again on the couch.

"So," I said. "You were gonna ask me something?"

"Yeah, I was wondering. I mean, just about everyone's heard of AIDS now. But it's all pretty confusing."

"I try to keep up with it," I said. "They think they've discovered the virus that causes it, but nobody knows when they'll come up with a vaccine. If they ever do."

"Are you afraid you'll get it?"

"Well, I worry about it, of course, same as everybody else. I got tested, as soon as they came up with a test for it. So far, I'm good. How about you, Zig? Are you afraid you'll get it?"

"Sure, but I'm more afraid for you, Josh. They say it mostly hits gay men."

"I know. That's what everybody's saying. That's why I've been cutting back on sex. Or trying to."

"Isn't that kind of, uh, impossible?"

"Well, yeah. But what I mean is, they're saying some kinds of sex are riskier than others. I'm not about to let anybody fuck me without a condom, you can bet your life on that. Oral sex seems to be a lot less risky. As long as you're not bleeding anywhere in your mouth. But even so, it's best to be cautious."

"Makes sense to me."

"There's always jacking off, of course. That's probably the safest sex of all." I thought about jacking off with Ziggy, and my dick started getting hard.

"Yeah," he said, "thank god for masturbation. What would any of us do without that?"

"Go crazy, I guess." We laughed. I noticed Ziggy's cock was growing, too.

"Okay, then," he said. "I've got another really personal question for you. But, Josh, don't answer if you don't want to, okay?"

"Go ahead, Zig; ask."

"When's the last time you fucked without a condom?"

"Um, it's been about five years, I guess. 1979. Five or six years."

"No way."

"Yeah, honest to god."

"Good for you, Josh. That's smart."

"As soon as they started talking about this stuff, I made up my mind to use them. Just being cautious, I guess."

"Well, I'm glad I asked," he said. "That makes me feel a lot better. Maybe you won't ever get sick, then."

"I hope not. Life's too short as it is."

We sat there for a couple of minutes without saying anything.

He put his arm up around my shoulder. Then he closed his eyes, and it just got to be magical. For me, anyway. I looked over at him and he seemed so relaxed. I thought maybe he was meditating. Then he opened his eyes and looked at me again and we both smiled.

He took his arm down and, instead, he leaned my way, putting the full weight of his head on my shoulder. I wondered if he was going to take a nap on me, like a little kid. Sitting there with him leaning up against me, it was almost like tripping.

—

I DON'T KNOW HOW LONG we sat there, snoozing. It could have been half an hour, or even longer.

Eventually Ziggy shifted a little and said, "Josh, I'm gonna take a quick shower and go to bed."

"Bed sounds good," I said.

He stood up, stripped off his underwear, and walked into the bathroom. I heard him turn on the shower as I got into bed.

Then he was gently lifting my arm up and slipping into bed in front of me. I saw his beautiful bare ass and I realized he was completely naked. That took me by surprise. I figured it was probably a good thing I still had my underwear on.

He sighed and held my arm to his chest, and then I guess after that, we were in dreamland.

Tuesday

WHEN I WOKE UP, Ziggy was already out of bed and getting ready for work. He made coffee; I could smell it. I glanced over just in time to see his naked butt disappear into the bathroom. Then I heard the shower running.

I was sitting there on the bed, still half-asleep, when Ziggy came out from the shower. He was drying himself with a towel. "You're awake."

"Yeah, trying to be."

"There's fresh coffee, Josh. I'll go get you some."

He went into the kitchen. I heard him get a cup from the cupboard, and the next thing I knew he was handing me a steaming cup of coffee with lots of cream, just how I like it. "Watch out," he said. "It's hot."

"Thanks, Zig."

I sat there sipping java while I watched him pull on some underwear. He saw me looking and smiled. "You're up early, dude."

"Yeah, time to find a job. Might as well get an early start."

"Well, let me know if there's anything I can do." He put on some socks and then pulled on his jeans. "I asked at work, but they don't have any openings. Not unless you want to sell cars."

"There's one thing I did want to ask you, Zig. About getting a phone."

"Yeah?"

"Are you against having one?"

"Not really. I just haven't felt a need for one." He looped his belt through his jeans and buckled it. Then he sat down to put on his shoes. "Why, you want to get one?"

"Well, not really, but these jobs I'm applying for, they'll want to get back in touch with me. At least, I hope they will."

"Yeah. Right. Okay, I'll call the phone company and set it up on my break."

"I'll pay for it," I said.

"I'm not worried about the money. Listen, I gotta run, Josh. Good luck today. I'll see you when I get home, okay?"

He took off, and then an hour later I was out of there, too.

I got a lot done that day. I called nearly every job I'd circled in the paper, and I typed up a resume at a copy store nearby. Then I headed for the second-hand stores. I found a suit that fit me, and enough shirts and ties to get me through at least a week of job hunting.

I came back home, dropped my new clothes on the bed, stripped down naked, and took a nice, long shower.

—

ZIGGY CAME HOME just as dirty and greasy as he did the day before. I'd just gotten out of the shower and put on a pair of his underwear.

He started peeling his clothes off, and then he saw the new stuff I'd brought home. "Dude. You're gonna wear a suit and tie to work?"

Josh Jango

"God, I hope not. You have to dress up when you're job hunting. After I get hired, it'll be different. At least, I hope so."

He shook off one of his shoes, and then the other, in different directions. "I hate wearing suits and ties."

"You and me both."

He sat down on the couch and pulled his socks off. "Ties are uncomfortable as hell. And they make me feel like I'm on a leash."

I laughed. "A leash! You know, that's exactly what they are. We're being led around on a leash by the corporate evil."

"I hate wearing clothes anyway." He stood up and took off his pants. "Wearing a shirt buttoned tight around your neck just makes a bad thing worse."

I had to agree.

"Hey, Josh, good news. They're gonna install the phone this Friday. Can you be here?"

"*This* Friday?"

"Yeah. But one of us has to be here between noon and 5 p.m. That's when the telephone dude'll be by." He stripped off his underwear and stood there naked.

"Hell yes. I'll make sure I'm here. That's great!"

"Also, I told them to make our number unlisted. I hope that's okay with you." He reached down and moved his cock and balls around to let them breathe.

"Yeah, A-ok, Zig."

"Alright, dude. I'm taking a shower."

I sat on the couch and did some reading. Ziggy hummed a tune while he washed off the dirt and grease from work. When he came out of the shower he asked me if I wanted to explore the neighborhood.

We walked the residential streets nearby and enjoyed the balmy weather. We got some pizza and carried it over to a grassy spot called Franz Park. We ate while we watched some guys play touch football, then we made our way back to the apartment.

98

Ziggy started stripping as soon as we walked in the door. Shoes and socks came off first, and then his jeans. That was fine with me; I took mine off, too. He took his shirt off, and mine came off, too.

We sat on the couch for a couple of minutes in just our underwear, reading. Then he said, "Hell, might as well take it all off." He stood up and stripped off his briefs. "You said you like going naked, too, right?"

"Uh, yeah, I do.' I stood up and pulled mine off. "I've always liked going naked. I never could do it at home, though. My mother didn't like any kind of nudity. This'll be great, having a friend who likes going natural as much as I do."

"Hell," he said, "you can't get much more natural than this."

We sat there bare-ass, reading, for an hour or so. I got a hard on, like, every five minutes, but I was starting to get used to it, being naked around him. He was right; you can't think about sex all the time.

Then he yawned. He said he was going to bed. Ziggy brushed his teeth and then I watched him scoot under the covers, still naked. He told me to stay up as late as I wanted, but I told him I was sleepy, too. So I brushed, peed, and turned out the lights. I put on my underwear and went over to the bed.

I thought maybe he was already asleep. I slipped into bed in front of him and snuggled back underneath his arm. He was awake after all, though. He said, "Josh, you like going naked as much as I do, so why put *on* your underwear to go to bed?"

"Oh," I said, "um, yeah, I guess that does seem weird, doesn't it?"

"No, it's okay. I don't mind. You should wear them if you want to. I was just curious." He snuggled up close behind me, fitting his soft cock against the fabric snug in the crack of my ass.

"Most of the time I do sleep naked. It's more comfortable," I said.

"Well then, why not now? You're not wearing them because of me, are you?"

"Um, well, yeah, sort of, in a way, yeah."

"But why? God, you don't think I would do something to you in your sleep, do you?"

"No! Of course not. No, it's nothing like that."

"So now I'm really confused. You put them on because of me, but it's not because of me?"

"Okay, it's kind of embarrassing, but I'll see if I can explain."

"Okay." He waited, listening.

"Zig, it would be almost too good. Snuggling up in bed with you, with both of us naked? I don't think I could even fall asleep. My dick would be hard all night long. Look, I would love to sleep naked with you. But I wouldn't get any sleep. I'm not afraid that you would do something to me. Jeez, it would be awesome if you *did* do something. I'm just afraid that I might do something to *you*. In my sleep. If I could even get to sleep. Jesus, that would ruin everything, wouldn't it?"

He still didn't say anything, but at least he was still holding me close; that was comforting.

"Ziggy?"

"Yeah, Josh?"

"Do you understand? Why I'm wearing underwear to bed?"

"Yeah, I get it."

"Okay."

He didn't say anything else.

I felt a bit weird, then, having said all that. I was afraid I said too much. I didn't want there to be an issue between us about me wanting something from him that he wasn't able to give. The more I thought about it, the more I worried. I started wondering if he would even want to sleep together, after this.

"Zig?"

Nothing. And then, half asleep, he said, "What, Josh?"

"I'm sorry. I think I probably shouldn't have told you all that."

"Josh. Bro." He was barely awake. "You worry too much, dude."

"You think so?"

"Damn straight."

I didn't know what to say.

"Sometimes you can think about something too much," he said.

"You think so?"

"I don't think so, I know so."

I didn't answer. What could I say? Neither one of us said anything for a while. Five minutes later I was still wide awake, and wondering if I'd ever get to sleep for worrying.

I figured Ziggy was asleep by then. His breathing wasn't deep, but it was steady and even, and he was relaxed as always, holding me close.

Then, almost like he was talking in his sleep, he said, "Josh?"

I said, "Yeah?"

"If it feels good, do it." That's all he said.

I tried briefly to reason out exactly what he probably meant by that, but I was sick of thinking about all this stuff, sick of worrying. If it feels good, do it.

On an impulse, I reached down and pulled my briefs off and threw them across the room. I snuggled back in close to Ziggy. He hugged me close. His bare skin against my bare ass felt marvelous. His dick rested in the crevice between my ass cheeks, and I thought I could even feel the tickle of his crotch hair against my butt. My cock was rock hard. I was in heaven.

Wednesday

WHEN I WOKE UP Wednesday morning, Ziggy had already gone to work. I wasn't sure of that at first, because I didn't open my eyes right away. I like to keep them closed for a few minutes when I first wake up. It makes it easier to remember what I was dreaming. I love to remember my dreams.

So I was laying there in bed with my eyes still closed. I could smell coffee, but there was no sound at all, no shower running, nobody tip-toeing around getting dressed. I could tell it was bright in there, so I figured the sun was up. That meant Ziggy was on his way to work.

In my dream, Ziggy kissed me. Now, wouldn't that be amazing? Something like that could only happen in my dreams.

He was the most wonderful friend I could ever have. I loved him. He was a friend who expected nothing of me, and a friend who likewise I expected nothing from, except the respect and care that we already shared.

All right, I thought, *time to find a job.*

I got up, ate, showered, dressed, and set out for my two interview appointments. And I handed out my resume to a bunch of employers. It was a long day, and I did a lot of walking, dressed in a corporate costume, wearing a corporate leash. Finally, I made my way back to the apartment. I was beat.

—

BY THE TIME I GOT HOME, Ziggy was already back from work, singing in the shower. I took off my jacket and my shoes and socks and collapsed on the couch. He probably didn't hear me come in. He sung loudly, the way I do sometimes when nobody's home. I was electrified by how beautiful his voice was. I sat there with goose bumps, listening.

I guess I dozed off. When I woke up he was sitting there next to me. Naked, of course; I was learning to expect that. "Hey," I said.

"Hi."

"I fell asleep, didn't I?"

"Yeah."

I sat there for a minute, waking up.

"How'd the job hunt go?" he said.

"Okay, I guess. Time will tell. I had two interviews, and I dropped off a bunch of resumes."

"Dude, you sure look fancy in those clothes. You look like a professional businessman. A handsome one." He smiled.

"Thanks, Zig." I stood up. "Speaking of clothes, I'm gonna lose these and get in the shower. God, I stink. I've been sweating all day." And it was a relief to get all my things off. I padded into the bathroom.

When I came out of the shower, he was sitting naked on the couch, reading.

"How's the book going?"

"Oh, just fine."

"Any different, the third time around?"

"Naw. Just as good as the first two times," he said.

"What's it about?"

"Oh, uh, well, it starts out, this guy is hitching cross country. There's this city that's cut off from the rest of the world, and that's where he's headed to."

"Cut off? How?"

"Um, it doesn't really say what happened. I guess it was some sort of catastrophe or something, but it doesn't say what, just that the city is isolated; they don't have communication with the rest of the world. No telephones, no radio, no TV. Most of the people have already deserted the place, but some stay. And a few people go there, on purpose, to check it out. So, it's a story about the people who keep on living there. How they get along and stuff like that."

"Sounds a little like *Lord of the Flies*."

"Well, these are mostly adults. And they don't go savage. They stay pretty civilized. It's kind of hard to explain."

"I guess I'll have to read it and find out myself."

"Yeah, definitely."

Ziggy wasn't wearing anything, so I didn't put any clothes on either. I picked up the book I was reading and sat down next to him on the couch. We both focused on reading. Neither one of us talked for a while.

Then he said, "You know, there's lots of cool things I like about this book. One thing is how the main character of the story, he's got a girlfriend and a boyfriend, both."

"Oh, yeah?"

"Yeah. Not only that, all three of them are lovers together. They're like a threesome. They have sex together and sleep together and everything."

"Really?"

"Yeah. What do you think about that?"

"I like it. How'd that happen? I mean, how did they all meet each other?"

"It just happens. They meet and . . . it works out that way. I think it's so cool, that Delaney put that in his novel, like it's a normal thing for people to do when the right people meet up with each other."

"Yeah," I said, "I used to think about that kind of thing all the time. I wanted to do that with my best friend and his girlfriend."

"You did? Really?"

"Oh, yeah. I wanted him really bad, Zig. But he was straight, and he was dating her."

"Did you want his girlfriend, too?"

"Oh, sure. She was a real cutie, and a lot of fun, too. You couldn't help but like her. Anyway, I didn't like the idea of being jealous. He was my best friend. I wanted him to be happy. I didn't want to break them up; I just wanted to be part of it."

"So, you wanted both of them?"

"Yeah, both of them. Especially him. I wanted him so bad I could hardly stand it. God, I can still remember what he looked like naked." My dick started getting hard.

"I guess you lusted for him big time, huh?" Ziggy watched my cock grow.

"Well, yeah, I did, but it was more than lust. I really loved him. I wouldn't have lusted for him so much if I didn't love him, too."

"I understand. So, it gave you a hard on, to think about fucking both of them together? Him and her together?"

"Hell, yes. I wanted that, really, really bad."

"That's wild, Josh." He looked again at my hard cock. "You really could have done that? You could have fucked her?"

"Yeah, I could."

Ziggy stared at me for a while without saying anything else. Then he went back to reading his book, so I went back to mine, too.

A couple of minutes later, Ziggy lowered his book and looked at me. "Really," he said, "you could have sex with a woman?"

"Well, sure," I said. "Why not?" He just looked at me. "Okay, I admit, she'd likely be my buddy's passion more than mine. She'd be for him more than for me. But yeah, I could definitely do it."

"But Josh. You're gay."

"So what? I could still have a relationship with a woman. If she . . . I don't know, if she understood."

"Understood what, that you're gay?"

"Yeah."

"You could fuck her?"

"Of course I could fuck her, Zig. If I thought she was sexy. If she wanted me to. If *you* wanted me to."

Ziggy stared at me like it was some kind of revelation. Then he raised his book up and started reading again. That's when I noticed his cock was not just hard, it was rock hard and standing up stiffer than I'd ever seen it before. It was so rigid it wasn't even throbbing. And he hadn't even touched it. Pre-cum was glistening on the head and starting to drip down the side.

"Holy shit, Zig."

He looked at me, and then he looked down at his cock. "I've got a stiffy, don't I?"

"If it was any stiffer, it would turn into a tree. God almighty!"

He put his book down and looked at his hard dick. Meanwhile, my cock had stiffened up and grown even bigger, if that was possible. It was way beyond hard and, like Ziggy's, approaching critical mass. Seeing Ziggy's beautiful cock rigid like that gave me shivers.

We both sat there, looking at his dick. He wasn't self conscious about it at all. "Zig," I said, "do you think I could take a really close look at it?"

"Aw, sure," he said, grinning. "Why not?" He got up and stood right in front of me, with his arms folded. Then he moved even closer, with his legs spread wide, straddling mine. I think he enjoyed showing off. "Don't touch it, though, or I'll shoot," he said. "I'm that close."

"And you were calling me a horny bastard," I said. "Look at you." His rigid, fat dick was about three inches from my face, with pre-cum fluid oozing out of the tip. I had one hand on my own hard cock, and I really wanted to wrap my other hand around his and bring him off. But we had never done that before, and I didn't want to presume too much.

"It doesn't get any harder than this," he said. "I feel like I could explode."

"You look like it, too."

"I need to come, really bad. It almost hurts, it's so hard."

"Well, that should be easy to take care of," I said, stroking my own hard cock.

"It's your fault, too, bro."

"My fault?"

"Yeah. Thinking about you and me, fucking some woman together, taking turns and stuff like that, that's what got it so hard."

"You'd like that?"

"Oh, yeah."

This was getting interesting! I slowly jacked my dick while I watched the clear fluid flowing out of his cock. It was all down the sides and was even dripping onto his balls. "You're driving me crazy, Zig, with this hard dick of yours."

"Fuck, how do you think I feel?"

A strand of pre-cum dripped down from his balls, slowly stretching all the way down until I felt it touch my bare foot. I reached out and slid my finger along the bottom of his ball sac to gather it up.

Ziggy shuddered and said, "Dude!"

I put the finger in my mouth and tasted his pre-cum.

"You almost made me shoot," he said.

"I didn't get it all," I said. "Uh, can I do it again?"

He shivered uncontrollably for a moment and stared at me, wide-eyed.

It was a constant flow of juice dripping down his dick. Another strand was already stretching down toward my feet again. I didn't mind. It could drip all over my feet; that was okay with me. "Your stuff is dripping off your balls, Zig."

"I can't help it, Josh. I need to come, bro."

He watched my hand as I reached out toward him again. I paused when my fingers were just an inch or two below his ball sac. I looked up to see his reaction. We looked each other in the eye for a few seconds; then he looked down again at my hand. He didn't shy away at all; he stayed right there, only a few inches away. Then he tilted his head back and closed his eyes and waited.

Chapter 8
CLOSER

NOW I KNEW he wanted me to stroke his balls again, and that's what I was going to do. But when I reached underneath, palm up, I went farther than I did before. I put my hand through his legs and gently touched the end of my finger right up into Ziggy's butt crack. Near his asshole.

Pulling my hand gently toward me, I caressed the skin between his asshole and his ball sac, stroked the bottom of his balls, and then slid my fingers halfway up the underside of his stiff cock, gathering up the dripping pre-cum so I could bring it to my mouth.

But I didn't get that far. As soon as I touched his ass crack he started moaning. As my fingers slid across his slippery balls he said, "Awww, FUCK!" The real surprise came when my fingers moved up the slippery base of his cock. I hadn't even taken my fingers off his slick boner when he groaned, his dick jerked and clicked, and it shot a huge glob of cum right smack into the middle of my face.

In a gut reaction I leaned back, but that didn't take me out of the line of fire.

One spurt right after another flew out of his cock and soaked my face and my hair and my chest. A couple of the last shots landed on my belly and my crotch, with him moaning and groaning the whole time.

He had his eyes closed until he almost fell backward on his ass, halfway through his eruption, but he caught his balance. After his dick was finally done shooting he turned around and plopped down on the couch next to me.

"Christ," he said.

I wiped the cum off my face, licking my hands.

"My god, I can't remember the last time I came that hard," he said.

I scooped dripping jizz off my belly and chest and licked my fingers.

"Josh," he said, "thanks. That was fantastic. Your touch, man, that's what did it. I owe you one."

"Oh, well, don't thank me," I said. "I hardly did anything."

"Yeah, you did. You sure as hell did. Hey, did I get some on you?"

"You shot your whole load on me, Zig."

"Oh, fuck. I'm sorry, Josh. I was pretty much out of control."

"No problem," I said. "It was awesome. You know I like your cum."

"I couldn't help it. That felt so good, bro."

I checked myself over for any more of his cum that I might have missed. Then he said, "You've still got some on your cheek, dude."

"Where?"

He reached over and moved his finger gently across my cheek to scoop it up. "There," he said. He held his finger out like he didn't know what to do with it, now that he had it.

"Here," I said. I grabbed his hand and put his finger in my mouth and licked it clean. He smiled and blushed.

"Have you ever tasted your own jizz?" I said.

"Naw."

"You ought to."

"What's it taste like?"

"Good. Yours, especially."

"Yeah, but what's it taste like?"

"Um, it's a little salty, like sea water, or tears. But it's kind of sweet, too, in a way. Yours, especially. A little bit like fresh broccoli, maybe. It's not a strong taste, though. It's good. I like it."

"Maybe I'll try it someday," he said. "But I don't think I'm ready for that, yet." He thought about it for a minute. "Jesus, why would I want to taste my own cum, though? If I ever tasted anybody's cum, it'd be yours, not mine." Then he looked at my hard dick. "Josh, you didn't come yet."

"Yeah, but it's no big deal."

"Yes it is! You've got to come, bro. I want *you* to feel good, too."

"Okay."

"Cool!" He leaned back and rested his arm on the back of the couch, around my shoulders. "Are you gonna jack off?" He seemed eager to watch. His dick was still big.

I looked at his dick while I started to stroke mine. "Yeah, I'm gonna jack off. Unless you want to help."

"Oh, hell," he said. "I wouldn't know what to do. I'll just watch." He was blushing again.

"I was just kidding. That's okay. I love to jack off." I stroked my cock for a minute or two, putting on a little show for him. He seemed to be thinking about something, though.

"I should help," he said. "You helped me; fair's fair."

"You don't have to, Zig."

"I want to. So tell me what you want me to do, Josh."

All sorts of things went through my head, but I couldn't ask for any of them. Ziggy was my straight friend. I couldn't ask him to jack me off, or to do any of the other things that came to mind. Just asking him to touch me seemed like asking too much.

Whatever he did would have to be his own idea. "Zig, you'll think of something. But really, you don't have to do anything. I'm getting off just on you watching me."

"You sure?"

"Yeah, I'm sure." I went on stroking for another couple of minutes, and, yeah, it was hot, Ziggy watching me. What an exhibitionist I was! His dick was getting stiff again, standing up straight, so I figured he was enjoying it, too.

"I've got an idea," he said. "Stand up." I stood up. He said, "Bring your dick over here, in front of me." I moved around so I was standing in front of him. "Yeah, like that. Like when you were sitting down and it was me who was standing in front of you. Spread your legs."

I moved my feet apart. I felt a pleasant, shivery tingling all over, from following Ziggy's orders.

"Get closer. Here." He put his knees together. "Closer." I stepped forward until I had one leg on each side of him, straddling his thighs. My dick was almost in his face. "Okay," he said. "Stroke your cock, slowly. Keep on stroking, and get yourself close to shooting off. But don't come yet."

"Okay." I jacked while he watched.

"You've got some nice abs, Josh." He reached up and gently ran his hand over my belly. "Have I ever told you that?"

I shivered. "Mmm. That feels good, Zig. You've got a nice touch. I'm really sensitive there."

"Yeah, I know, me, too." He caressed my belly a couple more times, then he leaned back in the couch and watched me jack my cock some more. He took hold of his own slippery cock. "You've got big balls, too," he said.

"Not any bigger than yours, Zig. I like your balls."

"Me, too," he said. "I mean, you know, I like your balls, too." He stroked his cock with one hand, spreading his slick pre-cum around the way he does, while he tugged at his balls with the other hand.

I was getting that tingly feeling all over from the way Ziggy was talking, and from him watching me, and from me watching him. My cock started feeling it, too. "I think I'm starting to get close, Zig."

"Good. Keep jacking. You're gonna shoot your load on me. But try not to come in my face, okay? I don't think I'm ready for that."

"Okay."

"You can come on me, that's cool, just not on my face, alright?

111

And make sure you tell me when you're close." He kept stroking his cock.

I was close already, but I figured what he meant was to tell him when I was really, really close. So I stroked gently for another minute or two, and then I started feeling like, this was it. "Zig, I'm gonna come if I keep this up."

"Okay. Keep on jacking." He watched my cock and he watched my face, and when he heard me start moaning, he took his hand off his slippery cock and reached between my legs and stuck his finger into my butt crack, right up against my asshole!

I groaned. I was past the point of no return. He kept his finger up against my hole and with his other hand he tugged gently on my ball sac.

"Ohhhhhhhh!" That was it. I leaned back, aimed my dick down at his chest, my hips bucked and my dick started spurting. Never had I felt so good. He kept his slick finger pressed right up against my anus while I was coming, and when I bucked and moaned and groaned his finger slipped inside an inch or two. That set me off even more. That, and him tickling my balls.

Once he saw I was shooting, he took his hand off my balls and furiously jacked his own cock, but he kept the finger inserted up my ass. He said, "I'm coming, too! Coming, Josh," and his second load started launching up into the air.

His finger slid even deeper into my ass while he was jacking and shooting and groaning. Most of his cum landed on me. Most of mine fell on him. When we were finally spent I stood there, straddling his legs, with my balls on his wrist and his finger still up my asshole. It was a very intimate moment.

Ziggy sat there with his eyes closed and his mouth open, dazed. We were both covered with cum. I liked having his finger up my ass. I closed my eyes, too. I felt marvelous.

"Oh, man," he said. I opened my eyes and he was looking up at me. "I didn't mean to do that, sorry." His face was red. He slowly, very gently, withdrew his finger from my butt. Then he casually held his finger up to look at it briefly, making sure it looked clean. It did. "Did I hurt you?"

"Not at all. It felt really good, Zig."

"Okay."

"In fact, it made me come extra good."

He laughed. "Well, that's good, then. Glad I could help."

"Oh, you did. That was amazing."

"Cool. Hey, let's take a shower," he said. "Get cleaned up."

"Okay." Did he mean, take one together? Now, that would be awesome.

He walked to the bathroom, and I followed. I waited in the doorway as he turned on the water and felt the temperature. He looked at me as he stepped into the tub. "What are you waiting for? Come on."

I was there in a flash, stepping into the shower right behind him. He stood under the spray and thoroughly drenched himself. Then he slipped beside me as we switched places. I got under the water while he soaped up.

Then I offered to wash his back, which was fine with him; he did the same for me. We took turns getting under the water until we were both done.

We finished drying off in the living room.

"Hey," he said, "you want to take a walk?"

—

WE DID A COUPLE OF BONG HITS first; then we threw on some clothes and headed out. Ziggy chose a different way out of the neighborhood this time.

"This is exciting," I said.

"Yeah?"

"Yeah. This is my home now. But there's so much I haven't seen yet. I like St. Louis so far."

"It's a good place to be."

"I'm lucky to have a friend to show me around. It's like having a welcoming committee."

"Oh, hell, I'm the lucky one, Josh. To have somebody to share it with."

"Maybe we're both lucky, then. But I couldn't have found a better friend. I could look for the rest of my life and I'd probably never find anyone like you. You're one of a kind, Zig."

"God, I hope so." He laughed. "One of me is plenty. But seriously, the same goes for you, Josh."

"Nah, not me."

"Yeah, really. You're different. You're not like anybody else. You've got a kind heart, bro; that in itself is a treasure. So don't ever sell yourself short, okay?"

"Sometimes I wonder."

"And I'm honored to know you, Josh. You could have your pick of friends."

"Now I'm gonna get embarrassed."

"And you're humble, too, just naturally." He put his arm around my shoulder. "You and me, pal. Maybe we're loners, or misfits, or freaks, but we found each other. And of that, I'm glad."

"Amen," I said. "I'm glad, too."

That's about the time I started believing I really had a brother in Ziggy, a true spirit brother. And I loved the way he was so relaxed with physical intimacy. He touched me all the time, casually, like it was the most natural and normal thing to do. I wasn't used to that, not even with my own family, but it was something I needed. Everyone needs that.

We walked across a highway bridge, crossed a busy intersection, and then we entered a path among some trees. We were in some sort of park.

"Do you know a lot of people, Zig? Here in St. Louis?"

"Not really. Not anymore. Not since high school. I tend to keep a low profile these days, Josh."

"That's hard to believe," I said. "I think you really stand out.

114

I'll bet lots of people want to be your friend."

"I don't usually give people much to remember me by. You'd be surprised how invisible you can be. Well, maybe you wouldn't be surprised. You probably know what I'm talking about."

"Yeah. I do. Sometimes people don't see me, even when I'm standing right in front of them. But with me, I think it's because I'm so shy."

"There's not that much difference."

"What do you mean?"

"You're shy because you don't want to get burned. Well, I don't want to get burned, either. Both of us could have more friends if we wanted to."

"I think being shy is part of my nature, Zig. I've tried to overcome it, but some things are just ingrained."

"It's okay. I like you fine just the way you are, Josh."

"Alright."

We were following a hiking trail through the park.

"Jeez," I said, "we're lucky we even met, you know that?"

"Yeah, that's a fact," he said. "Between you being shy, and me being cautious, we're lucky we even talked."

"Well, yeah, but what are the chances we'd even meet, with you living here and me in Memphis?"

"Slim to nothing."

"And in a gay bar, too."

"Well, it's an after-hours bar," he said. "Anything goes, in that place."

"So I noticed. Memphis doesn't have a club like that," I said.

"Do you go out to bars much?"

"When I'm lonely, I do."

"Yeah," he said. "Same here."

We walked for a while without talking. That was difficult for me to imagine, Ziggy being lonely. "Zig," I said, "tell me if it's none of my business, okay? But have you ever met a girl you thought about marrying?"

"Jesus, what made you think of that?"

"Oh, uh, I guess I was thinking about you being lonely. Sorry, I don't mean to be nosy."

"Nah, that's okay, Josh, I don't mind. Don't worry about getting too personal. Not with me, okay?"

"Okay."

"Yeah," he said, "I knew one girl who I probably would've married, if things had happened differently. She was a real sweetheart. And smart, too. We liked each other a lot."

"What happened?"

"She said we had to stop seeing each other. Said her therapist told her so. She needed to settle down and find a stable businessman to marry. In other words, some boring guy in a suit. Who wanted to raise a family."

"Weird."

"Yeah, I thought so, too. She said she used to be wild, hung out with bikers and did crazy shit and stuff, and she missed that kind of thing, but her therapist told her that wasn't what she wanted."

"So," I said, "you ended up in the same category as bikers?"

"I guess so. Life with me would have been too uncertain. She was looking for something predictable, I guess. The white picket fence and all that crap. That's not me, not at all. Not the married life, at least."

"You would have married her, though?"

"I thought about it later, and yeah, I probably would have. She could have talked me into it. She was definitely unique."

"Wow. Too bad, Zig. I hope she knows she missed out on something good."

"Yeah, well, maybe so, but it was probably for the best."

"You think so?"

"Definitely. I'm not the marrying type. I like being independent. You marry someone, all of a sudden you're obligated to sacrifice your individuality for the relationship. That might work for some people, but not for me."

"Yeah," I said, "I've seen how that works."

"Anyway, that's the only girl I ever came close to marrying. I don't expect I'll ever marry anybody, now. I'll just take my chances being single."

"I'll bet you don't have any problem finding a girl when you want one, though."

"Sure I do. I'm picky, dude. And most women are picky, too. I wouldn't have it any other way."

"I guess I was just curious. Maybe I didn't know straight guys get lonely, too?"

"Now you're really talking crazy," he said.

"Yeah. Okay. Everybody gets lonely sometimes. I guess I knew that."

"Sure." We kept walking. "But listen, Josh, you keep calling me straight. I don't think of myself that way, dude. I mean, I like women, but that doesn't mean I have to *only* like women, does it? It makes me a little uncomfortable when you call me that. Like I'm some dude trapped in a cage."

"Jeez, I'm sorry."

"No problem, bro. Just letting you know."

We were still in the park. I thought we'd have reached the other side by now. It had to be gigantic. Right in the middle of the city. I looked around and said, "Zig, what is this place?"

"Forest Park. Ever heard of it?"

"No. My god, it's huge."

"Yeah, it is. Close to home, too. I come here a lot." We kept walking. "So, Josh, you said you had a girlfriend, too."

"Yeah, I did."

"How'd that go?"

"She was really nice. And down to earth. An artist. We met at college. I was friends with her and her best friend both. I'd go over to the apartment they shared, like, almost every day, and we'd hang out."

"How far did it go?"

"It was never anything formal. We never said we were boy-friend/girlfriend. We never even had sex."

"Really?"

"See, the thing was, I knew I was horny for guys more than girls, but I wanted to be like everybody else. People thought it was wrong to be gay, and I guess I didn't want to be, you know, an outcast. So I thought I could fight it and overcome it and be normal."

"Normal, huh? What a strange concept that is."

"It was pretty crazy. Liking guys, that was part of who I was. I must have known that it wasn't gonna change. But I thought I could ignore it and be straight anyway. Stupid, huh?"

"Nah. You didn't want to be an outcast, nothing stupid about that. And you had a girl you cared about."

"Yeah. I really liked her, and she liked me. We had something special together, no doubt about that. I had this idea we could be a couple, if I could give up my yearning for, you know, a boyfriend."

"Did she know you liked guys?"

"We never talked about it. I guess she must have wondered why I wasn't trying to make out with her and stuff. It was a fucked-up situation, Zig. I didn't want to admit to *myself* that I was queer, let alone talk about it with somebody else."

"Josh, that is so sad, dude."

"I never would have made any moves on her. I figured that out later. I wasn't horny for her, Zig, or for any girl. But I was getting closer to her than I'd ever been to anybody else, ever, and I loved her for that. We were getting to be soul mates or something. Or at least it felt that way to me."

"So what happened?"

"She and her roommate went to Europe for a year. It was this hitchhiking trip they'd been planning since high school. While she was there, she met a French guy and they ended up getting engaged. Somewhere along the line, she gave up on me, and she was right to do that, but it still hurt me. A lot."

"Sure it did. You loved her."

"Yeah. I did."

We continued along the hiking path; still within Forest Park. Now we were next to the St. Louis Zoo. The park seemed to go on forever.

"I wish I knew you back then, Josh. I would have been real with you, dude, straight up."

"Yeah! That would have been so great, Zig, if we'd been friends back then."

"You could have talked to me about anything, bro." He put his arm around my shoulder. "Being horny for guys—I would have told you it was perfectly okay. I would have told you to go for it."

"Yeah. Damn, that would have been awesome. I sure wish *somebody* had told me that back then."

"Somebody sure as hell should have. There must have been some people who had a hunch you were gay." He took his arm off my shoulder and gently ruffled my hair. "Somebody should have had a heart and told you not to worry about it."

"Oh, well. Maybe I had to learn it on my own," I said. "Maybe in this life I needed to learn the lesson of being true to myself, of accepting myself. And to trust my own feelings."

"In this life?"

"Yeah, you know, reincarnation and all that."

"Okay. I wasn't sure if you believed in that."

"Well, I don't know what I believe, but I think reincarnation is definitely a possibility."

"I think so, too," he said. "Actually, I'm almost sure of it. I just don't know the details of how it all works, but I do believe in it."

We came to a road, and another bridge that crossed the highway back to our neighborhood. But the park went on, beyond the road. Ziggy said, "We'll come back and see the rest of the park later if you want to. There's a lot to see."

"Sure."

"This is one of my favorite places. I walk here all the time."

119

"Yeah, definitely. I want to see the whole park."

We left the hiking path and followed the sidewalk to the bridge. "So, Josh," he said, "have you ever fucked a woman?"

"I wanted to. Even after I admitted I was gay and I knew it wouldn't change, I still wanted to try it with a woman. To find out what I was missing. Just so I'd know."

"Makes sense to me," he said.

"So I did, sort of."

"Sort of?"

"Yeah, well, I found myself in a situation where it was now or never. There was this woman who took a liking to me, and I was pretty sure she knew I was gay, or bisexual, but she was interested anyway, so I didn't have to worry about her finding out the shocking truth, you know, if I, you know, couldn't get it up."

"Right, I get it."

"So one day we were alone and we started petting; you know, making out and kissing and taking our clothes off and, I don't know, it just seemed like a good time to see if my dick would go up her pussy."

"Damn, Josh, you did that? You've got nerve, my man."

"I was surprised, myself. But anyway, I tried for a couple of minutes, but it just wasn't finding a place to slide into. I don't know what I was doing wrong, to tell you the truth."

"Was your dick hard?"

"Yeah, it was hard. I wanted to fuck her. But after a couple of minutes of fiddling around, I began feeling like I didn't know what I was doing. And she just looked at me like, "You're on your own, buster, I'm not gonna give you lessons." And I started wondering, jeez, what am I doing here? So I eased off and we kissed and made out some more. Then, I don't know, we decided to do something else. And that was the end of it."

"That was it?"

"Yeah."

"Dude." Neither of us talked for a minute. "Well," he said, "maybe it was just as well."

"Pretty weird, huh?"

"No, not weird. At least you tried, Josh. I'm proud of you, bro. I'll bet most gay dudes wouldn't have the nerve to try something like that."

"Yeah. I did try."

We walked past a burger place. Ziggy said, "Are you hungry?"

"Yeah, I'm starving."

"Want to eat here?"

"Sure."

"I'm kind of curious, though," he said. "Just now you said you weren't horny for any girl. But earlier, you said you could fuck a woman if . . . you know, if—"

"If she was your passion, and you wanted me to? Damn right I could."

"But how is that different?"

"Because you'd be there! We'd all be naked together, and you and your fat dick and your beautiful ass would be right there, and I'd be putting my dick in the same place where yours had been, and I'd be knowing I was doing something that turned you on, and . . . I don't know, it would just be completely different. I'd be having sex with *you, that's* how it would be different."

"Josh," he said, smiling. "Josh, Josh, Josh. You really have a way with words, dude." He looked like he was trying not to laugh. "I think I'm getting it, now. Loud and clear."

We reached the counter and ordered. We took our food to a corner table and dug right in. Ziggy wasn't talking. Maybe it was just because he was eating, but I was afraid I'd said something wrong.

"I . . . I hope I didn't gross you out, Zig. Fuck, I told myself I would never put you on the spot like that. I'm sorry."

"What do you mean, put me on the spot?"

"You know. About sex."

121

"What are you talking about?"

"About you and me having sex," I said.

"What about us having sex?"

"I didn't want you to think I was expecting it."

"Oh, hell, I know that."

"You do?"

"Of course."

I just looked at him.

He put his food down. "Look," he said. "You're one of the most unassuming people I've ever met. That's one reason I feel so comfortable around you. You're not looking to see what you can get out of me. You're not expecting anything at all from me, except friendship. I really love you for that, Josh."

"Okay."

"And you know I like women. You accept that. You're okay with that. That's so awesome, Josh. You're the first gay man I've ever met who accepts me the way I am—and still wants to be friends. That means a lot to me."

"Well, yeah, of course I do, Zig. I wouldn't be a friend if I didn't accept you the way you are."

"You see? I'm the same way. I tell you, Josh, you and me have a hell of a lot in common. A lot. Look, I don't mind you wanting to have sex with me. Hell, it's flattering. I'd probably wonder if something was wrong with me if you didn't. And you know what? I like it. Sometimes it turns me on, knowing you're watching. So relax and don't worry about it, okay?"

"You sure?"

"Definitely. You're gay, and I like women, but so what? We're in this together, and any differences that come up are just gonna make it that much more interesting."

He picked up his food again and smiled. "I like things interesting." He took a big bite of an onion ring.

Chapter 9
CONNECTING

"AND LISTEN," he said, "as far as sex between you and me goes, we will, bro, we will. You know, when we fuck a woman together. I want that just as much as you do. That whole thing turns me on."

"Yeah, I remember. Jeez, I'll never forget! Your dick was about to explode, just thinking about it."

"Hell, yes. You know that turns me on. It would be so hot. I'd love to see you fucking somebody with that big cock of yours. And I know just what you mean about putting your dick where mine has been. I'd love that. You and me taking turns fucking the same pussy? That would be so awesome."

It sounded awesome to me, too. "Let's do it, Zig."

"Damn straight! Tell you what, I'm gonna check out this woman tomorrow, Eleanor, see if she's open to stuff like that. We'll find someone. We'll make sure it's a girl you feel comfortable with. We'll find someone you like." He looked at me and grinned.

"Okay," I said. "I think I'll need some pointers first, though."

"Yeah, bro, it wouldn't hurt to get you up to speed on a few things."

"I'm pretty ignorant about fucking, if you want to know the truth."

"But you fuck guys, though, right?"

"No. A couple of times, that's it."

"No way." He laughed. "You're kidding."

"It's true. I don't know the first thing about fucking."

He just stared at me for the longest time. I started to feel uncomfortable, wondering what the heck was going through Ziggy's mind.

Finally he said, "Dude. I had you figured for one of those shy, quiet types who take charge when you get another guy in the sack."

"Nah." I felt myself beginning to blush. "Not me. I haven't learned how to control the situation like that. Not so far, anyway."

He seemed truly surprised. We continued eating for a while. Then he said, "Okay, so, other guys fuck you, then. That's cool."

"No, hardly ever. It hurts too much, Zig." He just stared at me, until I said "What? What did I say?"

"Sorry. I guess I don't know as much about being gay as I thought I did. Hey, let's get out of here, Josh. Are you done?"

We went back outside, made our way across a few busy streets, and then we were back on Clayton Avenue.

As soon as it was quiet enough to talk I told him, "Zig, not every gay man is a top or a bottom. I know that's what a lot of straight people think, but there's much more to it than that."

"I guess there must be a lot of variation, huh? From guy to guy?"

"Sure. Everybody's different. And a lot of guys don't fuck at all. A lot of guys aren't even interested in fucking. There's other ways, you know. To get each other off. Good ways."

"I've heard all about guys sucking each other's cocks," he said, "so I guess I should have known better, I see that now. But I just figured all guys like to fuck. Or get fucked. Or do both. Even cocksuckers. That just shows how little I know."

"Not all guys. Not me."

"Why not?"

"Well, I like to suck. I do. I like it. And I like to get sucked. Another thing that's hot is jacking off right next to each other. Jacking each other off, that's even better. Those are my favorite things. Fucking, I don't know, I've never enjoyed it that much."

"But why?"

"Well, um, I guess because it hurts."

"Yeah, that would be a good reason."

124

"I've tried, but you can't enjoy something that hurts."

"But Josh, it doesn't have to hurt. You just had the wrong guys fucking you, dude."

"Maybe so."

"Seriously. Hell, getting fucked really feels good if the guy knows what he's doing."

"Yeah, so I hear."

"Dude. You don't believe me?"

"I believe you, Zig. But somehow I always get the guys who don't know how, or don't care. Bad luck, I guess."

"It's not luck at all. Listen to me, Josh. You've got to learn how to stay in control. If a guy wants to fuck you and he's not doing it right, then by god, you give him only two choices. *Don't* fuck you, or else do it *your* way. Either he lets *you* tell *him* how to make you feel good, or he doesn't get to do it at all. Period. That's just the way it's gotta be. You can't let people hurt you, Josh. You just can't."

"You make it sound so simple."

"It *is* simple. I know this sounds kind of crazy—a guy who likes women telling a gay guy how to get fucked—but I know what I'm talking about."

"But I wouldn't even know what to tell him, Zig. I don't know the first thing about fucking. All I know is, lube it up and stick it in. But that's what the guys who fuck me do, and it hurts. I don't want to be fucked if it's gonna hurt, and I don't want to fuck anybody else, either, if it means I'd be hurting them."

"Okay, okay. I understand. And that's right; you shouldn't do it if it's gonna hurt. But fucking is a good thing, Josh. It's an awesome thing! You need somebody to show you how good it can be. Show you how it's done. That's the only way you're gonna learn how to be a good fucker yourself. Tell you what, let me think on that for a while, okay?"

"You think you might know somebody who can show me?"

"Yeah, maybe I do. I'll have to work this out in my head, first. Give me some time to think about it, okay?" We stopped at the market on Clayton, and I picked up another newspaper. I still had a job to find. After we left the market Ziggy said, "You could watch me fuck, for starters. That way you could see how it's done."

I was speechless. Watch Ziggy fuck? I'd pay money for that. I tried to say something, but I couldn't get the words out of my mouth.

"It wouldn't make you a true believer," he said. "You'd have to be the one getting fucked for that, but you could watch how I do it. I don't want to sound like I'm bragging, but I'm really good at getting them to enjoy it."

I finally managed to get it out: "You'd let me watch?"

"Hell yeah, bro! Of course I would let you watch. Dude. My cock's getting hard right now, thinking about it."

"Mine is, too," I said. "I'd love to watch you fuck. But I don't know if the *woman* would want me watching."

"Yeah, therein lies the catch."

"Unless we find a girl who wants me to join in," I said.

"Well, that could happen. We were already looking for that kind of situation."

"Zig, listen. I really do want to learn to fuck. For me, at least, I know it's something I've been missing out on. It really turns me on when I watch guys do it in movies. Especially when they *both* have hard-ons. They look like they're having so much fun. No, not fun, what I mean is, pleasure. Ecstasy! I get off on imagining me being part of that. Either part. I would love to take turns, being top and bottom. I want to do both. But the pain spoils it for me."

"What part of it hurts?"

"All of it! It hurts my asshole when they push it in, and then it hurts inside, too. Maybe I'm not relaxing enough. Hell, I don't know what it is."

"Yeah, I'm sure that's what it is. You've got to relax, bro."

"I can't. Not when I know it's gonna hurt."

"But it won't hurt, if you relax."

126

"That's easy to say. And I know it must be true. But I guess my asshole doesn't know that."

"Okay, okay. Let me think a minute." We went inside our apartment building and walked up the stairs.

As soon as we walked into the apartment, we started taking off our clothes. Going naked at home was fast becoming the normal state of affairs. Ziggy dropped his shoes, one by one, and then he pulled his socks off. "Okay, let me ask you this, Josh. How did you learn about jacking off?" He unbuttoned his jeans and pulled them off. I did the same.

"Um, I remember playing with my dick a lot when I took baths. My dick would get hard, and it felt good for it to be hard, so I would try to keep it that way. Then one day, when I was flopping it back and forth, I had my first climax, and I was hooked forever."

Ziggy smiled. "Climax?"

I took off the rest of my clothes, down to my socks. "That's what it was called, in a facts-of-life book I found hidden in my dad's dresser drawer." I sat down and pulled off my socks. "It's weird to remember all this stuff again."

"Okay, so you played with your cock a lot, that's cool. Definitely a good start. Did you play with your ass much?"

"Um, no, I don't remember doing that."

"Didn't you ever tickle your asshole?" He pulled his briefs off, tossed them on the bed, and stood naked. "Run your fingers over your hole and tickle yourself there, stuff like that? Maybe even stick your finger up there sometimes?"

"No, I don't remember ever doing that."

"Okay." He went into the bathroom to pee.

I followed him to the bathroom door and watched. "Did you? Play with your asshole?"

"You bet I did. I played with my butt as much as I played with my cock, back when I first started getting horny. It felt good. I thought everybody did."

"Nah. I didn't."

127

"Okay, then, Josh. That's it. That's your homework."

He finished and I took his place, peeing in the toilet. "My homework is to play with my asshole?"

"Do you really want some help with this?"

"Yes. I do."

"Okay. You're the student, I'm the teacher. And I'm giving you some homework, okay?"

"Okay."

"The thing to remember in all of this is, it's all about feeling good. Right?"

"Right."

"So listen. Every time you shower, you play with your asshole."

"Uh, okay." I shook the last few drops off my cock and flushed the toilet. We walked back out to the living room.

"Seriously. I want you to soap up your fingers and play around with your butt. Be gentle. Do whatever what feels good. Let your fingers go inside there. You liked it when my finger went up your butt, didn't you? You said you did."

"Sure I did. That was awesome."

"Okay. So, do that to yourself. Play with your asshole. You don't have to put your finger inside at first. Only if it feels good. But play around. You and your asshole need to become really good friends. Explore! For at least five minutes, every time you shower, I want you to explore your asshole. Play as long as you like, if it feels good. Play until the hot water runs out, if you want to. Promise me."

"Okay, sure, I'll do it. I promise." I would have felt weird talking about this with anybody else, especially standing there buck naked like we were, but it seemed perfectly natural with Ziggy.

"Cool," he said. "You can do this. There's only one rule: no pain. Only do what feels good. You work on that, and let me know, um, Friday. How it's going. In the meantime, Teacher will be planning your next assignment."

"Okay."

Ziggy grinned. "We'll make you an expert fucker before you know it. One way or another. I guarantee it."

—

ZIGGY WENT INTO THE KITCHEN to get some soda, and I sat down with the newspaper. I didn't want to miss any new job listings. He sat on the couch and read his book for a while. Then he put the book down for a minute. "Hey, Josh?"

"Yeah?"

"Now that you've shared the bed a few nights, I was wondering what you think about it."

"I like it."

"Are you sleeping okay?"

"Sure. I'm sleeping great. How about you?"

"Oh, great. Better than ever."

"Cool."

"So," he said, "you're okay with how small the bed is?"

"Oh, sure. The way we sleep, it's all we need. Um, how about you? You want a bigger bed?"

"No, that one's big enough."

"Do you miss having it all to yourself?"

"No! Hell, no."

"Okay." I began to wonder what this was all about. It seemed like he was being very careful with his words.

"I was just wondering," he said.

"Wondering what?"

"If our apartment was bigger, say, and we had plenty of room, would you want a bed that was bigger? If we had room for it?"

I put the newspaper down. "If we had a bigger apartment?"

"Yeah."

"And plenty of room?"

"Yeah."

"In that case," I said, "I'd still want to sleep with you in that tiny little bed. Zig, it doesn't need to be any bigger. No matter how much room we have." Now Ziggy was grinning. "I love sleeping together like we do, Zig. But if *you* want a bigger bed, then we can get a bigger bed."

"No, dude, I never said I wanted a bigger bed."

"I know you didn't say it, Zig. But do you?"

"Jesus, no, Josh. I don't want a bigger bed, either. I like it just the way it is. I only wanted to make sure you're completely okay with it. That's all." He picked up his book again, smiling.

I was happy, too. Life was good.

When I was done with the newspaper, I started reading my book.

Another half hour went by, and then Ziggy yawned and stretched his arms. "I'm going to bed, Josh. Stay up as long as you want, okay? Don't worry, the light won't bother me. I can sleep through anything."

"You sure?"

"Yeah, sure, no problem. Don't worry about making noise, either. You won't wake me up. Raid the fridge or take a shower, you won't wake me."

"Okay."

He put his book away and went into the bathroom. He brushed his teeth and peed. Then he came back out and sat on the bed. "We'll be stopping by here when I get off work tomorrow. She's gonna drive me home so I can shower and put on some fresh clothes. Before we go out to dinner."

"Okay." I hadn't forgotten about his date. "No problem. I'll spend a few hours at the library so you can have the place to yourself."

"No, Josh, I want you two to meet each other. She knows about you. She wants to meet you."

"She knows about me?"

"Well, I didn't tell her you're gay yet. But yeah, she knows we're sharing the place. She's cool; she knows how much I like you."

"Well, okay. If you want me here, I'll be here."

"Definitely. If you don't have something else you were gonna do."

"I'll be job hunting, but I'll make sure I'm home by the time you get off work."

"Cool. I think you guys will like each other."

"There's one thing I better ask you, though, Zig. Just so I know in advance; um, what do you want me to say, if she asks me if I'm gay?"

"I was gonna ask you the same thing, bro. Do you mind if I tell her?"

"Hell no, you can tell her. I'm not ashamed of it. I just didn't know if *you* would be, you know, embarrassed."

"Embarrassed about what?"

"About having a gay roommate."

"No, dude. No. Never. If she has a problem with that, then that's her problem. Anybody who doesn't like who I hang with can take a flying hike."

"But she's gonna see that we sleep together, what about that? I hate to ask you about this stuff, Zig, but I want you to know what could happen. One person tells another. People like to talk. What happens if the guys you work with find out you're sleeping with a gay man every night? You wait and see, some asshole is gonna wonder if you're gay, too. And if he does, he'll wonder out loud. Maybe not to you, but he'll say it to somebody else. People can't help but talk about stuff like that. Some people, anyway."

"Fuck, I'm not worried about it, Josh. They know I'm not gay."

"Okay."

"At least I think they know. Hell, I don't care. Let 'em think what they want."

"Okay. Sorry. I guess I worry about stuff too much."

"Yeah, dude, you do."

"Anyway, I just wanted to make sure. You know, that you don't want me to lie about it."

"Josh. Dude. I don't want you ever to lie about anything for me. Hell, if I wasn't willing to own up to something, afterwards, I wouldn't do it in the first place. Including sleeping with my best buddy."

"Okay. That's good to know. You're the best, Zig."

"Besides, she already knows we sleep together. And cuddle up together. I told her."

"No way!"

"Yeah, I did. I told her. She laughed. She said more guys ought to do that, instead of pretending to be so macho. Maybe there'd be fewer wars. You'll like her, Josh, wait and see."

"Wow. That's wild."

"Damn, bro. I'm excited. I know she wants to fuck, I just know it." His cock was growing stiffer as he talked. "Your pal Ziggy is gonna get some pussy tomorrow. Me and her, we're gonna eat, and then we're gonna fuck!"

I smiled. His happiness was contagious. So was his wood. My dick started to get hard, just from looking at his. "I'm happy for you, Zig."

"Hey, don't worry, little brother, we're gonna make sure you get plenty of sex, too. I won't forget about that. Tomorrow is my turn, but you'll get your share."

"I'm not worried about it, Zig. So, listen, I'll be here when you get home from work, and then I'll take off before you get back from dinner. Just tell me how late to stay out. I don't want to come in when you're in the middle of something. Is midnight late enough?"

"Josh, dude, you are so cool. I might take you up on that some other time, but not tomorrow. We're going over to her place after dinner. Her roommate is out of town, so we'll have the place all to ourselves. She's already got it all planned out."

"Oh. Okay."

"I'll be home after that, but it'll be late. You'll probably be asleep way before I get back."

"Any chance you'll spend the night over there?"

"Oh, hell no. I mean, not even if she asks me to. That's not part of the plan."

"Okay."

"You think I should?"

"No, no, I didn't mean it that way."

"I guess I'm like a homing pigeon. I like to come home to my own nest."

"Nothing wrong with that."

"I can hardly wait!"

"I can tell you're excited." I kept looking at his hard-on.

"Well, sure I am. She doesn't know what she's in for. But I do."

"Are you gonna tell me about it, later?"

"Oh, sure! You bet."

"Cool."

He folded the covers back on the bed. "Okay, Josh. I guess I'd better get some sleep, dude. Gotta be rested up for tomorrow." He crawled into bed and pulled the covers up to his chest and looked at me.

"Alright," I said. "Good night, Zig. Sweet dreams."

"'Night." He closed his eyes. A few minutes later, he switched to his other side, facing away from the light. I turned off the lamp at the end of the couch, leaving only the dresser lamp on. That was enough for me to read by.

I went on reading for another half hour or so. Then I started feeling drowsy, but I was sticky from the long walk we took. A nice long shower seemed like just the thing for a good night's sleep.

I put my book away, turned on the shower, and stepped into the tub. Then I remembered my "homework." Put my finger up my ass. Okay, so I gave it a try.

I took it slow and gentle. Plenty of soap. No force. I remembered Ziggy's one rule: no pain. I finally relaxed enough for one
finger to go in, but then my asshole slammed shut again around
my finger. No problem; I left it up there and waited. My butthole
finally relaxed again, and after that, I began having a little control.

It actually felt kind of good. A little more fooling around like
that, and then I finished my shower. I dried off and turned out all
the lights. Ziggy was asleep facing the wall, so I lay down on the
outside of the bed and snuggled in toward him, facing his back.

This was a switch. We usually faced outward, with the guy
who was near the outer edge of the bed in front. The guy behind
him would sleep with his arm wrapped around him, and that kept
the one at the edge from feeling like he might fall off the bed.

Switched around, though, facing the wall like this, also
worked well. I put my arm around Ziggy, and that kept me feeling
secure. My dick got hard, snuggled up against his butt with both
of us naked, but I knew he didn't care. I was glad he talked me
into sleeping nude.

I was almost asleep, starting to dream, when Ziggy changed
positions. He turned in his sleep to his other side, and he put his
arm around me in the process. Now, incredibly, we were front to
front with our arms around each other and our faces inches apart.
And, wonder of wonders, our cocks were pressed up against each
other!

His cock was stiff and hard, like mine. His eyes were closed,
but even more telling was his breathing. It was slow, deep, and
steady. He was still asleep.

I didn't dare move. I didn't *want* to move. This was like a
dream come true. My dick started leaking pre-cum, and I realized
I could shoot my load like this. Hell, just feeling his hard cock
against mine, just *thinking* about it, would be enough to make me
come, and it wouldn't take long, either.

His dick was every bit as hard as mine was. Maybe he was
close to coming, too. Hell, maybe a little movement was all it

would take for both of us to shoot off, rubbing our cocks against each other.

No, no, no. He was asleep. As incredible as it would be, I didn't want it to happen, not that way. There would be a sticky mess, and worse than that, there'd be hell to explain. I couldn't do that to him, I just couldn't. It would almost be like rape, even though it was him who put us in this position.

It was probably the most difficult thing I'd ever done, but reluctantly I turned myself around to face in the other direction. Ziggy gave out a quiet moan when I moved. As I positioned myself facing outward, with my back to him, he pulled me closer again.

He pushed his pelvis forward a little and pressed his hard cock up into the crack of my ass. *Let him,* I thought. *Maybe he's dreaming about his date tomorrow. Let him go ahead and shoot his load on me. Hell, I'd like that.* At least I wouldn't have done something I'd have to explain or apologize for. My cock was stiff as a board.

Neither of us moved. I listened for any signs that would tell me if he was asleep or awake. If he was still asleep, I could relax and maybe my dick would go down and eventually I would fall asleep, too. If he was awake? Hell, I didn't think this would have happened, if he was awake.

His breathing sounded like he was asleep. After pulling me up against him, his arm relaxed. Every sign seemed to indicate he was asleep, except his hard cock, and it was normal to get a boner during sleep. Guys do that several times a night. So I decided yes, he was asleep.

I relaxed. You would never hear me complain about Ziggy's cock being hard. I enjoyed feeling his boner snug up between the cheeks of my ass.

As for my own boner, it was so hard it was almost hurting. I still couldn't get over it. Ziggy's stiff cock had pressed up against mine! I needed to come really bad. I wanted to come while this was absolutely fresh in my memory. I wanted to shoot a load

Josh Jango

thinking about it, how it had felt. Get off on it while I was still
absolutely sure it really did happen. Jeez, I was so close to coming,
my balls would be aching for days if I didn't get off now.

I gently started stroking my cock. Very gently. I didn't want to
wake Ziggy. Not that he would mind, I knew he wouldn't mind; I
just didn't want to disturb his sleep. This wouldn't take much. I
tickled the underside of my cockhead, stroked it a few times,
played with my balls, and stroked my dick some more.

Then I felt Ziggy move behind me, and I stopped. He was
moving his hips, slowly. Pressing them forward, and then relaxing
them back. Forward and back, in rhythm. Jeez, he was dreaming.
Unless by chance he was awake. Either way, I liked it.

He didn't stop. I was sure he was dreaming. I started stroking
my cock again, gently like before. My hands were already slippery
from my pre-cum. Ziggy kept pressing his cock against my ass,
relaxing, and pressing into me again.

I had to come. This was too much. I went on stroking, gently
but surely, and then I felt the tingling all over, and then I was
there. My whole body shivered uncontrollably, and then I started
shooting. I stroked my dick as cum spurt out, catching it in my
other hand, thinking about my cock touching Ziggy's cock. My
hips jerked; I couldn't help that. It felt so good.

I finally finished shooting, and Ziggy was still moving his hips
against my ass in a steady rhythm, pressing harder than before.
My god, it was getting slippery back there. His cock must have
had its own pre-cum flowing, for it to be slippery like that. It was
stiff as it could be.

His boner slid back and forth in the crack of my ass, and of
course he still had his arm around me. His hand moved around a
bit, and I imagined maybe in his dream he was feeling for tits.
Then his fingers found one of my nipples.

Oh, jeez, I didn't know until then that my nipples were so
sensitive. His fingers hardly moved at all, they just flicked back
and forth a little, the way people move in a dream, but he was

136

tickling me, and it felt wonderful. Nobody had ever played with my nipples before. Meanwhile, his cock continued to move back and forth.

My own dick didn't go down much after I came, and now I felt it growing harder again. Ziggy wasn't even awake and he had me wondering if this was how good it felt to have an expert getting you ready to be fucked. But no, I wasn't ready for that.

His movements became more purposeful, and his cock was moving farther down my ass now. Still there was nothing to indicate he was awake. His movements were slow, and without the forcefulness of someone awake and conscious.

When he moved his cock downward, the head of it went down as far as my asshole. Then, when he moved it upward again, it slid deeply up the crack of my ass. I realized, then, how close I was to getting fucked. Hell, with a little maneuvering I could probably get my asshole right where his cock wanted it to be. He might not even wake up.

No, no. There were a lot of things wrong with that idea. First of all, as much as I would have loved to be fucked by Ziggy, I knew my asshole wasn't ready for it. No matter how slick his cock was with his pre-cum, my asshole wasn't going to relax enough to let it in. And even if it did go in, it would hurt. I didn't want to be hurt by anyone, but especially not by Ziggy. I didn't want anything I did with him to hurt.

And I knew Ziggy didn't want to hurt me, either. If he found out he had hurt me, even if it was in his sleep, he'd probably never forgive himself. Was that wishful thinking? No. He really loved me that much, straight or not. In fact, as far as I could tell, he didn't want to hurt anybody.

Meanwhile, his cock never stopped moving up and down my ass, and it was getting slicker than snot, as they say.

Another thing wrong with that idea was, no condom. If there was anyone in the world I would let fuck me without a condom, it was Ziggy, but I knew that was exactly the kind of thinking that got people in trouble. And besides, a condom wasn't just for the bottom's benefit; it was to keep the top safe, too. I didn't think I had any diseases at all, but when was the last time I was tested for STDs? Six months ago?

And Ziggy continued moving his slippery hard cock up and down against my ass, and his fingers still had a hold of my nipple, and now my own cock was stiff and hard again. Ziggy moved lower, and now the head of his dick was actually pushing briefly on my hole as it slid upward. Something had to give here, and I knew it wasn't the right time for it to be my asshole.

I moved my body upward an inch or two and lifted one leg a little. Hallelujah, just as I hoped, his stiff boner slid right in between my legs. I lowered my leg again, and then Ziggy's slick cock was moving in and out between my legs. He moaned softly and moved his hips forward and back, adjusting to the new angle.

I lifted my ball sac up out of the way of his cock, which peeked out an inch or so every time he pushed forward. He was breathing heavily, sliding his cock between my legs, and he moaned again. His fingers started moving again on my nipple, pinching it gently.

I held my own dick with one hand, squeezing it a little bit. I was sure I could easily come again, Ziggy had me so aroused, but I didn't want to yet. Not with Ziggy still fucking my legs like this. I wanted to wait and come at the same time he did.

I hoped he wouldn't wake at all. Or at least shoot his load before waking up. He might stop if he realized what he was doing. Or what he was fucking. Or would he? "If it feels good, do it." We both believed in that, or at least he did, and I was trying my best to adopt that attitude myself. Maybe if he woke up he would keep on fucking me?

Enough of thinking about it. I wanted to come, and I wanted him to come. I kept one hand on my cock and put my other hand down where his dick was poking through my legs. I wanted to feel his cock, and I did. My fingertips stroked its slippery head each time it poked through.

Then he gave out a long moan, pressed his cock forward all the way, and held it there. Cum started spurting out, one squirt right after another.

When he started shooting I grabbed my own cock a little tighter and I was over the edge, too, spewing cum everywhere. He moaned as his dick kept coming and I'm sure I did some moaning of my own.

Finally, after we were spent, I lay there with his dick between my legs, wondering, what now? I didn't know if Ziggy could actually sleep through an orgasm. I didn't know if that was even possible, unless you were drunk and passed out or something.

I was licking the cum off my hand when I felt his cock slip out from between my legs. I didn't move. There was a minute of silence, and then I heard him whisper, "Josh?"

Should I pretend to be asleep? No, of course not. Time to face the consequences. Quietly, I answered, "Yeah, Zig?"

"Josh," he said softly, "did I just do what I think I did?"

"You were dreaming, Zig. People do all kinds of things in their sleep."

"Yeah," he said. "I was fucking Eleanor. I was fucking her on my boss's desk at work. You were there, too, dude, you were watching me fuck her. You were right there, up close, watching my dick going in and out of her pussy, and I was digging the hell out of it. I wanted you to watch."

"Yeah," I said. "I figured you were dreaming about fucking."

"You were awake?"

I couldn't lie. "Yeah."

"Josh," he said, "I was fucking Eleanor, and then I came. I came inside her, dude. But when I woke up, it was you! I can't believe I did that, Josh. Did I hurt you?"

"Nah. Don't worry. It didn't hurt. I liked it."

"Were you asleep at first? Fuck, I feel like I raped you."

"That's funny. I was thinking about rape, too."

"Oh, man," he said. "I knew it! Josh, I am so sorry. You should have stopped me, dude. Fuckin' punched me in the mouth, if you had to. I was asleep; I didn't know what I was doing!"

"No, Zig, I don't mean that you raped me. I meant, I was thinking about raping you."

"What?"

"No, what I mean is, I was thinking about how I couldn't do something to you in your sleep, because it would be too much like raping you."

"I don't get it," he said. "Why were you thinking about that?"

"You were asleep and then you turned around and your hard cock was pressing right up against mine. And I got really horny and I needed to come really bad, but more than that I wanted to make you come. You had a big, stiff boner that wouldn't quit, Zig. And so did I. And I wanted so bad to do something to you. But I couldn't. Because it would have been like raping you in your sleep."

"Okay, I guess I get it. But Josh, you worry too much. It wouldn't be a big deal if you horned in on my cock when I'm asleep. Especially if I already had a hard on. Fuck, bro, if it's hard, that means it *wants* to come."

I just looked at him. I guess I must have looked surprised.

"Really," he said. "I'd be asleep, dude. You'd be doing me a favor. Think of the good dream I'd have." He grinned.

"Zig," I said, "do you really mean that?"

"Sure I do. You're my buddy, Josh. If it happens again . . . hell, go for it."

"But you don't know what you're saying!" The thought of what might lay ahead astounded me. "Um, you better set some limits, at least. My god."

"What do you mean, limits?"

"Like, what am I allowed to do? And how often?"

Chapter 10
ELEANOR

"DUDE," he said. "No need to spell it out. I wasn't thinking of specifics. I'm just saying, generally speaking, if a situation like that comes up again, go for it. If you want to. Only if you want to. I'll be asleep; you'd just be doing me a good buddy thing, doing me a favor. I won't mind. I'd enjoy it."

"Um, okay," I said. "I'll, uh, keep that in mind."

"You're talking about jacking me off, right?"

"Oh, uh, well," I said, "okay, yeah, if you want to limit it to jacking you off, I'm cool with that."

He thought about that. Then he said, "You set your own limits, Josh. Do what you want, just don't fuck me in my sleep." He smiled. "That would be taking it just a little too far."

"Okay then." I smiled, too. "I won't play with your asshole, only your dick."

"Oh, you can play with my asshole if you want. Just don't put anything in it, not without my permission, okay?"

"Sure, Zig. I can't believe we're talking about this. But I'm glad we did."

"Back to *me* fucking *you*, Josh. I still can't believe I did that. I came up your ass, bro. Fuck!"

"No you didn't. Your cock wasn't in my ass. It was between my legs, not in my asshole."

"Oh. Okay. Wow, that makes me feel a lot better. I thought I fuckin' raped your ass, Josh. I would never forgive myself."

"No, hell no."

"How did my cock end up between your legs?"

"Well, you almost raped me."

"Dude!"

"Just kidding. It wouldn't have been rape, believe me. You were moving your hard dick up and down the crack of my ass in your sleep, pressed up against my asshole, and I almost let you. I really wanted to let you, but I just don't think I'm ready for that yet. I was afraid it would hurt. And I didn't have any condoms."

He just looked at me, grinning from ear to ear, blushing like crazy.

"What?" I said.

He could hardly get the words out. "You would have let me fuck you in my sleep?"

"Well, like I said, I wanted to, Zig. You must know how much I like you." Now I was the one doing the blushing.

"Dude." He ran his fingers through my hair, ruffling it up. "Josh. Dude," he said. He seemed like he was choked up. "You are so special."

"Nah," I told him. "That's you."

—

AFTER WE CLEANED UP a bit we got back under the covers, snug up against each other, just like always. Ziggy seemed like he was at a loss for words. He had his arm around me, holding me close.

I lay awake for a while, replaying everything through my head, feeling lucky to have such a friend.

I was finally falling asleep, when I thought I heard him say something.

I woke up a bit and then I did hear him say, "Josh?"

I said, "Hunh?"

"Josh," he said, "I wouldn't trade you for a million dollars."

Thursday

ZIGGY WAS IN THE SHOWER when I woke up, singing a happy song. It made me feel like singing, too. He stopped when I walked into the bathroom. Then he said, "Good morning."

"'Morning, Zig. No need to stop singing on my account." I stood at the toilet, watching my aim, and out of the corner of my eye I watched him, naked in the shower, rinsing shampoo from his hair. "Did anybody ever tell you that you sound like Randy Travis?"

"Nope. Nobody but you has ever heard me sing, bro."

"Well, you do. You ought to bottle that up and sell it. I know where they'd put it, too, right on the shelf between the honey and the molasses."

He laughed. "You can flatter me all you want, dude, but I'll tell you what, I'm still gonna keep my day job." He turned off the shower and opened the curtain.

"What if I got you a recording contract, would you believe me then?" I finished up and flushed the toilet.

"Now you're really talking crazy, bro." He grabbed a towel and started drying off.

"No, Zig, I'm serious. I love your voice."

"Maybe we should move to Nashville, then. That's where the Grand Ole Opry is, right?"

"Okay, let's go. Will you let me be your manager?" I followed him out to the living room.

"I don't know," he said, "maybe. What kind of percentage would you want?"

"Not much. Hell, I'll do it for free, if I get to sleep with the man himself on a regular basis."

"Hmm. That does sound like a good deal," he said, grinning. "I guess I'd be a fool to pass that up." He sat down on the bed and dried between his toes with the towel. "Wait a minute, does that include sex, too?"

"Oh, um, well, no, sex would not be required."

"No sex? Damn, I'd have think twice about that, then. I thought managers were supposed to take care of every need." He took a t-shirt out of the dresser and slipped it over his head.

"We can leave that up for negotiation, then," I said. "How's that sound?"

"Okay. I'm sure we can work something out."

"Alright, then. Grand Ole Opry, here we come!"

"Yeehaw!" He put his arm around my shoulder and hugged me close. "Josh, you'd be the best manager a guy could ever want."

"You do have a good voice, you know."

"I'm just glad you like it, little brother. That's good enough for me." He let go of me and went into the kitchen. Next thing I knew, he was putting a fresh cup of coffee in my hands.

He took some briefs out of the drawer and slipped them on. "Got to wear clean underwear, especially today."

"Yeah, you're gonna have a good time, I know." I sat down on the couch.

"Well, it might not go like I think it will. But I'm pretty sure I'm reading her right. Hell, it'll be good, anyway, even if we don't fuck. I like her. She's a lot of fun."

"With an attitude like that, you can't go wrong, Zig."

He put his jeans on and fastened his belt. "I'll be fine, once I get through the razzing at work."

"They're gonna be razzing you?"

"Dude, they already started. Every one of those jokers had something to say yesterday about my big date. It'll be twice as bad today."

"Hell, Zig, they're just jealous."

"Aw, I know." He went into the closet and came out with a shirt. "I don't mind. It's a nice change from what they usually ride me about."

"They razz you on a regular basis?"

"We all tease each other. All the time. Unless we're listening to baseball. It's just shop talk. Makes the day more interesting."

"What kind of stuff do they say?"

"Oh, just about anything." He sat next to me to put on his socks and shoes. "It's kind of funny. They give me a hard time about being single; just about all of them are married. They tell me I'm missing out on the good life. But let them find out I'm going out on a date, and one by one they come up to me begging for the details. Like they don't want the other guys to know how long it's been since they fucked their own wives."

"Do you razz them, too?"

"Oh, sure. I always think of something. It's all in good fun."

"It's just guys, right? All guys?"

"Sure, back in the shop, at least." He stood up. "I'd better get going, Josh. I'll see you when I get off work, okay? She's gonna bring me home to shower and change. That way she'll get to meet you, too."

"I'll be here."

"Cool. Alright, bro." He was on his way out the door and I followed along behind him. He turned around and hesitated, and then, awkwardly, he held his hand out. So I shook hands with him. Then he laughed and said, "Oh, hell." He let loose of my hand and gave me a nice big hug instead. A long one. Long enough for both of our dicks to start getting hard.

Then he let me loose and said, "Look, I just want to thank you for last night."

"Aw, hell, Zig . . . ."

"No," he said, "I mean it. Thanks."

Then he was out of there.

And I had a job to look for. After I finished my excellent cup of coffee.

—

I WAS TAKING A SHOWER, getting set to go job hunting again. Then I remembered my homework. Play with my butt. I didn't have to rush off, so why not?

I was beginning to believe I could actually do this. I got my asshole relaxed enough to squeeze two fingers in at once. I still had a way to go before I could actually enjoy having a cock up my butt, but I was in no hurry for that. Not in a hurry to let some stranger fuck me, no matter how good he was. I'd rather cuddle with Ziggy, without any sex.

What I liked better was the thought of me doing the fucking. I was beginning to understand it could feel good. Imagine. I could make a guy feel good by fucking him. A new concept for me.

I finally got out of the shower, put on a suit and tie, and hit the streets for a job. I did a lot of walking, rode a lot of buses, and gave out a bunch of resumes. It ended up being an exhausting day. I interviewed at a temp agency, too, and by the time I got out of there it was time to head home to Ziggy and Eleanor.

I stripped off my clothes as soon as I walked in the door. I slugged down a soda, then I got in the shower to wash off the sweat. I thought I had plenty of time, so first I did my homework again. I was halfway through my shower when I heard Ziggy holler hello. Then he walked into the bathroom.

"Dude!"

"Hey, Zig."

"It's the moment I've been waiting for, bro! Eleanor's out in the living room."

"I thought I'd be done showering by the time y'all got here. Sorry."

"No problem. Take your time. We're not in a hurry, Josh. Not to eat, anyway." He grinned. "I'll introduce you guys when you get out. Then you can chat while I get cleaned up."

He went out to Eleanor, closing the door, and I finished my shower. I felt a little funny about meeting a stranger with nothing on but a towel, but what the heck.

Eleanor was pretty. She had an attractive, smiling face with sparkling eyes. As soon as I came out of the bathroom she stood up and said hello. Ziggy introduced us.

She held out her hand. "It's so good to finally meet you, Josh. I've heard so much about you."

"Same here, Eleanor." I gently shook hands with her.

She said, "My, goodness. Ziggy told me you were a good-looking guy, but he didn't tell me how sexy you are."

I blushed at that, even though I knew she was probably just saying it to be nice. "Well," I said, "you're every bit as pretty as Ziggy said you'd be."

That seemed to please both of them. Score one for me; sometimes I trip all over my words. I was off to a good start this time.

Ziggy began taking off his clothes. He told us he was going to take a quick shower while we got to know each other. He stripped all the way down to his briefs, right there in front of us in the living room, and Eleanor gave out a wolf whistle. Ziggy grinned and then he disappeared into the bathroom.

He left the door open a few inches. That was just like him. Privacy was not a big issue. Or maybe he *wanted* her to see him naked. Lord knows, I remembered the first time I saw him nude; I wanted to lick him from head to toe.

Eleanor and I both watched through the open door for a few moments, hoping to get a glimpse of a naked Ziggy. Then she turned to me and we smiled at each other.

"So, Josh. Ziggy said you're from Tennessee?"

"Yes, I moved here from Memphis."

"Ooh. That's where Graceland is, right? Where Elvis lived?"

"That's right. Home of Elvis. Also the home of the Blues, and the birthplace of Rock 'n' Roll."

"Have you been there? To Graceland?"

"Yeah, I've been there."

"What's it like?"

147

"Well, uh, it's not a huge house, but still, it's impressive. It's at the top of a little hill, on about a dozen acres of land. There's a stone wall around it, and a wrought-iron gate with big musical notes on it. It's a cool-looking place."

"My mother was a big fan of his. She wanted to see him, but she never did get around to it. And then it was too late."

"I guess your mother never went to Las Vegas, then."

"My mother never goes anywhere. Born and raised in Indiana, and happy as a bug right where she is."

"Well, that's good. If she can be happy with what she's got."

I was still standing there with nothing on but a wet towel around my waist. Eleanor was looking me over the whole time we talked, and I started to feel self-conscious.

She said, "Well, don't let me keep you from getting dressed, hon. Don't be shy. I've seen men naked before. I grew up with four brothers running around the house, so I've seen everything."

"Okay," I said. But then I *really* felt awkward. And crazy as it sounds, my dick started to get hard. I couldn't change in front of her, no way. The kitchen seemed like the best choice. If I went into the bathroom, then Ziggy would be in plain view to her while the door was open, naked in the shower. Not that he would mind, but . . . .

I got some briefs out of the dresser. "I'll just go in here for a minute," I said. Around the corner in the kitchen I dropped the towel and pulled on the underwear, and then I was back out in the living room almost before I'd left.

She took a good look at my briefs, and then she looked up, smiling. She wasn't embarrassed at all, but I was, a little. I picked up my jeans and pulled them on.

"Ziggy said you'll be a famous writer some day."

"He told you that? Jeez!" I started blushing like crazy. "Well, if he's going around telling people that, I guess I better go ahead and give it a try."

"Now, don't be modest. He said you're already halfway through your first novel."

"Well, halfway through the first draft, yeah. I've got a long ways to go still."

"This is so exciting! I've never met a writer before."

"Oh, god," I said. "He's got so much confidence in me, I don't know whether to laugh or cry. Ziggy's the greatest guy ever."

Then we heard the shower stop. "He'll be out in a minute. He's been excited about this all week."

"I have, too," she said. "Ziggy's a real doll." She leaned over and whispered, "I've been trying to get a date with him for months. I was almost ready to give up."

"Really?"

"Yes! For the longest time I thought he would want to be the one who asked. I didn't think he'd like it if I asked him out. But then I finally did, and here we are."

"I'm glad you did. I guess he's, um, cautious, sometimes."

"Shy, you mean. Yes, he sure is."

That really surprised me to hear her say that. I never thought of Ziggy as being shy. I was the one who was shy, not him.

Then the bathroom door opened and Ziggy came out, with a wet towel around his waist.

"Squeaky clean," he said. He raised his arms in the air. "Now I'm ready for anything!" Then his towel slipped off and fell on the floor and he stood there naked to the world. Eleanor giggled, and Ziggy, in no hurry, reached down and pulled the towel up around his waist again. "Oops," he said, grinning.

They laughed about it, and I laughed, too. Ziggy had a knack for breaking the ice, I'll have to say that.

"It'll just take me a minute to get ready," he said. "Don't y'all look, now." He went over to the dresser and pulled out some underwear. He dropped the towel and then he put on the briefs, and we got a nice view of his sexy ass. He turned his head, saw us watching, and grinned. "You guys weren't supposed to watch."

Eleanor said, "Are you kidding? I wouldn't have missed that for anything."

"Well," he said, "maybe we can arrange another peek later, then. But only if you show me yours, too. Fair's fair." He stood there with his hands on his hips, so very sexy in just his briefs. I couldn't help it; I envied Eleanor for the good time she was going to have with him that night.

Eleanor pretended to be shocked. "Show you my derriere? You cad! A lady has to worry about her reputation."

"Nobody'll know! Will they, Josh? You won't tell anybody, will you?"

"Don't worry," I said. "All your secrets are safe with me. Unless they tickle me. Then I'll tell them everything." They both laughed at that.

"So *that's* the way to get the truth out of you, huh? Okay," Ziggy said, "I'll remember that, pardner."

"Uh, oh. Now I'm giving up my own secrets." I hoped he was serious, though. I couldn't think of anything I'd like better than for Ziggy to tickle me. Mercilessly.

He put on a fresh pair of jeans, and then he took some socks to the couch and sat down next to Eleanor. "We were talking about Josh's novel," she said.

He looked at me and grinned as he pulled on a sock. "Oh, yeah?"

"Yes." Then she looked at me and said, "Josh, you'll let me read it, won't you? I'd be so honored."

"Um, well," I said, "I don't know if you'd really want to read this one. The subject matter might not appeal to you."

"Of course I'd want to read it. If you wrote it, I would. Why, what's it about?"

I looked at Ziggy and he looked at me, and he shrugged his shoulders, as if to say, go for it. He was tying his shoes.

"Well, see, it's sort of a practice novel. A special interest novel. It's about two guys in high school, best friends. They fool around with each other while they're on a field trip."

"They fool around with each other," she said. She thought about that. Then she said, "Oh, you mean, like," and then she moved her hand up and down in front of her crotch, just as good as any guy with a dick could do to imitate jerking off.

Ziggy and I both burst out laughing, and she laughed right along with us. I said, "Yeah, you've got the idea, alright. They do that, and more."

"Well, that wouldn't bother me. Except in a good way. I'd love to read it."

"Okay, then. Wow. I've already got two fans, and I'm not even half finished. I guess I better hurry up and get to work on it."

"Damn right," Ziggy said. Then he looked at her. "Josh and I are driving down to Memphis this weekend to bring it back. Along with his other stuff."

"Oh, that sounds like fun. Are you going to visit Graceland while you're there?"

"Nah, not planning on that," he said. "Not unless Josh wants to." He looked at me.

"We weren't planning on staying long. But hell, Zig, I guess I really should give you a little tour while we're there. What do you think?"

"Sure. I've never been to Memphis. You can show me the sights."

"If you're an Elvis fan, we should definitely go to Graceland. Another place we could go is Beale Street. That's where the Blues clubs are. And we'll absolutely have to eat some good barbecue. Memphis barbecue is the best anywhere."

"Sounds good to me," he said. "Speaking of food, I'm starving." He stood up. "Josh, ol' buddy, I guess we're out of here. I'll bring you a doggy bag, if there's any left."

Eleanor stood up and held out her hand. "It was a pleasure meeting you, Josh."

"The pleasure was mine." Routine stuff to say, but hell, we both really meant it.

They walked to the door and Ziggy held it open as Eleanor walked out. Then he turned and looked at me and grinned. "I'll talk to you tomorrow, bro." He held up his hands to show me his fingers crossed, and then they were on their way.

—

AFTER THEY LEFT I stripped off my clothes and found some food to snack on. Then I settled in for a good reading session. I read for an hour or so and then I thought, what the hell, might as well have a toke. So I got the bong out and took a couple of hits. I got a nice buzz going and then I continued reading another hour.

I was beat from walking all day, though. By the time it started getting dark I was ready for bed. Waiting up for Ziggy was out of the question, since he wouldn't be back till midnight. So I put the book up, turned out the lights, and hit the sack.

I hadn't been in bed more than fifteen minutes when I heard footsteps come up the stairs, and then someone tried the door. The hair on my neck stood on end. I was freaking out, wondering if someone was trying to break in. Maybe they thought no one was home.

I heard the door open. I knew there was more than one person because I could hear them whispering to each other. I stayed where I was and pretended to sleep. Maybe if they saw someone was here, they'd turn around and quietly creep back out.

The door closed, and someone said, "Shhhh." Then it sounded like one of them was walking through the living room.

I put my hand in front of my face; that way maybe I could open my eyes and look between my fingers without them knowing I was awake. Someone turned on a light in the kitchen, probably the dim one over the stove. The guy tip-toed back out of the kitchen toward the front door, and he looked my way when he passed. That's when I realized it was Ziggy.

Then I heard Eleanor say softly, "Is he asleep?"

Ziggy said, "Shhhh." He whispered, "Yeah, he's asleep. He won't wake up, but let's be quiet anyway."

She whispered, "Okay."

I thought, *Alright, if they want me asleep, I'll be asleep. Or at least pretend to be.* I kept watching through my fingers.

Eleanor had changed into some jeans. Ziggy motioned her over to the couch. He took off his shoes and pointed at Eleanor's feet. She took her shoes off, too, while he pulled off his socks. Eleanor tried not to giggle. Then he leaned over and kissed her, briefly. He looked at her, grinned, and kissed her again, with his hand resting on her shoulder.

When they came up for air, he got up and moved the coffee table back a few feet. He took off his outer shirt, then he sat down and kissed her again. A long one. When they came up from that kiss, Eleanor whispered, "I need to freshen up."

Ziggy whispered, "Okay. I'll be here." She got up and took her purse into the bathroom and closed the door. Ziggy came over to the bed and bent down. He whispered in my ear, softly. "Josh, if you're awake, dude, pretend you're asleep, okay?"

I didn't say anything.

He whispered, "Whatever you do, don't let her know you're awake." He looked at the bathroom door. "It's cool if you watch, okay? But don't let her know you're watching. Not this time, dude."

I made a quiet little noise like "mmmph," and that seemed to be enough for him. He stood up, with a big grin on his face, and went back to the couch and sat down. He sat there for a minute or two, then he took off his t-shirt, wiped under his armpits, and tossed the shirt over the back of the couch.

A few minutes later she came out and sat down next to him. He whispered, "I hope you don't mind me taking my shirt off. It's kind of warm in here."

She whispered back, "You can take everything off, sweetheart. I won't complain."

They whispered back and forth like that the whole time they were there. They never did talk in anything above a whisper, because I was asleep. Or was supposed to be.

He said, "Oh, no. Fair's fair. I'm not taking anymore off until you do. It's your turn." He grinned.

"Do you think he's really asleep?" she whispered.

"I checked him out while you were in the bathroom. He's out like a light. He had a rough day. He's been job hunting."

"Poor guy. He's such a cutie," she said. "Somebody's bound to hire him, just for his good looks."

"I know. He's smart, too," Ziggy said.

"Maybe they have something where we work."

"Naw, I already checked. Not unless he wants to sell used cars."

"He's too sweet to sell cars. He'd end up giving them away."

"I know. That's exactly what I thought. Hey, I gotta pee, babe, don't go anywhere, okay?" He smiled.

"You better hurry back," she said, "or I might rape your little friend here."

"Oh, he'd like that."

"But you wouldn't."

"What makes you think that? I wouldn't mind at all, as long as I get to join in."

"Go pee, you animal. I'll be waiting."

He went in and stood at the toilet, leaving the door wide open, and after two or three minutes of silence, he finally managed to let out a long, steady stream of piss. Meanwhile Eleanor was looking at me. I thought she might have seen that my eyes were open, but no, I guess she was just checking me out.

154

Ziggy came back and sat down.

"Is that what they call pee-shy?" she said.

"No," he said. "That's what they call not being able to pee because your dick is so hard."

She leaned over and kissed him, long and heavy. And when they came up for air she took off her blouse. All she had on underneath was a thin little bra. Ziggy caressed her everywhere he could find bare skin, starting with the soft skin of her neck and shoulders, moving up to her ears and her cheeks. Every place he touched with his fingers, afterwards he kissed gently with his mouth.

It was cool watching a pro at work. He wasn't in a hurry at all, I noticed that right off. He took his time and gave her all the attention she wanted. He didn't take her bra off until she started to take it off herself. You could tell she was just as eager as he was. He wanted her, that was obvious by the attention he gave her, but she was the one calling the shots, or at least setting the pace.

It was exciting to watch. I felt like a pervert, a peeping tom, pretending to sleep so I could see everything, but my dick was hard and I was enjoying this. There was no way I was going to turn to the wall and try to actually sleep. Fat chance of that, anyway. I'd be awake, and I'd still be able to hear them.

I'd seen my share of sex in movies at the adult book stores. You sit in a booth and feed it quarters to keep the movie playing. And these days you could even rent fuck movies, on VHS or Betamax, and watch them at home on your TV if you could afford a VCR.

This wasn't like watching movies, though. This was the real thing, right in front of me. In the same room.

They were doing a whole lot of kissing and caressing and licking and nibbling. Neither one of them was in any great hurry. I swear they did that for another thirty minutes before Eleanor unfastened Ziggy's jeans. Now, that was a magical sight: Ziggy in nothing but bright white briefs, with a big, stiff boner inside. I would have loved to put my hands on that. Like Eleanor was doing. Ziggy moaned softly, and gently lifted her hand away so he wouldn't come yet.

They were less than eight feet away from me. I could see everything. I could even see the entire front of his briefs were wet with pre-cum. No wonder, after half an hour of kissing and nibbling and slowly making love.

Now that he was down to just his briefs he went ahead and removed her jeans, and she seemed happy to get out of them. Then they both had plenty of bare skin to play with, and that's what they did. They took turns kissing and licking each other all over, everywhere. They did that for at least another fifteen minutes, swear to god.

Then one time when Ziggy licked down below her belly button she pulled her panties out a little so he could lick farther down. She moaned softly and moved a little on the couch to give him better access. He went ahead and pulled her panties all the way off and then he went to it, licking all over her pussy area. She was breathing heavily and moaning and sighing softly, and he kept licking and kissing and nibbling and licking some more.

I could tell things were really heating up. Ziggy got down on the floor on his knees and he was lapping and licking at her cunt like there was no tomorrow. Then, while he used one hand to continue caressing her there, he used his other hand to pull off his briefs. Damn, his boner was as big and stiff and straight up as it could be, and shiny with pre-cum.

He went back to licking her, and now she was moaning louder. I thought I heard her say "Fuck me" but I couldn't be sure. Her moaning was more insistent now, like she was experiencing some kind of need, and Ziggy was doing everything he could to keep her feeling that way.

Meanwhile, with his free hand I saw him reach under the couch and pull something out. He stopped licking her briefly and put it up to his mouth to tear it open, and then I realized what it was. A condom. He was getting a condom ready!

He went back to lapping at her pussy and then while she moaned and whispered his name, he put the condom over the head of his cock and rolled it down and then he was ready. But he kept on licking her, and she didn't stop moaning. Except now it sounded more like wailing.

She was getting so loud, the neighbors probably heard her. Wailing and moaning and then she said, loud and clear, "Fuck me. Ziggy, fuck me!" And then she was moaning and wailing again.

Ziggy stood up and he lifted her up in the air, and she let him. He turned her completely around and put her down again and now she was on her knees on the couch, with her back and her butt toward him. He didn't waste a second; he got down on his knees again and put his face up in her ass and he lapped at her pussy again, and she was absolutely loving it. I could tell by the noises she made.

His cock was still rigid and I wanted to put my mouth on it. It seemed a shame to let that beautiful boner throb in mid air, with no attention, but of course I stayed right where I was. Eleanor faced away from me but I thought I better not move, in case she turned around.

Then Ziggy stopped licking her pussy and turned his head my way. He put both of his hands to work between her legs, but he looked directly at me. Was he trying to tell me something? Or maybe he was just checking to see if I was watching.

Eleanor was still facing the other way, with her head lowered, moaning and sobbing with pleasure, so I moved my hand away from my face so Ziggy could see I was awake and watching. When I did that, he got a big grin on his face and raised his eyebrows as if to say, Can you believe this? He took one hand from her pussy and gave me the thumbs up sign, still grinning like crazy. I gave him the thumbs up back. Then I put my hand back in front of my face and continued looking between my fingers and pretending to be asleep.

Ziggy licked up the pussy juices now dripping, almost squirting, out of her cunt. He was using his mouth and his tongue and his hands to make this woman delirious, and all three of us enjoyed the hell out of it.

Then she started telling him to fuck her, in no uncertain terms. She wanted his cock in her NOW. Ziggy kept a hand at her cunt while he stood up from his knees and got close up behind her. He grabbed his cock with his other hand and pushed it down just enough to aim it right into her pussy, and then he moved forward. His rigid cock slid right inside her, and she started wailing again. He pulled it out and slid it back in. Pulled that stiff dick almost all the way out and then pushed it all the way in again. And again. And again.

Now she started saying, "Yes, fuck it, fuck it, fuck it, Ziggy, fuck it HARD." So that's what he did. He fucked her hard and fast, with a loud slapping noise each time his body slammed against the cheeks of her ass.

I thought, *Holy shit, this is fantastic.* I wanted so bad to jack myself off, but I couldn't take a chance on her seeing me awake. So I just lay there watching, with my own stiff boner lurking underneath the bed covers. God, I loved looking at Ziggy's beautiful ass moving back and forth like that.

Now they were both moaning, with Ziggy still slamming his cock into her, doggy style. I figured if Ziggy was moaning then he must be close to coming, and sure enough, after another minute of groaning and moaning he finally let out a really loud "Ahhhhh!" and slammed his cock into her and held it there, pushing hard up against her, going "Ahhh! Ahhh! Ahhhhhh!"

Chapter 11
GETTING THE IDEA

I COULD IMAGINE Ziggy's cum flying out of his cock into that condom deep down inside Eleanor, spurt after spurt, while he moaned and pressed his shaft in as far as it would go. After a minute or so he slowly resumed fucking her, moving in and out, much more gently now. She was still moaning softly, but I think she was through with her orgasm, too. Ziggy gently pulled his cock out. He wrapped his arms around her, hugging her.

This was my cue to look completely passed out, sound asleep, so I closed my eyes and willed myself not to open them no matter what. I moved my hand away from my face so if Eleanor looked she could see that my eyes were closed.

I heard them shuffling around a bit. It sounded like they were kissing or something. Then I heard Eleanor whisper, "Baby, we're gonna have to do this more often."

Ziggy chuckled, and then he whispered, "You know where to find me, girl."

Then I guess she was putting her clothes back on. Ziggy whispered, "No need to rush off."

"I know," she said. "I'd better get going, though. Thanks."

"Thank you," he said. "For everything. Dinner was great, and dessert was even better."

"See you at work tomorrow," she said.

"No, wait, I'll walk you out to your car."

"Oh, that's okay, I'll be alright."

"No, I insist." I heard him throw on his jeans and then they walked on out, shutting the door.

I heard their footsteps going down the stairs. I waited for a minute, then I got up and went to the bathroom to pee. It took a while, because my cock was still hard, but I finally managed to do it.

Ziggy came back while I was peeing. He walked into the bathroom and said, "Dude!"

I looked back at him. He had a huge grin on his face. Made me grin, too. "Dude, yourself," I said.

"Did you get to see much?" He unzipped his jeans and pulled them off. No underwear on, so that left him naked. He stood at the sink and washed his face.

"Hell, yeah. I saw everything." I finished up and flushed the toilet. My cock was still big and hard.

"Did it turn you on?" He took my place at the toilet, standing there naked with dick in hand, letting it flow.

"Are you kidding? Good god, Zig, I was so turned on I thought I was gonna shoot my load without even touching my dick."

He laughed. "I'm glad you got to watch. That part couldn't have gone any better even if we'd planned it."

"Yeah, what happened, anyway? I thought you guys were going over to her place."

"We did. Her roommate was supposed to be out of town, staying at her parents' house. But when we got there her roommate was home and her *parents* were there, too. Fucking unbelievable."

"So you came over here."

"Right." He shook his dick, flushed the toilet, and followed me out to the living room. "I told her you'd probably be asleep, and if you were, nothing short of a tornado would wake you up. Especially if we kept it quiet. She likes you, anyway, bro."

"Well, it was awesome, Zig. Really incredible. You sure knew how to make her feel good."

"Did you learn anything, li'l brother?"

160

I sat down on the bed. "Sure! Um, let's see. I learned never be in a hurry. Let her set the pace."

"Right on, Josh. You picked up on that, huh?" He stood there right in front of me.

"Sure I did. I couldn't miss it."

"What else?"

"Umm, well, she really got off on you licking her pussy. That was amazing. You must have licked her for at least fifteen minutes, Zig. Doesn't your tongue get tired?"

"Yeah, it does. But you have to make them happy. That's one of the best ways, if you do it right."

"I really don't know if I could do that."

"What are you talking about? Of course you could do it." He sat down next to me and put his arm around my shoulder. "Why couldn't you?"

"What does it taste like?"

"What, her pussy?"

"Yeah. And her, uh, pussy juice. I've never seen that before. Do they all squirt it out like that? I've never seen anything like that in the porn flicks."

"Some do more than others. They all get wet if you turn them on enough. That's a good thing, Josh. Don't worry, bro, you can get used to it. Guys get wet, too, when we get horny; you don't mind that, do you?"

"No, of course not. I like your pre-cum. And your cum, too."

"Because it tastes good?"

"Yeah, it tastes good, but also I like it because it's yours."

"Really?"

"Yeah." I started blushing. "Especially 'cause it's yours."

"Mine's special, huh?" He smiled.

"And also knowing how it makes you feel. I like making you feel good, Zig."

He thought that over. "Okay," he said, "I can understand that. When you like a guy a lot, you want to make him feel good. That's

Josh Jango

why you want to lick up his cum, especially since you know it'll give him some pleasure. Am I right?"

"Yeah. Exactly."

I thought he was going to say something else, but he just sat there thinking, like something new had occurred to him.

I looked at the clock. "Zig, you have to work tomorrow."

"Yeah, let's go to bed," he said.

I pulled back the covers and got in.

He went and turned out the kitchen light, then he curled up under the covers with his back to my front, skin to skin, my arm wrapped around him.

Then he said, "Oh, hell, I didn't even take a shower."

"Don't worry about it," I said. "I like the smell of your sweat, especially when it's fresh like this."

"But I probably have Eleanor's smell on me, too."

"No problem."

We lay there for a minute or two, and then he said, "Listen, Josh. You like cum because it's part of what happens when you make a guy feel good. It works the same way with a woman. Licking on her pussy makes her feel good. And you don't stop just because she starts getting wet. There's nothing to it; you get accustomed to the taste pretty quickly."

"What does it taste like?"

"Oh, jeez. It's hard to describe. It varies. It's not a strong taste."

"Can't you give me any idea at all?"

"I guess somewhere between chicken soup and oysters, maybe. Usually it's a little salty. Sometimes a little tangy, the way lime is tangy. Sometimes it even has a little bit of a chocolaty taste to it. But it's not a strong taste, Josh. It's very easy on the palette, little brother."

"I guess I'll find out for myself, one of these days."

"Look, tell me. Did you always like the idea of drinking a guy's cum?"

162

"No. The first time I heard of somebody doing that, it sounded really gross."

"See?"

"I had to get used to the idea. It took . . . time."

"But now you like it."

"Yeah. Now I really like it."

He didn't say anything after that, and neither did I. I had a lot to think about. He probably did, too.

—

MY DICK WAS STILL HARD, and it got harder when Ziggy snuggled up against me, pressing his fine ass up against it. We were both used to that, though. It wouldn't keep either one of us from getting a good night's sleep.

Tonight my dick was extra hard, though. It was rigid and stiff the whole time Ziggy and Eleanor were making out, and it never really went soft. I wished I had a chance to jack off somewhere along the way so my balls wouldn't ache tomorrow. I didn't feel like getting up, though, now that we were curled up together.

Ziggy wiggled his ass against my hard boner. If he did that a few more times, I'd probably shoot my load right there.

He said, "You didn't come tonight?"

"Nah," I said. "No big deal, though. It'll give me good dreams."

He didn't say anything after that.

Sometime later in the night, I woke up and realized I'd been dreaming about fucking Ziggy. And then I woke up more and I realized my cock was between his legs. My cock was rock hard and it was slick and it was between his legs, probably poking up against his balls!

My first thought was, here I was doing the same thing to him in my sleep that he did to me the night before, except tonight he was surely asleep and not even aware of it. Which meant I was basically raping him, or at least raping his legs.

Then I realized he wasn't breathing the way he usually does when he's asleep. I whispered, "Zig?"

"Aw, hell, dude. I was hoping you wouldn't wake up."

"What's going on?"

"I was trying to give you a good dream, bro."

I thought about that for a minute. "You put my dick between your legs?"

"Well, fair's fair. You let me fuck your legs last night. But no, listen, it's not just that. I want to make you feel good, Josh. I was hoping you would have a fuck dream while you were fucking my legs. Don't you love it when you come in your dreams?"

"Oh, jeez, Zig! Damn, you never cease to amaze me."

"So listen," he said. "Go back to sleep. Leave your cock up there next to my ass and go back to sleep, okay?"

"Zig, you are so crazy!"

"Oh, so now I'm crazy, huh?"

"In a good way."

"Okay."

"Zig, I love you."

"I know. I love you, too, Josh. Now go back to sleep."

"Okay."

The idea of falling asleep now seemed unlikely, but I wanted to give it a try. I wanted to go ahead and do what Ziggy had dreamed up in his unconventional, heart-of-gold, best-buddy way. I closed my eyes and held him close to me, gently pressing my dick forward, keeping it snuggly inserted between his legs just below his asshole. And Ziggy pushed back on his butt a little, doing his part to keep us connected.

The amazing thing was, it worked. I did fall asleep.

The next thing I remember, I was sitting on the couch, Ziggy was kneeling in front of me, and my cock was stiff and sticking straight out at him. He was holding it with one hand, examining it really closely, studying every little freckle and the way it was shaped and everything. And then he said, "I wonder what it tastes like." And before I could stop him, he had my cock in his mouth, with his tongue underneath the head, and he made an "mmmmmm" noise. I couldn't help it; I came in his mouth, instantly. I had no control over it at all. I came and came and came, and he gulped it down as fast as it shot out.

And of course I woke up then, and I was actually shooting off between his legs, not in his mouth. And that felt just as good. We were laying there in bed, our positions the same as before. And my brief dismay about accidentally coming in his mouth was replaced with the wonderful ecstasy of shooting my load, and the pleasure of knowing this was exactly what Ziggy wanted to happen.

"Ahhhhhh." My spasms finally subsided. I felt the last of my cum oozing out. I sighed, and kissed Ziggy's back a couple of times without even thinking. Then I just lay there, recovering, getting my wits back. Was he awake?

Ziggy's fingers grasped the head of my slippery cock. My cock was still poking through his legs. Jesus, what was he doing? Then he put his hand up to his face.

"Zig," I said, "thanks."

"Were you dreaming when you came?"

"Yeah. I was. It was super. Thanks."

"Gotta take care of my best buddy," he said.

"Zig, I'd follow you to the end of the world."

He laughed. "Same here, Josh. We sure do make a pair, don't we?"

"Yeah."

"We have kind of a mess here, though."

"Let me see." I pulled my dick out from between his legs, and he turned over onto his back. He lay there with his hands behind his head. Jeez, there was cum all over him. "My god, Zig, did all that come out of me?"

"Nah," he said, "some of it's yours, some of it's mine."

I looked at him and grinned. "You horny bastard."

"Yeah, that's me, alright."

"Here, I know how to clean that up." I started licking, and I didn't stop until I had it all slurped up. It took me a while to get it off his belly because he was so ticklish, but I finally managed to get it all. Then I lay back down next to him.

"I tasted your cum," he said.

"What?"

"You heard me, bro. I tasted your cum."

"No way."

"Sure I did."

Would wonders never cease? "What did you think?"

"It wasn't bad. Not bad at all. Better than I expected."

"You amaze me, Zig."

"Hey, with you enjoying licking up mine the way you do and eating it all, I figured it's not gonna hurt me to give yours a taste."

"You didn't have to do that."

"I know. I wanted to." He looked at me and smiled.

I shook my head and smiled, too. "You're something else, you know that?"

I lay back down, and we stared at the ceiling for a few minutes.

Then he said, "Come on, let's get some sleep." We turned on our sides, him in front, and I held him up close to me.

Friday

I DON'T KNOW HOW HE DOES IT, but Ziggy managed to get up and get ready for work and leave without even waking me up.

He left a note about driving my car to work to do the tune up, and he said there were leftovers in the fridge from his dinner last night with Eleanor, and he reminded me this was the day the telephone guy would come.

He said if I felt like washing clothes for the trip tomorrow, there were quarters in a jar in the dresser, and laundry soap under the sink. That was a great idea. I'd already used up all of my own clean clothes and was borrowing his, so there was plenty of laundry.

I chowed down on the leftovers, then I gathered up all of our dirty clothes and got that done. No job hunting today. That could wait until next week. The telephone guy showed up in the afternoon; I had him install the phone in the walk-in closet, so we could forget about it when we wanted to.

Ziggy got home a little after four, in a great mood, as usual. He began stripping clothes off before he even closed the door, starting with his overalls. "TGIF, dude!" He handed me my car keys.

"Yeah, finally, the weekend," I said. "Hey, is Monday a holiday for you?"

"Yes! They'll be selling cars like crazy the whole weekend, but the shop is closed until Tuesday. How about you? Have any interviews on Monday?"

"Nope."

"Alright. Fantastic! A road trip and a long weekend. This ought to be good." He sat down on the bed and pulled off a sock.

"Yeah. It'll be good to get my stuff back, too."

"Definitely." He pulled off the other sock and tossed them into the laundry basket. "Hey, you haven't talked with Fred since Sunday, right?"

"That's right."

"What do you think is going through his head by now?"

"He probably thinks I'm laying low and feeling sorry for myself. That I'll come crawling back when I can't stand being without him anymore." I sat down on the couch.

Ziggy stood up and took off his belt. "That guy must think he's the center of the universe."

"I know what he's planning to do. He's planning on acting like he didn't even miss me, hardly knew I was gone."

"Jesus, what a bastard."

"That's the way he is."

"Do you think he's worried about you, though?" Ziggy pulled off his jeans.

"I doubt it. If he's worried at all, it's about not having someone to do housework."

"Is he gonna freak when he sees us carrying your stuff out to the car?"

"Well, he won't be happy about it," I said. "Losing his live-in maid."

"We should talk about scenarios of what might happen. Walking into stuff like this is easier to deal with when you've worked out the possibilities ahead of time."

"Sounds like a good idea. Just because we don't know what's gonna happen doesn't mean we can't be ready for it."

"Exactly. Plan ahead when fucking with assholes. That's my motto." He pulled off his underwear and stood there in just his t-shirt.

"Maybe we can do it when he's not there," I said. "That would simplify things."

He pulled off his t-shirt, wiped his armpits, and threw the shirt in the basket. "You have a key, right?"

"Sure. And I paid my rent for this month, too. I have every right to go in there, whether he's there or not."

"That might be the way to go, then. There's no use asking for trouble. You know what he'll say later, though." He sat down next to me on the couch. "That you didn't have the guts to show your face. The standard thing for a bully to say in a situation like that."

"That's exactly what he'd say."

"Well, here's what I think. It doesn't matter what he says, or what he thinks, as long as we get out in one piece with your stuff. His opinion isn't worth shit, and he doesn't get to make the choice here; you do. There's nothing wrong with avoiding trouble when it wouldn't serve a purpose anyway. But you're the one who calls the shots, dude. We can make sure we see the bastard, give him another chance to be a jerk, or we can go in when he's not there. Or we can wing it and be ready for either one, Josh. I'll be there to help, no matter what."

"I guess I oughta think about it," I said.

"Don't let it worry you too much, okay? It's gonna work out, bro. No matter what happens, we'll get through it."

"Okay. I appreciate you helping me with this, Zig. I won't feel so on my own, with you there."

"You'd do the same for me, Josh."

"That's right, you bet I would."

"Is there a way to know when he'll be gone, if we want to go that route?"

"No, not on weekends." I thought about that for a minute. "Wait, I remember now, we were talking about going to Atlanta on Labor Day weekend!"

"One week after St. Louis?"

"Yeah, I know, that's a lot of traveling. They've been making plans for weeks, though. St. Louis was the spur-of-the-moment trip. Atlanta is like a dream destination. At least if you're gay in Memphis. Atlanta has an established gay community, plenty of gay bars, and a bathhouse. Everything Fred could want. It even has a Six Flags amusement park. I'll bet they go."

"You have any friends you could call, to find out?"

"Only the ones who'd be going with him, and they're most likely leaving right about now, soon as they all get off work. I could try calling Tony. Maybe he hasn't left yet." I went to the closet and brought out the phone and set it on top of the dresser.

"You had them install the phone in the closet? Dude!"

"I hope that's alright."

"It's great. Perfect. I like it."

Tony's answering machine kicked in on the fourth ring. Then halfway through his usual outgoing message, Tony himself picked up. He sounded out of breath, like he'd run to the phone. "Hello?"

"Tony?"

"Yeah. Hey, Josh! Is that you?"

"Yeah, it's me. How you doing?"

"I'm great! Are you home?"

"No, I'm not back yet. Still in St. Louis."

"Oh. Damn, that's a shame. I thought you was home. Fred told us he talked to you Sunday, but that's the last I heard."

"Why, what's up?"

"We're all fixin' to go to Atlanta! Well, Fred says he might not go, but you know he wouldn't miss a trip to Atlanta. I wish you was coming with us, though."

"Me, too. But I know you'll have lots of fun."

"Yeah, we will, no doubt about that. It won't be the same without you, though, Josh."

"You're one of the good ones, Tony." I brought the phone over to the coffee table. "Hey, listen, is Fred still pissed off at me?"

"You haven't talked with him?"

"Not since Sunday." I sat down next to Ziggy.

"Oh. Wow. Well, I haven't talked with him much, either. Josh, I really feel bad about last weekend."

"Tony, it wasn't your fault. You didn't have anything to do with it."

"I know, but I should have stayed there with you instead of taking off with Fred. I don't know what I was thinking. I realized it after we left, but it was too late then. Jerome was driving. When shit like that happens, he always sides with Fred. You know how that is. I'm sorry, Josh. I never should have left you alone."

"Don't worry, Tony. Everything happens for a reason. You're the best friend I've got in Memphis; nothing will ever change that."

"I thought you'd be back by now," he said. "Didn't nobody tell me you wasn't going to Atlanta. What are you doing still in St. Louis?"

"Getting to know the place better. There's some really good people here, Tony." I looked at Ziggy and smiled.

"When are you coming back?"

"Oh, jeez. I don't think I can tell you that, now. It might be soon, though."

"Fuck, I sure hope so. Listen, I'm sorry to run, Josh, but I gotta go. Jerome is picking me up in a few, and I ain't even packed my stuff yet. I'll talk to you when we get back, okay?"

"Okay, Tony. Let's keep in touch, no matter what happens, okay?"

"Of course we'll keep in touch," he said. "What the hell are you talking about?"

"Okay. I'll call you. If I don't see you first."

"Okay. Bye, Josh."

I hung up the phone and looked at Ziggy.

"Did you find out anything?"

"Yeah, they're going to Atlanta, but Fred might stay home."

"Might?"

"Yeah. Sounds like he hasn't made up his mind yet. Fuck."

"Would he really do that? Pass up a trip to Atlanta?"

"It wouldn't be like him, that's for sure. But you never know with Fred."

"So, we don't know any more than we did before."

"Right."

"Well, I'll be with you, Josh. What's the worst he can do, if he's there?"

"I don't know. I've never known him to get physical with anybody, but he sure does act like he wants to sometimes. He's chickenshit by nature, but he still manages to come across threatening."

"Probably just a big baby who learned how to scare people."

"Something else I realized is, I'm gonna miss Tony. That's the only bad thing about leaving Memphis. He's my closest friend there. I hope we don't lose touch."

"Yeah, I figured you must have some friends there, still."

"Not that many. Not close friends, at least. But Tony is, for sure. He's really a good person. I wish he'd be home this weekend. He's the one person I'd want you to meet. But he'll be in Atlanta with the rest of them."

"Maybe he'll want to come up here and visit us in St. Louis."

"Yeah, that would be great!"

"Friends are precious, bro. Hang on to the ones you've got."

"Yeah."

—

ZIGGY SNIFFED UNDER HIS ARM and frowned. "God, I stink." He stood up and said, "You wanna take a shower?"

"Yeah, sure!"

"Well, come on, then," he said, smiling, walking toward the bathroom.

We stood at the tub while Ziggy felt the temperature; then he got under the water, with me right behind him. I rubbed his back. I didn't even ask; I just started rubbing his shoulders.

He sighed. "Feels good, bro."

I massaged his back for the longest time, getting hard from all the touching. Then I reached for the soap and lathered him up. Then I slapped his ass.

"Thanks, Josh." He took the soap. His dick was hard, too. "Now it's your turn." Massaging my back, he said, "How's the homework coming along?"

"Fine. I've been practicing each time I shower. I'm learning to relax."

"Is that right?"

"Yeah. I can get two fingers up there, no problem at all. I'm working on three."

He laughed. "That's exactly what I wanted you to do. I've been working on your next lesson plan, dude. If you're ready."

"Okay."

"The next step involves someone else playing with your butt."

"Someone else? Oh, jeez, I don't know, Zig. I don't think I'm ready for that. That doesn't appeal to me to much right now, to tell you the truth."

"You'll never like getting fucked if you don't let the guy play with your butt first. Getting you to relax is part of making you feel good, Josh. That's what this is all about, is making you feel good, right?"

"Well, yeah, sure. I guess so."

"You guess so?"

"It's just kind of hard to imagine a stranger doing this to me. Who do you have in mind, anyway? I mean, jeez, if the guy is gonna be fucking me, don't I get to meet him first? I should have some say-so in it."

"Don't worry. You'll get to meet him first. And then you can tell me what you think."

"And I'll have the final say?"

"Definitely. You'll be calling the shots, bro. You're in control, every step of the way."

"Uh, who is it? What's he like?"

"There's a guy at work who would probably be good."

"Probably?"

"Well, yeah."

"What do you mean, 'probably'?"

"Well, he's really nice, polite, and not bad-looking, either. He's an older guy, but sexy."

173

"And he's gay?"

"Yeah, he is. He doesn't necessarily want people to know, though."

"Oh, great. Another closet case."

"Well, the important thing is if he's good at fucking, and if he'll let you be in control. And I think this guy probably fills the bill."

"It's the 'probably' part that worries me."

"Well, I understand, but there's no way to be sure. Not unless I let him fuck *me*, first, and I'm not too thrilled with that idea, to be honest."

"Well, join the club. I'm definitely not thrilled about the idea of *any* stranger fucking me. And the same goes for him putting his fingers up my ass."

"Okay, pal. Don't worry. Relax. I wouldn't let anybody hurt you. We'll figure something out."

"Okay." I sighed. "I just don't know how I'm gonna relax enough to let a stranger into my butt. I can barely let *myself* in there."

"Yeah," he said, "I guess I didn't really think it through enough." He massaged my back for a while. Neither one of us said anything. I was so relaxed I was starting to feel drowsy. "Hey, listen," he said, "why don't you go ahead and play with your ass now? Show me what you can do, bro."

"You serious?"

"Yeah."

"Right now? With you here?"

"Yeah, why not? You're gonna have to get used to doing sex stuff with me, anyway, sooner or later. If we're gonna fuck a woman together."

"Uh, okay." I soaped up my hands and reached behind and tried to put one finger up there, for starters, but I couldn't relax enough. "I think I'm too nervous, Zig."

"Because I'm here?"

"I guess so. Maybe I'm embarrassed or something?"

"Yeah, maybe. That would explain it." He thought about it. "Do you get embarrassed sitting on the shitter in front of someone else?"

"God, yes."

"Why?"

"Jeez, I don't know, I just do. It's so, um, personal."

"But peeing is personal, too, isn't it? You don't mind peeing in front of somebody."

"Actually, I used to get embarrassed about that, too. But that was because I'd get a hard on."

"Embarrassed about your dick getting hard? Oh, right. Jeez, I keep forgetting about your mother. Yeah, okay, of course you would get embarrassed about taking a shit. You learned that from her, too. Jesus, Josh, what a sicko she was. You gotta realize how ill that was, for her to be ashamed of her body."

"That's her, alright."

"We didn't have anybody like her at the orphanage, thank god. And we didn't have much privacy, either. When you share a bathroom with a dozen guys getting ready for school all at the same time, sitting on the can is just something you do whenever it becomes available. Before someone else grabs it."

"Oh, god. I would be so embarrassed."

"Because that's what you learned. It's all about learning, and what you learn, you can unlearn, Josh. Granted it's difficult sometimes, but you can unlearn stuff like that if you work on it. It's easier if you get somebody to help you."

"Just sitting on the toilet wouldn't be so bad. It's wiping my ass in front of everybody, that's what would mortify me. Oh, and the sound, too. The sound of shitting. I don't know why I get embarrassed, everyone does it, but I do. Get embarrassed."

"Well, don't feel bad. Lots of people are like that. That's why they put doors on bathroom stalls."

"Yeah."

"But Josh, it would be a good thing if you could get over it. At least when you're with family. That's you and me, bro; we're family, now, right?"

"Right."

"Wanna try playing with your butt again?"

"Okay."

And I tried, but I guess I was still too embarrassed. Or at least self-conscious.

When I still couldn't do it, Ziggy tried to get me over my embarrassment by doing it to himself. Right there in the shower, in front of me, he stuck a finger up his asshole, then two fingers, and then, when he was good and relaxed, he put three fingers up inside himself. With me watching! It was funny. And sexy.

I still couldn't get myself to relax, though.

"Okay," he said. "I think I know what I'm gonna have to do."

"Uh, oh. I don't know if I like the sound of that."

"Oh, don't worry, bro, you'll enjoy it."

"If you say so." *Now* what the hell did he have planned?

"Here's what we're gonna do. I'm gonna get out of the shower and wait in the living room. I'll close the bathroom door so you know nobody's watching. You stay in here till you can relax enough to get two fingers up your butt easy, just like you've already been doing. Take as long as you like. I want you to be nice and relaxed, and make sure you're squeaky clean, too, inside and out, okay? Whenever you're ready, come on out."

"Uh, okay. I'll do it. But jeez, Zig, what have you got planned? What the hell am I getting myself into?"

"Don't worry, Josh. You'll see, buddy. You're gonna love every minute of this."

Chapter 12
RELAX

I DID FINALLY get my asshole to relax, once he wasn't there watching. I soaped myself up good, moved my fingers around, and got totally relaxed. And totally clean. I finished showering and came out of the bathroom.

Ziggy was lying on the bed with his eyes closed, naked.

"I did it," I said. "I still don't understand why I couldn't relax with you there, though."

"Oh, well, we'll get you over it." He got up. "It's just stage fright or something."

"What do you want me to do now?"

"Lie down here on the bed, Josh. Face down. Put some pillows underneath, so you can totally relax and still breathe. I'm gonna give you a full-body massage."

"For real?"

He grinned. "Yes, dude, for real. You can do the same for me sometime, okay?"

"Okay." I lay down, belly down, and positioned the pillows.

"That's it," he said. "I want you to let yourself completely relax. Completely." He climbed up on top of me, with a knee on each side of me, and sat on my butt. His bare ass, sitting on my bare ass. "It might take you ten minutes, it might take you thirty. However long it takes, you're gonna get so relaxed, you might even fall asleep. If you do, that's okay."

"Alright."

"Somewhere along the line I'll get a little, uh, intimate with you. Just letting you know ahead of time, so you don't freak out. Okay?"

"Okay. But you're giving me a hard-on already."

He laughed. "Hard-ons are completely okay, bro. I'm getting one, too. But this is gonna be about relaxing."

"Okay."

He started at my shoulders and neck. He had a knack for finding the tight spots. He went at them gently but firmly, working until I felt each muscle relax.

My cock was hard and I thought his was, too. Then when he moved down lower I could feel his cock moving across my ass, and it was definitely heavy and hard. This was not supposed to be about sex, though, so I didn't focus so much on his cock or mine; I just relaxed and let my mind wander.

He moved down, little by little, getting one part to relax, then another. He worked on the muscles in my butt. "Anybody ever tell you you've got a nice ass?"

"Yeah," I said, "but people will say anything."

"Well, you do. You sure enough do. Is this what they mean when they talk about 'bubble-butts?'"

"Jeez, I don't think so."

"Damn, I wish my ass was this hot."

"What are you talking about, Zig? You've got a beautiful ass. I love your ass."

My legs were next. They were just as sore as my shoulders, maybe more. He worked on them till they loosened up, then he moved down to my feet.

He did one foot at a time. He found muscles I never knew I had. He spent a lot of time on each one, and the biggest surprise was him licking them. He licked my feet all over. Now, *that* I would definitely call intimate. By the time he was done with my feet, I did feel totally relaxed. Except for my cock, which was so hard and stiff I thought it might break off.

He moved up my legs again. When he reached my butt he worked the cheeks of my ass as if they were bread dough. Gently. Then he eased up and caressed my skin lightly, running his fingers

178

all over my ass. He gently caressed every inch of my butt, and it felt so very good. Like tickling, but better. He said, "Is your cock hard?"

"Are you kidding? You know it is, Zig."

He laughed. "So's mine, Josh. You've got one sexy butt, dude. I like your feet, too."

He kept on with my ass, and spent more and more time on my ass crack, caressing all the way from my balls to my back and everything in between. If I ever tensed up, he backed off to give me more time to get used to the idea of being touched. Touched in unfamiliar, secret places. Then he'd move ahead.

He kept coming back to that spot between my balls and my asshole. It felt wonderful. Sometimes he would spread my ass cheeks to get better access there. Occasionally his fingers would brush against the ring of my asshole itself, and it was total pleasure. Until then I had no idea there were so many nerve endings there. Who knew?

He wasn't trying to push his finger inside, although he probably could with lubrication. I was half in a dream state, half in nirvana, and totally relaxed. He was rubbing gently all around my asshole, and I was in ecstasy.

I imagined doing the same to him, later, but mostly I wasn't thinking about anything; I was just enjoying the sensations. Then, incredibly, I felt licking again. Not my feet this time, but my asshole! "Jesus, Zig!"

"Shhhhh."

I had an impulse to resist, but then I relaxed and went with the flow. If he wanted to lick me there, who was I to complain? Oh, my god, it tickled, but it felt so much better than tickling.

He focused on my asshole and under my balls, licking, then rubbing with his thumb and fingers. Then licking again. I thought I was relaxed before, but it wasn't until my anus unclenched and allowed his tongue inside that I realized *now* I was totally relaxed.

Oh my god, Ziggy had his tongue up my ass. And I was relaxed enough to let him do it. Two wonders in one.

I was relaxed, but my cock was rock hard. I pushed my butt backward to give him better access. I didn't care whether I came or not. It felt so good I just wanted him to go on. Keep on doing what he was doing. He kept licking and rubbing. Except now, when he rubbed, his thumb would go inside a little.

His thumb was going inside my asshole, and I was still relaxed. In fact, I raised my butt higher. I probably looked like a cat in heat, but I didn't care. I liked what Ziggy was doing to me.

Then I felt him put two fingers in, instead of his thumb. He must have had some lube; his fingers were slippery and went right in.

My ass was in the air and my cock was stiff, dangling between my legs. I could have come with just a few strokes, but I was happy as I was. This was fantastic. He held one cheek of my ass with one hand, and with the other he moved two fingers in and out. Or was it three? Then he took his fingers out and used his tongue some more. I wondered what he was doing with his free hand, because I felt the bed shaking. Then I realized what it probably was. He was stroking his own hard cock.

He kept this up for a while, alternating from licking to using his fingers and then back to licking again, stroking himself when his hand was free. Then one time, instead of his own dick, he grabbed *my* rigid cock. Oh my god! He yanked my stiff dick twice and that was it. I was shooting my load. Euphoria.

I moaned as my cum started flying everywhere. Meanwhile he gently continued pulling on my cock and pushing his tongue in my hole. When I was just about spent, he let loose of my dick and jacked his own hard cock. Then he groaned and I felt his warm cum landing all over my back.

I looked back at him, just as he opened his eyes. He looked at me and smiled. I lowered myself down flat on the bed, and he collapsed on top of me. We lay there like that for at least five minutes.

Then he got up and said, "Let's go get cleaned up, Josh."

—

I COULD HAVE STAYED IN BED and slept, I was so relaxed. Spent and relaxed.

Ziggy walked to the bathroom, and then I heard the shower start. He said, "Come on, Josh." When I got to the bathroom he was feeling the water. He looked at me and smiled, stepped into the tub, and I followed.

"You go first," he said. So I squeezed past him and got under the spray. Then he lathered me all over with soap. After a couple of minutes he said, "Why so quiet?"

"Oh, just thinking about how good that was."

"Yeah. It was."

"Were you planning on that from the start? Us getting off?"

"No, I just wanted to get your butt to relax, but I guess it was bound to happen. That licking thing always makes everyone horny. I didn't plan it, though. Just helping you with your home-work, bro." He continued rubbing my back.

"And you got horny, too, huh?"

"Hell, yes." He reached down and squeezed my butt and massaged it. "Are you still relaxed?"

"Yeah. Very. I could fall asleep."

"Tell you what. Let's get some fingers in there again, while you're still relaxed. Are you okay with that?"

"Uh, sure, I guess."

"Don't worry, I won't hurt you."

He slipped his soapy hand into the crack of my ass and gently rubbed my anus. He moved his fingers around, but he kept coming back to my asshole. He touched my balls and my cock. It felt good. He concentrated more on my anus, massaging all

181

around the ring of it, and then he eased one finger right inside. I might have tightened up just a little bit, briefly, but then I relaxed again. He had a great, gentle touch. I was surprised how relaxed I still was.

"Does that feel okay?" he asked.

"Yeah."

"Does it feel good?"

"Yeah."

"Okay." He kept moving his finger around, and in and out. He really knew what he was doing. He had me totally relaxed. I didn't even flinch when he added a finger, making it two in there. "You okay?"

"Yeah. I'm fine. You're good at this."

"Thanks." He moved his two fingers around, being careful and gentle. "We'll get you up to speed on this, partner. You'll see."

I was ready for anything. I leaned forward against the wall, standing under the hot shower, thoroughly enjoying an anal massage.

"You really *are* relaxed," he said. "Is your cock hard?"

"Is the Pope Catholic?"

He laughed. "Good. That's the whole idea." He gently pushed three fingers against my hole, and they went right in. "You okay?"

"Yeah. That's three fingers?"

"Yeah. And you're still relaxed as can be."

"It feels good."

"Sure it does, you bet." He held his three fingers in there, making sure I stayed relaxed. He reached around with the other hand and felt my dick. "Three fingers and you're still hard. That's good." Then he started moving his fingers around. "You still okay?"

"Yeah."

"Feel good?"

"Oh, yeah."

"See how good it can feel to have someone up your ass?"

"Yeah. It's amazing. I'll bet you could fuck me right now, Zig, and it wouldn't hurt at all." I thought, *I wish. That's one thing that'll never happen.* But at least I could fantasize.

He laughed. "All in good time, bro. We've got your anus relaxed, that's the hardest part. But you've got more muscles in there to work through. You've made a lot of progress. Enough for today." He gently took his three fingers out and massaged my ass some more. "There's no sense in rushing it," he said. He soaped me up all over. Then he said, "Okay, dude, my turn."

We switched places. My cock stuck straight out, stiff and hard. It brushed up against him when we squeezed past each other. He grinned. "You're ready to go again!"

"Well, jeez, what did you expect?"

"I'm telling you, this stuff is like magic."

He faced the wall, and I soaped up his back. "When you said 'my turn' did you mean for me to play around inside your butt, too?"

I was beginning to think he hadn't heard me. Then he said, "You can if you want to."

"Yeah," I said, "but do you want me to?"

Another half minute went by. Then he said, "Yeah." He looked over his shoulder at me, and I looked at him. He said it again: "Yeah. Okay." He turned his head forward again, put his hands on the wall, and pushed his ass back a little farther. "Play with my ass, Josh. Make me feel good."

Chapter 13
TANGLED UP TOGETHER

I TRIED TO DO IT the same way he had. I massaged Ziggy's ass cheeks, caressed his ass crack, rubbed his anus, and fondled his balls. Gently, I pushed a soaped-up finger against his anus. It went right in, and he sighed. I said, "Are you okay?"

"Yeah, Josh. Keep going, dude."

I moved my finger around, feeling the inside of him.

"Go ahead with two fingers, bro."

I took my finger out, soaped up some more, and then I pressed two fingers inside. It seemed unreal, that I was doing this to Ziggy. Of all people. Yet at the same time it seemed like the most natural thing in the world.

His asshole was holding my fingers, but not with a tight grip. I imagined how wonderful just that much pressure would feel, if my cock was in there instead of my fingers.

"That's it," he said. "Don't be afraid to move your fingers around in there, Josh. Push them in as far as you want."

I did like he said, and he moaned softly.

"I'm not hurting you, am I?" I reached around to see if his cock was hard. When I touched it, he moaned again. His cock was stiff as a board.

"You're doing great, Josh." He took a deep breath. "It's been a long time since anybody did this to me."

"Okay, then." I moved my fingers in and out.

"Try three fingers," he said.

I put three fingers together and they went in with only a little resistance.

"Ahhh. I forgot how good this can feel," he said.

I moved the fingers in and out a bit, and with my other hand I reached under and gently cupped his balls in my palm.

"Oh, Jesus, Josh. Yeah, touch me there, dude." I felt him start stroking his cock. Pretty soon he said, "Josh, do me a favor?"

"Sure."

"Kneel down and put just two fingers in, turned around the other way, so you're kind of pressing toward my belly button instead of my tail bone, okay?"

"Okay, sure." I knelt down behind his ass and put two soapy fingers in, just like he said. I was getting drenched by the shower spray, but that was okay.

"Ahhh, yeah, dude, that's it, that's it. Move your fingers around. And put your other hand back on my balls like you did before, okay?" He was still stroking his cock.

So I did what he said. He moaned when I touched his balls, and I felt him stroke faster on his hard dick.

"Dude," he said. "I'm gonna come." He was breathing hard. "Josh, I'm coming." He kept stroking and groaning. His asshole clenched tighter. With my fingers up his ass I could *feel* him coming. It was amazing. I could feel him shooting one spurt after another. He was still gasping and moaning and stroking.

I saw his cum splash against the wall, and I thought, *Damn. I'd love to gulp down every drop of that stuff,* but I was thrilled just the same, absolutely. I had a hand on his balls, two fingers in his ass, and I felt each spurt of his dick. What more could I ask for?

He stopped moaning and took a long breath. "Okay, Josh." Finally he was finished erupting. "You can take your fingers out now. Jesus, that was awesome. Thanks, dude." I stood up, and he turned around. He looked at my stiff, swollen cock, bobbing up and down, and said, "You didn't come?"

"Nah." I was grinning from ear to ear. My cock was stiff and rigid as a board and I was probably leaking pre-cum like a faucet, but I didn't even care. I was so happy. "Both my hands were busy,"

I said. "But it doesn't matter. I helped you get off!" I felt like a kid with a new toy. "I'll do that again anytime you want, Zig."

"That's cool," he said, "but it's your turn, now, Josh." He grabbed hold of me and turned me around; then he pulled me against him, my butt to his balls. I could feel his dick, big and full, pressed up against my back.

The way he took over my body, it sent me into a trance. Some sort of alpha-wave state of mind. I just surrendered to it. Let him do what he wanted. A shivery feeling ran through every inch of my body.

He reached around, grabbed my cock, and slowly started stroking it. He reached around with his other hand and gently tickled my balls. His chin was resting up near my neck and he softly said in my ear, "I'm gonna make you come, Josh."

My god, he didn't know how close I was. And the feel of our bodies together, it was incredible.

"This is what my buddy used to do to me," he whispered in my ear, "while he fucked me in the closet." I felt Ziggy's dick pressing stiff on my back. I imagined his dick up inside my butt, pushed in as far as it would go. I was pretty damned sure I would love it.

"He'd grab me from behind like this, while his slippery cock was inside me. Moving up and back, in and out, fucking my ass, and I loved it. He'd bring me off at least once, maybe twice, before he got off himself. One time he fucked me for over an hour and jacked me off three times."

"Jesus!" That was all it took. "Ahhh!" My cum started flying.

"Yeah, Josh, shoot a good load." He kept stroking me, and tugged the skin of my ball sac, which just about sent me through the roof. I was gasping and moaning. My body jerked with each spurt, but he held me close so that we never lost contact.

Finally I shot my last squirt of cum and I began to relax. Ziggy held me till he knew I could stand on my own. Then he loosened his hold. I turned around. "Wow."

"Good one, huh?"

"You got that right. Thanks, Zig."

"No problem, bro. We're in this together. You help me come, I help you come."

"Sounds good to me," I said.

"Let's get done before the hot water runs out."

We quickly rinsed off, stepped out of the tub, and took our towels to the living room.

—

ZIGGY LOOKED OUT the window. "Hey, want to go for a walk? It's not even dark yet. And the sky's clearing up."

"Sure!"

"You might even see a surprise later, Josh. If the weather holds up."

"You're just full of surprises," I said.

"Yeah, sometimes I even surprise myself."

"Maybe we can get something to eat while we're out?"

"Yeah, for sure," he said. "I'm starving." He opened the dresser drawer for some underwear. "Hey, you did the laundry!"

"Yep."

When we got outside there were some nice colors in the sky. It looked like maybe a nice sunset in the works.

"How's onion rings and cheeseburgers sound?"

"Perfect. Zig, I gotta tell you, that massage on the bed was fantastic. The best I've ever had in my life. And not just the last part, either. All of it."

He smiled. "I'm glad you liked it."

"But you surprised me. I'm kind of, uh . . . confused. No, more like, amazed."

"Amazed and confused, huh?"

"Zig, you keep on amazing me. I never would have thought in a million years that you would put your tongue up my, you know . . ."

"Your asshole?" He laughed. "Well, you might be the only guy I would do that with, Josh, but hell, I figured, why not? I've done it to women before, lots of times, so why not my best buddy?"

"I'm not complaining, Zig. Believe me, I'm not complaining. It was awesome."

"That's one of the tricks I learned. It's how you get the other person to want it more. You lick and you lick, and you keep on licking until she's all primed up and ready. And even then, you still don't stop, except to trade off with using your fingers, and then you go back to licking. There's more to it, of course. But it works whether it's a pussy or an asshole, believe it or not. On guys or girls."

"Oh, I believe it."

"With a few differences, of course. And it's not just the hole you're working on, it's the person. You make her feel good enough, Josh, and she'll be begging you, dude, begging you to fuck her silly. Or him, as the case may be. And then, both of you end up happy."

"I wish somebody had explained it to me like that before. It makes so much sense, but who knew?"

"Well, I want you to learn how to fuck, bro. Nobody ever explained it to me. My buddy in the orphanage didn't explain it, he just showed me. That's basically how I learned."

"Yeah, that's one of the best ways to learn."

"I learned from an expert," Ziggy said. "He might not have known he was an expert, but he was. What I learned from him is, if you're gonna fuck somebody, you do it right. You make sure the other guy enjoys it as much as you do. If you don't do that, then you're not honoring him, you're using him. Anyway, the more the other person enjoys it, the more you enjoy it. That's just the way it works."

"Makes sense."

"You remember how he showed me, right?"

"Oh, yeah. My dick gets hard in about two seconds when I think about you and him fucking."

We reached the restaurant, got our food, and went outside again, eating while we walked.

He ate a few onion rings and then he said, "Two seconds, huh?"

"Hell, yes. Are you kidding? That's so hot, what you and your buddy did together. I'd have given anything to be either one of you."

Ziggy smiled. We ate a few more bites of food, then he said, "When you imagine yourself being a part of that hot little scene, what turns you on more, being the teacher, or the learner? The fucker, or the one being fucked?"

"Uh, I don't know. I'll have to think about that."

We crossed over some busy streets, and then the bridge over the highway. That put us inside Forest Park. We ditched our trash and picked up the path where we left off the last time.

"So, have you decided? When you think about us fucking, which makes your dick harder, giving or receiving?"

I shrugged my shoulders. "Either one. I don't know. I like the idea of being on either end of it."

He laughed. "That's a good sign. Good. You like both."

"Yeah." He had me grinning. Zig was so easy to talk to.

We were following the path eastward, away from the sunset, but we took our time, stopping to check out the changing colors in the west.

Then he said, "Listen, Josh, let's forget about some random guy fucking you. How about if I teach you, the same way that I was taught?"

I stared at him, astonished.

"I can't think of any better way for you to learn," he said, "if you're okay with me doing it. I can really make a believer out of you, bro."

Chapter 14
NEW PLAN

"OH, MY GOD."

"If you're willing."

"Zig, you're freaking me out!"

I felt like screaming. He was suggesting the very thing I had thought was impossible. I know it's crazy to be scared of pleasure, scared of happiness, but my life was about change forever.

I had that moment of panic, but then I experienced something like a transformation. The timid part of me jumped right out of my skin and took off and left me behind. The fear just left me.

I felt a calmness, a steadiness. By god, I was going to stay right here. Ready or not. Here with my buddy Zig.

Who was going to show me how to fuck. Oh my god.

"Josh," he said, "I can't think of anyone better to teach you. I wouldn't trust anybody else, anyway. Someone else might hurt you."

"Zig . . . ." I was so elated I could hardly get the words out. "Zig, listen. If I'm gonna get fucked, there isn't anyone else in the world I'd rather have fuck me. Hell, you're the *only* guy I'd want fucking me."

"Just think about it, okay? Don't let me rush you, Josh."

"My god, this is so crazy. Sure, I'll think about it, but Zig . . . didn't you hear what I just said?"

"There isn't any better way to learn how to fuck than to be on the receiving end of some good fucking. This I know. You want to learn how to fuck good, don't you?"

"Yeah, I do. Sure I do. But—"

"If you and I are gonna be fucking women together, I know you want to make us both feel good, right?"

"Us?"

"You and me and her. We're gonna be all tangled up together, bro. You know that. And we'll be switching around. I know you wouldn't just fuck one of us and forget about the other."

"Uh, no, of course not. I wouldn't do that."

"The more we make each other feel good, the more we enjoy it ourselves. That's the way it works."

Now the sunset was on our left. We were cutting across a golf course.

"Unless you just want to watch," he said. "But, bro, I want you to be part of it. We ought to be in it together. Fuck, I've got a hard on again, thinking about you and me and her."

"I really do want to be part of it," I said.

"Take your time and think it over, then. You'll like it, you'll see. I can teach you so much, Josh. I promise I won't ever hurt you."

"Zig. I know you won't hurt me."

"Fuck! Look at what I'm doing. The last thing I want to do is pressure you. I'm sorry, Josh. Listen, you're my buddy no matter what, dude. Don't ever forget that, okay?"

"Okay, Zig."

"It was just an idea."

"It's a great idea!"

"Okay."

Neither one of us talked for a few minutes. I couldn't believe he thought I needed to be talked into it. Then again, just a couple of minutes ago I wanted to run from it. So maybe he knew how scared I might be.

We got through the golf course and came to another road. The path turned left again. Now we were walking straight into a spectacular sunset in its last stages.

"Zig?"

"Josh?"

"Listen, don't feel like you have to answer this, okay?"

"Okay. What's your question?"

"Well, uh, have you ever fucked a guy before?"

"Just once." He looked at me. "Dude. You don't think I'll be good?"

"No, no, that's not what I was getting at."

"Josh, I learned from an expert. And I've fucked women in the ass. If I can get a woman to like it, I know I can get a guy to."

"Zig, I believe you. I was just curious." We were still walking along the path. We came to a big greenhouse, went up and took a closer look, then we got back on the path and continued walking.

"How'd it go," I said, "the one time with the guy?"

"It was really great."

That's all he said. I looked at him and I was surprised to see that his eyes were shiny, glossy, like you get when you're trying not to cry. "Zig. What's wrong? What'd I say? I'm sorry if I . . ."

"No problem. It's okay. He . . . he really liked it. I went slow, and I made sure he was enjoying it the whole time, and he really got off on it. I *know* he liked it; he shot off without even touching his cock. And then he got off again when I got off, from me jacking him. It was . . . great. For both of us."

"Well, I'm sorry if I said something wrong."

"You didn't. I'm glad you asked. That's something I really like to remember."

We walked along for a few more minutes, both of us lost in our own thoughts.

Now that the sun was down it was getting dark.

Our path meandered around, and then we came out on a road next to a lake. We walked in silence a few more minutes, and then I said, "It's kind of funny, when you think about it."

"What's funny?"

"Here's the straight guy, trying to talk the gay guy into having sex. Meanwhile, the gay guy, maybe he's not so sure—like he has

192

to make up his mind whether he really wants to get fucked by the nicest, sexiest, most lovable and wonderful guy on earth. It's kind of backward, isn't it? Shouldn't I be the one who's trying to talk *you* into fucking *me*?"

"Yeah." He grinned. "You should be."

"Well, listen, Zig, I've already made up my mind."

"You have?" He stopped and looked at me, waiting for the news.

"Yeah, silly, jeez, of course I want you to do it! I wanna learn everything, Zig. And if you're gonna be fucking me, well, that's even better. Yes, I'm scared. I admit it, I'm scared. But absolutely, I'm in."

"Dude!" he said, grinning.

"I want to learn, Zig. You be the teacher, I'll be the student."

"Alright, bro, that's what I wanted to hear!" He had a huge grin on his face. I put my hand up in the air, palm toward Ziggy, with a big smile. High five! He raised his hand up and slapped my palm, and then we gave each other the warmest, closest, best hug ever.

I was happy and excited. Our relationship had a new element to it. I think Ziggy was as pleased as I was.

We followed the road along the lake, and now it was really getting dark. I could even see a couple of stars. We came to another road off to the left, and went that way. As soon as we turned I saw an enormous, familiar surprise rising up through the trees. "Jeez, Zig. Look at that moon."

"Yeah, isn't it great?" He grinned.

"My god, it looks so huge when it's low to the horizon like that."

"Makes you realize how close it really is, doesn't it?"

"It looks like we could get in a plane and fly there in a couple hours."

We stopped and watched it move up out of the treetops.

"That's got to be a full moon," I said. "Look how perfectly round it is."

As it cleared the trees and rose higher, wisps of clouds occasionally passed in front of it, adding to the show. Really beautiful. Ziggy put his arm around my shoulder, and then I put mine around his. We just stood there and watched.

Eventually we got to walking again. Everything seemed more magical now.

Chapter 15
GETTING CLOSER

WE WALKED ALONG the road beside the zoo, and then we saw the highway bridge ahead of us. Time to head back.

We got inside the apartment and started stripping down to our normal state of nakidity. Pulling my socks off, I said, "Still want to drive to Memphis tomorrow?"

"You bet. I'm looking forward to it." Ziggy pulled his t-shirt over his head and tossed it.

"I'm gonna pack some clothes before I go to bed. We might stay the whole weekend, right?" We unzipped our jeans and took them off. "Maybe I should make reservations for a hotel room."

"Yeah, definitely, all weekend, dude. Till Monday." He pulled off his briefs. "You're gonna give me the grand tour of Memphis, remember? As soon as we rescue your stuff from the enemy."

I laughed. "Okay. I'll pack plenty of clean underwear, then. If you don't mind me borrowing some of yours, that is."

"Go ahead, I've got plenty."

"Me, too, but they're in Memphis."

"Not for long."

"I like wearing your underwear, anyway."

"Is that right?"

"Yeah. It gives me a hard on, putting my dick and balls where yours have been so many times."

He laughed. "Dude!"

I smiled. "Just telling the truth."

"You gay guys are something else," he said, grinning.

"That's not so weird. Think about it. You'd probably get a boner, too, if you were wearing Eleanor's underwear, right?"

"Wear a girl's panties? No way!"

"Okay, okay. But what if she borrowed some of *your* briefs, and she wore them all day, and then she gave them back to you?"

"Um." He had to think about that. "First I'd smell them, of course. That's only natural."

"Okay, and then what?"

"God, leave it to you to think of this kinky stuff." He thought for a while. "Yeah, okay. I'd put them on. Maybe I *would* get a boner."

"See? It's not so weird, after all."

"No, I guess not. Kinky, but not weird. I like that idea, actually. Wearing other people's underwear."

Ziggy went into the kitchen and slugged down some milk. He came back and picked up his book and sat down to read. I got my backpack out of the closet.

"Zig," I said, "I'm just wondering."

"What, dude?"

"When it comes down to actually, you know, showing me how to fuck, will it really, uh, work? For you?"

"You worry too much, bro." He smiled. "Why wouldn't it work?"

"Well, you know. You liking women and all."

He looked at me. "Josh. Are you wondering if I'm gonna change my mind? You know me better than that."

"No, that's not what I meant. You've made up your mind to do it. I know you won't change your mind."

He thought about it some more. "So, maybe you're wondering, like, if I'm gonna be able to stay hard? While I'm fucking you? Is that what you're talking about?"

"I don't know. Maybe." I tried to picture Ziggy going soft while he was fucking anyone, or anything, but I couldn't. It was unlikely. "No, not that, either. I can't imagine *that* ever happening once you got started. That's one thing I like about you, Zig, is how you're so totally uninhibited about sex."

196

"Okay. Then give me a clue here. What do you mean, will it work for me?"

"It's just that, well, you know. You like girls. I'm a guy. Jeez, Zig, you're straight. You're not ever gonna feel weird about it?"

"There you go with that 'straight' stuff again." He put down his book and said, "Come over here, Josh, ol' buddy. Let's talk about this. I want us to be on the same wavelength."

I came over and sat down. He turned toward me, putting his knee up on the couch. "Are you saying I *should* feel weird about it?"

"No! Jeez, I didn't mean it like that."

He looked at me. "Are *you* gonna feel weird about it?"

"No, not at all," I said. "Well, I don't know. Maybe a little."

"But why?"

"I don't know."

He just looked at me.

"You're right," I said. "I worry too much."

"It's your mother, I'll bet, lurking in the back of your brain."

"No, I don't think it's the sex. I'm fine with sex, at least when it's with another gay man. Maybe it's because you're . . . well, you know, because you mostly like women."

"Why would that make a difference?"

"I don't know. Jeez, most gay guys would give their left nut to get fucked by a guy like you. It just doesn't happen very often. It's unusual for a straight guy to be so okay with having sex with another guy."

"Well, there you go again, calling me a straight guy. I'm not straight, okay?"

"Okay, okay, but you do like women mostly. I know that much."

"Maybe you're wrong about that, as well."

"Oh, come on. You're not the slightest bit gay!"

"Well, maybe I'm partly gay. Hell, sometimes I think I must be."

"Oh, jeez. All I'm saying is, I don't think of you that way. And so maybe I'm gonna feel a little funny about two guys having gay sex when one of them likes women so much."

"Well," he said, "we'll be having sex, no question about that, but remember, the idea is for you to learn how to fuck, the same way I learned. Then we can have three-way fucks with a woman. So it's not just gay sex; there's also a long-range goal in mind."

"Right, right, I remember. In order to be a good top, you have to know what it's like to be the bottom."

"Well, yeah. That's one way of putting it."

"I've heard gay men say that, too. Hell, maybe I don't really feel weird about it; maybe I just feel lucky. It's not something your average, uh, guy who likes women knows about."

"Well, for what it's worth, I'm not your average guy."

"You sure got that right." I smiled.

"You won't regret it, Josh, I promise. It's gonna be good. You'll see. And I'm gonna enjoy it just as much as you do, bro!"

"Oh, jeez. Now I'm gonna worry about turning you gay."

"Dude." He laughed. "Chill out. Sex is sex. You worry way too much about this gay-versus-straight stuff. It's just words people use, Josh. They're just words."

"Words that have meanings."

"Listen, 'straight' is just a category, a label. What does it really mean? Who makes the rules for being straight? And even if I was straight, why would I have to go by the rules anyway? I never agreed to any fucking rules. Whatever I am, it's not like I signed up to be that way ahead of time. I shouldn't have to follow somebody else's rules. I am what I am."

"Well, no, I didn't mean you should. It's just that, you know, that's my perception of you, that you're sexually attracted to the opposite sex, exclusively."

"Oh my god, Josh, get real! That's just not true! George, my buddy in the orphanage? I couldn't even look at him without getting a hard on. I used to go find him, if he didn't come looking for me first."

"Okay, one guy."

"No, not just one guy." He reached over and tickled one of my nipples. "Two guys. You turn me on, too. You know that."

"Are you talking about the time you were dreaming about Eleanor?"

He looked at me, surprised. "Josh. Bro. Dude." He had a hurt look on his face.

"What?" We sat there, looking at each other.

He reached over and ran his fingers through my hair. "Josh, I can't believe this. You know you turn me on. You know it. Don't you?"

"I don't know. Yeah, maybe I do. Do I?"

"Of course you do. You couldn't have missed it."

"But I thought you were straight."

"Oh, this is crazy."

"What do you mean?"

"You're trying to convince me that I'm straight, and I'm trying to convince you that I'm not. Something about that sounds so backward." He thought about it a minute. Then he put his hand on my shoulder. "Look, it's true, I like sex with women, and that's not gonna change. So, somebody could say I'm straight, and maybe he'd be partly right. Or maybe not. People are just too complicated to fit into narrow little slots like that."

"Alright."

"Maybe I'm partly straight, but that's not all I am. I'm more than that. Same with you. Maybe you're gay, but you're more than that, Josh. Way more." He moved his fingers back and forth, caressing the back of my neck. "Labels can really fuck things up sometimes."

I put my hand on his knee, feeling the curves of his skin, the soft hair on his leg. "Yeah," I said, "labels are really confining. It's like being put in a box."

"It is. We shouldn't have to try to live up to our labels. That's totally bass-ackward."

"Wouldn't it be cool," I said, "if people didn't get classified by who they have sex with? I'll bet we all start out bisexual when we're born, anyway. Maybe that's what you are, is bisexual."

He thought about that for a minute. "Sure. That's what I am. Bisexual. But it sounds so clinical. And generic." He gave it some more thought, and then he continued. "Not only that, it makes it sound like I'm sitting on a fence. Like I can't make up my mind. But that's not me. I don't have any problem knowing who I want."

He ran his fingers through my hair again, then he put his arm around my shoulder. "If I have to wear a label," he said, "I guess 'bisexual' is as good as any. But it sounds weird. Like I have two sexes. I don't understand why people think sex with a guy is so different from a girl. Fuck, either way, it's the same thing, sex with another human being. Hell, it's people who *don't* have sex with one whole gender that could be singled out as different. *That's* who ought to have some kind of label. They ought to call people like that 'monosexuals'."

"Yeah," I said. "I like that."

"Those dang monos." He smiled.

"From what I've heard, they're in the minority, too," I said. "Hardly anyone is completely straight. Kinsey had a scale. He said most people are somewhere in between." I put my hand on his thigh. "Maybe that goes along with what you're saying, Zig."

He thought about that, frowning. "Not really. What I'm saying is none of those labels and scales and graphs can tell you anything about one person. If you try and figure out where somebody is on one of those scales, you never will, because it's always changing.

"Like me, for instance. Last night when I was with Eleanor, okay, I was being straight. But maybe not completely straight, because I liked it that you were watching. Tonight, when I licked your asshole, someone could say I was being gay, because I was doing it to a guy. But maybe not completely gay, because I was thinking about licking your ass while you were fucking Eleanor."

"Okay," I said, "so maybe it depends on who you're with or who you're thinking of at the time."

"Yeah. That's right. It's always changing. But see, all that is nebulous in another way, too, because I didn't lick your asshole because you're a guy, I licked your asshole because you're Josh, my pal, my buddy."

"Okay, I guess I follow that."

"But on the other hand, you probably wouldn't turn me on as much if you were a girl. I *like* it that you're a guy. You see how complicated it is?"

"Yeah, it's definitely complicated, you're right about that. That's what makes it confusing."

"One thing I know for certain," he said. "If you live your life doing things—or *not* doing things—just because people expect it of you, your life isn't yours anymore."

We sat there for a while without saying anything. Thinking about it all.

Then he said, "Have you ever met a girl who turned you on?"

"Yeah, I have. More than once."

"Did you think to yourself, 'No, I can't be attracted to her, I'm gay'?"

I laughed. "No, of course not. But I did kind of wonder what my gay friends would think of me, if they knew."

"That's what I'm talking about. It's not right to let labels limit us like that. It's self-defeating. I'm not ashamed that you turn me on, Josh. Why shouldn't you? I want to get inside your skin every way I can. I'm not gonna turn away from that, just to live up to a label. If the thoughts don't fit the label, then the label's wrong, not the thoughts."

—

ZIGGY HAD HIS ARM AROUND ME, stroking my shoulder, and I had my hand on his leg, playing with his thin furry hair. It was one of those moments no one is in a hurry to end. Five or ten minutes went by. By then we were so relaxed and comfortable, he almost nodded out. I was sleepy, too. "I guess I'll get back to my packing," I said. Ziggy yawned and stood up.

I started going through dresser drawers. He had more than enough underwear for both of us, so I thought what the hell, I'll leave my underwear here and wear his. Not just because wearing his stuff was sexy; I liked it because it was like getting inside his skin. I grabbed some of his socks, too.

I heard him peeing in the bathroom, then the sound of him brushing his teeth.

I picked out a few of his t-shirts, too. Might as well fill out the wardrobe with his stuff. I would have snagged a couple pairs of his baggy jeans, too, but they fit Ziggy better than me. I really liked the way they hung on his butt and showed it off.

When I came out of the closet he was sitting on the bed. "I'm gonna turn in," he said. "It's been a long day, bro. I'll pack my stuff in the morning, while I fix breakfast."

"Okay."

"Stay up for a while if you want to. We're not on any schedule. I'm just kind of beat."

"Yeah, alright. I think I'll read a bit, after I pack."

He went to the bed and slid under the covers. "See you in dreamland, Josh."

"Good night, Zig."

I put the clothes in the backpack, and decided to get the rest of my stuff in the morning.

I took my credit card into the closet and sat down on the floor next to the phone. Where should I make reservations? I couldn't remember the names of any hotels in Midtown Memphis. The only name I could come up with was the Peabody Hotel, downtown, which was way classier than what we needed. I was looking for a place that was clean and safe but cheap, not some fancy place with fancy prices.

Then I thought, why not? I had a little money saved up, and the Peabody wasn't *that* expensive. I'd always wondered what it would be like to stay there. I couldn't think of any better occasion for it, either: our first road trip together.

No problem. The Peabody still had rooms available, including the usual with two double beds, but we didn't need two beds. So I reserved a room with just one bed. For a second I wondered if I should ask Ziggy about it, but I couldn't see either one of us wanting to sleep apart in separate beds.

With the reservations taken care of, I grabbed my book and sat down on the couch. I read for a few minutes, but I kept looking at Ziggy. Was he dreaming yet? It would be so wild if we really *could* meet in dreamland. Not just be in each other's dreams, but actually share the same dream. Now, that would be freaky.

Not gonna happen, though. Which was fine. We were just about as close as two people could get. Better to keep a little distance, a little separation. Better to maintain a bit of mystery in the mix. We could snuggle up and sleep in each other's arms, but our dreams would always be our own. That was a good thing.

I put my book away, turned out the lights, and slid into bed. I snuggled myself in, in front of him. Ziggy barely woke up, only enough to pull me up close to him. Then he sighed, and was back in dreamland.

Saturday

I SMELLED BACON frying and coffee brewing. Ziggy was quietly humming a tune while he walked back and forth, getting things ready. I stretched, and then I sat up in bed.

He saw that I was awake and said, "Good morning!"

"Good morning. You're full of energy this morning."

"Oh, sure. I'm all ready to go. This is gonna be fun," he said. "I haven't been on a road trip since I went to Washington, D.C."

"Really?"

"Really. Only time I've gone anywhere since high school was training for work."

"Wow."

"The disadvantages of not owning a car, I guess. Not that I've really wanted to go anywhere. Most of the time I'm happy right here in St. Louis."

"Yeah, I wondered about that. You work on cars, but you don't own one?"

"I used to. I had a raggedy old 1968 Mustang that I fixed up super nice. I didn't drive it much, though. It stayed parked most of the time. So when a guy offered to buy it I thought, what the hell. Why not?"

"You had an old Mustang and you sold it?"

"I wasn't using it, Josh. Really, I got more enjoyment out of fixing it up than driving it. Hey, are you ready to eat? This food's almost ready."

"Let me wash up first, it'll just take a minute."

After breakfast I offered to wash the dishes, but Ziggy told me to finish getting ready. His backpack was by the door, and he was ready to go.

I finished packing, took a quick shower, and then I was ready, too. Half an hour later we were in my car, tooling down I-55 to Memphis.

Chapter 16
ON THE ROAD TO MEMPHIS

"So," ZIGGY SAID, "is there any cool stuff we can see on the way down to Memphis?"

"Not a thing that I know of," I said.

"No way! What is it, 300 miles? There's gotta be something we can stop and gawk at."

"Three hundred miles of farmland. Corn, soy beans, cotton, rice, and not much else."

"Jesus. But we're driving alongside the Mississippi River. There must be something we can look at, right?"

"Well, check out the map, maybe there's something I don't know about. It's in the glove box."

Ziggy pulled out the map and looked at it for a while. "Doesn't look too promising," he said. "Cape Girardeau is the biggest city we'll go anywhere near, but it doesn't look like much."

"We can stop there and check it out, if you want. Take a look around."

"Wouldn't hurt. It would give us a break from driving."

"Okay."

"Let me know when you want me to take the wheel, okay?"

"You really want to?"

"Sure I do. Why, are you getting second thoughts about me driving?"

"No, not at all."

"I really do have a license. Here, I'll show you." He reached into his jeans for his wallet.

"You don't have to do that, Zig. I believe you."

He pulled his license out and held up so I could look. "See?"

It looked like a picture of some kid on it. "Let me see that." He let me take it, and I held it up so I could glance at it while I drove. "Jeez, Zig. How old are you in this, sixteen?"

"It wasn't *that* long ago. I was nineteen. Have I changed that much?"

I looked at it again. "No, I guess not. Maybe it's the hairstyle. Your hair was really long."

"Yeah, well, after a few years the same old look gets boring."

I looked at the license again to see when his birthday was. Then I noticed his name. "Ziggy is your real name?"

"Yeah, sure. Why? What did you think it was?"

"I don't know. I figured Ziggy was a nickname, like maybe for Sigmund or Siegfried or something."

"Nope. It's my real name. But you can call me Siegfried if you want to."

"Nah. I like Ziggy better."

I looked at his I.D. one more time. "June, 1964. I'm older than you, then. But not by much. I was born in October '63." I handed the license back to him. "You're still like an older brother to me, though. The way you look out for me, Zig. I've learned a lot from you."

"Gotta look out for my buddy. But I'm learning from you, too, Josh. It goes both ways."

We went on driving. "Did your mother name you after Ziggy Stardust?"

"No. I was born way before that."

"Oh, yeah, of course. Duh. The comic strip, then?"

"No, dude. That was later, too. I don't know how she came up with the name. She never told me."

"Okay. It doesn't matter, anyway. It's yours, and I like it."

"At least it's different."

"I was the only Josh in my grade at school, but I guess it's not an unusual name these days."

"Is it short for Joshua?"

"Yeah. That's my middle name, Joshua." Ziggy just looked at me, waiting for the rest of it. "Okay," I said, "well, I've got sort of a weird first name."

"Dude, it couldn't be much weirder than Ziggy. What is it?"

"Zacharias."

"I like that. Sounds like the old frontier days. Or, knowing your mother, maybe it was somebody from the bible?"

"It was her father's name. But they never called me that. Never called me Zack, either. Just Josh, which is fine with me."

"Josh it is, then. Hey, what were the chances of two guys with Z names hooking up with each other like we did?"

"Pretty slim, I would say. A coincidence, huh?"

"That's right, dude. We coincided."

"Against all odds."

"Makes you wonder if it was supposed to happen."

"Because of our names?"

"No, but think about it. What are the odds that two guys like us, strangers who live 300 miles apart, would end up in the same bar, on the same Friday night? And then actually hook up with each other? And get along with each other as awesome as we do? It's like long-lost brothers meeting by accident. You know, like, maybe it wasn't an accident."

"Yeah. I know. It makes reincarnation seem believable. If we were friends in the past, it makes sense that we'd meet again."

"Right, that's what I'm talking about."

"It was Saturday night, though, remember? We met on Saturday night."

"That's when we got to know each other, but we met the night before."

"What?"

"Yeah, Friday night." He smiled. "You were drunk, though. I guess you don't remember it."

"Jeez, you gotta be kidding. I wouldn't forget somebody hot like you! Drunk or not. Where was it, a different bar?"

"No, same one."

"No way. Let me think for a minute." I concentrated, trying to remember. Friday night?

"You were with your friends," Ziggy said.

"Remembering that night is like remembering a different life," I said. "Everything changed the next morning. Completely. Friday night I was still with Fred and Tony and the other guys. Fred was still my boyfriend. I met you that night?"

"Yeah. We talked. You don't remember?"

"I wasn't even there long, I remember that much."

"Long enough to have two drinks."

"You were watching us?"

"Wasn't just me. People noticed, when you guys came in. Your accents and your southern ways stood out."

"God, I guess I was out of it. I was already buzzed when we got there, I know that. I only remember talking to one guy. I felt really bad, too, because he wanted to get to know me better, but I wouldn't hang out with him."

"Is that right?" Ziggy smiled.

"Yeah."

"What do you remember about him?"

"Not as much as I'd like to. He was really hot, but he wasn't stuck up or anything. He was wearing a baseball cap. He had beautiful eyes, I remember that."

"What color were his eyes?"

"Um, I don't remember. But I remember the way he looked into mine; like he was looking into my soul. That sounds crazy, doesn't it?"

"Nah. Not crazy."

"The weirdest thing was, it seemed like I already knew him. Even though we'd never met. Strange, huh?"

"You never know. Maybe in another life."

"So, when did you and I talk?"

"You were standing at the bar, buying drinks, and I was sitting on the stool there right next to you. You don't remember?"

"Was that when we first got there?"

"No, it was later. You were buying your second drink."

"That was when that other guy talked to me. You were there, too?"

"Well, yeah." He grinned. "And I remember the guy you're talking about. I didn't think he was all that hot."

I really wanted to remember this. It was as difficult as trying to remember a dream after you wake up, but if it was still there, I had to pull it up.

Ziggy said, "Do you want a clue to help you remember?"

"Yes. Please."

"Okay. I was wearing a baseball cap."

"You were? I only remember one guy in a baseball cap."

"That's your clue, then."

I thought about that for a while. Then I figured it out. "Oh my god, that was you?"

He laughed. "Yeah, dude, that was me."

"I remembered you different."

"Well, I was dressed up for a Friday night. Really, I looked that different?"

"Yes! You had that baseball cap on, for one thing. That really changes the way people look. And you weren't wearing any glasses."

"Yeah, that's my preppy redneck jock look. I have the best luck at picking up foxy ladies with that look. But then I saw you."

"I'll tell you what I remember," I said. "This guy, he smiled at me and it felt like the sun came out on a cloudy day."

Ziggy grinned. "And then what?"

"I smiled back. And he said hi, and I said hi."

"Yeah, and then what?"

"Then I got really, uh, self-conscious. I couldn't think of anything to say."

"Yeah. At first I thought you were being snobby, but then I figured out what it was. You were just shy."

"That's the way I am. Especially when I meet somebody so perfect. Sometimes I feel outclassed, Zig. You were so awesome."

"But I thought you were awesome, too, Josh. Didn't you know that?"

"I remember being surprised how, um, straightforward you were. How friendly you were. At first I thought you had mistaken me for someone else. Then I wondered if we had met before, but I knew we hadn't. It was like we were friends at first sight. I've never had that happen before. Except in dreams."

"We connected, dude. I'm glad you remember it."

"I thought about you the whole rest of that night, Zig. I didn't even realize I was lonely until I met you. When I walked away from you I felt like I turned my back on the first ray of sunshine I'd seen in the last two years."

"I wish we could have talked more that night," he said, "but that's okay. Everything turned out all right. It doesn't get much better than this. Now we're buddies, closer to each other than most brothers are."

"I know. We couldn't have it any better."

We drove for a while, thinking about things.

Then I said, "We're really lucky, aren't we? Friday night could have been the end of it, if we didn't both go back on Saturday."

"Yeah," he said, "you would have gone back to Memphis the next day. So, why did you go back to the bar Saturday night?"

"Hell, I was lonely. I hoped I would run into *you* again, even though you said you only went there on Fridays. But I didn't see you inside. When did you get there?"

"Around 1 a.m. You were already there."

"You saw me? Why didn't you say hello?"

"I tried! I nodded to you at least four times, dude, and spoke to you, but you hardly noticed. You weren't interested. It was almost like you didn't know who I was."

"I didn't! I didn't know who you were. If I even saw you. That's so crazy. I was *looking* for you, Zig. I looked at every person in that place, looking for you."

"I guess sometimes I'm too good at keeping a low profile."

"And I'm too shy."

"It's okay. We hooked up, anyway."

"I should have talked to you more on Friday night," I said. "But it seemed so impossible."

"What, to talk to me?"

"No, not that. I could have done that. What I mean is, to get to know you."

"What do you mean?"

"Well, you asked me if I wanted to hang out for a while."

"Yes, I did. That's exactly what I said. You do remember."

"I didn't know if you wanted to have sex, or just to talk, or to go outside and smoke a joint, or what, but no matter what it was, I wanted to. I wanted all of those things. But I couldn't. I was committed. I had a boyfriend who would get pissed, and even if he didn't get pissed, I had a boyfriend. It couldn't have worked out, not the way I wanted it to. And anyway, until then, I didn't even know I was lonely. And on top of all that, I didn't live around here. It just seemed totally impossible."

"You said, 'I'd better get back to my friends. My boyfriend's probably wondering what happened to me.'"

"Yeah. What else could I say? But I felt so lonely after that. The whole rest of the night. I didn't know how lonely I was until you said hi. Then when I went back to my friends, it hit me like a ton of bricks. Jesus, I felt like I turned down a miracle."

"Yeah. I could tell you were pretty miserable, but I didn't know why."

"You could tell, huh?"

"I watched you with your friends. Hey, I'll bet I know which one Tony was. He was the only one of them who could make you smile."

"Yeah, Tony's the greatest."

"At first I thought *he* was your boyfriend."

"He probably would have been, if I hadn't met Fred first."

"And I know which one Fred was, too; that one's easy. The guy who treated you like shit. The one who hated that you were getting more looks than he was."

"He does treat me like shit. But I didn't know it was so obvious."

"Well, not everybody would notice. It's just that I pay attention to stuff like that."

"You were watching, huh?"

"Everybody was. I noticed you guys when you came in. You were obviously from out of town, visiting up here from somewhere down South. I, for one, thought your little group was interesting. Especially you. And the more I watched you the more intrigued I got."

"It's amazing how things work out sometimes."

"Really, Josh, you didn't recognize me Saturday night? Outside, when I walked up and you were talking with those two guys we bought weed from?"

"No. You looked familiar, but you looked a little like an actor I saw in a movie a couple months ago. I thought that explained it."

"Yeah, I know who you're talking about. I wear a cap sometimes just so nobody will tell me I look like him."

"You don't really look like him. It was just my mind, playing tricks."

"It's okay. He's good looking. I don't mind looking like him."

"You're better looking than him."

Ziggy laughed. "Alright, now. Stop. You can't bullshit a bullshitter."

"Alright, you win. You're butt-ugly. But I love you just the same, Zig."

"I love you, too, Josh."

We drove on in silence for a while.

Then I asked him, "If I'd hung out with you that Friday night, what would we have done?"

"Oh, well, I guess we'll never know, right? That's one of those alternative universes they talk about. Who knows?"

"No, really, Zig, what did you have in mind?"

"Before I knew you had a boyfriend?"

"Yeah."

"Um, well, you know. Hang out together. Talk. Maybe get buzzed. Get to know each other. Like we did Saturday night."

"Okay."

"I don't know exactly what it was, but to me, you seemed different from most of the guys I see there. You seemed complex, and deep. And nice, too. Kind. Sensitive. Hell, I don't know. You just seemed like a real sweetheart. And thoughtful. Intelligent. I figured we'd probably stay up all night talking about stuff. I knew you had a lot to say. It's been a long time since I had somebody to talk to."

"You wanted to talk, huh?"

"Sure."

"Did you know I was gay?"

"Not at first, but it didn't take long to figure it out. No big deal."

"That didn't bother you?"

"No, of course not. You know that."

"Okay."

"How about you? Did you think I was straight?"

"No. Not Friday, anyway."

"You thought I was gay?"

"No, I didn't think that, either. I couldn't tell. I wanted you to be gay, but I couldn't tell. I mean, you didn't act gay or anything, but I was hoping."

"I can relate to that."

"Have you ever heard of gaydar?"

213

"Um, that's when a gay guy can recognize another gay guy, right?"

"Right. And my gaydar is lousy."

"Well, you're not the only one. Guys always try to pick me up when I go there."

"Jeez, Zig, it's a gay bar, you gotta expect that."

"I know. I don't mind. It's flattering."

"Sure it is."

"You're the only guy there I ever spoke to first, though."

"For real?"

"Yeah."

I just stared at him.

"What?" he said. "What did I say?"

"You just made my day, that's all. My week. My year."

"Dude," he said, "I've been telling you all along, you're different. You're special. Of course I talked to you. I couldn't not talk to you."

"Zig," I said, "there's nobody like you. You make me feel so good. So worthy. You're the best. The absolute best."

"Naw. That's you, Josh."

—

THIS WAS GOING TO BE A LONG DRIVE, five hours, but it would be fun. I couldn't have asked for a better companion. There'd be plenty of time for us to talk, and no doubt some quiet time as well, when we could let our minds wander and daydream. Of course, whoever was riding shotgun could take a nap if he felt like it, but for the time being we were wide-awake and in the mood to talk.

I was curious. "Zig, how did you find out about that bar, anyway?"

"I was in one of the clubs in St. Louis, on a Saturday night, and when it was time for last call, this couple I'd been talking to asked me if I was going to Faces. 'Faces,' I said, 'what's that?' They told me it was an after-hours club across the river, and I ought to check it out, people from all over St. Louis went there to keep on partying late. I asked if they would let me ride over there with them. They said sure, no problem."

"Were you surprised by the place?"

"Well, yeah. It was bigger than I expected, and it was cool to see so many different kinds of people having a good time together."

"Was that the first gay bar you'd been to?"

"It's the *only* gay bar I've been to. And I didn't know it was gay until after I got there. There were guys dancing with guys, which I had never seen before. I asked the people who took me there, and they said yeah, it's a gay bar most of the time, but after hours it's anything goes. Which didn't bother me. I thought it was pretty cool."

"How long ago was that?"

"A couple of months ago. When I turned twenty-one. I liked the place, but I like it better on Friday nights. Saturdays are too crazy, and there's too many people from out of town. Fridays are better for meeting local people."

"So, were you going there, like, every Friday?"

"Nah. Only when I was horny, or lonely. I've been there, like, four times, max, before last weekend."

"Okay."

We rode on in silence for a few minutes.

"How about you," he said, "did you go out to bars much in Memphis?"

"Yeah, at least once a week. Saturdays, without fail. Fred loves to go out on Saturday night. It's part of his social life. It can be fun, I guess. You get to know the other regulars, and you always run into friends. Fred can be a lot of fun, when we're out and about like that. Besides, if I didn't go with him, he'd get so plastered he wouldn't remember a thing the next day."

"You kept him from drinking?"

"No, it wasn't like that. He could drink all he wanted, I didn't interfere or criticize. Hell, I drank, too. He just didn't like to get shit-faced when I was around, for some reason."

"How about before you met him, did you go out much?"

"Not to the bars. I wasn't old enough. Sometimes I hung out at the malls. And I went to the adult book stores; you only have to be eighteen to get into those. You can meet guys that way."

"You went there to meet guys, huh?"

"Well, sure. If I went somewhere, I'd be looking at guys, not girls."

"No, I mean, to meet guys, you went to the adult book store?"

"Yeah."

"I never would have expected that," he said. "Every time I've ever been in one of those places, nobody would even look me in the eye, let alone talk. I didn't really care, but sometimes I felt like I was the only one who wasn't embarrassed to be there."

"You're talking about out in the bright-lit part, where they sell the books and magazines and movies, right?"

"Yeah, and the dildoes and vibrators and blow-up dolls, all that stuff. And the condoms and lube."

"At first," I said, "I went there for the gay novels and magazines. But eventually I figured out sometimes you can meet guys there. Guys as horny as you are."

Ziggy laughed. "How old were you when you first figured out you were horny for guys?"

"Oh, man. Let me think about that for a minute."

"Or maybe you always were?"

"Well, I was always fascinated if I saw someone naked, even when I was three or four. Boys, girls, men, women, anybody. Probably because I never got to see anybody in my family naked. Nudity was not allowed, except when nobody else could see you. We learned from a very early age to hide our bodies, to not let anyone see us. Not 'that' part of our body, anyway."

"So sick. Your mother's doing, right?"

216

"I guess. Maybe my father was a prude, too, I don't know. Anyway, that just made me want to see people naked all the more."

"Of course. That's the best way to get a kid to do something, is to forbid it."

"Yep."

"She must have been pretty clueless."

"I think it was sixth grade."

"Sixth grade?"

"That's the first I remember being horny for guys. Listen to this: I used to pretend I was being initiated into a club by my two friends. They would hold me stark naked under a cold shower for five minutes. They were stripped down, too, in just their underwear. And they would get all wet and soaked while they held me under the water."

"That sounds pretty horny to me," Ziggy said.

"It was. Of course I struggled, but they grabbed me and wrestled me into staying right there under the cold water."

"Of course they did. It wouldn't have been fun, otherwise."

"It's funny, remembering all this. I'm glad you asked. I'd forgotten about it. I used to practice at home, in the bathroom shower upstairs. My dick would be hard the whole time. And I'd pretend to be so embarrassed. They would laugh at my hard cock and slap at it, to be mean."

"They slapped at your boner? Jesus, I'm surprised you didn't come. Oh, wait; you *did* come, didn't you! You sly rascal."

"Yeah, it always ended in embarrassment, and a really great orgasm. I practiced doing that for days on end. Weeks."

"So you were horny for guys that early, huh?"

"Yeah. Except I didn't exactly know it yet. That initiation scene, that was conveniently out of my control. I didn't have to admit I liked it, I was just practicing for torture."

"You didn't want to know it. But I can understand that."

"Zig, I didn't even know what gay was back then. Boys wrestle each other at that age, gay or straight. The thing I understood to be naughty was sex. Period. Playing with my dick, and the good feeling I got, that was the forbidden thing, not the wrestling with my buddies."

"Dude. That's so sick. Your mother, right?"

"Yeah, I guess. It wasn't anybody else."

"Forbidding ejaculation. Fuck, that's evil."

"No, it's just stupid. My mother was stupid her whole life. She died of stupidity."

"Your mother was, uh . . . wait, I think I'm confused."

"I don't mean that she was retarded. Retarded people aren't stupid. Retarded people are pretty smart, actually. Maybe she just didn't know how to think for herself. Or maybe she was misguided."

"She must have been, if she thought shooting your load was bad. That's an essential part of being a guy. And it also happens to make the world go round."

"It's not a completely bad thing, though."

"It's not a bad thing at all!"

"No, I mean, my mother being stupid is not a completely bad thing. It gives me an excuse for being the way I am."

"What are you talking about, Josh? There's nothing wrong with the way you are, bro."

"I'm talking about being naive. And innocent."

He laughed. "You are, dude. And I love you for that."

"Alright." I sighed. "I'm confusing myself now. I criticize my mother, but I guess in her twisted mind she really did have good intentions. Maybe."

"Sure she did. So did mine. We need to believe that, Josh, whether it's true or not."

I just looked at him.

He nodded his head. "We make it true. By believing."

He had the gears in my brain turning every which way, but what he said sounded right, somehow.

We drove on for a while without saying anything.

"Zig, what were you like in sixth grade? What kind of stuff was going on in your life?"

"Um, I might have had a little bit different environment at home from yours. But school was probably about the same. And I was having orgasms, too, like you. I don't know if any cum actually came out at first, but I was definitely having orgasms."

Then I remembered, he was getting fucked by another kid at the orphanage. Holy shit. That was way different from what I was doing. "What was school like for you, back then?" I said.

"It was okay. Sometimes kids picked on me, but I didn't care." He shrugged his shoulders. "Everybody gets picked on. That's just how school is."

"My two buddies and me, we were patrols in the sixth grade."

"Patrols? What are those?"

"You know, crossing guards."

"No way."

"Yeah, we were. For a while. Then we got tired of it. David quit first, and then Franklin and me. It gave us more time to hang out after school."

"Is that when they tortured you?"

"That's when we talked about having a club, but I never got tortured. That was just me fantasizing."

"Okay. But you guys really did hang out?"

"Sure. But we weren't gay or straight; we were too young to even know much about sex. I didn't, at least. My parents never told me anything about sex. My dad had a teenager sex-ed book, but I had to steal it from his dresser drawer to read it."

"But you were horny for your buddies."

"Yeah, I guess I was. But I didn't think of it in those terms."

"Okay."

We drove on.

He said, "When was the first time you *really knew* you were horny for guys?"

"That would be ninth grade. Somehow I got picked to be basketball manager, which I really liked. It was the next best thing to being on the team. I went to all the games, even the away games. I was right there on the sidelines. And I got to pick up in the locker room, before and after the game."

"So you got to see all the guys naked, under the showers, changing clothes, horsing around, right?"

"You got it. Every one of them. Every day. And there were at least half a dozen of them I would have done anything with. Anything they wanted."

"And you knew it."

"Hell yes, I knew it. That wasn't the reason I signed on as a manager, but yeah, that's what came out of it. I wanted so bad for one of those guys to walk me home and talk me into doing something really perverted. Anything, as long as it involved him and me both getting naked, and both of us getting our rocks off."

"Damn, Josh. I can picture it. You have a way with words, dude. You've got me with a fucking hard on, talking the way you do."

"I was horny."

"Except the way I imagine it, I'm one of the guys who walked you home."

"Really?"

"Yeah. Hell yeah. I was horny in ninth grade, too, really horny. I was willing to fuck just about anything that presented itself. If you had let me walk you home, we would have gone at it, I guarantee."

"Really?"

"Hell yes! Me, the big basketball star, letting the lowly manager walk home with me? The first time you looked at me that way, I would have found a way for you to show me your gratitude." He grinned.

"Damn, Zig. We really should have known each other back then. That would have been so awesome."

"We could pretend," he said.

"What do you mean?"

"We could pretend that we're in ninth grade together, some-time. Do what we would have done then. If you want to. Just for fun."

I looked at him. "Zig," I finally said, "That would be so great."

He said, "You want to?"

"Yeah, hell yeah. You're the best, Zig, the absolute best."

"It'll be fun," he said.

Chapter 17
CAPE

IT TOOK US A COUPLE HOURS to reach Cape Girardeau. We were definitely ready to stop and stretch. Cape is a river port, one of the few between St. Louis and Memphis. It was bound to have some history to it. Who knows, maybe Mark Twain stopped there.

We parked the car downtown, bought some carry-out, and walked to Riverfront Park, which is on the other side of the flood wall. It was cool being so close to the mighty river. We sat there and ate our lunch, watching the river go by.

"Reminds me of when I was in fourth grade," Ziggy said. "I used to go down to the river and sit there and watch."

"You started the contemplative life at a young age."

"I did contemplate. It was my favorite place to go when I wanted to think about stuff, or to be alone. For years I went there."

"I can picture you," I said, "like Siddhartha, contemplating life and the universe."

"It was a little like that. I did get a sense of how the universe works, from a human perspective. Or at least from one kid's perspective."

"Had you started your, uh, teachings with your buddy at the orphanage yet?"

"George didn't come to the orphanage till I was in fifth grade. But we hit it off almost as soon as he got there. I spent just about all of my free time with him or down at the river by myself. I learned a lot, both ways."

"I'm trying to imagine it: Buddha having sex every day."

"Well, you'd be surprised. They're not mutually exclusive. Yes, the stuff I was doing with George was a very different kind of experience from the contemplation and meditation I did down by the river. Yet there were some elements that overlapped, some experiences supported by both. Not just sensations, but states of mind. And in any case, they didn't get in the way of each other. Not at all."

"Well, from what I remember, Buddha believed life for most people leads to suffering, due to greed or craving of worldly pleasures. Something like that, anyway."

"Attachment to worldly pleasures can definitely lead to suffering, I'll agree to that. And George and I had plenty of pleasure together, that's for sure. But every time we did anything, we thought of it as a gift. We reminded each other of that, each time. The very first time, he made it clear that pleasure is one of the greatest gifts we can give someone, next to love."

"Um, yeah, okay, I'll go along with that."

"And he said we should never take it for granted. We should always consider the possibility that this time might be the last time. We should always experience each moment of pleasure as if it might be the last. Then we'd remember, every time, how precious a gift we were giving each other."

"Wow."

"It went along perfectly with what I worked out down by the river on my own. Craving things, wanting things, that leads to suffering. Better to treat each thing you receive as a gift. That way you're happy with what you have. You can even be happy if you lose what you have, because after all, it was a gift to begin with, a gift that came with no guarantee that you could keep it forever."

"I like that. So, pleasure is okay, if you don't crave it ahead of time, and if you appreciate it as a gift when you're fortunate enough to get it."

"Sure. As long as nobody's getting hurt by it, of course. And George never, ever hurt me. He was very careful of that. And of course I never hurt him, either."

"That's amazing."

"Not really. George was a very loving person, and he really looked out for me."

"No, I mean, the concept of not wanting, not craving, together with the appreciation of pleasure."

"Oh, right. Yeah, it *is* amazing. It can almost be godly, when you put them together."

We sat there for several more minutes in silence, watching the river flow.

—

EVENTUALLY we had to get back on the road, or we'd never get to Memphis. So we filled up the tank with gas, stocked up on drinks and snacks, and found our way back to the highway.

"Zig," I asked, once we got going, "your friend at the orphanage, is there any chance he might have been gay?"

"No, he wasn't gay. He was more like me," Ziggy said. "You know, bisexual. He liked girls as much as I do. I was the only guy he ever fucked around with. Until later, in the army, but that's different. Military guys sometimes help each other out when they get horny. It doesn't mean they're gay."

"How long did you and him do it?"

"Oh, I don't know, maybe three years? That sounds about right. Three years, on a daily basis. Then he discovered girls and things changed."

"He lost interest in you?"

"No, George was like my big brother. He never lost interest in me. But we didn't fuck as much after that. After he got to high school he started using his expertise more on girls. We still stayed close, though, all the way up until the end."

"Did it hurt your feelings when he switched to girls?"

"Well, yeah, at first. Because I didn't know what happened. We used to hang out together all the time. Even when we started going to different schools, we still met every day afterward. Then all of a sudden he stopped showing up at our usual spot. All week long, I went every day, hoping he'd be there, but he wasn't.

"For a while I wondered if I'd done something wrong. Then I decided, maybe it's not me. Maybe in high school you make new friends, and it's tough-titty for the friends you had before. It didn't make me feel any better, but I thought, you know, life goes on."

"I think that would have broken my heart."

"Oh, it worked out okay. Just when I thought he'd given up on me, he came back looking for me. He was excited about girls and all, but he said he really missed me."

"So you guys started fucking each other again?"

"I didn't fuck him, Josh. Except for one time, years later. It was always George fucking me."

"Um, okay. So, did he start fucking you again?"

"Yeah, once in a while, for old time's sake, which I think he liked as much as I did. But it was way less than before. Like, once a week, instead of every day. Mainly, what happened was, he introduced me to girls."

"Oh. Okay."

"I never should have doubted him. He really did care about me. He was in tenth grade and I was only in eighth grade. I was in middle school, he was in high school. Also, by that time he wasn't living at the orphanage anymore; he was with foster parents. And he had lots of new friends. It would have been so easy, Josh, for him to leave me out of the picture completely, but after that one week apart, he took me along with him everywhere he went."

"Wow. He really did like you."

"Dude, I'm telling you, I was on top of the world. He and his friends treated me like their favorite mascot or something. The girls flirted with me and everything. It really worked out okay. That was a great time, a really great time for me."

"Wow. You were lucky. But hell, you deserved it."

"Maybe. But I knew I was lucky, believe me."

"Did you, uh, do anything with any of the girls?"

"Hell, yes! Before it was all over, I fucked every one of those girls. And more than once, too. They must have liked what I was doing because they came back for more. And it wasn't because I have a big cock, either; I'm pretty average in that department.

"Can you imagine a short little eighth grade squirt, not even full height yet, fucking full-grown high school girls? George taught me everything he knew about fucking, and then the girls filled in the missing details. Each and every one of them told me, right out, how to make them feel good, how to use my tongue, stuff like that, and I did everything they asked. I did whatever they told me to do. With pleasure."

"Jeez, Zig, you're giving me a hard-on. Um, how about the guys, did you ever do anything with them?"

"Nah. Just jacking off together. We did that if we got horny and there weren't any girls around. Which was pretty often."

"Really? You and your friends jacked off together?"

"Sure. Didn't you?"

"Not too often. Hardly ever."

"You're kidding."

"No, I'm not kidding."

"Why?"

"I don't know. Maybe I thought it was naughty."

"Jesus, Josh. All the more reason to do it."

"Yeah, I know. I wanted to, believe me. I don't know why we didn't. Maybe we were just afraid."

"I'll bet every one of you was waiting for somebody else to start it, and then nobody did."

"Yeah, I think you're right. We were all chickenshit. Or at least I was."

"No, you weren't chickenshit, just cautious. Let me guess: all of your friends were quiet, cautious types. Like you."

"Yeah, I guess they were."

"See? It was different with me. All of George's friends were rowdy punks. And if none of them started the ball rolling, then I

226

did. I took it for granted every one of those guys loved sex; hell, what teenager doesn't? Every one of us probably jacked off three times a day or more, and we all knew it, so there wasn't any reason to be ashamed of it. Doing it alone is okay, but not a requirement. It's sexier sometimes to do it in front of each other. Why not?"

"Wow. My god, the stuff I missed out on. So, how did you start the ball rolling?"

"Oh, I don't know, no special way. It didn't take much. The first time it happened, I didn't know any better. They were talking about sex and cocks and cunts and fucking and we all had huge boners. Back at the orphanage, when everyone was hard, we did something about it. So, me, the little mascot dude, I said something innocent like, 'Damn, I'm horny, I sure would like to jack off.' The other guys laughed, but I knew they wanted to, too. One of them said, 'Well, what are you waiting for?' I said, 'Not your sorry asses, that's for sure,' and I pulled out my cock right there and started stroking."

"Damn."

"Everybody stared at me, watching me jack my cock. Pretty soon they were all, like, fidgeting and squeezing their cocks through their pants and basically horny as hell. One of the other guys finally said, 'Hell, why not?' He pulled his cock out, too. In another five minutes every one of us was stripped down naked, with nothing on but our socks, jacking off."

"Damn! I wish I could have been there."

"It was horny, for sure. We did it a lot after that. Those guys talked all the time about fucking girls left and right, but I don't think any of them really got any pussy more than, say, once a week at the most. Me neither. When everybody lives at home with his or her parents, or like George and me, in a home with an adult watching you most of the time, you just don't get that many chances to sneak away somewhere and fuck. Not with a girl. Maybe if you're fucking your brother or your best buddy, sure. But

227

if you bring a girl over, grownups watch you like a hawk. Where can you go? So you end up horny most of the time. It's only natural to jack off a lot. And doing it by yourself is fine, but sometimes it gets boring."

"I think I missed out on a lot when I was a kid," I said.

"Yeah you did. Blame your perverted parents for that. But, hell, there's no use crying over spilt milk, as the saying goes."

"I guess not."

"Sure. The best thing to do is realize where you went wrong, do what you can to fix it, and go on from there." He shrugged his shoulders. "Look at it this way. At least you've got a friend now you can jack off with."

I laughed. "Yeah. I do. I guess I'm lucky after all."

—

WE DROVE ON. I was starting to get tired of it, and then I remembered. "Zig, do you feel like driving for a while?"

"I thought you'd never ask, dude. Sure, I'll drive."

"Thanks for tuning the car up, by the way. It's really running smooth."

"No problem."

We took the next exit and pulled into a gas station. When we took off again, Ziggy was at the wheel. He said, "Anything to see in New Madrid, while we're here?"

"Well," I said, "this is where there was a big earthquake, back in 1811, but besides that, there's probably not much going on here."

"Yeah, the great New Madrid Earthquakes."

"You've heard of it?"

"Fuck," he said, "who hasn't?"

"I hadn't. Not before I moved to Memphis. So, then, I guess you know about the river flowing backward?"

"Dude. Think about it. The Mississippi River flowed backwards?"

"That's what they say."

"That has to be a crock of shit. What the hell could make it do that?"

"Yeah. I know what you mean. I wondered the same thing. But it really did happen."

"You sound pretty sure about that, bro."

"I did some research at the library, Zig. I found an explanation for it."

"For real? Don't tell me, okay? I want to see if I can figure it out."

"Okay." This would be fun.

Ziggy thought about it for a couple of minutes. Then he said, "Okay, let me take a guess."

"Alright." I was smiling.

"Backwash. If a fault line rose up across the river, there'd be backwash. And since the ground is so flat, it could wash back for miles."

Now I was grinning. "I'm impressed, Zig. Somebody had to explain it to me before it made any sense."

"Well, it was easy, once I pictured it in my head."

"Yeah, well, it was easy because you're smart."

"Oh, hell. I guess I do have at least two or three brain cells up there that work." He smiled. "Only on a random basis, you understand."

I laughed. "Okay, but you can't fool me. You'd be right at home in any college, if you ever decide to give it a try."

"Well, if I ever get tired of fixing cars, maybe I will."

"You could."

"Only if you go with me, though."

"Okay, deal," I said. "I'll go back to school if you do."

"For real?"

"Cross my heart."

"Cool," he said. "I might just take you up on that someday."

"That would be an adventure, wouldn't it?"

"Definitely."

—

ZIGGY DROVE US ONWARD, with both of us in deep thought for a while. Eventually, though, I started feeling sleepy. I was thinking about taking a nap when he said, "Is Memphis close to the river?"

"It's right next to it," I said. "But it's above it, on a bluff, so they don't need a seawall or anything."

"No flooding?"

"Not on the Memphis side, but Arkansas floods sometimes. They have levees to keep it from flooding inland."

"Is the river wide there?"

"Yeah. Half a mile, at least."

"That's pretty wide."

"And the current is strong, too. Stronger than it looks. But there's a backwater channel at the Memphis waterfront. Boats tie up there. There's an old paddlewheel boat you can take a ride on, and the Delta Queen stops there on a regular basis."

"Have you ever gone out on the river?"

"No. I wanted to, but I never got around to it. One year they had a gay river cruise, but Fred didn't want to go."

"Why not? That sounds like it would have been fun."

"He said it would probably just be a bunch of nelly queens. He's kind of a homophobe."

"What?"

"Yeah. He still thinks there's something wrong with being gay."

"But that doesn't make sense. Isn't *he* gay?"

"Oh, sure. And he'll admit it, at least to other gay men, but he makes fun of the ones who are more effeminate than he is. He gets really uncomfortable around, you know, swishy guys."

"Really!"

"He does. He gets all nervous. I think it makes him doubt his own manhood or something. To him it's only okay to be gay if you're masculine. But actually, he doesn't think it's okay even then. I know, it doesn't make sense. But that's Fred."

"That's crazy," Ziggy said. "That's just the opposite of me. I don't mind effeminate guys at all. I admire them, actually."

"You do?"

"Sure. It takes a lot of balls to be that way out in public. And I don't mind being around them, either; it's no big deal. They have a lot of fun with each other, from what I've seen. At the bar they do, anyway."

"Yeah."

"Hell, Josh, I admire *anybody* gay who has the nerve to be honest about it. That takes guts."

"It's not easy. The first time you tell somebody is the hardest."

"You know what else I like about gay guys, Josh?"

"What?"

"Your attitude about sex."

I looked at him. "Uh, what do you mean, Zig? What attitude?"

"There's something really hot about it. The way you just do it, and the hell with what other people think. Guys fucking each other, sucking each other's cocks, stuff like that. "

I must have been looking at him like he was crazy.

"Don't look at me like that," he said, blushing. "I just think it's sexy. Oh, hell, I don't know how to explain it."

"Alright," I said. "I guess I can relate to that. I think it's sexy, too."

"You know, this probably sounds strange," he said, "but sometimes I've fantasized about it. You won't believe this, but I think maybe I have this secret desire to be queer just for one guy. Isn't that crazy?"

"Uh, jeez, Zig, I don't know. Maybe, maybe not." Good thing I wasn't driving, or we might have wrecked.

"I don't mean in an effeminate way. We'd both be masculine. If I was gonna be queer for a guy, it would be somebody who was masculine, like me. Or like George. Or like you, Josh."

Jesus, was he kidding? "Umm, well, hell, I'm the same way. About liking masculine guys."

"Yeah."

We drove on, silent for a few minutes. I couldn't believe he said that.

"But girly men are okay," he said. "It's weird, that Fred could look down on somebody else for being gay."

"Well," I said, "it's not as weird as it seems. When you grow up thinking everybody considers you inferior, it's easy to internalize that. So if you don't counteract that somehow, or at least recognize it, you end up believing it yourself. The same thing can happen to black people. And women. And individuals, too, like for instance kids who are slow in school."

"Okay. I think I get it. If enough people tell you you're worthless, you begin to believe you're worthless."

"Exactly."

"Jesus. That's awful," he said.

That led to more silence and thought as we drove on.

After a while, he said, "Josh?"

"Yeah?"

"You don't feel that way about yourself, do you?"

"I used to." I held up my thumb and finger. "I came *this close* to killing myself once, in high school, when I thought my big secret was finally out. I thought life wouldn't be worth living if people found out I was gay."

Ziggy looked at me with tears in his eyes. "Oh, Josh."

"I'm glad I didn't."

"Me, too," he said. He wiped his eyes with his shirt. "I'm so glad you didn't."

"Then I knew I had some work to do. I had to get used to the idea that I'm gay. So did other people. And I lost some friends, but not as many as I expected. And I made some new friends. And after that I knew my friends liked me for who I am."

"The friends you lost weren't worth having," Ziggy said.

"Yeah. I figured that out, later."

"Damn right."

"One day I finally came to an astounding realization. It changed everything. I finally realized I was the same animal as everyone else. I mean, it sounds so simple, but before that, I was thinking I was some kind of inferior species or something. But ever since I realized I'm like everybody else, I've felt good about it. I mean, so what if I'm gay? It's part of who I am. I'm still the same animal as everyone else. No matter what color or gender or preference, we're all the same animal."

"There you go," Ziggy said.

"Maybe one of these days Fred will realize that."

"Maybe," Ziggy said.

"In any case, it's his problem now, not mine. It's gonna be such a relief to have him out of my life."

We drove on in silence for a while.

"I sure hope he's not there this weekend," I said.

Chapter 18
WHAT HAPPENED

"WHAT WAS IT that happened last week," Ziggy said, "that got him so pissed off? You never told me."

"Uh, do you really want to know?"

"Well, I might be meeting the dude. It might be good to know what's going on between you two. But hell, it's really none of my business. I already know he's an asshole; maybe that's all I need to know."

"No, I don't mind telling you. We were spending the night at the house of a couple of guys he knows, a gay couple in St. Louis. No, wait; let me tell you about the baths first. It'll give you a better perspective on this."

"Okay. Yeah, I was gonna ask you about those, too."

"Basically, the baths are a place to hook up for sex."

"Okay, I kind of thought that's what it was."

"Guys walk around with nothing on but a towel, and when they meet someone they want to have sex with, the towels come off. Sometimes in a private room, sometimes not."

"Do any women go there?"

"No, it's guys only. No women allowed."

"Okay."

"I don't think it would work with women. Guys are such horndogs, but it's a whole different thing with women, I think."

"That does kind of make sense."

"So, you can rent a tiny little room with a little bed, or you can just get a locker and put your clothes in there. Either way, most people walk around with just the towel on. If you meet a guy you want to have sex with, you can go to your room or his. Or if neither one of you has a room, they have dark places where you can go."

"Dark places?"

"Well, not completely dark. You can still see what you're doing. And so can everybody else. Like, they have one room called the orgy room. That's one of Fred's favorite places, but I stay out of there most of the time."

"Okay."

"And they have showers there, open showers, which are kind of cool. You can watch other guys take a shower, and they can watch you. I like that part."

"I can relate to that," he said.

"And most baths have a steam room, or a sauna, or both. And maybe a hot tub."

"Okay, that figures."

"As far as sex goes, you can be as picky as you want, like me, or you can be as slutty as you want, like Fred. Or anywhere in between. Fred goes wild there. He sucks dicks all night long, and he usually gets fucked at least two or three times, and every one of the guys is a complete stranger. Fred's not the slightest bit interested in meeting any of those guys ever again. He doesn't even want to know their names."

"Jesus. Isn't he worried about disease?"

"He claims he always uses condoms, but Tony told me he's seen Fred get fucked without one. More than once. I think he's convinced it can't happen to him. Or else he thinks it's still the seventies, when people thought you could get rid of anything with penicillin. Or Rid."

"Wishful thinking."

"Yeah, you know it."

"Still, nobody's getting hurt by the sex," Ziggy said. "If it wasn't for AIDS and stuff like that, I'd say there's no harm in it."

"Right. Each to his own. That's why I don't criticize Fred for being that way. There's nothing inherently wrong with sex. Sex is a good thing."

"You've got that right."

"Anyway, now you know what the baths are like. That's where we went Friday night, after we left the bar. Friday afternoon we cooked out, at Dennis and Craig's house, then we went bar hopping to see what all the gay clubs were like, and then we headed over to the baths. We spent a few hours at the baths, and then, after the guys were all fucked out, we went back over to Dennis and Craig's house and crashed there."

"Okay. So far, so good. Did you and Fred sleep together?"

"Oh, sure. We didn't do anything, but we slept together. I was so horny my balls ached, and Fred had come so many times his dick was worn out. Not to mention his ass. But that's the way it usually works when we go out of town. I'm used to it. I could have worn myself out, too, if I'd wanted to."

"But you didn't want to."

"Well, I didn't find anybody I wanted to do anything with. Except for maybe one or two guys who weren't interested in me."

"Nothing wrong with being selective."

"So, anyway, Saturday morning we slept in. I was one of the last ones to wake up. Everybody else was downstairs, Fred included, getting set for breakfast. Everybody but Dennis, one of the two guys who lived there. He had just woken up, too, I guess.

"He came out of the bathroom and walked by my bedroom and the door was wide open. So he came in. All he had on was a t-shirt, nothing else. It was his house; he could walk around naked if he wanted to. He came over to where I was still in bed and he said, 'I think they're getting breakfast ready.'

"I said something like, 'Is everybody down there?' He said, 'Yeah, everybody but you and me.' And he just stood there, and I was looking at his cock, and it started getting hard. Pretty soon it was big and stiff and horizontal, sticking straight out, and it was at least eight inches long, longer than mine, with a nice knobby head on it. About six inches from my mouth. The next thing I knew, it was in my mouth, and I was sucking on it."

Ziggy just looked at me.

"Am I freaking you out?"

"No, dude, go ahead. Sex is a good thing. Don't worry, I'm following you."

"Okay, so, about ten seconds later, Fred walked in on us. He saw me sucking on Dennis's cock, said, 'I don't believe it,' and turned around and stomped right back out. Then Dennis pulled his cock out of my mouth and he walked out of the room, too. I'm thinking, Jeez, what the fuck was that all about?

"Ten minutes later, I'm washed up and sitting at the dining room table, waiting on my pancakes, and nobody's talking. Nobody's saying anything about anything. Fred is obviously very pissed, and everyone knows it. Then Dennis comes out of the kitchen and puts some pancakes on my plate, and some on Fred's plate, and he says, 'Chill out, guys, nothing happened.'

"I said, 'At least, nothing that didn't happen to Fred a couple dozen times last night.' But Fred says, 'It's not the same.' What the hell is that supposed to mean? Fred must have sucked off at least a dozen guys that night, and got his own dick sucked on by another dozen or two. No doubt he had three or four guys fuck him, too, he usually does. And he does it out in front of anybody who wants to watch, so it's not like nobody's supposed to know.

"On the other hand, I didn't have sex with anybody the whole night. Not one single person. That's what usually happens with me. I don't really mind Fred having sex with all those guys if it makes him happy. But that's crazy, him getting pissed off about me sucking Dennis. I don't get it."

Ziggy looked like he was trying to sort it all out in his head.

"Anyway, that's what Fred got pissed off about."

"Did you guys have some kind of agreement? Like, I've heard of open relationships. Did you guys have an open relationship?"

"Well, we had an agreement. We weren't allowed to have sex with anyone else when we were in Memphis, but if we went out of town, we could have sex with anybody we wanted."

Ziggy laughed.

"I know, it sounds funny. But that's what we agreed to. It was Fred's idea."

"So if you were both out of town, together, both of you could have sex with anybody you wanted?"

"Yes. That's why they go to the baths, to have sex with anybody they want. It's okay with me, except when I go to the baths, I'm always looking for that one guy, that one special guy I can connect with. That's why most of the time I end up not having sex with anybody."

"But you could if you wanted to. Have sex with anybody you wanted. Fred wouldn't have objected to that?"

"Not at the baths. As far as I know, anyway. Who knows? I don't like having sex in public, so Fred's never seen me have sex with anybody else. Not until he saw me with Dennis."

"It sounds like Fred wanted to be the only one who was allowed to have sex with other people."

"Yeah, it's got to be something weird like that."

"That's not weird. It's not fair, but it's not weird. That's human nature. People find it easy to make different rules for other people than the rules they set for themselves."

"That's so evil," I said. "Well, maybe not evil, but it's, um, weak. Putting different standards on others. If you're gonna expect other people to be strong, you should be willing to be strong yourself."

"*You* know that," he said, "and I know that, but still, it's hard to do. A lot of people don't even try. A lot of people don't even see a reason to try."

Neither one of us said anything for a while.

Then Ziggy said, "Well, he should be happy about one thing. Now he can have sex with anybody he wants, even when he's at home in Memphis."

"And he will, you can believe that," I said. "Although I think he already was, to tell you the truth."

"I wasn't gonna say it, but yeah, I think so, too."

"I wanted to believe the best of him. I'm so naive."

"You are, Josh. And like I said before, I love you for it. You just need to find the right person to put your belief in, that's all."

"Zig, I have. I already have."

He looked at me, and I looked at him, and we smiled.

—

AN HOUR LATER we reached the Missouri border, and the "Welcome to Arkansas" sign. I felt like turning around and staying in Missouri.

Ziggy said, "We're almost there, right?" He took the turnoff into the Welcoming Center. "How much longer, an hour?"

"More like an hour and a half," I said. "But you're right. It's not far, now."

"I'll bet you're getting excited, huh?"

"No. Nervous maybe, but not excited."

"You lived in Memphis for what, two years? You don't feel any of that 'coming home' feeling?"

"No. If I feel anything, it's more like a 'returning to hell' feeling."

"That bad, huh?" He pulled around into a parking space and turned off the engine.

"It's not Memphis, it's Fred. Memphis is okay. There's lots of good people there, but Fred isn't one of them."

"He really did a number on you, didn't he?"

"I don't want to be around him. I don't want to ever see him again. All the times he's gotten pissed off at me when I didn't deserve it—fuck, I can't believe I stayed with him so long."

"You were hoping for the best. And giving him the benefit of the doubt. Probably more than he ever gave you."

"He never gave me anything. Nothing that he didn't turn around and take back. Once in a while he eased up and did something nice, but he always found a way to ruin it, later."

"Like he didn't want you to be happy."

"And I put up with it, too. I let him do it to me. Jeez, I must have thought it was my lot in life. Like I deserved it."

"Dude. You know better than that now, don't you?"

"Yeah, I do."

"You have to believe in yourself, Josh. Always. Believe in your worth, even when it seems like no one else does. Even when you're all alone. You have to. It's really important."

"Alright."

"Give yourself a pat on the back once in a while for a job well done. Jesus, Josh. You're a beautiful person. And you've got a heart of gold. You didn't get that way by some stroke of luck, dude; you got that way because of your ideals. Because of who you want to be, who you try to be, what you believe in. Those are the things that make you who you are."

"Okay."

"Let's get out and stretch, bro."

—

WE WENT TO THE RESTROOM and took a leak, and then we putzed around for a few minutes, looking at the Arkansas brochures.

"Look at this one," Ziggy said. "Crowley's Ridge State Park."

"Yeah. Looks peaceful."

"A little out of our way, but not by much. We could go through there on the way back to St. Louis. The brochure says there's a road that follows the ridge most of the way."

"Sure, I'd be up for that."

"Something to keep in mind, at least."

"Okay," I said.

"Dude, you're still nervous."

"Yeah, I am. Fuck, I can't help it. What if Fred decided to stay home? What if he's home when we go there to get my stuff? I don't want to see him again, Zig. He makes me feel so worthless. I don't ever want to feel that way again. God, it's like he's got some kind of power over me."

"Come on," Ziggy said. "Let's take a walk."

He led the way. We followed the walkway away from the restrooms. We went past some trees and a picnic table. When we got to the end of the path, we crossed the drive and went on walking, away from all the other people.

"We're gonna get you relaxed, Josh. One way or another." He reached into his pocket, grinned, and pulled out a thin little joint. "Wanna catch a buzz?"

"Jesus, Zig, I didn't know you brought any." I looked behind us and all around us. "I guess we're alright. Unless someone's got binoculars."

"We'll be okay," he said. "Better to smoke here than in the car. The smell really lingers inside a car."

"Okay, sure. Let's get high." We sat down cross-legged on the grass, facing each other. "Are you still gonna be able to drive?"

"Yeah, I'll be okay. I'll be extra careful. We're not gonna get blitzed anyway, this is only a tiny pin joint." He flicked his lighter and put the flame to it.

We passed it back and forth until there was nothing left of it. It didn't take me long to start feeling it.

"Great idea," I said. "I'm feeling better already."

"Sometimes a little herb is all it takes to give you a better perspective on things."

"You know what? Fuck Fred. If he's there, he's there. He's not gonna do anything anyway. He's too chickenshit."

"There you go. That's the spirit. And I'm gonna be right there with you, Josh. The bastard better not try anything, or he'll have me to deal with."

I sighed. "I appreciate you doing this. You're the best thing that ever happened to me, Zig."

"No problem."

"I wish I'd met you to begin with, instead of Fred."

"Oh, well, everything happens for a reason. That's what I think."

"Yeah, I guess so. I sure wouldn't want to change anything, if it meant I didn't end up meeting you."

"Right. Sometimes the littlest thing can change the direction your life goes."

"Still, I wonder how things might have been different if we'd known each other sooner."

"That would have been cool, for sure."

"Or if I'd known somebody like your friend George."

"Or," Ziggy said, "how about if all three of us knew each other back then? That would have been a real trip. Twice the fun."

"Oh, jeez! No telling what kind of wild stuff the three of us would have done together."

"For sure."

"Zig," I said, "where is George now? Will I ever get to meet him?"

Ziggy just looked at me.

"Zig?"

Chapter 19
RELEASE

"GEORGE DIED, Josh." He looked down at the grass. "Almost two years ago."

He looked up at me briefly, and then he looked away, over at the cars on the interstate.

"My god, Zig. What happened?"

Ziggy turned back to me, with a look on his face I'd never seen on him before. Sadness, but behind it something worse. Despair.

"He died in the Grenada Invasion. He was an Army Ranger."

"Oh, Zig."

He looked down at the ground again. "We were gonna live together when he got out."

"My god." I leaned forward and put my hand on his shoulder. "Zig, I am so sorry."

"It's not your fault." His eyes were shiny, starting to fill with tears, and he picked at the grass.

"Zig, that's the saddest thing I've ever heard."

"I know," he said. He raised his head and looked at me. Tears were running down his face. "Josh, sometimes . . ." He could hardly get the words out. "Sometimes it hurts so much, I can hardly stand it."

I took hold of him and pulled him toward me. "Zig. Oh, Zig."

When I held him against me, he grabbed me and held me so tight it almost took the breath out of me. We hugged each other close, and he began wailing, just completely let loose crying.

We held each other like that for five minutes at least. He went on crying, hard. He finally eased up a bit and tried to say something, but he couldn't get it out. Then he cried some more, still holding on to me.

Eventually he seemed cried out. He sniffled a little more, and slowly let loose of me. "Sorry," he said.

"Zig, you can cry on my shoulder anytime."

"I know." He pulled his shirt up to wipe the tears away. "Thanks, Josh." He finished wiping his face. "I really needed that."

"Anytime, pal."

He sniffled some more, trying to clear his nose. "I wondered if that was ever gonna happen. It'll be two years next month, and I still hadn't cried. I couldn't. I don't know why, but I couldn't."

"Sometimes a thing hurts so much, you can't cry. It sounds weird, but it's true."

"I guess so," he said.

"You must still miss him so much."

"I will *always* miss him. *Always.*"

"You were gonna live together?"

"Yeah. See, when he turned eighteen, he didn't have anywhere to go. He had this bright idea to join the Army and be a Ranger. He liked the idea of 'Special Operations,' they called it. He passed the tests and they signed him up. I got letters from him all the time. He was really gung-ho. But he wasn't gonna make a career of it or anything."

"You were still in school?"

"Yeah. I still had two years to go. I got a part-time job at the dealership, and then after graduation I took classes at the tech school. I got my first apartment. He visited me there when he was on leave. He liked the place. He asked me if he could live with me when he got out of the Army. I said, 'Hell yes! Of course!'"

"Damn."

Ziggy sighed. "After he was killed, I got depressed every time I walked into that apartment. I had to move out. Hell, I wanted to be happy when I remembered him, not sad. So, I found the place I have now."

"I can understand that."

"So, anyway, that's what happened to George."

"It's really tough to lose someone like that," I said. "But, Zig, at least you had those years together. That's something to be thankful for."

"Yeah. Six years, we were like *this*." He held up two fingers together. "Actually, nine years, counting while he was in the Army. I wish you could have met him. You would have liked him. He would have liked you, too."

"Nine years. Lots of people don't get nearly that many."

"Yeah, I guess you're right." He sighed, looking down again.

"I hope you and I get nine years together," I said.

Ziggy jerked his head up and looked at me. "Roger that! Fuck nine; let's shoot for ninety, Josh. Might as well aim high, bro."

"Yeah, ninety sounds good, Zig. At least for starters."

Ziggy held up his palm, and I slapped it with mine.

—

BY MUTUAL AGREEMENT, Ziggy took the driver's seat when we got on the road again. He could probably drive perfectly well when he was stoned, but I wasn't sure if I could. Things get so distracting.

Not that we were zonked. I was perfectly able to count all the toes on one hand, for example, but sometimes caution is prudent.

"I had one more remedy in mind for your nervousness, in case the weed didn't work," he said.

"Oh, is that right? And what would that have been?"

"Sex."

I laughed. "Damn. I should have pretended I was still nervous."

"I always feel more relaxed after sex," he said.

"Me, too."

"Sex is good."

"Sex is fucking great," I said.

"Jesus, don't make me get a boner while I'm driving. Let's talk about something else."

"Have you ever jacked off while you were driving?"

"Jesus H. Christ, no. I'd probably have a wreck."

"People do it. At least, I know some people who claim to have done it."

"I don't even want to try it," he said.

"I know this one guy in Memphis who used to drive around naked. For like an hour or two. At night, but still."

"Fucking pervert! Just kidding."

"After he told me that, I really wanted to try it, but I never did."

"Not yet, anyway." Ziggy looked at me and grinned.

"Well, you're right, I might still do it; who knows?"

"We oughta do it together sometime. That sounds like fun."

"Yeah! Definitely," I said.

"Okay."

"Cool!"

"Fuck," he said, "I've got a hard on."

"You fucking pervert."

"It's your fault."

"Do you want me to take care of it?"

He thought about that for a minute. "Some trucker might see us. Besides, it would be too messy. I don't want to get cum all over your dashboard."

"I know how to take care of it without any mess at all."

Ziggy looked at me, and then back at the road. And then at me again. "Um," he said. "Maybe some other time."

"Okay."

"Really. I'd probably wreck."

"I understand."

"For real. You know what I'm talking about. I'd probably stomp the brake and the gas pedal both, forget to watch the road, flip us over or something. You know how I am. Hell, you're that way, too, when you come."

"Okay," I said.

"Some other time, okay?"

"Alright."

We drove on in silence for a few minutes. Apparently he was still reluctant to have my mouth on his cock, but I was okay with that.

Then he asked, "Did you and Fred have sex very often?" But before I could answer, he said, "No, never mind, I don't want to know. Forget I asked."

"Well . . . ."

"Seriously, don't tell me. I don't want to know."

"Okay."

"I'm sorry," he said.

"For what?"

"For not wanting to know."

"No problem."

"How about Tony, did you and Tony ever fuck?"

"Nah. We sucked each other off one time, but we've never fucked."

"Really?"

"Well, you know me. Fucking is not my specialty. Not so far, anyway."

"But you, uh, blew each other?"

"Yeah, we blew each other."

After a few minutes of thought he said, "How does that work, anyway?"

"What do you mean, how does it work?"

He looked at me, and then back at the road. "Sorry. I'm not used to talking about stuff like this."

"It's okay. Just say it."

"Well, correct me if I'm wrong, but when you sixty-nine, aren't your tongues on the wrong side of each other's cocks?" He started to blush a little.

"Yeah, they are. That can definitely be a disadvantage."

"That's what I thought. Can you come that way?"

"Well, I'm sure it's possible, but I never have."

Ziggy looked at me with a puzzled face.

"It's very pleasurable, it's just not the best way to make each other come. It's definitely hot, especially for somebody like me. And especially with someone I really like. There's something almost magical about it."

"What do you mean, somebody like you?"

"Well, you know. I like sucking. A lot."

"Oh." He started blushing again.

"And I like getting sucked, too, so sixty-nining with someone I'm hot for would be fantastic, especially if he was into it, too. I could do it for hours, I'll bet."

"Jesus." Ziggy reached into his pants and repositioned himself.

"There's nothing quite like receiving at the same time you're giving," I said.

"I'll bet." He put his hand to his boner and squeezed it a little.

"But really, for actually getting each other off, taking turns works better than sixty-nining."

"Oh. Okay. Is that what you and Tony did?"

"Yeah. Well, actually, we did both. First we sixty-nined, then we took turns."

"Okay."

Another few miles in silence.

"So, Zig," I said, "since we're talking about sex, I'm curious. What would we have done back at the rest stop, if you decided sex was the remedy I needed?"

"Oh, I didn't think it through that far. I don't know. We would have figured something out, bro. We always do."

"Okay."

We drove on in silence for a while, each of us lost in our own thoughts. Or maybe our thoughts were about the same thing: sex.

I could tell his hard dick hadn't gone down at all, and neither had mine.

He was resting his hand gently in his lap. Maybe he was trying to hide his boner, but more likely he just couldn't resist putting a little pressure on it once in a while to make it feel good.

Twenty minutes later, we approached another rest area.

Ziggy said, "Fuck, let's stop, okay? I gotta use the rest room."

"Me, too. And maybe I'll find a way to lose this boner I've got."

"Oh, Jesus, you, too? My cock's been stiff ever since we left the last place."

"Yeah, same here." I laughed.

"Plus I have to piss."

"Same here."

Ziggy pulled the car into the rest area and parked, and we headed for the men's room.

We went straight to the urinals and stood at two, side by side. I unzipped, and my pee started flowing as soon as I got my semi-hard dick out, but I didn't hear anything from Ziggy's direction. I looked over and he was looking down at his cock. Then he looked up toward the ceiling and closed his eyes.

I must have been halfway done by the time I finally heard the sound of his piss hitting the porcelain. He said, "Ahhhhhhhh." I looked over at him and he still had his eyes closed. Then he opened them and smiled at me. "That'll take care of one problem." He looked around to make sure no one else was in there with us. "I was beginning to think I wouldn't be able to pee, with this hard on." He turned slightly toward me, so I could look, and wagged it a little. A steady stream of golden piss was still flowing out of it.

"Jeez, Zig." I quickly looked around to make sure we were alone, and then I looked back at his hard cock. It was so incredibly erotic, watching him pee with a hard on. My own dick started stiffening again instantly. "My god, let me finish peeing!" I looked back to my own piss stream and tried to think of anything but Ziggy's stiff cock, for just a few seconds more, please, god.

We stood there like that for at least another half-minute, listening to each other piss. Mine slacked off and stopped long before his. When I was done, I dared to look over at Ziggy again, and my dick immediately stiffened right back to full wood at what I saw. He had his eyes closed and he was gently stroking his enlarged dick as the pee continued to flow. God, he had a beautiful cock.

I stood with my rigid dick in my hand, staring at his beauty. My dick already felt like it had been hard for hours. Looking at his wood again turned me on even more. I was so close to coming, I could probably shoot off with only a couple of strokes. I felt that tingling you get when your dick starts taking over.

I watched as his piss finally slowed to a trickle, and then it stopped. He gave it a few shakes, and then he started stroking it again!

"Jeez, Zig." I shuddered involuntarily. "What are you doing?"

He opened his eyes and looked at me. "Beat off with me, Josh. Come on." He looked over the little divider so he could get a good view of my dick. "Come on, dude! Your cock is just as stiff as mine is. Let's shoot a load right here, want to?" The whole time he talked, he was slowly stroking. And checking out my cock.

I thought, *Hell yes.* "Okay." I started stroking my dick, but I was already on the verge.

He said, "Cool! Let's see who can shoot first."

I was already there. The tingly feeling was starting to run through my whole body. Two more strokes and I was past the point of no return.

Then out of the blue Ziggy said, "Last one to shoot has to lick the other one clean!" Looking at me with an evil grin, he started in with some serious jacking.

By then I couldn't have kept from shooting my load if my life depended on it. I let out a groan as the first volley of cum shot out of my dick.

Ziggy looked down at my cock in surprise and his grin turned to a wide-eyed look of disbelief. All I could do was continue to moan as my body jerked and one cumshot after another spat out of my dick onto the porcelain.

"Fuck, Josh! How'd you do that?" He stroked his dick frantically as he watched my cock erupt. Then he started to shoot, too. He yelled, "Here I come! Ahhh! Ahhhhhhhh!"

Then the door to the bathroom opened, and we instantly drew up closer to the urinals to hide our dicks. I was pretty much spent by then, but Ziggy closed his eyes, his hips jerked uncontrollably a couple of times, and I knew he was still shooting.

The man who came into the bathroom went straight into the first stall, peed briefly, and then he came back out and left the bathroom without even washing his hands. We were still standing at the urinals.

We moved back a step and looked at each other's big dripping cocks. Ziggy still had a surprised look on his face. "Dude. I didn't know you were so close."

Sheepishly I said, "You don't have to do it, Zig. You were probably just joking anyway, right?"

"No, I wasn't. Fuck, I was dead serious. I just didn't expect it to turn out this way. A deal's a deal, though. Come on, before somebody else comes in." He knelt down on his haunches so his mouth was at dick level, and before I even had time to think he grabbed me by the base of my dick and gently pulled me toward him.

He paused for a couple seconds, like he was gathering up his courage, and then he put my cock in his mouth. Oh my god. He pressed his lips snugly around it, and I felt his tongue underneath it. Incredible. Gently, slowly, he pulled his lips and his tongue backward over the swollen head, gathering the cum off my dick and into his mouth. Then I saw him swallow.

He was still kneeling down, only a few inches in front of me, staring at my cock. Both of us looked at the shiny head of my dick, shiny with Ziggy's spit, hardly believing he did that. Then another pearl of cum oozed out. "Jesus," he said. With a wipe of his tongue he licked it up, then he stood.

We were standing there facing each other. Ziggy wiped the cum off his dick with his hand. Then he stood there with gooey fingers, looking over at the sink. Instinctively I grabbed his hand and put his fingers in my mouth.

"Dude." He laughed. "You got my cum after all!"

Then we heard a cough from back in the last stall! We looked at each other with bugged-out eyes. Somebody was here in the bathroom the whole time? Holy shit!

We frantically did the best we could to stuff our semi-hard dicks back into our jeans. Then the restroom door opened and another guy walked in. He looked at us briefly, but he didn't seem to think anything unusual was going on. He went into the first stall and we heard the sound of piss hitting water. We heard him go, "Ahhhhhhhh."

Ziggy grinned at me as he pushed the door open, and we hightailed it out of there.

—

"I CAN'T BELIEVE YOU DID THAT," I said, once we got back on the highway again.

"Me neither," Ziggy said.

"You didn't have to."

"A deal's a deal. Hell, it was my idea in the first place."

I was about to say, what were you thinking, but then I realized: he thought I would have to lick *him* clean. Which meant he *wanted* me to lick the cum off his cock. At least for that one brief impulsive moment, Ziggy *wanted* my mouth on his dick.

We were quiet for a few minutes, lost in our own thoughts.

Then he said, "What is it they say? 'Never bet more than you're willing to lose.'" He laughed. "Hell, it's okay. I already tasted your cum once before, remember?"

"Yeah, that's right, you did."

"Sure I did." He looked at me and smiled. "So, it's no big deal. I just got it from a little closer to the source, this time."

"Well, it doesn't bother me if it doesn't bother you. I just don't want anything to put a snag in our friendship."

"Oh, I don't think you have to worry about that, Josh. We're close enough now, anything that comes up, we can work it out, one way or another."

"I sure hope so."

"Sure we can. We just have to make up our minds ahead of time, to do whatever we have to do to fix things if anything ever does come up."

"I'm all for that," I said.

"Me, too. Want to shake on it?"

"Okay, sure."

"Okay. So listen," he said. "Here's what we're shaking on. No matter what happens, no matter how much one of us pisses off the other and acts like a complete, worthless asshole piece of shit, we're gonna remember that we love each other, and we want to keep on loving each other. No matter what stupid selfish thing one of us does, we're gonna remember that neither one of us would ever do something like that to the other one on purpose. Right?"

"Amen."

"We're gonna remember that no matter what happens to piss us off, our friendship is bigger and better and more important. So if something does come up, we're gonna talk to each other, and we're gonna tell each other right out, what pissed us off, and why it hurt, and then we're gonna make it better. Agreed?"

"Damn right," I said. I put my hand out and Ziggy took hold of it.

It started out as shaking hands, and then it turned into something more like letting the energy flow. We held hands like that for half a minute or more. Not that macho tight-grip handshake that hurts, and not a wimpy handshake either, but a nice, warm, gentle, firm hold of each other's hand.

It seemed like the natural thing to do at the time, but after we let loose I felt . . . different. Better. More complete. It was like we had filled up the empty spaces in each other. It felt fantastic.

"Zig?"

"Yeah?"

I was smiling, feeling really good. "Uh, I'm not sure how to say it." I wanted to ask him if he felt something, too.

"That's okay," he said. "Take your time."

I watched Ziggy drive my car, watched him as he watched the road and looked at me occasionally, and it was odd. I mean, he had this goofy grin on his face.

"When we shook hands," I said, "I felt something really awesome go between us."

"Me, too." He smiled at me, and looked back at the road.

After a few minutes of silence I said, "Have you ever seen one of those old westerns where two guys become blood brothers? You know, where they mix their blood together, to show how close they've become?"

"Yeah, I've heard of that."

"This probably sounds kind of weird, so don't laugh, but I feel like we're blood brothers now."

"Dude! You nailed it! That's exactly how I'm feeling right now."

"It feels awesome."

"Yeah, same here," he said. "Absolutely."

We drove on for at least ten minutes without saying a word. Smiling.

—

HALF AN HOUR LATER we were minutes away from Tennessee. We reached a fork in the road; it split into two interstate highways. Both of them led to Memphis.

"Which way should I go?" Ziggy asked.

"Route 40. It'll take us straight into downtown Memphis."

"We must be pretty close," he said.

"Oh, yeah. Five miles. Maybe less."

"Josh, listen, I'm gonna stop and let you drive."

"Uh, okay."

"Yeah. You should do the driving in Memphis. You know the roads, and besides, you've seen it before. I want to be a tourist and gawk at the sights."

"Okay, Zig. I'll be your official tour guide."

He got off the interstate and turned into a truck stop. We traded places and got back on the road.

Then we were crossing over the Mississippi River into Tennessee. And Memphis.

Ziggy stared out the window at the city's downtown skyline. "Nice, huh?"

"Yeah," he said. "Pretty impressive. Looks like a postcard, with the river and the tall buildings and all."

At the end of the bridge I took the Riverside Drive exit. Ziggy said, "You're gonna give me a tour of downtown first, huh?"

"Well, this is where our hotel is."

"Dude. I thought you'd save a few bucks and put us out in the boonies."

"Nah. Only the best for the Z Brothers. But it's too early to check in. I thought we could park by the river and walk around a bit."

"Okay, sure."

"You know, it does feel kind of nice to be back, one last time. There are definitely a few things I'll miss about Memphis."

"Like what?"

"Um, the food, for one. And the people, too. Strangers say hi to you when you pass each other on the street. Nobody did that where I grew up."

"Yeah. It's good when people aren't afraid to smile and say hello."

"This is the park I was talking about." I pulled in and found a parking spot away from the other cars.

"Are you sure we can't check into the hotel yet? It's almost three o'clock."

"Yeah, I'm sure. Not until four."

"Maybe this would be a good time to get your stuff out of Fred's house, bro."

"Oh, jeez, Zig. I'm not ready for that. Couldn't we get settled in at the hotel first?"

"Sure, no problem. He's not gonna hurt you, though, not with me there, little brother. Not unless he's got a gun, in which case we're both in deep shit."

"He doesn't have a gun. He's as scared of them as I am. But we need to talk before we go over there."

"Okay."

"You said so yourself, it's best to plan ahead when you're fucking with assholes. Remember?"

"Yeah, and this guy sounds like a first-class asshole, no doubt about that."

We locked the car and took a stroll next to the mighty Mississippi.

First we just watched the river. It's wide in St. Louis, but by the time it reaches Memphis it's huge. Really impressive.

Ziggy said, "Okay, let's be logical about it. Either he's there, or he's not. Or else he comes home while we're there. Is there a way for us to know, ahead of time, if he's home?"

"Sure. We could call," I said. "He always jumps on the phone when it rings. He hates to miss a call."

"Does he have an answering machine?"

"No. We talked about getting one, but he was against it. He didn't want me listening to his messages."

"Oh, nice. Nothing like keeping secrets from the guy who's supposed to be the love of your life."

Another revelation for me, although it should have been obvious all along. "Zig," I said, "I'm so stupid. Fuck, I should have been out of there a long time ago."

"Don't feel bad, Josh. You wanted to believe the best, that's all."

"I wish I met you or Tony first."

"Yeah, but who knows? If you hadn't met Fred, maybe you wouldn't have met Tony or me, either. You never know how those alternative universes are gonna go."

"Yeah, I guess so. Hey, we could try calling Tony. He's got an answering machine. Maybe he'll say something in his message about who went with him to Atlanta."

"Okay. And we can call Fred, too, before we go over there. If he doesn't answer, then he's probably not home, right? Either that or he's sitting on the can. So we call again five minutes later, and if he still doesn't answer, he's probably not there. Unless he's working out in the backyard or something."

"The only time he ever goes in the backyard is when he wants to pee off the back porch."

"Will you need to sort out your stuff from his, when we get there?"

"No, it's all separate. I have my own bedroom where I keep my stuff."

"You guys didn't sleep together?"

"Most of the time we did, except for when he camped out in front of the TV. My bedroom was for appearances. Like for when his mother came over, or somebody from where he works. He doesn't want any of them to know he's gay."

"Christ. That's fucked up."

We reached the end of the park and started back the way we came.

"Well, anyway," Ziggy said, "it sounds pretty simple. We go in, get your three boxes first, take those out to your car. Those are the important things. Your novel, and sentimental stuff. Then we go back in and get the rest of your stuff. Shouldn't take more than half an hour."

"Unless he comes home while we're there," I said.

Chapter 20
PLAN OF ATTACK

"WELL, WHAT'S THE WORST that could happen if he does come home, Josh? If we do meet Fred face to face?"

"He's not gonna be happy, that's for sure. Especially when he figures out I'm leaving," I said.

"Yeah, but what will he do? Argue? Pick a fight? Try to beat you up? Kill us with an ax?"

"I don't think he would use a weapon. But I've never tried to leave him before. I don't know what he'll do if he gets really crazy."

"Well, what does he do when he gets radically pissed off?"

"Shout. Accuse. Condemn. It's like a mind-fuck. It's his way of hurting people, and he's good at it. He twists everything around, makes you feel like *you're* in the wrong, and it's *you* who's worthless, and somehow he always ends up looking like the good guy. All that, while he's calling you every nasty and hurtful thing he can think of. It's intense. It's not just words, either. The whole time, you feel like any second he's gonna punch you."

"Nice guy," Ziggy said. "I wonder who he learned that from."

"His mother, no doubt. She can be a real bitch. Everyone is afraid of her. Even him."

"Anyway, listen. The whole time we're there, we stay together. I'll be right beside you. If he does come home, don't let him involve you in any kind of discussion about anything. Don't talk about where you've been, or what you're doing, or anything else. Pretend you're completely deaf if you have to, but don't talk to him about anything. And don't stop doing what we came there to do."

"Um, okay. Ignore him, right?"

"Damn right, ignore him. Let him say whatever awful, terrible stuff he wants to say, but don't respond. He'll do everything he can to get you engaged in an argument, but you're not gonna fall for it, okay?"

"Okay."

"It'll probably piss him off all the more, but that's life. And if you forget, Josh, if you start talking to him, I'm gonna get between the two of you and tell you to shut up and get back to work. Are you okay with that? You can pretend I'm your new master and you're *my* slave now."

I laughed. "Alright."

"And one thing you've got to remember, bro, is he doesn't mean shit to you any longer. You might still care about him, that takes time to get out of your system, but remember: he's lost any right he ever had to tell you what to do. Okay?"

"Okay."

"Hell, he never *did* have any right. Nobody does. You've got to be the one in control, Josh. You know that, right?"

"Yeah, I do. But sometimes I forget."

"It's your *life*, Josh. *Your* life to live."

"Jimi Hendrix, right?"

"You got it. 'If 6 was 9'. Hendrix had the right idea, for sure."

"Alright. So, I know I can do this. Having you there, Zig, really helps. I appreciate you doing this."

"You'd do the same for me, Josh. You know you would."

"Yeah, I *would*, Zig. If anybody ever tries to hurt you, I'm gonna be there for you, you can count on that. Nobody's *ever* gonna hurt you, if I can help it."

"You've got spirit, Josh. Maybe you're shy and quiet, but you're brave. You might not think so, but you are, brother."

We stood there and watched the river.

—

WE STILL HAD TIME to kill before check-in, so we drove down Union Avenue and worked our way to Overton Park. I wanted to show it to Ziggy. It's only a fourth the size of Forest Park but still, it's big. I showed him all my favorite spots. We followed the road all the way through, and came out on North Parkway.

We needed empty boxes, and I knew a liquor store on Summer Avenue that might have some. When we got there, though, some guy was breaking down all the boxes and loading them into the back of his ancient pickup truck. Ziggy opened the door and jumped out before I'd even come to a complete stop. By the time I got out of the car he had four boxes in his hands.

"I got the last of them." He handed them to me and said, "I'm gonna run in and get some whiskey or rum or something. I'll be right back." Five minutes later he came out with a paper bag in his hand.

"They ought to have our room ready by now," I said. "Wait till you see this place, Zig."

"Nice, huh?"

"Yeah, it is. It's old, like from the 1920's. They restored it just a few years ago, so it's in excellent shape."

"I wonder if it has any ghosts," he said.

"Oh, jeez, no doubt. I'll bet plenty of people would want to haunt the Peabody Hotel. Even if they didn't die there. It was famous for ballroom dances and parties. The Peabody was a popular place in the big band era."

"Is it like that hotel in 'The Shining'?"

"No." I laughed. "Well, actually, yeah, maybe it is. But it's in the middle of downtown Memphis, so, no outside grounds, no mazes to get lost in."

"Oh, well." He smiled. "I guess we'll just have to make do with the ghosts."

"You think there really is such a thing?"

"I don't know," he said. "Maybe. If people's spirits leave their bodies and go somewhere else when they die, then I guess it only figures that some people wouldn't want to go. You know how ornery some people are. If there's any choice about something, there's always somebody who doesn't want to do it. Out of stubbornness, if nothing else."

"Yeah, and then, some people might be afraid to leave. You know, afraid of where they'd be going."

"Right."

"And there's people who die suddenly, unexpectedly. They might not even know they're dead. They might not know it's time to move on," I said.

"Jesus. How could you not know that you're dead?"

"Well, people are good at fooling themselves when they're alive," I said. "Maybe it's the same way when you're dead? At least for the ones who haven't, you know, moved on."

"From what I've heard about ghosts, I think they're probably just as dumb as live people. I mean, think about it," he said. "There must be a lot better things to do when you're dead than haunt some old house. That would get boring really quick."

"Maybe time is different somehow, when you're a ghost."

"You mean like, slow motion?"

"No, more like, maybe the past and present and future are all kind of together somehow."

"That would be extremely weird."

"For us, maybe. But for a ghost, who knows?" I said.

"Yeah, who knows what's weird and what's not to a ghost?"

"Exactly."

"Well," he said, "I guess we might find out someday, but I'm not in any hurry. Life is short enough as it is."

"That's for sure."

"I'd rather skip the ghost part, though. That would be sad, to do the same thing day after day for centuries, and not even have enough sense to get bored with it."

"Hopefully," I said, "when the time comes, we'll both have enough sense to go to the light."

—

WE REACHED THE PEABODY HOTEL, parked the car in the garage, and found our way up into the lobby. We were still a little early, so we strolled around, checking the place out.

"Nice place," Ziggy said.

"Check out that fountain, Zig."

"No way! Ducks?"

I laughed. "Yeah, this place is famous for the ducks. People really love 'em."

We walked over to get a better look. Five mallard ducks, paddling around or standing up on the edge preening themselves, pretending to ignore us. When we got close, though, they started quacking nervously.

"They live in the fountain?"

"No, up on the roof. That's where they stay at night. Every morning they come down the elevator, spend the day here, and then in the evening they take the elevator back up. They have a red carpet and everything. It's a big ceremony."

"I want to see that."

We checked in and got our room key. The clerk told us the ducks go up at 5 p.m. and they come down at 11 a.m. He said expect a big crowd.

We were on the way to the elevator when Ziggy said, "Wait a second, Josh. I want to ask you something, before we go up to our room." We found a couple of empty chairs in the lobby and sat down. "Josh, wanna pretend we're in the ninth grade?"

I grinned. "You remembered!"

"Well, sure I did. You want to?"

"Yes! Definitely."

"Okay." He smiled. "I guess it won't really work to pretend the whole time we're here, but how about just while we're in the hotel room? That should be easy."

"Yeah. That sounds excellent."

"Alright, then. So, when we walk through that door into our room, we're in the ninth grade. And we go to the same school."

"Okay. And maybe this is the first time we've ever really met each other? Like, we're part of different crowds, and maybe we've seen each other around, but we didn't meet until now."

"That ought to work. Let's see, in ninth grade I was hanging out with George and his punk buddies."

"And I was hanging out with my nerdy friends."

"Okay. But why would we share a hotel room in Memphis? Any ideas?"

"Um, some kind of convention? Maybe we belong to a student club that's having a convention."

"The only club I ever belonged to was Distributive Education. I had to, if I wanted to work part-time while I went to school. But that wasn't until I was in eleventh grade."

"I've heard of that. I knew a couple of guys who were in D.E. Well, let's pretend I'm in D.E., too. And let's say we're in the eleventh grade, then, instead of ninth grade. We're on a trip to Memphis with the other students for the yearly convention. You and I got a hotel room together just by random luck of the draw. We didn't know each other until now."

"Okay, cool. That'll work."

The lobby was starting to get crowded. "Zig, look. People are grabbing their spots already. To watch the ducks."

"Let's take our stuff upstairs," he said; "then we'll come down and grab a spot, too."

We took the elevator up and located our room. Before he unlocked the door he said, "Remember now, we're in eleventh grade, the whole time we're in this room."

I grinned. "Okay."

He opened the door and we went in.

"Dude! Look at this shit. Only one bed? Didn't they know there are two of us?" Ziggy was hamming it up already.

"That's okay," I said.

"Fuck, I guess you'll want to take turns sleeping on the floor or some stupid shit like that. You probably have a bed all to yourself at home, right?"

"No, I don't. I share a bed with one of my brothers. I always have."

"You're used to sharing a bed with another dude?"

"Oh, sure."

"You don't mind?"

"I don't mind. It's no big deal."

"Well, okay," he said. "Alright. I'm used to it, too, so I guess it won't be a problem." We took off our backpacks and set them on the floor. "What did you say your name is?"

"Josh."

"Good to know you, Josh." He held out his hand, and we shook.

"And you're Ziggy, right?"

"Yep, that's me."

"Good to know you, too, Ziggy. I was hoping I'd get to meet you someday. I've seen you in the halls at school."

"That's cool," he said. "You look kind of familiar, but I don't think I've ever seen you in the lunchroom. Or in Gym."

"No, we have different schedules."

"That explains it. Hey, I'm gonna unpack later. I wanna go see those crazy ducks do their march to the elevator."

"I'll go with you! Um, I mean, if that's okay with you."

"Oh, sure. Hell yeah. We're gonna be roommates, we might as well hang out together while we're here, right?"

"Sure! That would be great. If you don't mind. I figured you probably had your own friends here you'd want to spend all your time with."

265

"Nah. I don't really know any of these guys. All the dudes I used to hang out with graduated last year."

"Really? Two years older than you?"

"Yep. I got to know them through a buddy of mine at the orphanage."

"Wow."

"Yeah. Those were my friends. I don't know anybody in my own grade. Hell, I'll probably know you better than anybody else in our whole school, by the time we get back home."

"I know a few people," I said, "but I don't really have too many friends. Not as many as I'd like. I guess I'm kind of shy."

"What for?"

"Jeez, I don't know. I just am."

"Well, no problem, dude. I'm not shy at all, so it'll work out. Now if we were both shy, then we'd have a problem."

"I never thought of it that way before. I guess it would be a problem, wouldn't it?"

"Two shy people together? Of course. But, hey, I'll bet you're not as shy as you think you are."

"I don't know about that. I'm pretty shy."

"Well, I'll be the judge of that. Hey, let's go see those ducks."

We locked up the room and headed down the hall to the elevator.

Ziggy grinned and said, "How am I doing so far?"

"Excellent! You're perfect. How about me?"

"Great. This is gonna be fun. Pretending to be classmates in school. It's almost real."

"Yeah, it is. It's like, what I missed out on. This is great," I said.

"But you did have some friends in school, right?"

"Yeah, I did. Guys who were just as quiet and clueless as I was."

"I had lots of friends," he said, "and a best friend, too. But they were all older than me, and more experienced. You're the first time I've ever had someone like a little brother."

The door to the elevator opened, crowded and with barely enough room left inside. But the real surprise was when it reached the ground floor. It opened up and the lobby was packed full of people.

"Jesus, fuck! What are all these people doing here?"

"I don't know. To see the ducks, I guess. They told us it would be crowded."

"I'm getting claustrophobic," Ziggy said. "Let's skip the ducks for now. We can see them tomorrow, okay?"

"Okay."

I looked at him, and he looked at me.

"Josh, we might as well go get your stuff."

"Yeah."

"You'll be glad when it's over with. So will I, to tell you the truth. Then we can enjoy the rest of the weekend without worrying."

"Okay." I really didn't want to go. "Let's go," I said.

When we passed a pay telephone booth I said, "Wait. I'm gonna call Tony's apartment. He always leaves a special message when he goes out of town. Maybe he'll say who went." I called Tony's number. The phone rang, and rang, and rang. "That's weird. The machine's not picking up at all." I finally hung up after a dozen rings, and looked at Ziggy.

"Don't worry," he said. "He probably forgot to turn the thing on. That happens sometimes, right?"

"I guess. But he always leaves it on, even when he's at home."

"It didn't play when you called him yesterday, did it?"

"Yeah, it did. It started playing his usual recorded message, but then he picked up."

"Maybe he turned it off when he answered. Or maybe he turned it off to record a new message and forgot to turn it back on."

"Yeah, maybe."

"I wouldn't worry about it, Josh. Anyway, why would any of them want to stay home?"

"Alright. Fuck it," I said. "Let's go."

—

WE WENT TO THE GARAGE and cranked up the car and headed on out.

"His house is in Midtown, pretty close by."

"Nice house?"

"Naw. Average. A little run down. It used to be his mother's house, until she remarried."

"So now the house belongs to Fred?"

"No, his mother still owns it."

I pulled into the parking lot at Krystal, next to the phone booth. "I'm gonna stop here and call the house."

"All according to plan, right?"

"Yeah."

"You're really nervous."

"He's a sick bastard, Zig."

Ziggy put his hand on my shoulder. "I'll be with you, Josh. I won't let him hurt you, bro. Okay?"

"I know, Zig. I'll be alright. I know I have to do this."

"Did you ever read the book *Dune*, by Frank Herbert?"

"Yeah. Why?"

"Did you like it?"

"I loved it. I've read it twice. One of these days I'll probably read it again."

"Remember what Paul does when he's afraid?"

"Uh . . . ." I had to think about that one.

"What he says? The litany he recites?"

"Oh! Yeah, of course. 'Fear is the mind-killer.' That is one awesome saying. I used to have the whole thing memorized."

"Used to?"

"Let me see if I can remember it." I thought for a minute. "'I must not fear. Fear is the mind-killer. Fear is the little-death that brings total obliteration. I will face my fear.'" I looked at Ziggy for his reaction.

"Dude! You are incredible." He shook his head in wonder. "Now I know we were meant to meet up. Jesus, how many people would memorize that?"

"That saying has helped me through some tough times, Zig."

"Do you remember the rest of it?"

"Um, 'I will face my fear. I will permit it to pass over me and through me. And when it has gone past I will turn the inner eye to see its path. Where the fear has gone there will be nothing. Only I will remain.'"

"You got it!" Ziggy held up his palm, and I slapped it with mine. "Dude." He grinned from ear to ear.

I felt relieved. Calm, for a change.

Calm enough to wonder: what was I thinking? I'd gotten through scary shit before. I knew I could do it again. "Zig, let's forget about calling ahead. Let's just go on over there, right now."

"Alright! I'm with you, brother."

The more I thought about my relationship with Fred, the angrier I got. Fred had manipulated me into cowering like a kicked dog. And I let him.

Not anymore. "If he's there, he's there," I said. "Like they say around here, 'Ain't nothin' but a thing.'" I started the car and got back on Union Avenue. "Zig, how about if I do the talking? I'm the one who got myself into this mess."

"Whatever you want, Josh. But it'll be easier for me to take his shit than it will be for you. He doesn't mean anything to me."

"I know. But sometimes the easiest way is not the best way."

"Ah. Said like a true Jedi Master."

"I'm glad you'll be there to back me up, though. In case I need it."

"No problem, little brother."

I turned at Rembert Street, and again at Courtland Place. I pulled up in front of the house and parked, right behind Fred's old Dodge Dart.

"This is it. That's his car in front of us, but it doesn't mean he's here. He doesn't take that junk heap anywhere unless he has to. If he went to Atlanta he would have gone with everybody else, in Jerome's Lincoln."

We got out of my car. Ziggy waited for me to come around; then he fell in right beside me as we walked up to the house. I tried the door to see if it was locked. It was. So I opened it with my key and we went in. Ziggy followed close behind me. I called out, "Fred?"

Silence.

The house was very quiet. "The windows are shut, that's a good sign," I said. We walked through the dining room and into the kitchen, and back to the living room. "Let's go upstairs." Ziggy was right behind me the whole way. I looked into Fred's bedroom, checked the bathroom, and checked my own bedroom. "He's not here. Unless he's hiding in a closet."

"What about the basement?"

"There isn't any. They don't have basements in the South, I don't know why."

"Okay," Ziggy said. "Well, no time like the present, right?"

"Yeah, let's get started. First thing is my boxes, right?" I went into the closet. I gave one to Ziggy, and picked up a second one.

"Put that one on here," he said. "I can carry two." So I put it on top of the other one, and then I picked up the third one. He said, "Lead the way, bro."

We put them in the trunk of the car, then we brought in the empty liquor store boxes. We emptied out my dresser drawers and put all that in the backseat of the car. Then we went back, got all my shirts and coats, and took those out, too.

I closed the trunk of the car and looked at Ziggy, and he looked at me.

270

"Let's go back in one more time," I said. "To get my mail. And take one last look around."

Fred had my mail scattered around everywhere, as usual. I looked through it, but it was all junk mail. I was going to toss it when I saw a letter in the trash in Fred's handwriting. A note. To me. I pulled it out and looked at it. I read it over, silently.

"What have you got there?" Ziggy said.

"A note, from Fred. Take a look." I handed it to Zig.

> Josh: Where the hell have you been? You
> missed the trip to Atlanta, asshole. I hope
> whatever the fuck you've been doing was
> worth it. It won't stop the rest of us from
> having a good time, you can be sure of that,
> but you better have a good explanation.
> And don't forget the laundry has to be done
> by Monday night so I can have clean clothes
> for Tuesday. And you haven't vacuumed the
> carpet for weeks.

Ziggy handed it back to me. "That's all he had to say?"

"You can tell he really missed me, right?"

Ziggy snorted. "Yeah, sure he did."

"See what I mean? He treats me like hired help."

"No kidding. 'Wash the clothes, vacuum the rug.' I'm surprised he didn't threaten to dock your pay."

"What pay? But it's weird, that it was in the trash. He wrote me a note, but then he threw it away."

"Maybe he knew you'd see it in the trash?"

"No, that wouldn't make sense." I dropped the note back into the trashcan. "I'm glad he mentioned the laundry, though. I almost forgot my dirty clothes." I went through the kitchen to the utility room, and started separating my clothes from Fred's.

271

I had laundry scattered all over the floor when Ziggy came in and said, "Josh, there's someone at the front door. Some old lady."

"Shit. That's all we need." I stood up and went into the living room, expecting it to be Fred's mother. But when I opened the door, there was my favorite neighbor.

"Mrs. Rainey! How are you doing?"

"Just fine, sweetheart. I hope I'm not intruding?"

"No, of course not, come on in. Zig, this is Mrs. Rainey. She lives down the street. Mrs. Rainey, this is Ziggy, a very good friend of mine from St. Louis."

"Nice to meet you, ma'am."

"Good to meet you, too, dear. Josh, hon, did Fred come back yet?"

"No, ma'am. I think he went to Atlanta for the weekend."

"I don't think so, dear. Not unless he just left. I saw him not more than an hour ago."

"You did?"

"He was walking down Cooper Street, towards Overton Park."

"Darn. I hoped he wouldn't be around today. I'm moving out of here, Mrs. Rainey."

"Well, good for you. Goodness, don't let me slow you down, then. I'd best be going. Unless there's something I can do to help."

"Aw, thanks, but we can handle it."

"You two come over and visit with me when you're all done here, okay?"

I looked at Ziggy, and he nodded his head. "Sure. We'd love to, ma'am."

"You know where to find me then, Josh."

"Okay," I said. "We'll see you a little later, then." She went out the door and down the walk. I looked at Ziggy. "Fuck. It figures. He could walk in the door any minute."

"Looks like you were right, Josh. You had a feeling he might still be here."

"Well, the hell with him. He's not gonna run my life anymore. I'm gonna finish getting my stuff together. If we're still here when he comes back, so be it. Maybe it'll be better anyway. I can tell him straight to his face what I think of him."

"Your call, bro. I'll back you up, whatever you want to do."

"I'm almost done going through the laundry." We walked to the back of the house, and Ziggy watched while I finished sorting clothes. I put my things in a couple of grocery bags and carried them into the living room.

"I guess that's it, then," I said. We turned off the lights and locked the door on our way out.

We walked to the car and squeezed the bags of laundry into the back, on the floor. "I almost wish he had been here," I said. "I'd like to tell the bastard to his face what a waste of time the last two years have been."

"I can relate to that," Ziggy said. "If you don't call people on their bullshit, they feel like they got away with it."

"Yeah."

"Well, we can come back later, if you really want to talk to him face to face."

"Nah. He's not worth it. Once I drive away from here, I'm gone. He's out of my life."

We got into the car and I started the engine. As I pulled out, Ziggy said, "Where's Mrs. Rainey live?"

"Just down the street."

"Are we gonna stop in?"

"You want to?"

"Yeah, she's nice. And we told her we would."

"Okay. Sure." I pulled the car over again and parked. We got out and locked it up. Then we noticed two people down the street, walking our way.

I recognized one of them. "That's Fred."

Chapter 21

FRED

ZIGGY WATCHED FRED approach and said, "Dude, are you sure you're ready for this?"

"No," I said, "but what the hell."

Ziggy moved up closer beside me. We stood there and waited as Fred walked toward us. The guy who was with him, I had never seen before.

Fred spoke first, as soon as he was close enough to be heard. "Where the fuck have you been, asshole?"

"Gee, thanks, Fred. I'm glad to see you, too."

"You didn't answer my question."

"It's none of your business anymore."

He walked right up in front of me and stopped. "What the fuck are you talking about? You've been gone a week and you won't tell me where the fuck you've been? *What* the fuck you've been *doing*? Of course it's my business."

I stood my ground. "I just came back to get my stuff, Fred. I'm moving out."

"You can't move out. You're my fucking lover, remember?"

The guy who was with him said, "Your lover? Jesus! You said he was just your roommate!"

"Lover, roommate, whatever." He turned back to me. "Look, you're not moving out, so stop talking crazy shit." Then he looked at Ziggy. "Who the fuck is this?"

"He's a good friend of mine. But that's none of your business, either."

"The fuck he is. You brought some trick home. You thought I'd be in Atlanta, but here I am and I caught your ass."

"No, Fred, I believe that's you. You and your friend here."

"He's not a trick."

"Why don't you introduce us, then? What's his name?"

He looked at the guy and said, "Uh . . . ."

Sure enough, Fred didn't even know his name.

The guy looked at Fred, and then he looked at me. "My name's Corey. And I'm really sorry. He told me he didn't have a partner. I asked him. He said he was single. I didn't know."

"No problem," I said. "It's not your fault. And anyway, he *doesn't* have a partner. Not anymore."

"Look," he said, "I didn't bargain for any of this. Sorry, guys. Sorry for everything, but I'm out of here."

Fred said, "No, you're not! You stay right here, goddamn it." The guy looked at Fred in surprise, but he didn't leave. "And you," he said to me, "take your trick someplace else, asshole. You're not bringing him into my house."

"He's not a trick. He's my friend. And you won't be telling me what to do. Not anymore. I told you, Fred, I'm moving out."

"The fuck you are."

"Listen, Fred. I know it probably doesn't mean anything to you, but I loved you. Two years I loved you, but now I've finally figured it out. You don't love me. You never did. And guess what? Now I don't love you anymore, either."

"You're full of shit," he said.

"No. I'm not. I'm telling the truth. You never have loved me."

"Yes, I did. Just because I don't show it doesn't mean I don't feel it."

"Now listen to who's talking shit. You don't love anyone, Fred. Not even yourself. You don't even know what love is."

"And I guess you do, huh? You're the expert, huh?"

"I didn't say I'm an expert. But I know enough to know one thing: you don't care about me or anyone else. Only yourself. And I'm through with your selfishness. Two years of my life I wasted on you."

"I know what it really is," he said. "Somebody new came along, and he fed you a line of bullshit. Told you he cares for you more than I do, and you fucking fell for it, hook line and sinker. What a stupid fuck you are, Josh. Everyone in this fucking world is only out for himself, and if he tells you anything different, he's a liar.

"I let you share my house with me, are you forgetting that? And all the good times we've had together, you're gonna throw all that away? For a new lover? Some stranger you just met?"

"I didn't say he was my lover. That's not who he is. He's my friend. That's even better. That's something you've never been."

"Aw, bullshit."

"As for sharing your house, that's nothing. I had to pay rent. Your mother lets you live there for free, but you made me pay rent."

Corey and Ziggy both looked at Fred in surprise.

"Well, uh, hell," he said, "we could probably work something out, as far as that goes. Lower your payment, maybe. If you do more work around the house."

"What work would that be? I've already been cleaning the whole fucking house, and doing your laundry, too. Not anymore, though. I'm out of here, Fred. And I won't change my mind, either."

"Fine! See if I fucking care. Give me your goddamn house key, then. Right now."

"Okay." I pulled out my keys and started pulling the key off the ring.

"But know this, asshole. This is it. No changing your mind later. Are you sure you want to do this? After all the good times we've had?"

"Yeah, I'm sure."

"You won't find anybody half as good as me, Josh. I hope you know that."

"God, I sure hope not. If there's anybody more worthless than you are, I sure as hell don't want to meet him." I handed him the house key.

He grabbed it from my hand. "Alright then. That's it, mother-fucker. Stay the fuck out of my house."

"My pleasure."

"And forget about coming in to get your junk. Stay the fuck out of my house."

"Oh, yeah? What are you gonna do with my stuff? Sell it?"

"No, asshole, nobody would want to buy that shit. If you want it, I'll be putting it out in the street. When I fucking get around to it. In the meantime, I don't even want to see your ugly face around here." He turned away and stomped up the street toward his house.

Corey, the guy who walked up with Fred, stayed with us and watched him walk off.

When Fred realized Corey wasn't with him, he turned around. "Come on, bubba," he said. "Damn it, do you want to fuck, or not?"

The guy looked at Ziggy and me, shook his head, and said, "Unreal." He turned in the other direction and walked back the way he came.

Fred shouted, "Fine!" We watched him walk to his house. When he got to his porch he looked back, saw that we were still watching, and flipped us off. Then he went inside and slammed the door so hard one of the panes of glass shattered.

Followed by silence.

It took a few moments to process.

Was it over?

It was hard to believe, but, yes. It looked like Fred was out of my life.

I turned around and looked at Ziggy. He stood there next to me looking like he was ready to pound the hell out of somebody in a heartbeat. When he saw me smiling, he relaxed. It was then that I realized: he was ready the whole time to jump in instantly if Fred went off the deep end.

He stretched and loosened himself up. "What do you think he'll do when he figures out you already got your stuff out of there?"

"I don't know. Punch a hole in the wall, probably."

"Josh, you were great. Just perfect, dude. I couldn't have handled it any better."

"Thanks, Zig. Sorry you had to listen to all that crap."

"No problem."

"Let's go visit Mrs. Rainey."

—

SHE WAS STANDING AT THE FRONT DOOR of her house, watching.

"Hello, boys." She held the door open for us. "Come right on in."

Zig said, "Hi, Mrs. Rainey."

"Hello, Ziggy."

"We got all of Josh's stuff out."

"Well, that's good. Sit down, make yourselves at home."

Ziggy and I sat down on the sofa, next to each other.

Mrs. Rainey sat in the armchair and looked me over. "Josh, hon, I saw you talking with Fred. He looked angry."

"Yeah. I finally told him I was through with him. Poor guy, now he'll have to do his own laundry."

"Well, he had his chance, Josh. He doesn't deserve someone as nice as you."

Nobody said anything for a few moments. I think Ziggy and I were both letting our pulse rate get back to normal.

"Honestly," she said, "I've often wondered what you ever saw in him. But of course, it's none of my business."

"I thought he was good looking, I guess."

"Handsome is as handsome does, dear."

"I didn't know any better. He was nice at first. Kind of domineering, but he said he cared about me."

"Maybe he did, but it never looked that way to me, hon."

"I think he *wanted* to care. Maybe he didn't know how."

"Well, at the rate he's going, he never will."

"He was my first boyfriend."

They both looked at me then. Didn't say anything, just stared at me.

Then she stood up. "Goodness, you boys must be thirsty. Can I get you something to drink? Iced tea?"

"We can't stay long," I said.

"Well, no matter. I'll be right back." She walked into the kitchen.

Ziggy and I looked at each other. "She's so nice," he said.

"Yeah. She really is."

She came back and gave us each a glass of tea. "There you go." She watched Ziggy as he chugged down half of his. "My, my, you *were* thirsty."

"Yes, ma'am."

"Aren't you the handsome one, too! You remind me of one of my grandsons. That boy can't keep the girls away. I'll bet you have the same problem, good-looking as you are."

"Oh, no, ma'am. I get lucky once in a while; that's good enough for me." He raised his glass to his mouth again and finished the drink.

"Would you like some more?"

"No thank you, ma'am. That was delicious. Thank you."

She sat down. "You're from St. Louis, Ziggy?"

"Yes, ma'am."

"Is that where you've been all week, Josh? In St. Louis?"

"Yes, ma'am."

"And now you've come to get your things and go back."

I looked at Ziggy, and he looked back at me. "Yes, ma'am. That's where I'm going to live, now."

"Well, I knew you'd get your fill of that other one. Just a matter of time."

"You knew, huh?"

279

"Oh, yes. Selfish and hateful, that boy." She looked around as if to make sure no one else was listening, and then she leaned toward us and whispered, "Just like his mother."

"Yeah, I finally figured that out. That's why I'm leaving."

"Well, goodness, Josh, you don't have to leave Memphis to put that stinker behind you."

"I know, but I like St. Louis. And Ziggy and I have really hit it off great. He's like a brother to me now."

She looked at Ziggy, and then back to me. "Well, I hope he treats you better than Fred did. You're such a sweetheart."

Ziggy said, "I will, ma'am. I promise you that. He means a lot to me."

"We're gonna live together," I said.

"Well, if that's what you two really want, then you shouldn't let anything stop you."

Ziggy and I grinned at each other.

"Goodness, you young folks move around so much these days. But I guess you're used to it. I'm going to miss you, young man."

"I'm gonna miss you, too, Mrs. Rainey. You're the best neighbor I've ever had."

"I packed a lunch for you boys."

"Oh, Mrs. Rainey, you didn't have to do that."

"I know, dear." She walked into the kitchen and came back with a big paper bag. "It's only some sandwiches and a few other things, nothing special."

I stood up, and then Ziggy stood, too. "You're so nice," I said. "Thank you." The bag was heavier than I expected. "Jeez, what all do you have in here?"

"Just a few odds and ends. Ziggy, you take good care of Josh, you hear?"

"Yes, ma'am, I sure will. You can count on that."

"All right, then. Best of luck to you, Josh, dear. And you, too, Ziggy."

"Same to you, Mrs. Rainey." I wanted to hug her so bad. I knew I might never see her again. But I just stood there, looking at her.

"Josh, dear," she said, smiling. "Aren't you going to give me a hug?" She held her arms out. I rushed over and held her tight. She wrapped her arms around me and hugged me close. "You're such a nice boy."

We let loose of each other, and then she looked at Ziggy. "You, too," she said. He went over and they gave each other a good hug. Then we made our way out the door.

"Josh, you call me as soon as you get back to St. Louis, you hear? Just so I know you got home alright."

"Yes, ma'am, I will. I'll call you Tuesday, okay? We'll be home by then." She stood at the door and watched us walk down the steps. I looked back and we waved to each other. I told Ziggy, "I really am gonna miss her."

"She's nice," he said.

I unlocked the car and we got in. "Sometimes when Fred was really pissed off at me and screaming and cussing, right in the middle of everything she would knock on the door, bringing us something to eat. I think she did it on purpose, to get him to cool down. It happened too many times just to be a coincidence."

"She could hear him this far down the street?"

"Well, with the windows open, sure. People probably heard him the next block over."

"Jesus, what an abusive jerk. There's no excuse for that." He looked back toward Fred's house. "Well, bro. It's time to get you out of here."

"Yeah." I started the engine, and we left Courtland Place behind. I turned west onto Union Avenue, heading back towards downtown. "I'm glad Fred was there," I said. "I got to face the enemy after all."

"You were awesome, Josh."

"Let's go back to the hotel. Hell, it's Saturday night. We should celebrate."

"Definitely," Ziggy said, grinning. "Time to party, dude!" Ziggy was in a great mood. "You did it, Josh. You really did it."

"We did it," I said. "You and me, Zig."

"You're the one who dealt with the asshole. Without any help from me. I'm proud of you, dude. That took balls. That took courage."

"Hell, I'm just glad it's over. Now I won't ever have to see that bastard again."

"Yep. He's part of your past, now. And we're gonna celebrate." He was grinning.

"Yeah." I started to smile, too.

"There you go. Things are looking up, bro. Am I right?"

"You're right, Zig." We high-fived each other. I was feeling better and better by the minute.

I was just now starting to comprehend it: I really was single. Free. Free to do whatever I liked, free to be with whoever I wanted. Another thing Ziggy and I had in common now.

We reached the Peabody Hotel, parked the car, and walked into the lobby. What a change from the earlier crowd. It was quiet, not at all crowded. The ducks had gone up to their penthouse suite. People sat around drinking cocktails, talking softly.

When we reached our room Ziggy said, "Back to the eleventh grade, right?"

"Right." We went inside.

"What's on the agenda?"

"We're on our own tonight," I said. "It's sign-in night. Half the other students aren't even here yet."

"So, in other words, we can do whatever we want to tonight, right?"

"Sure."

"Cool. Want to go see if we can pick up some chicks?"

Chapter 22
THE TWO OF US

I WAS SPEECHLESS.

He looked at me, smiling, waiting for an answer.

I couldn't think of one word to say. Pick up some girls? Was he serious?

He said, "You want to?" Still waiting.

Oh, my god. This was the part of eleventh grade that I didn't like at all. "Jeez. Um, I don't know."

"You don't know?"

Oh, hell with it, I thought. *Just say it.* "Ziggy, I'm just not into girls that much. Not the way most guys are, anyway. I don't know why."

Now he looked puzzled. "Are you serious?"

"Don't tell anybody, okay? Fuck. You're not gonna want to have anything to do with me now. I should have kept my mouth shut. You think I'm weird, don't you?"

"No, dude, no, I don't think you're weird." He went over to the window and looked out.

"Yeah you do."

He turned toward me again. "Look, it's okay." He went over to one of the chairs and sat down. "It's not weird. A little bit unusual, maybe, but not weird. I've met other guys the same way. No big deal."

"Really?"

"Yeah, really. What, you thought you were the only one?"

"Well, I didn't know. Yeah, maybe. Everyone else seems so girl-crazy."

"Tell you what, dude. Let's forget about chicks this weekend. We'll just hang out together and get to know each other, okay? Forget about girls. Don't get me wrong, I do like the girls, but I can do without them just fine, no problem. Okay?"

"You sure?"

"Hell yeah, bro." He got up and walked over to me. "This weekend, it's just you and me. Deal?" He held out his hand to shake on it.

I grinned and grasped his hand. "Deal."

We dug in to the food Mrs. Rainey gave us. Two sandwiches, an apple, and two slices of cake, for each of us. We saved some of the cake for later, but polished off the rest of it.

"Alright," Ziggy said. "It's Saturday night. Let's get cleaned up and see what kind of trouble we can get into. Together. Just you and me, bro." He started peeling off his clothes while I watched.

Soon he was down to his underwear. Blue briefs, with white trim. They looked so sexy. I didn't know he even owned any colored briefs. He looked up at me and grinned. "What's the matter, you never seen a grown man in underwear before?" He threw one of his socks at me and hit me in the face.

"You're not grown, wise ass." I threw his sock back at him.

He grinned and let it fall to the floor. He pulled off his underwear. "You're right about my ass, at least."

"What do you mean?"

He turned around and mooned me with his bare butt. "My ass is very wise."

"Get in the shower, you nut."

He laughed. "Okay. I'll make it quick. Then it's your turn." He disappeared into the bathroom, leaving the door open a few inches.

I picked up his blue underwear off the floor to take a closer look. Yeah, sure enough, they were mine. Ziggy was wearing *my* briefs. Well, that was fair enough, since I was wearing his.

I unpacked the clothes from my backpack while he was in the shower. Then I heard the water stop, and a minute later, Ziggy walked out of the bathroom naked, toweling his hair dry. "Your turn, dude."

I shucked my clothes, too, and got in the shower. By the time I came out, Ziggy was dressed and ready to go.

We didn't go far that night. Over to historic Beale Street, where we looked around for a while, checking out the blues clubs. Then we came back to the hotel. We had a drink at the bar in the lobby and soaked up some of the atmosphere. Then it was back to our room.

As soon as we closed the door, Ziggy plopped down on the bed. He put his hands behind his head. "What do you want to do now, bro?"

"Um, I don't know. Go to bed?"

"Dude. It's not even ten o'clock yet. You're tired already?"

"No, not really. I just thought since we have a big day ahead of us tomorrow . . . ."

"Fuck, we can sleep when we get back to St. Louis. Don't you want to party?"

"Well, sure. Okay." I smiled.

"That's the spirit." He went over to his backpack and took out a brown paper bag. "And speaking of spirits, dude, look at what I brought." He pulled a bottle of rum out and held it up for me to see. "Let's get some sodas and ice and mix up a strong one, want to?"

"Okay," I said, grinning. "Sure."

We went out to the ice machine and came back with a bucket of ice and two Cokes. Ziggy made the cocktails, and we sat down to drink and shoot the shit.

It was fun, pretending we were in high school together. It was therapeutic, too. All the stuff I kept secret back then, now I could talk about. Maybe it was like that for Ziggy, too.

"So," he said, "you're not girl-crazy, huh?"

"No, I guess not."

"How do you know?"

"It's not too hard to figure out. The other guys talk about how big Mary's titties are, or how they'd like to get into Sarah's panties, or what a knock-out Irene is. Me, I'd rather look at the guys naked in the locker room. Titties just don't do much for me, Ziggy."

"So, when you look at pictures of women in Playboy or Penthouse, you don't want to, like, feel their breasts? Touch them? Lick them?"

"It's just that I don't go nuts over them like most guys do. When I see a beautiful woman or a pretty girl somewhere, I know she's beautiful, but it doesn't even occur to me to wonder what she looks like naked."

"Oh." Ziggy looked at me, took a sip of his drink, and looked at me some more. "Yeah, okay, maybe that *is* an indication of . . . something. But like I said, you're not the only one like that. It's not as weird as you think."

"Well, I wish I knew some other guys like me. Even just one."

"You probably already do, and you just don't know it."

"I doubt it. Not the way they all talk about girls."

"You can't just go by talk. Hell, every guy on earth talks about titties, just so the other guys won't think he's different. But just because they talk about them doesn't mean they go nuts over them."

"Really?"

"Guys learn real early how to talk the talk, Josh. Even the guy who sounds more girl-crazy than anybody else might just be saying it because he doesn't want anybody to think he's different."

"Aw, no way."

"Dude, it's true."

"But that's . . . that's like lying. Taking it that far would be nuts. It doesn't make sense."

"It *does* make sense, Josh, for somebody who's afraid to be different. You're lucky. And brave. You're not so afraid to be different.

That's one thing unusual about you, bro. You're not afraid to be yourself."

"My god." Another revelation. If only I knew this when I really *was* in eleventh grade. "So, you're saying you can't believe what guys say?"

"What I'm saying is, not always. Some guys will say anything. Some of them mean it, others just say it whether they mean it or not. Girls can be the same way, I guess. But I don't understand girls as well. They think different than guys."

"Yeah, I don't understand girls at all."

"I haven't met a guy yet who does. It's like they're a different species or something."

I laughed. "I'm glad to hear somebody else say that. I thought maybe it was just me."

"It's not just you, believe me. Girls are different."

I finished off my drink, and Ziggy downed the rest of his. Then he stood up and said, "Want another one?"

"Not yet. That one really went to my head."

"Same here. I think I'm tireder than I knew."

"Do you want to go to bed?" I asked.

"Yeah, I guess we could. Might as well. If you're ready to."

"Yeah, I'm ready." We started taking off our clothes.

When I was in eleventh grade, just the thought of sleeping in the same bed with a hot-looking guy like Ziggy would have given me an instant hard-on. It wasn't any different now. Our role-playing put me right into that shy, horny, desperate frame of mind I was in constantly, back in school.

And just as I would have done in eleventh grade, I got embarrassed about my erection. Crazy, but I did. I could feel myself blushing so hard I must have been red as a beet. I would have turned away from Ziggy so he couldn't see my boner, but I had to see him strip down all the way to his briefs, I just had to.

He watched me out of the corner of his eye while he pulled off his socks and his jeans, and I knew he saw my hard dick, tenting out my briefs. Seeing him in his briefs again just made me harder. He looked up from my underwear to my face, and he saw I was blushing. "Don't be embarrassed, Josh. You've got nothing to be embarrassed about, bro."

But I was. I slipped in under the covers, still in my underwear and t-shirt, and turned facing away from him.

"Josh. It's okay. Really. So what if you got a hard on?"

"You probably think I'm a fag, now," I said. This role-playing was freaky. It really seemed real.

"I didn't say that, did I?"

"No, but it's probably what you're thinking. Only fags get boners from watching other guys undress."

"I'm not thinking anything. Maybe you're gay, maybe not. I don't care, dude. I like you either way."

"Really?"

"Really."

I turned around and looked at him. "You really mean that?"

"I really mean it. And besides, it's no big deal, getting a boner. I get boners all the time. It's part of being a guy. Look, I'm getting one now, see?"

He was, too. I looked at the outline of his big, hard cock in his underwear, and my own boner got twice as hard. I lay back down on my side, looking the other way again, even though I would have rather stared at the bulge in his briefs for another hour or two.

He got into bed and pulled the covers up over us. "You worry too much, bro. It's nothing to be ashamed of. I've slept with other guys, too, and they all get boners." He reached over and turned out the light on his side of the bed.

I lay there facing away from him, not having a clue what to say. I felt like I ought to say something, but all I could think of was, "I'm sorry."

"You're not hearing what I'm saying, Josh. There's nothing to be sorry about, dude."

"Yeah," I said, "but listen, I think it's true, Ziggy. I think I *am* a fag. I'm so embarrassed." Like I said before, this role-playing was freaky-real. I was on the verge of crying.

"Hey, hey. Who cares, Josh? If you're gay, you're gay. So what? It's not the end of the world. I still like you."

I lay there for a while, not saying anything, feeling sorry for myself, wondering if he was just saying that to be nice.

"Josh?"

"What?"

"Are you gonna turn out your light?"

I reached over and turned out the lamp.

Five minutes later, he said, "Josh?"

"What."

"Would you do me a really big favor?"

"What favor is that?"

"I'll sleep better if you come over here closer, and put your arm around me."

"No way," I said.

"What?"

"No, what I mean is, you're kidding, right?"

"No, I'm not kidding. I'll sleep better."

"For real?"

"Yeah, for real. Pretend like I'm your teddy bear, okay? Your teddy bear needs his pal Josh to hold onto him."

"You're making this up."

"No, I'm not. I really want you to. Will you? Please?"

"You sure?"

"Yes. I'll sleep better."

"Well, um, okay. If you're sure." I rolled over toward him onto my other side, and then I was right behind him. I reached over and put my arm on top of him, but I wasn't used to touching people. Not in eleventh grade, anyway. Plus I still had a hard dick.

"Get closer," he said. "Don't just put your arm on top of me. *Hold* me."

I snuggled up closer to him and wrapped my arm around his chest, holding him close.

He sighed. "That's it."

My hard dick hadn't gone down a bit, and when he wiggled his ass a little to get snug up against me, I almost shot my load. My dick was lying right in the crack of his ass. If he wiggled one more time, I would have had to get up and change my underwear.

He sighed again. "Thanks, Josh."

"No problem, Zig."

"Sweet dreams, dude."

"You, too."

It was like reliving eleventh grade all over again. Except it was different this time. This time, I found somebody who liked me for who I really am. Finally.

Sunday

WE SLEPT THE WAY WE ALWAYS DO: one of us holding the other one close, in a cuddle. We stayed that way all night. It was a bigger bed, but we hardly used the extra space.

When morning came we lingered in bed until finally, hunger got us going. Once we were up, we were eager to get out and see the sights.

We went to the Lorraine Motel, where Martin Luther King was killed. Then we drove by the train station, and the Orpheum Theater. And we drove past Sun Studio, where Elvis and Carl Perkins and Howlin' Wolf and Roy Orbison and a bunch of other famous artists recorded music.

Then Ziggy wanted to see Graceland, so we drove by there, too.

Then we stopped at the Buntyn Cafe for a hearty brunch, including some of their excellent homemade rolls. We stuffed ourselves and then we got back to sightseeing.

We drove farther east, to the Japanese Garden, which Ziggy really liked. He said he could stay in a place like that for hours, deep in thought.

When we left the garden we talked about what to do next. Ziggy said he'd like to see some of the places I used to hang out. I told him we'd already seen some of them, like for instance Overton Park.

"How about that place you went to meet guys, before you were old enough for the bars? Is that place still around?"

"The adult bookstore? Yeah, it's still there. Why, you want to see it?"

"Yeah!" He grinned. "I want to take a look at your hook-up place."

"It's not far from here. We can go, if you want to."

"Yeah, let's go. I wanna see where your hormones raged."

"Oh, well, jeez. I didn't go that much, after I met Fred. But before that, I went fairly often. I had some good times there."

"Cool. I want to see it."

So we got in the car and headed out Summer Avenue.

"Zig, I don't want you to think I spent all my time here. I probably didn't go more than once a week, tops. Sometimes way less."

"Only when you were horny, huh?" He smiled.

I laughed. "Well, that goes without saying. But if I'd gone every time I was horny, I'd have been there every day. And then it wouldn't have been so special."

We reached the store and I parked in the lot.

"This is gonna be cool, bro. Seeing where you used to hang out. Who knows? If I'd been living in Memphis, we might have seen each other here. Stranger things have happened."

I put the gearshift into park. "What a thought. I can picture it, Zig. You come into the store, just to look at the girly magazines, and I see you and, naturally, I just about melt into a puddle because you are so incredibly hot looking, and I try my best to let you know I'm interested . . . ."

"And I'm looking at the naked women in the magazines, and then I notice this cute little shy guy, following me around everywhere in the store . . . ."

"And then you nod at me, just to be polite, and go back to looking at the magazines, and god, you've got a huge hard on, and you're not the slightest bit embarrassed about it . . . ."

"I keep on looking at one magazine after another, and I see you smiling at me, and staring at my hard-on, and I begin to wonder if you really want what I think you want . . . ."

"Oh, jeez, Zig. I'm gonna come right here in my pants if we keep talking like this. Let's go inside." I turned the engine off. "You wanted to go inside, right?"

"Oh, definitely, dude. I want to see this place inside and out. Lead the way." So we walked in through the front door. Ziggy looked around and said, "Where is everybody? There were at least eight or ten cars parked outside."

"Oh, they're back in the video booths, probably."

"How can you meet people when everybody's inside a booth?"

"Well, let's get some quarters and I'll explain how it works."

I led Ziggy to the back, into the video area. A couple of guys were hanging out back there, one a little younger than us and the other in his forties. We found an empty corner over near the Coke machine, and we talked quietly while we watched what went on.

I told Ziggy, "Sometimes you can meet someone out where the magazines and videos are, but usually they don't want to talk out there. I don't know why. Maybe they're afraid someone they know will walk in and see them with a stranger."

"So, if a guy wants to meet up with somebody and talk, he comes back here to the backroom?"

"Well, some guys will talk back here, yeah. But actually, there's a lot that goes on without talking."

"Oh." He thought about that. "Okay, so how does that work?"

"Well, the best way is eye contact, I guess. You see somebody you want, you look at him and try to catch his eye. Like that young guy here has been doing. You saw him, right? Walking back and forth, smiling at you?"

"That guy is trying to hook up with me?"

"Yeah. No doubt about it."

Ziggy looked at the guy, the guy smiled at Ziggy, and Ziggy quickly looked back at me. "Jesus. I think you're right."

"Anyway, so, if you want a guy, you get his attention with eye contact. If he wants you, he'll look back at you. Not just once; more than once. You know how that works. Or, yeah, sometimes you do say something. Anything. Just to break the ice. Then, after you both know that you're both interested, you find a booth."

"The two of you go into a booth together?"

"Well, sometimes you do, yeah, and sometimes not. If you do share a booth, usually one of you goes in first and leaves the door unlocked, and then, like, ten or fifteen seconds later, the other guy goes in. That way it's not so obvious what's going on."

"Okay, so, if the two of you go into a booth together, then you talk?"

"Maybe, maybe not. Sometimes you don't need to talk. It depends on whether you just want sex, or more. Me, I was always on the lookout for getting to know the guy, so I was always willing to talk. I wanted sex, but I also wanted a buddy. Ideal would have been a friend I could have sex with on a regular basis. Even better if we could get together somewhere else besides these tiny little booths."

"Did that ever happen?"

"Hardly ever. It's like, guys who come here don't really want to know anybody who would come to a place like this."

Ziggy burst out laughing. "That sounds like something Groucho Marx would say."

"I know. But it's still easy to think that way. I've caught myself, once or twice, thinking that way about somebody. Then I realize, of course, *I'm* one of the people who come to a place like this."

"Yeah. Hell, I guess it's human nature."

"Silly monkeys, aren't we? Anyway, yeah, a couple of times I did make friends with guys here, but it didn't last too long either time. But I never gave up trying. Sex is great, but sex with a buddy is even better."

"I can relate to that," Ziggy said. "I really like the sexy stuff you and I do together."

"You and me both."

"What are these booths like inside? Is there even *room* for two people?"

"Come on, I'll show you." Ziggy followed me along the little hallway and I found a booth that was empty. He followed me in. I locked the door, fed some quarters to the machine, and a movie started playing.

We sat down beside each other, so close that we were touching. It was either that or press against the walls.

"There's not a whole lot of extra room," he said.

"No, but it's enough. One time I saw *three* guys fit into one of these, believe it or not."

"Three? In one of these booths? That must have been a trip."

"Yeah, I wish I could have watched whatever they were doing. They were in there a long time, fifteen minutes at least. They came out looking like they'd been in an oven, but they were smiling."

Ziggy watched the movie playing. There was a guy and a girl; the guy was licking her in her private parts. Some other guy was in it, too, peeking through a doorway, watching all the action.

Ziggy seemed fascinated. He saw me looking at him. "I saw an old eight-millimeter stag-party film once," he said. "One of the guys at work had me over when his wife was out of town. But it wasn't anywhere near this good." He stared at the screen, watching the action.

"That's the only one? You've never seen any other porn flicks?"

"Nope. This is the first time I've ever been inside one of these booths. Fuck, it sure is warm in here. Don't they have air conditioning?"

"Take your shirt off, Zig." I smiled. "You won't hear me complain."

"I think I will." He pulled his t-shirt off over his head, wiped his armpits, and continued watching the video. He had a nice big hard-on in his pants, and I did, too, from looking at his. He glanced over at me and saw me looking at his bulge, and he smiled. He saw my hard dick, too. He said, "We might just have to take these big boys out and whack off, bro."

"Sounds good to me," I said.

He unbuttoned his jeans, pulled down his zipper, and uncovered his beautiful, rigid cock. He looked at it, and then he looked at me and grinned. He looked back at his cock and then he pushed his jeans and briefs down so it could stand up free and unfettered. He spit in his hand and wrapped it around his dick and gently stroked. Then he turned to me and said, "Come on, dude, take yours out, too."

"Okay." He watched me pull my jeans down and push the band of my underwear down below my balls, and he grinned when my dick stood up, high and hard.

I wrapped my fingers around it and squeezed. Zig saw me do that and went back to his own cock, stroking. We watched the movie, but I think we were watching each other more.

All of a sudden Ziggy said, "Jesus Christ Almighty!" He frantically pulled his underwear and jeans up. "Josh, there's a fucking hole in the wall, and somebody's waving a finger at us! Jesus! Let's get the fuck out of here!" He grabbed his t-shirt and unlocked the latch.

"Wait, Zig." I pulled my pants up; as soon as he saw I was decent he opened the door and he stood out there, shirt in his hand, waiting for me. When I came out he started down the hallway, and he made sure I was following him. "Zig, wait up a minute."

He didn't stop until he was all the way down at the other end of the hall, past the booths, down at the Coke machine. When he got there he turned around and looked at me, still wide eyed. "Jesus. Did you see that? Fucking incredible." He pulled his t-shirt on over his head.

"Zig," I said, "I am so sorry. I should have told you."

"You knew there was a hole in the wall?"

"I didn't know about that one, no. The last time I was in that booth, it didn't have any holes. I'm sorry. I should have checked. It's been a while since I've been here." Seeing how upset he was, I was starting to feel bad.

"Christ. That totally freaked me out."

"Zig, I'm sorry."

"Aw, don't worry about it. You didn't know."

"I should have checked."

Ziggy reached into his pocket for some change. "You want a soda?"

"Yeah, sure."

He bought a Coke for each of us, and we stood there, drinking. "So, what's up with the holes? People put them there to watch?"

"Well, I guess people do watch through them, but that's not what they're mainly for."

"No?"

"No."

He just looked at me.

"Zig," I said, "haven't you ever heard of glory holes?"

"Well, I heard a guy at the bar one time say he put his cock into the glory hole. I thought he was talking about somebody's pussy or asshole."

"Nope. He was talking about a hole in a wall, Zig, one that's big enough to put your dick through."

"Jesus, why would somebody want to do that?"

"Think about it."

"I'd be afraid somebody would chop it off or something."

"Remember I told you, when two guys here make eye contact, and decide they want each other, sometimes they go into a booth together?"

"Yeah, sure."

"Well, sometimes they don't. Sometimes they go into two booths that are next to each other."

Ziggy looked at me. "Uh, two booths that have a hole in the wall between them?"

"Now you've got the idea."

"Oh. Wow."

"Yeah."

"They fuck through the hole?"

"Well, I guess sometimes they fuck, but mostly, it's, you know, blow jobs."

"Oh, wow."

"Yeah."

"But you can't even see each other," he said. "I mean, okay, maybe you can know who's on the other side of the wall, but still, you can't see each other while you're doing it."

"Yeah, that's right."

"That sounds so weird."

"It's part of the attraction of it, actually. A lot of guys think it's really erotic. It's not like anything else, that's for sure."

"I'll bet."

"And sometimes, you *don't* know who's on the other side of the wall. All you can see is his dick, and maybe his belly and his thighs, enough to get an idea of what kind of body he has, but you really don't know who it is.

"It could be your next-door neighbor, or your teacher, or that hot guy you work with, or hell, it could even be your brother. Or the jerk down the street who's such an asshole, but has such a nice body. And if you don't know who he is, he probably doesn't know who you are, either."

"Fuck," Ziggy said. "I had no idea this kind of stuff went on."

"That's what the finger through the hole was all about. Whoever that was, he wanted you to put your dick through, Zig. So he could suck you off."

"A complete stranger wanted to suck me off?"

"Yeah. And when he got through with you he might have done me, too, likely as not."

"Jesus."

I looked at Ziggy's crotch and was surprised to see that he had a raging hard on. "Zig, something tells me this is really turning you on."

"I can't help it," he said. "Yeah, like gangbusters. Crazy, huh?"

"No, not crazy. I like it, too, sometimes. Glory hole sex is really hot."

"My cock is stiff as a board."

"I'm horny, too."

Ziggy said, "You know what? I wanna try it!"

Chapter 23

A Different Kind of Connection

I WAS ASTOUNDED. "You want to try it?" Surprised that Ziggy, who is basically a straight guy, would even consider doing something like that.

Then I remembered, half the guys who come into that place are straight. That's what makes it so interesting. They go inside the booths alone, knowing no one can really say with certainty what they do in there—except the guy in the next booth over, of course.

I was disappointed. Disappointed that Ziggy was gonna let some stranger suck him off before I got a chance to do it. He was my pal, though, my buddy. If it would make him happy, then by god, I thought he should do it.

"Do you want me to wait here? While you go back there?"

"What are you talking about?" he said.

"You want to try it, you said."

"Yeah, I do." He smiled. "You okay with that?"

"Sure, Zig, if that's what you want."

"Cool! Well, come on, then." He grinned.

"You want me to come with you?"

"Dude. Of course I want you to come with me."

"Okay." I felt a little better then. We'd find some stranger to do both of us. Maybe that younger guy was still there.

Ziggy walked down the hall and I followed right behind him. "Wait," he said. "How many quarters you have?"

"Um . . . ." I pulled out what I had left. "Six."

"We'll need way more than that. Wait here, I'll get more."

I stayed there and tried to decide which booth would be our best bet.

A few minutes later he came back. "Here. This ought to last us a while." He handed me at least ten dollars in quarters. "I don't want to run out in the middle of something good," he said, smiling.

He looked inside the booth we were in before, then he went to the booth beside it. The one where the guy who wiggled his finger had been. It was empty, now. He looked at me, grinned, and went on in.

I started to follow him into the booth, but when he saw me coming in behind him he said, "What are you doing?"

"What do you mean, what am I doing? You wanted me to come with you, didn't you?"

"Yeah, but not in the same booth!"

"I don't understand." I moved closer to him and whispered, "You wanted to find out what it's like for a stranger to suck you off, right?"

He whispered back, "Yeah, but not a *real* stranger, for god's sake. Get in the next booth, and we'll pretend you and I are strangers, okay?"

"Oh, okay." He waved me over to the other booth and closed the door to his. I heard him lock it. It was just starting to sink in, what he wanted to do. I hurried into the next booth and locked my door. This was really going to be freaky, but freaky in an excellent way!

I put some quarters into the slot and then I sat down. I looked through the hole in the wall and Ziggy was still feeding quarters into his machine. Jeez, he planned on being here for a while. I got up again and fed in some more quarters. By the time I heard him stop, I'd spent every last quarter I had. This was gonna buy us a *lot* of time.

I sat down again, and he sat down, too. He changed his channel a few times, until he found a movie he liked. Then he squeezed his hard cock through his pants.

I figured he was watching me through the hole, like I was watching him, so I rubbed my hard dick inside my jeans. I heard him say, "Yeah!" He immediately started giving his dick more attention. Stroking it, pushing the fabric down to show the outline of it.

We kept that up for a minute or so and then I unbuttoned my jeans. I stuck my hand inside my pants for a better feel of my cock. As soon as Ziggy saw me do that, he did the same thing. He fondled that beautiful boner of his inside his open jeans.

I pulled my zipper down all the way and spread my jeans to show him the bulge of my cock inside my white briefs. I rubbed it through the fabric. I heard Ziggy say, "Oh, yeah. Stroke that monster."

He opened his pants, exposing his underwear—a pair of *my* briefs, again—and, of course, he showed off the thick boner inside. I said, "So damn hot. Look at that big dick!"

We rubbed our hard-ons for a minute or two. Then I pulled the waistband of my underwear out to look at the skin of my shaft. It was still hidden, though, from Ziggy's view. Ziggy said, "Yeah, come on, dude, let that puppy free."

Zig lifted the front of his briefs the same way, exposing his hard cock and balls to himself but still out of my sight. I could imagine that awesome dick of his. I could picture it in my mind, but I wanted to see it for real. "Fuck," I said, "I want to see what you've got!"

It was so cool. We both had stiff boners, but we took our time, not rushing it.

I reached into my underwear and fondled my stiff dick, and then I thought, *What the hell, it's time to show some flesh.* I pushed my underwear down under my balls and let my hard dick stand up straight, in plain view. I heard Ziggy say, "Oh, man, what a fucking beauty!"

Once he got a good view of mine he went ahead and freed his up, too. He pushed his jeans and underwear down to his knees and his stiff cock was out in the open. In the process he ended up with his bare ass resting on the seat. His beautiful, bare ass.

I quickly pushed my jeans and briefs down, too, and then we were totally exposed, with nothing between us but a flimsy wall and a nice big open hole to see through.

It was awesome. My dick was so hard it could just about get up and walk on its own. Ziggy looked just as excited. He pushed his jeans and briefs farther down, all the way to his feet, and spread his legs open wide. "So damn sexy," I said. I looked at his rigid cock pointing up and said, "Fuck, I want that."

I pushed my pants to my feet, too. Then Ziggy pulled his t-shirt off. "My god," I said. "You're beautiful, buddy." He was almost completely naked now, and I loved it. I took off my shirt, too, but it was Ziggy's skin I wanted to touch. He sat there bare ass, wagging his cock back and forth, knowing how much I enjoyed watching it. I don't know if he knew he was torturing me, but he was. I said, "I want it."

"You want it?"

"Yeah. Really bad."

"What do you want to do with it?"

"I wanna suck it! Please, let me suck it. I'll make it feel good. You'll like it, I promise."

He waved it again a couple of times, and then he whispered, "You sure?"

"Yes. Please." I stuck my fingers through the hole, motioning for him to bring it to me. "Please."

He stood up and turned toward me, gently stroking it. I stared intently, hardly able to stand waiting any longer. "Come on," I said. "Let me suck it."

He stepped closer to the hole, almost within reach of my fingers. He was definitely torturing me, but I didn't mind. It was all in fun, and in pleasure, of course. Then he stepped closer, close enough for me to touch the head of his cock. I felt it, gently. The skin was so soft, and yet so full and stiff, and it was already leaking pre-cum.

I pulled my fingers back and whispered, "Put it through the hole."

He leaned forward, carefully, holding his cock to aim it, and gradually approached the hole. Slowly, so slowly, he moved forward, and finally the head of his cock came through and was on my side of the wall. I started stroking it again. He didn't stop—he kept moving forward, putting more and more of his shaft through the hole. I stroked the underside of it, gently caressing the silky smooth skin, even as it moved closer toward me.

I intended to do everything I could to make this the most enjoyable experience ever for Ziggy. I knew this might be my only chance. It might be the only time he ever allowed me to do this. I wanted so much for him to enjoy it. And, as he liked to say, the more he enjoyed it, the more I would. That's just the way it works.

I used every trick in the book, everything I knew about making a guy feel good. I knew he expected it to go in my mouth, but I knew I could take my time. He wouldn't stop now, not till I got him to shoot his cum one way or another.

So I wasn't in a hurry. First I fondled and stroked him, ran the back of my fingers gently along the underside of his cock, getting him really hard, making him feel great, but letting him wonder when the hell I would finally put my lips around it.

Then I started licking. I licked the shaft, and I heard him say, "Jesus!" I licked the head, and I used the tip of my tongue to tickle that sensitive spot underneath. He moaned. I licked the entire length of the shaft, then I held it and admired it a while. It was simply beautiful. As far as I was concerned, Ziggy's cock was perfect.

There would be plenty of other times when I could stare at it again. Right now I wanted to make him feel better than he'd ever felt before. So I gave it one more long lick, and then I started using my lips. First I kissed the head, then I nibbled the other parts of his dick with my lips. He said, "Oh my fucking god."

I put my mouth back on his cock head, but this time I let the head go inside, wrapping my lips snugly around it just below the ridge of the head. That's when he really started moaning. I moved slowly down the shaft, taking it deeper into my mouth, keeping my lips snug against his cock. I wrapped my tongue underneath. Then I drew back, slowly, and then forward again. I heard Ziggy gasp.

His cock got extra hard and stiff. I didn't want him to come yet, so I eased off a bit. I took it out of my mouth, licked the shaft a few times, and then I gently reached for his balls. The hole in the wall was big enough for cock and balls both to fit, so I pulled them through and held the sac by the bottom and started licking his nuts.

That got him moaning again, so I guessed I was doing something right. I licked his balls until they were thoroughly wet and then I went back to his cock. I gave it more of the same attention I'd given it before. Once again, when he got extra big and stiff, I eased off. This time I licked underneath his balls. I took one and then the other inside my mouth gently, and hummed. He gasped again. Then I went back to licking below his balls. I went further and licked behind them, right up next to his asshole. Then he was groaning.

Eventually I moved back to his cock, repeating all the stuff I'd done before, but this time I figured it was time to get serious. I had his shaft inside my mouth, and I moved my lips and tongue up and down, just like before, but this time I did it in a steady rhythm. I went forward until the head of his cock pressed against the back of my throat, then I pulled back with my tongue and my lips, until only the head was inside. Then forward again, back and forward again, in a regular rhythm.

I could tell he was getting close again because the head of his dick was extra big and his whole cock was extra stiff, but this time I wanted him to come. If we'd been at home, or in the hotel room, I might have made it last even longer, but Ziggy was ready now, and I wanted it as bad as he did, so I kept up the rhythm. He moaned, non-stop.

I could taste his pre-cum, flowing steady now. He was breathing heavy. I relaxed my throat and let his cock go deeper, as deep as it could go. I flexed my throat and then he said, "Uuuhhhh! Coming, Josh! Uuuhhh! Ahhh! Ahhhhhhh!"

His hips jerked and he pressed up flat against the wall, his cock pushed as far as it would go inside my mouth, and I felt the first sudden spurt of cum launch into the back of my throat.

I pressed the curve of my tongue around the underside of his cock and I quickly slid up and down his shaft, so he would have the best orgasm ever. And this way I'd be sure to taste it. And taste it I did. Spurt after spurt flowed into my mouth, with him moaning the whole time. It was sweet and a little salty and it couldn't have tasted better if it was honey. It was Ziggy's cum, and it was shooting out of his cock straight into my mouth. I was so happy I almost cried.

I could barely swallow fast enough. He must have shot at least nine or ten spurts before he finally slowed down, and even then his cock was still pulsing.

When he was finished, I took my mouth off his cock and started licking it clean. I was extra careful with the head—I knew how sensitive guys can get after we shoot our loads, especially with an uncut cock—but I wanted to do what I could to extend the pleasure for him.

I kept giving his dick my loving attention, until he hesitatingly moved back a little. Then I carefully supported his cock and balls with my hand while he stepped back and withdrew from the glory hole.

He plopped down with a sigh and said, "Incredible." He leaned back, like he was exhausted.

I stood up, but he said, "Wait, Josh. Sit down a minute while I rest up, okay?"

So I sat back down and played with my own dick. I hadn't come yet. I knew my balls would hurt all day if I didn't come, so I started jacking off while I sat there. As soon as Ziggy saw what I was doing he said, "No, Josh, don't. Let me do it, bro. Just give me a minute, okay? I want to do it. Let me get you off."

We sat there next to each other for another minute or so, and then he whispered, "Okay. Put it through, man."

He wouldn't get any argument from me. If he wanted to jack me off instead of me doing it, that was super with me. It would be like a gift from the gods. I stood up and moved over to the hole.

"That's it," he said. "Let me have that monster cock."

I slowly put the head through the hole, and inched my way forward until I was all the way up against the wall. Ziggy took hold of my dick and it seemed like he was examining it. He moved it up and down, side to side, like he was looking at every inch of it. He gently squeezed it, stroked it, and squeezed it some more. I didn't know exactly what he was doing, but I liked it.

"Beautiful," I heard him say. "Fucking beautiful." He started stroking it, gently, slowly.

I could relate to what he was doing. When you're playing with a dick through a glory hole, all your attention is focused on the dick. It's like you've never seen a dick really well until you see it that way. It becomes this thing you want to look at, play with, and examine every inch of. And then, make it come.

Ziggy stopped, but he was still holding it. I felt him switch hands, holding my dick by its head now. He could do anything he wanted, as far as I was concerned. All he had to do was keep doing what he was doing, and I was bound to shoot my load. It was such a thrill to have Ziggy handling my dick.

I felt him hold my dick up high, and then I got the surprise of my life. I felt his tongue lick the bottom of my cock!

He licked it once, and then he paused. Half a minute went by. Then he licked it again. And again. I was just about delirious. Then he switched hands again, and I felt his tongue on my dick head.

My body shivered uncontrollably. Ziggy was licking my cock. I could hardly believe it. He paused again, then he went back to stroking it gently with his hand. Then he stopped again, for half minute.

Then I felt something warm and wet surround the head of my cock, and I said, "Zig!" He had my cock in his mouth! He kept it there, and pressed his lips around the shaft. Ziggy had my cock inside his mouth, using his lips to make me feel good.

"Zig," I whispered, "I'm gonna come if you keep that up." But he just kept on going. Now he was moving his mouth farther down, sliding his lips along the shaft, and pressing his tongue underneath. "Zig," I said, "I mean it, I'm gonna come if you keep doing that."

He made a noise somewhere between a moan and a hum and went on, sliding his lips and tongue up and down my cock in a steady motion.

I knew what he was doing. I sucked him off, so now he was returning the favor. I wasn't so sure he would like it, though, if I actually came in his mouth.

I held back as long as I possibly could, but it wasn't for long. This was probably the first time he'd ever had a dick in his mouth, barring that quick clean up in the highway restroom. But being a man, he sure as hell knew how to make a dick feel good. What he was doing with his lips would have been enough as it was, but using his tongue and lips together was driving me crazy.

"Zig," I said, louder this time, "I swear I'm gonna come any time now, no kidding." I shivered again, and I know he felt it, because my whole body shook. But he kept moving his mouth up and down my cock, and now he was flicking his tongue under my shaft from one side to the other, like he was trying to wrap his tongue all the way around it.

I couldn't take any more. I felt my cum building up and then another shiver ran through my body. "Zig!" I said it really loud this time. "Zig, I'm coming! Right now!" He just seemed to get more serious about keeping his mouth on my cock.

Another shiver, and then my first spurt of cum shot into his mouth. I gave him fair warning. He wanted my cum, and he was getting it. One mind-blowing spurt after another.

I felt him swallow, and I heard it, too. He kept his mouth on my dick as my balls emptied, doing his best to take everything I gave him. That was my longest orgasm ever. And the best, too. One spurt after another, while Ziggy moved his tongue up and down my dick. Amazing.

And then when I was done, he cleaned me up, too, just like I had done to him. Incredible. I withdrew slowly and I sat down, totally spent. Ziggy was still kneeling down, looking through the hole, smiling. "How'd I do?" he said.

I was just about speechless. "Zig, that was incredible. Just incredible." I felt totally drained. And gratified.

He stood and pulled his underwear and jeans up. When I saw him getting dressed I figured I'd better do the same. I couldn't imagine us doing anything else together just then, not at least until we recharged, and those booths were starting to feel awfully small. Yeah, time to go.

We emerged from our booths and looked at each other, full of big grins.

Ziggy said, "You ready?"

"Sure," I said. "Let's go."

We left the video area, stepped into the brightly lit part of the store, and headed out the front door.

When we got to my car Ziggy said, "Hold on, I'm gonna run back in for something. It'll only take me a minute." He came out again a few minutes later, and we got back on Summer Avenue, heading back into Memphis.

"What'd you get?"

"Lube."

We drove on for a couple of minutes in silence.

"Zig," I said, "you surprised the hell out of me in there, I hope you know that."

He laughed. "I surprised me, too. But what the hell, Josh. Life's too short to stay in a rut your whole life. That whole scene in there was making my cock super hard, so I had to try it."

"How'd you like me sucking you off?"

"Oh, man. I wish we had done that sooner. That was fucking incredible!"

"You liked it that much? Really?"

"Hell yes! Jesus. You can suck me off anytime you want, bro. I mean it, Josh. Anytime you want. I had no fucking idea a blowjob could feel so good."

"Zig, you really mean that?"

"Hell yes I mean it!"

I was so happy, my eyes started filling up with tears. It was like chains were lifted off my shoulders. "Okay," I said. "You got it."

"Hell yes. That was incredible."

"So were you," I said. "You didn't have to do that, you know."

"I wanted to."

"Yeah, I know. 'Fair's fair.' But really, you didn't have to do that. Sucking you off is plenty enough to make me happy."

"I didn't do it just to be fair. I wanted to. I wanted to try it. Hell, seeing how much you enjoyed doing it to me, I *had* to try it. Just to find out what I was missing."

"How did you like it?"

"It was hot. My cock got hard again while I was sucking you, thinking about how good I was making you feel. I was really getting into it. Did I do okay? I didn't scrape you with my teeth or anything?"

"It was fantastic, Zig. That was your first time ever, doing that?"

"First time, bro."

"Well, yeah, that's what I thought, but you did really great. I guess it's true what they say; guys know better how to give head because we know what feels good."

"I'll say one thing, Josh, you sure as hell do shoot a lot of cum. Surprised the hell out of me. I could hardly swallow fast enough. Jesus."

"Sorry."

"No, that's okay. I just wasn't expecting so much, that's all."

"I hope it didn't taste bitter or anything. Did it?"

"No, not at all. It tasted good."

"Okay."

We drove on in silence for a while. I felt like a million dollars. Ziggy said I could suck him off anytime I want. He liked it *that* much. I had a best buddy who was closer than a brother, and now he was going to let me get him off, too. I couldn't imagine how I could be any happier.

"Zig" I said, "just remember, you don't have to do it to me, when I do it to you, okay?"

"We'll see."

"Seriously. I'll feel much better doing it if I know you won't feel obligated to return the favor. You can understand that, can't you?"

"Um, yeah, I can understand how that would work. Okay. I promise I won't feel obligated."

"Great. Thanks."

"But we'll make sure you get off, too, one way or another, okay?"

"Okay," I said. I was grinning. I was so happy.

—

WE WERE HUNGRY. We returned to the hotel, then we walked over to the Rendezvous restaurant to eat some Memphis barbecue. Pork ribs, red beans and rice. Ziggy raved about it.

310

We took a stroll down Beale Street, then we headed back to the hotel. When we reached the lobby Zig said, "We still haven't seen the ducks do their walk."

"Tomorrow morning's our last chance," I said. "Eleven a.m."

"When's check-out time?"

"Uh, same time."

"Could be a problem, dude."

"All they really do is get out of the elevator and walk down a red carpet to the fountain."

"It wouldn't break my heart to miss that," he said.

"Me neither." So we made plans to check out early, around 10 a.m.

When we reached our floor Zig said, "Eleventh grade again?"

"Yeah, definitely," I said. "If you still want to."

"Oh, sure, I'm enjoying it."

We walked into our room, and suddenly we became four years younger. Students in high school again.

"Fuck, I need a shower," Ziggy said. "You want to go first?"

"No, go ahead. I can wait."

"Alright." I watched him strip to his underwear. He knew I was watching. "You ought to take a picture," he said, grinning. "It'll last longer."

"Oh, jeez. I'm sorry." Caught.

"Hey, I was just kidding, dude. I don't mind you looking. Guys look sexy in just their underwear, don't you think?"

"Yeah." Still, I felt embarrassed.

"Dude, listen. You gotta understand, being sexy is a *good* thing. And so is *looking* at sexy people. Don't ever be embarrassed about looking, okay?"

"Thanks, Ziggy. I wish everybody felt that way."

"Well, you just have to be subtle about it. It helps to know who likes to be looked at and who doesn't. Me, I don't ever mind somebody looking at me. Let 'em. But some guys do get self-conscious about it. Either way it's not something to be ashamed of, wanting to look. Hell, I look at guys in the locker room all the time."

"You do?"

"Yeah. Are you kidding? Sometimes I get a hard on from looking at the guys." He rubbed his dick, and it looked like it was growing bigger. "It's happened to me lots of times. Especially in the showers."

"God," I said. "That's my biggest fear, the showers. I'd be so embarrassed, I think I'd just about die. Sometimes I don't even take a shower after P.E. 'cause I'm afraid I'll get a hard on."

"Dude, all the guys get a boner in the showers sooner or later. It's part of being a guy. Jesus, you see all those cocks flopping around, and all those bare asses, you can't help thinking about fucking, and when you think about fucking, *boinng*, there you go. Boner. No big deal. If anybody says anything about it, I just say something like, 'Hey, a stud like me, it's part of the territory, dude. Just thinking about the chick I fucked last night. Why, you want some of this?' That usually shuts them up."

"Wow."

Ziggy reached down and squeezed his dick inside his briefs again and rubbed it, like it was the most natural thing in the world to do in front of another guy. And now I knew he was getting hard. Hell, it was obvious. And he kept his hand on it, squeezing it while he was talking.

"When somebody gets a woody in the showers," he said, "we end up laughing about it. The guys start cracking jokes. It's no big deal."

"Really?"

"Sure. Hell, sometimes it starts a chain reaction. Another guy gets a boner from looking at the first one, and then somebody else does, and pretty soon everybody's got wood. And then we're all comparing. We make fun of the guy who's got the biggest dick for being such a freak — like we're not all jealous of him! Hell, it's all in good fun." He was still fondling his cock through his briefs.

"Wow. All this time I was afraid people would call me queer if they saw me in there with a hard on."

"Well, I'm not saying there wouldn't be some asshole who might call you queer, but those kinds of guys are jerks. They have problems of their own, so they take it out on other people. Nobody pays much attention to guys like that. Hell, I've been called queer a couple of times myself. I tell them, 'You wish.' Or, 'In your dreams.'"

"Really?"

"Yeah. No big deal. Hey, I'm telling you, you shy guys miss all the fun sometimes."

"I guess so." Jeez, he was still squeezing his boner.

"Anyway, dude, I'm getting into the shower." He stripped off his underwear and walked nude into the bathroom, hard-on and all, leaving the door open a few inches. Then he came back out, stood there buck naked with his big boner defying gravity, and said, "You don't mind if I leave the door open a bit, do you? It gets so steamy in there."

God, he looked beautiful. I wanted to touch him all over. "No, I don't mind."

"Okay." He walked back into the bathroom, leaving the door wide open, and turned on the shower.

Was he inviting me to watch? I couldn't tell. I wanted to, but hell, I didn't want to act creepy. This role-playing was something else. Here I was worrying about invading Zig's privacy, but just a few hours earlier we were as intimate with each other as two people can be.

I sat down in one of the chairs and picked up something to read. A few minutes later, the shower stopped. He opened the shower curtain and stepped out. His cock was still half-hard. Maybe he knew I'd be watching. He stood there right in my line of sight while he dried himself off.

Then he came out of the bathroom, still naked as a jaybird, toweling his hair. He said, "You're turn, Josh." He went and stood in front of the mirror, giving me a great view of his beautiful butt and his big dick, too.

By the time I was done with my shower, he was completely dressed. I dried off and got dressed, too. "Are we going somewhere?"

"You want to?"

"If you want to," I said. "We're on our own tonight, aren't we?"

"Yeah, no dinners, no speeches, no workshops, not until tomorrow at least," he said.

"What did you have in mind?"

"Well, we haven't been up to the roof yet. I thought we could check it out."

"Oh, yeah! Cool. Let me put some shoes on and we'll go."

"When we get back we can make some drinks. There's still plenty of rum left."

"Excellent. I'm definitely up for that," I said.

So we took a look around on top of the Peabody Hotel. There were great views of Memphis from up there. Beautiful at night. And the Skyway Ballroom was there, a popular place for dances with live music all the way back since the twenties.

On the way back in we raided the ice and Coke machines and then, back in the room, kicked off our shoes. We were ready to settle in and get tipsy. We made drinks and then Zig surprised me again and pulled out a joint, so we smoked that, too—in the bathroom, with the fan on and the door closed, so the smell wouldn't give us away.

One drink and one joint later, we both had an excellent buzz. It was too early to go to bed, of course. We didn't have to get up early, anyway.

So I asked him, "What do you want to do?"

Ziggy reached into his backpack and pulled out a deck of cards. He held them up to show me. "Wanna?"

"Yeah! Great idea."

"Okay. You want to play on the bed, or on the floor?"

"The floor's good. The bed's too soft for cards."

"Yeah, they'd go everywhere."

We sat cross-legged on the floor, facing each other. Ziggy shuffled the cards.

"What do you want to play?" he asked.

"I'm flexible. Hearts, Spades, Rummy, Poker, whatever. You might have to refresh my memory on the rules, though. Unless we play Poker. I know draw poker."

"Let's play Poker, then," he said.

"You have any change?" But as soon as I said that, I realized what we were going to do.

"No," he said, "not a dime. You?"

"No, me neither. Uh, maybe we'll have to play something else, then. Poker's no fun without anything to bet."

And Zig's next line was . . . "I know what we could do."

"What?"

"Dude, we could bet our clothes."

Chapter 24
PLAYING THE CARDS RIGHT

"STRIP POKER?" I couldn't help but smile. He remembered. Ziggy remembered that I wanted to play this.

"Yeah! One piece of clothing, each hand," he said. "That'll be the bet. The first guy to lose all his clothes has to kiss the other guy's ass." Ziggy grinned.

This was going to be fun. And sexy. "Okay," I said, "you're on." I couldn't stop smiling. "But you better get ready to kiss my butt, 'cause I'm gonna beat your ass." Really, though, I didn't care who won, as long as we both ended up naked.

"We'll see about that," he said. He shuffled the cards and let me cut the deck, then he dealt them out. "Five card draw, nothing wild."

We picked up our cards and looked them over. The bet was already determined, of course. All we had to do was draw cards once, and then we show our hands.

Ziggy won the first hand. He laughed. "We'll just see who has to kiss ass."

"We've got a long way to go, my friend." I took off one of my socks and then I gathered up the cards. I shuffled, Ziggy cut, and I dealt.

Ziggy won that hand, too. "Alright, no sweat," I said. I took off my other sock. "Your luck can't hold out forever."

I won the next hand, and Ziggy lost a sock. Then Ziggy won, and my t-shirt came off.

He chuckled as he gathered up the cards. "You're losing, dude. You're already half-naked."

"Game's not over yet."

Ziggy dealt, we picked up our cards, and this time, Ziggy lost. And there went his other sock. Damn, his feet were sexy.

He saw me looking at them. "You like my feet, huh?"

"Fuck you," I said, smiling, as I cheerfully dealt the next hand.

"It's okay. Feet are sexy." He looked through his cards, frowning. He drew three cards, but it didn't help. He lost the hand, again. He pulled his t-shirt over his head.

"Okay," I said, "now we're even-steven. But not for long."

Ziggy gathered up the cards. "That's right. You'll be naked before you know it." He shuffled the deck and dealt.

My hand looked good, but Ziggy frowned. Sure enough, he lost again, third time in a row. "Jesus. What the fuck!" He stood up and unbuttoned his jeans.

Closely I watched as he unzipped his fly and slowly pulled off his pants. He was almost nude, now—all he had on was his underwear. He reached down inside and rearranged his hard cock before he sat down again.

As I gathered up the cards and shuffled, I studied every bulging inch of his briefs. He saw me looking, again. "You like what you see?"

I was starting to blush, but what the hell. "Yeah. I do. You're a good-looking guy, Zig. All over." My dick was hard.

"Aw, I'm just average. I'll bet you're the one who has to fight off the ladies. And the guys, too, no doubt." He smiled and winked.

"I wish." Damn, my dick was stiff. Zig was sexy in just those briefs.

"You're a handsome dude, Josh. No need to be modest."

"Well, thanks. Wish I had a body like yours, though."

I handed out the cards and we looked at what we were dealt. My hand looked pretty bleak. All Ziggy had was a pair of sevens, but he ended up beating me.

I pulled off my jeans and sat back down, embarrassed about having a boner, even though he had one, too.

"Whooeee! Look at that monster." He grinned.

No doubt I was red in the face from blushing. Now we were both in just our briefs, and my dick felt like a steel rod.

"Dude," he said, "don't be embarrassed. Don't ever be shamed by your cock getting hard. Be proud of your dick! A boner's a good thing. Look, mine's hard, too, and I'm not embarrassed."

"I know. That's what I've been looking at." Ziggy's dick was so big and stiff. And it just made mine stiffer, to look at it.

"See? No reason to get embarrassed. I'm not."

"You might not feel that way," I said, "if you knew what I was thinking."

"Oh, I don't know about that. Why, what's the big secret?"

"It's what we talked about last night. You know."

"You mean about being gay? I told you, dude, I don't care. I still like you."

"Yeah, but don't you understand? My dick is hard from looking at you, Zig. And thinking about what I'd like to do to you! You and your cock. That's why I'm so embarrassed."

"So? What's wrong with that? I don't get it."

"You don't mind?"

"Nah. I don't mind. I'm flattered. A dude like you, if your cock gets hard from looking at me, that makes me feel good, knowing you think I'm sexy. I'm honored. I don't have a problem with that."

"You don't? You're sure?"

"Yeah, I'm sure. Hell, I *like* it if I give you a hard-on. Anyway, it's nothing to be embarrassed about, Josh. Be proud of your cock. Okay?"

"Okay," I said. "If you're really sure."

"Sure I'm sure. Now, who's deal is it? I wanna make you take off your underwear, bro. Get a look at that big ol' thing in the flesh. You're making me horny, Josh. Damn, you're sexy!"

That made me laugh. "It's your deal, Zig. God, you're the best, you know that? Nobody's ever made me feel good the way you do."

"Aw, now you're getting me embarrassed. I'm just telling you the truth." He gathered up the cards and shuffled. I cut the deck and he dealt out the cards.

"This is it," he said. "At the end of this hand it'll be you or me, Josh. One of us kisses the other one's sweet ass. In addition to losing all of his clothes and playing the rest of the game naked. Bare-ass naked."

He picked up his hand.

And I picked up mine. Bleak, very bleak. God, I was so turned on. It was so sexy, both of us sitting there in our bulging underwear. Nothing else. So much bare skin. Both of us with big, stiff boners. And in another minute, one of our raging hard-ons would be totally exposed for all to see.

Ziggy won.

"Ha haa!" He cackled with glee. "Josh has to kiss my ass! Josh has to kiss my ass! Lose your underwear, bro. From here on out, you is butt naked."

I tried my darnedest not to be embarrassed. My dick was rigid, but hell, so was his. I pulled down my briefs and my hard cock stood straight out. It was so hard it was throbbing.

Ziggy whistled. "What a beauty. And you say that thing is hard 'cause of me?"

I nodded my head.

"I am truly honored. A sign of appreciation. It's like winning a trophy or something."

I sat back down and crossed my legs, my stiff dick jutting straight out toward Ziggy. "Yeah," I said, "except you can't take this trophy home with you." He was looking at the tip of my cock, and I realized it was wet with pre-cum.

He looked up. "Who says I can't?" He grinned.

"Anyway," I said, "now what?"

"What do you mean, 'now what?' Now you have to kiss my ass, bud. Pucker up!" Zig stood up and came over, turned his butt around in front of my face, and pulled his briefs down past his balls. "Kiss My Ass!"

I did. I kissed each cheek, and blushed even more. I wanted to kiss his balls, too.

He pulled up his briefs and sat back down, smiling.

"*Now* what?" I said.

"We keep playing. If I lose, I lose *my* briefs, and I have to kiss *your* ass."

"But what if *I* lose again?"

"Uh, if you lose, since you already kissed my ass, you have to kiss my cock."

"Oh, jeez. You have to promise not to tell anybody." I was still playing like we were in eleventh grade.

"Dude, we're high school best buddies now. Right? When we do something like this, it stays strictly between us. I promise, how about you?"

"Yeah. I promise, too."

"Cool," he said. "Deal."

So I dealt out the next hand, and he lost. I laughed nervously as he stood up and pulled his briefs off. Damn, he had a hard on that was just as stiff as mine. Stiffer, maybe.

"Okay," he said, "you stand up, too." I did, with my dick still sticking straight out, and he walked over behind me and looked at my ass, waiting. He said, "You're supposed to say, 'Kiss My Ass.'"

"Kiss My Ass!" And I meant it.

He bent over and kissed each one of my ass cheeks, just like I did to him. Then he sat down again.

"My deal," he said. "Same rule I already told you about. Whoever loses this time has to kiss the other guy's cock." He passed out the cards, and we picked up our hands. This time, he lost the hand.

"Damn. Okay, Josh, bring your cock over here."

I went over and stood right in front of him, my hard dick pointing right at his face. He looked at it, and then looked up at me. "Go ahead, Josh. Say, 'Kiss My Cock.'"

So I said it. "Kiss My Cock!" And that's what he did. He was blushing like crazy, but he put his hand on my dick to steady it, and then he gave it a kiss, right on the head. When he took his mouth away, there was a drop of my pre-cum on his lip, until he licked it away.

I sat back down, my dick stiffer than ever. Ziggy had kissed my cock! His lips had actually pressed against the head of my dick. "My deal," I said. I started dealing the cards and then I stopped. "Wait. What's next? What happens if you lose this hand?"

"You're gonna lose this time, and next time, too, dude, wait and see. Um, after kissing the other guy's cock, the next bet is sucking the other guy's toes. All ten of them!"

"Oh, jeez."

"You'll like sucking my toes, dude." Ziggy laughed. "But first you have to kiss my cock. Go ahead, finish dealing."

"You're the one who's gonna be sucking toes, pal."

I dealt the hand, and I lost.

"Ha! See? I told you you'd lose." He stood up, and his dick stood rigid and ready. He came over and stood right in front of my face and said, "Kiss My Cock!" And I did. I touched it with my tongue when I kissed it, but I don't know if he noticed. I saw him shiver, though.

He was blushing like mad when he sat down. "My deal," he said. "Whoever loses this hand has to give the other guy a toe job." He passed out the cards.

He looked at his cards and gave me a smirk. Maybe he had a good hand, but so did I. I drew one card, which seemed to surprise him. He drew two cards.

When we lay down our hands, he had three jacks, but I beat him. I had three kings. I laughed. "My toes are waiting for you, Zig."

He smiled. "Dude. Have you ever had anybody suck your toes?"

"No. I never have."

"Okay, then, I'm gonna show you how it's done." He put the cards aside, and got on all fours. "Lean back, bro, and put your feet out."

I leaned back on my hands and straightened my legs out in front of me. When he first mentioned sucking toes I figured it was supposed to be humiliating for the guy doing the sucking, but now I wondered what I was in for. Were toes ticklish?

"You know what to say," he said.

For a few seconds I didn't know what he was talking about, and then I realized. "Oh, right. Suck My Toes!"

He lowered his head down and positioned his mouth at my big toe. He licked it, slowly. Then he put it inside his mouth and started sucking on it while he moved his tongue all around it.

I said, "Oh, my god." He kept sucking and licking, and then he moved down to the next toe. "Jeez." It was incredible. I had no idea it would feel so good. So sensual. Hell, it was downright sexual.

I imagined him sucking on my dick the same way he was sucking on my toes, and a shiver ran through my whole body. Jeez, best not to think anymore about that or I might shoot my load without even touching my dick. The way he was making me feel, I might come anyway. I shivered again. "Jeez, Zig!"

He stopped sucking briefly and looked up, smiling. "Feel good?"

"My god, who knew?"

He didn't answer, he just lowered his head and resumed where he'd left off. And when he was done with that foot he started on the other. One toe at a time. It felt so good I thought I was going to faint. So I lay down flat on my back.

Eventually he sucked and licked every last one of my toes, thoroughly. He sat back, then, crossed his legs, and smiled. I sat up again, speechless.

He said, "Good, huh?"

I nodded my head.

He picked up the cards and gave them to me. "Your deal."

"God, that was incredible." I started dealing out the cards, and then I stopped. "I forgot to shuffle."

"No problem. Keep going."

"Okay." I continued dealing cards, but then I stopped again. "What's next? After sucking toes?"

"Um, the next bet, after toes, is licking the other guy's ass-hole."

"No way!"

"Yeah, dude. Way. Don't worry, we took showers, remember? It's just a game."

"Jeez. What comes after that? I'm afraid to ask."

"I'll tell you when we get there."

I finished handing out the cards. "I had no idea this game was so, uh . . . ."

"Kinky?"

"No, sexual. And, yeah, kinky."

He laughed. "Hell, it wouldn't be any fun, if it wasn't kinky."

I didn't know what to say.

He looked at my crotch. "Your cock sure likes it well enough."

I looked and not only was my cock stiff and hard, it was still leaking pre-cum. I looked at him, wondering if I should be embarrassed, but then I thought, *Fuck it*. This was the sexiest fun I'd ever had. Might as well abandon all shame and enjoy it to the fullest. I said, "Zig, I'm so horny I could explode."

He laughed. "Don't do that! There's better ways to come."

"And I have a feeling I'm gonna learn what they are."

"Stick with me, bro, and you'll learn a lot of things." We picked up our cards and looked them over.

This time, I lost. He cackled with glee. "Suck My Toes, dude! Suck My Toes!" He leaned back and stuck one of his feet in front of my face. I held it with both of my hands, and started with the big toe. "That's it," he said, with a sigh. "You learn fast, Josh."

I kept it up, taking my time, giving his toes the same loving treatment he gave mine. After a few minutes he shivered and lay back flat on the floor, with his hands behind his head. I held his foot in the air while I slowly sucked each toe. Then I gently lowered his foot to the floor and picked up the other one.

Ziggy sighed again. "You suck toes good, bro."

I looked at his dick and it was marble hard, moist with pre-cum. That's what I wanted to suck on next, but I didn't know if I'd get to do it. That was okay, though. I was having enough fun already with his sexy toes. My dick was rock hard.

I finished the last toe and was thinking about going back to the first toe again when Ziggy rose up to a sitting position. "Awesome, Josh."

"That was cool," I said. "I liked that." Both our dicks were stiff and throbbing.

"Fucking toe-sucker," he said, grinning. Then he stood up. "Hang on, I gotta pee."

He went into the bathroom and stood at the toilet, trying to pee with a hard cock. After a while I guess he finally softened up a bit and got it going.

I had to pee, too, boner or not. I got up and stood at the door, waiting for him to finish. He looked over and saw me and said, "Come on in, there's room for two."

So I went in and pointed my hard dick down toward the bowl. Nothing came out.

"Same problem I had," he said, a thin stream of his urine flowing into the bowl. "I'm horny as a motherfucker. It's hard to pee with a hard on."

I tried my best not to be embarrassed. I had never peed together with anyone, ever. Even with a soft dick. But both of our dicks were hard, and only inches apart. Jeez, I'd never be able to pee this way. The longer I stood there looking at his stiff cock, the harder I got.

"I'll bet your pee-shy," he said. "Am I right? A lot of guys are, you know."

"Yeah," I croaked. Jeez, I could hardly even talk, I was so horny looking at his cock.

"No problem, dude. Maybe we'll get you over that too, one of these days. But I understand pee-shy. It's okay." He finally finished, and he wagged his big cock up and down a couple times to get the last drops off. "I'll be in the other room. Take your time."

After he left it still seemed to take forever, but finally I was able to do it.

When I came out, Ziggy was sitting where he'd been before, grinning at me. He said, "Whose deal?"

"Yours."

"Okay." He picked up the cards and shuffled. Then he dealt them out. "Okay, like I said before, whoever loses this time has to lick an asshole." We picked up the cards.

I lost. "Oh, god."

He started giggling. "You have to lick my butt hole!"

"Okay," I said. "Okay. Uh, how do you want to do this?"

"Let's get on the bed. The floor's too hard." He got up and lay down on the bed, ass up. "Come on up and straddle my legs. Spread my cheeks apart, then stick your face right up in my ass and lick my hole. It's easy."

"Oh, fuck."

"Don't worry, bro. We just showered, remember? I'm squeaky clean."

I just looked at him.

"I promise you, Josh, I'm clean down there. And I won't tell anybody, I already told you that."

I still hesitated.

"If it'll make you feel better, listen. I've done it before, lots of times. If I can do it, you can do it. We used to play this at the orphanage."

"You played *this* at the orphanage?"

"Yeah. Except we called it Kiss My Ass. We played it a lot."

I looked at his ass, his beautiful ass, and I thought, *What the hell, I can do it.* Then a wave of relief flowed through my whole body, changing everything. I realized I *wanted* to do it. I wanted to push my face into that beautiful ass.

"Okay," I said. "Okay, I'm ready." I got up on the bed and positioned myself over his legs.

"Alright." He raised up his ass a little. "Go ahead, Josh. Lick My Asshole, dude."

I reached down and held his cheeks. This was very cool, actually. Not only was I putting my hands on his hot, sexy butt, I was also going to stick my face into it. I pressed my face firmly into his ass and gave his asshole one really nice, slow lick. Then I raised my head back up.

I felt like a different person. I felt like I was the guy I would have been all along, if Zig and I had met each other when we were younger. I wanted to lick his asshole again. I didn't want to stop. I lowered my head to lick it again.

Then I remembered our role play. This was supposed to be my first time doing this, and I probably ought to be timid about it. I took my face out of his ass and looked at him. He was looking right back at me. He didn't say anything, he just looked at me kind of hopefully. Then I realized: this really *was* my first time doing this, and I didn't feel timid at all. I pressed my face back into his ass and licked him again.

I heard Ziggy say, "Yeah!"

I thought, *I'm enjoying this, he's enjoying this, so why stop now?* It was sexy as hell. So I went on licking him, and I loved it. I really did. I licked him at least a dozen more times.

Then I got up and got off the bed. Back to the card game. Maybe I'd get my ass licked this time.

Ziggy sat up on the bed and his dick was rock hard. "Dude, that was awesome!"

"I guess you were right," I said. "It wasn't so bad."

"Wasn't bad, hell. Josh, you loved it! But listen, that's totally cool. Just between you and me, I like doing it, too."

I wiped the moisture off of my face. "Whose deal?"

"Yours," he said. "Unless you wanna lick my ass some more. That was incredible, bro. You think maybe I could talk you into doing it a little more?" His cock was as stiff as it could be.

I picked up the cards and started to shuffle, but I couldn't keep my eyes off his cock. I couldn't make my mind up which I wanted more, to lick his ass again, or to try and figure out some way to get him to let me suck his dick.

"Tell you what," he said, "lick my asshole for ten more minutes, and then I'll do it to you. I promise. I'll show you how good it feels. You won't want me to stop, I guarantee."

I put the cards down and said, "Oh, hell, why not."

Ziggy chuckled. He got flat on the bed again, this time on his back. He brought his knees up toward his head, which put his ass right out there, ready for my attention. "Lick my ass, little buddy."

I climbed up on the bed and knelt down in front of him. I put one hand on each cheek of his ass and I wet my lips. Starting at the small of his back, I licked along his ass crack, across his hole, and all the way up to his balls, but I didn't stop there. I licked across his balls and along the underside of his dick, too. All with one slow, loving swipe of my tongue.

He moaned in pleasure. "Fuck, Josh, you can do that as long as you want to, bro. All night, if you want."

I licked him again, the exact same way.

"Jesus. Dude, you're gonna make me come if you keep licking my cock like that."

Well, I wanted to make him come, but not so soon. So the next time, I licked all the way to his balls, but not his dick. I held the skin of his ball sac between my lips and tugged gently. He moaned.

I licked the underside of his sac, gently pushing his balls around with my tongue, and that made him moan all the more.

Then

Then I licked his puckered-up asshole, and licked it again. "That's it," he said, "lick my asshole good. See if you can get your tongue in there."

Put my tongue inside his asshole? Very kinky, I thought. *Hell, why not?* I'd gone this far, and enjoyed it every step of the way. My dick felt stiffer than ever. I was loving it.

His hole resisted at first, but it didn't take long to relax. Then the tip of my tongue went right in. I stuck my tongue out as far as it would go, as deep into Ziggy as I could, and I wiggled it around. Ziggy gasped. I wiggled it some more, and he groaned.

Ziggy tasted sweet. Honestly. His asshole was perfectly clean, freshly showered, and it tasted sweet. Or at least it tasted sweet to me. I loved it, and he loved it, too. He was squirming and moaning in pleasure. I wondered if I could make him come this way. He sure sounded close, the way he was moaning and groaning.

I kept it up until my tongue got tired, and then I wet my thumb and used that instead, to give my tongue a rest. That brought forth another loud gasp from Ziggy and a whole new level of moaning. I gently pressed my thumb into his hole and it opened right up. He gasped again and moaned. I pushed my thumb in farther, another inch, at least, and he moaned louder.

I wondered if Ziggy was unusually wired for this, or was everybody's asshole this sensitive? If everybody's was, that meant mine was, too. That was an intriguing thought.

I took my thumb out and I was getting ready to use my tongue again when Ziggy said, breathlessly, "Josh?"

"Yeah?"

"Do me a favor?"

"Sure, of course."

"Your cock, Josh. Put your cock in there."

I was speechless.

"You can do it. There's some condoms in my backpack. And get the lube, too."

Chapter 25
YOU CAN DO IT

I GOT UP and headed for his backpack, but I could hardly believe he wanted to do this. I had never, ever expected to fuck Ziggy. I knew, sooner or later, he would fuck *me*; we had agreed to do that at some future time. But never had I considered the possibility of fucking *him*.

The wild thing was, I really wanted to! My dick was so hard it ached, and I *wanted* to put it inside him. That surprised me almost as much as Zig wanting it. After eating his ass and getting us both so incredibly horny, I really did want to fuck him.

I found the lube and brought it back to the bed, along with some condoms. He had his legs lowered down to the bed, watching me, stroking his cock. I tore open the package of one of the condoms.

Zig reached for the lube. "Here, Josh, let's put a little bit of this on your cock first." He turned it upside down over my dick and let some drip on it. Then he set the lube down and put his hand on my dick and spread the lube around.

"Jeez, Zig, be careful. You'll make me come."

He took his hand away and wiped it on himself. Then he took the condom out of my hand. "Here," he said. "I'll show you how to put it on." He unrolled an inch of it and held onto the end while he put it up against the head of my dick. Then he unrolled the rest of it down the sides of my shaft, all the way to the root. "You leave some slack at the tip, that way it's less likely to break while you're fucking me."

Wow. To hear him say it. I was going to fuck him! Put my cock inside his ass. I was going to fuck him until I shot my load, inside a condom inside his ass. "Oh my god, Zig," I said. "I'm really gonna fuck you. I'm gonna fuck your ass."

"Damn right you are."

He picked up the lube again and squirted more over the condom, gently spreading it over my entire cock. "Careful," I said.

Ziggy handed me the lube. "Put some inside my asshole, okay?" He lifted his legs up in the air again. "This is gonna be . . . um, well, it's been a couple of years since I had a cock up my ass, bro. You'll want to go slow at first."

I kneeled in front of him. "Are you sure you really want me to do this?"

"Definitely. Yeah. I do. You do, too. You're cock is the stiffest I've ever seen it."

"Damn right, I want to. Surprise, surprise, huh?"

"No, not at all. I knew you could do it. Fuck, this is gonna be so awesome."

I dripped lube on my hand and spread it around his asshole. Then I carefully pushed my slippery thumb inside, getting him slicked up and relaxed at the same time. His asshole resisted slightly at first, and then it relaxed all the way. I took my thumb out and gently put a couple of lubed-up fingers in there.

"Do it," he said. "Go ahead and put your cock up my ass." He was looking at my slicked-up dick, looking at how stiff and hard it was. His cock was just as stiff. "Go slow, bro, at least until it's all the way in, okay? Go ahead, do it."

I put the head of my dick to his anus and pressed very gently.

"A little bit harder than that. You have to kind of trigger it, sort of."

I pressed a little harder, and moved the head around in a small circle, following the ring of his anus, tickling it a little and pressing forward at the same time. When I brought it to the center again, I pressed inward. He relaxed, briefly, and it was just enough for me to get the head inside. Oh, the pleasure!

"Hold it right there, okay? I'll tell you when," he said, breathing heavily.

"Am I hurting you?"

"Nah. Just want to get accustomed to it, that's all."

We stayed like that for a minute or so, me kneeling in front of him, him with his legs up, the head of my cock inside his ass. Connected.

I wanted to go in farther, but I wanted to wait. No way did I want to hurt him, not Ziggy.

"Okay," he said. "Go slow, but go ahead. Slowly. Keep going unless I tell you to stop, okay?"

"Alright." I gently pushed forward, pressing my dick farther and farther into his hole. Slowly. A half-inch at a time. The feeling was exquisite. Different from a mouth, but just as good. I kept going deeper, watching my cock disappear into his ass. Incredible.

"That's it, Josh. You're doing great, dude. It feels good."

He didn't say stop, so I kept going in. His cock was hard and wet with pre-cum. I had an urge to put it in my mouth, but I wouldn't be able to reach it with my dick in his ass. I could hold it, though. I touched his cock with my fingers but he said, "No, Josh. I'll shoot. I don't want to come yet. Let's make it last as long as we can." So I left his cock alone.

And I kept pushing deeper. Then I was all the way in. I couldn't go any farther. My pelvis was pressed up tight against his ass. I couldn't even see my dick, but I sure could feel it.

"Incredible," he said. "That feels incredible, Josh. Keep it there for a minute, don't pull back yet. Stay in there, good and deep. How does it feel?"

"Awesome, Zig."

"Yeah, same here."

"Doesn't this hurt your legs, though?"

"Nah. I might feel a little sore tomorrow, but it'll be okay. We could do it doggy-style, but I like this way better." He smiled, bashfully. "We get to look at each other, this way."

"Yeah. I like that, too," I said. "And I can look at your awesome cock, too. I wish I could suck it while I fuck you, but I can't bend over far enough to reach it."

"Good thing you can't. I'd come in a second."

"Coming is a good thing, Zig." I grinned.

"Yeah it is, you got that right." He smiled. "But so is staying close to the edge, until you can hardly stand it any longer *not* to come."

"Yeah, that does sound good."

"There's another way we could do it, too; you leaning back with me sitting on your cock."

"Really?"

"Yeah. It's kind of wild. The guy getting fucked does most of the work, and the other guy basically sits there, getting his cock worked over. That was my favorite way with George, but he liked this way better. He really liked pounding my ass."

I didn't know what to say.

"Alright, Josh. I think I'm ready. Pull your cock out a couple of inches, slowly, and then push it back in, slowly."

I did what he said.

"Beautiful. Feels good. Do it again."

So I did. Out, and then forward, slowly, until I was all the way in again.

"That's it. You're doing great, Josh. Try pulling out almost all the way, and going back in."

I kept pulling back, pushing in, pulling back, pushing in, slowly each time.

"You can go faster now if you want. Like, you know, harder."

I increased my pace, and in the process, started making slapping sounds every time I smacked against his ass. "That doesn't hurt?"

"Hell no. It feels good!"

I guess it did. His cock was as stiff as it ever gets. "Alright." I kept fucking him, faster now, and harder. "Zig, if I keep this up, I'm gonna come."

"Are you squeezing your ass cheeks together when you go in?"

I took a couple more thrusts into his beautiful, soft round ass, to see if I was. "Yeah, I am."

"Don't. You'll last longer if you don't clench your ass while you're fucking. Not until you're ready to shoot, then you can squeeze your ass together all you want, it'll make your orgasm better. I learned that trick on my own. Move your hips, but don't flex your butt until you're ready to come."

That sounded odd, until I tried it. "You're full of tricks, aren't you?"

"I learned most of them from George, but a few I discovered on my own."

I went on fucking him, and now I felt like I could go a lot longer. "What else did you learn from George?"

"Um, kissing."

"You guys kissed?"

"He kissed me all over, Josh. While he was fucking me. Not on my mouth so much, but everywhere else. It was really erotic. I told you he had tricks. Well, that was one of them. It felt good."

"I'm surprised."

"Why?"

"Jeez, Zig, I've heard of straight guys doing just about anything, if they think nobody will find out about it. Even getting fucked. But they usually draw the line at kissing. That's what I've heard, anyway."

"Well, they're missing out, if they do. Anyway, I never said George was straight. Remember? I told you. George was like me."

"Okay."

"So, go ahead, bro. Try it. Kiss me all over."

"Um, there's not a whole lot of you I can reach, from this angle."

333

"That's okay, just kiss whatever you can reach."

"Okay." While I continued fucking him I pulled his legs closer. I could reach his feet, so I kissed those. And then I started sucking on his toes.

"Jesus, Josh!" He shuddered involuntarily, and moaned.

I sucked all of his toes, and then I kissed his feet some more, but I never stopped fucking him.

"You're good at this!" he said.

"I had a good teacher." I leaned down and kissed one of his nipples, and he moaned again. So I kissed the other nipple, too, and then I started licking them. Then I moved to an armpit, and that set him off, too.

"Aw, fuck! Where'd you learn this stuff, Josh? You're awesome, dude. I love that. It tickles like hell, but it feels fantastic."

After a few more minutes of that I leaned back and put all my focus into fucking him.

"Yeah. Hard as you want, bro. Fuck me hard, I can take it."

So I smacked into him fast and hard. It was really intense. Both of us were grunting and groaning. Then I slowed the pace again. I leaned forward and kissed his nipples some more. He closed his eyes and moaned. I flicked each nipple with my tongue, and then I moved up to his neck and shoulders and ears. I kissed him in all the places I knew were so sensitive. He moaned some more, so I kept it up.

He had his eyes closed. I kissed him on his cheeks, and his forehead. I even kissed his closed eyelids. He kept moaning.

Then I kissed him on his lips. He didn't seem to mind. In fact, he seemed to move his head forward a little to give me better access to his mouth, while he still kept his eyes closed. So I kissed him again. I kept fucking him, and I kissed him again on his lips. He moaned and kissed me back.

I leaned back and started fucking him harder again. He opened his eyes and said, "Yeah, give me everything you've got, Josh. Fuck me hard." So I started smacking up against his ass with every thrust. I thought for a few seconds maybe I was fucking him too hard, but he said, "Yeah, that's it. Fuck, you're gonna make me come, Josh! Keep going! Fuck me good. Don't stop now."

He closed his eyes again, moaning, and he sounded like he was getting close. I kept thrusting into him, as hard as I could, which probably wasn't all that hard since I wasn't used to this. He was really getting off on it. I leaned forward again and kissed him on his mouth, and he kissed me back, this time with passion. Then he gasped and went, "Ahhhhhhhh! Oh, Jesus." He opened his eyes and said, "I'm coming, Josh, oh, god, I'm coming!"

I leaned back, still fucking him, squeezing my ass cheeks together now with every thrust because I wanted to come, too. Cum started flying out of his cock, shooting everywhere, and he gasped and moaned and went "Uhh! Uhh! Uhh!" Some of his cum hit my face, some of it hit his face, and the rest of it flew everywhere.

I kept fucking him hard. And then I felt myself go over the edge. "Zig, I'm coming!" I kept slamming into his ass as I began shooting my load, but the orgasm seemed to get better and better until it was taking over my whole body. I never felt so good in my entire life as I did right then.

I closed my eyes and I made one more deep thrust into Ziggy and held it; I pressed hard against him while my balls emptied and my cock went on shooting and my hips jerked. It felt like it lasted for five minutes.

Eventually I slowed down, and finally I stopped, with my dick still deep inside Ziggy. I opened my eyes and he was looking up at me, grinning.

"Dude," he said. "That was incredible."

"Yeah. It was, wasn't it?"

"Fucking incredible. You did it."

"I never would have believed I had it in me."

"Hell, I knew you did. From the very beginning, I knew."

"You did?"

"Pull your cock out slowly, okay? Slowly."

So that's what I did.

He looked at my dick and said, "Fuck, it's still hard. I'll bet you could go again."

"I don't know about that," I said. "I'm kinda worn out." His dick was still hard, too. I pulled the condom off my dick. "I guess I'll go flush this."

"No, just throw it in the trash, and then come back here and cuddle with me."

When I turned out the lights and came back to the bed, he was already under the covers. I crawled in and we lay on our sides, facing each other. We were so close I could feel the warmth of his breath. I said, "That was good."

"It was awesome. I knew you could do it, bro. Fuckin' A, I didn't know you were gonna be *that* good at it, though. You made me come without even touching my dick! I wasn't expecting that, not with this being basically your first time."

"That's unusual, huh?"

"Yeah, I think so. And you lasted a long time, too. Just like a pro."

"I thought it was you who'd be fucking me, Zig. I never thought I'd be fucking *you*."

"Well, you might as well get used to the idea, because that was good. I want to do that again."

"Okay."

"You should be proud of yourself, Josh. You're a natural."

"You're still gonna let me suck you off sometimes though, aren't you?"

"Sure, whenever you want."

"I don't know which I like better. Fucking you, or sucking you."

"Tell you what. When we have plenty of time, we can fuck. The rest of the time, we'll do blow jobs."

"Works for me." I grinned.

"Oh, man. We're so lucky, you know that? Josh, I'm so glad I met you."

"Same here, Zig."

We lay there for a couple of minutes, facing each other.

Then he said, "Who's gonna be the teddy bear tonight?"

"Me," I said. I turned the other way so my back was to Ziggy, and he wrapped his arm around me and pulled me up close.

We lay there like that for a few minutes, lost in our own thoughts. I realized I was seeing myself in a different way now. "Zig, I didn't know what I was missing."

"Yeah, sometimes it's like that. Just makes you appreciate it all the more when you find out."

We lay there for at least another fifteen minutes, not talking. Ziggy held me close. Eventually I heard him breathing slow and deep and steady.

—

THIS IS WHAT I DREAMED: I was in a Japanese Garden, standing on the bridge, watching big, orange fish weave around each other in the water below.

I walked to the end of the bridge, strolled along the path, and then I sat down on one of the benches.

There was no reason to hurry. I sat there for quite some time, enjoying the birds, the flowers, the wind, and the trees. Color, song, and fragrance swam in and out of my focus. My mind shifted, gently, from one thought to the next, and sometimes to no thought at all.

Eventually I noticed someone approaching. He was coming from one of the paths I had not yet explored.

I thought, *I know this person. It's Ziggy.* He saw me smiling, and returned the smile.

He walked up to me and stopped. "Hi," he said.

"Hi." I told him, "I saved a seat for you."

"Thanks." He sat down. "You come here often?"

"Every chance I get."

"I found my teddy bear," he said.

"You did?"

"Never thought I would, but I did."

"Never give up, right?"

"That's right."

"I was hoping I would see you here," I said.

"I want to show you something." He pointed far, far away into the distance. "Look over there."

I looked in the direction he was pointing. I could just barely see two people, sitting next to each other on a bench. I couldn't tell if they were men or women, let alone who they might be. "Who is that?"

"That's Zig."

"The real Zig?"

"Yes."

"Who's that with him?"

"Well, Zig thinks it's you."

"But it's not?"

"No."

"Okay," I said.

"Do you understand?"

"I don't think so."

He looked at me, smiling. Then he said, "I'm not who you think I am."

"No?"

"Nah."

"Who are you, then?"

"I'm you."

"Well, you sure could have fooled me," I said. "You look just like my brother Zig."

"Yeah," he said, "but remember, this is dreamland."

"What difference does that make?"

"You're dreaming."

"Yes, but . . ."

"This is your dream. And that, over there, is his dream."

"So, I can't meet the real Zig in my dreams?"

"You understand, then."

"But why not?"

"It would be highly unusual. Under the present circumstances."

"Because . . ."

"This is your dream. And that, over there, is his dream."

"So if I have something I want to share with the real Zig . . ."

"It would actually be very easy to do, in your present situation," he said.

"But not here in dreamland."

"Correct."

We sat next to each other for several more minutes. Finally I stood up. "Well," I said, "I guess I'll be getting back."

"Okay," he said, still smiling. "Nice to see you."

—

ZIG HAD HIS ARM AROUND ME, sound asleep. That's the way we always slept. Together, front to back, like one spoon inside another. I could tell he was having a good dream. His dick was stiff, pressing against the crack of my ass.

Usually I would have let myself fall back to sleep, but this time was different.

I carefully lifted his arm, slid out from under, and tiptoed into the bathroom. It was very early in the morning, probably not even 4 a.m. yet. I closed the bathroom door, because I didn't want to wake him. Then I turned on the shower.

First I sat on the can for a couple of minutes. Then I stepped into the shower and took a nice, long, hot one, taking the time to get squeaky-clean in the process.

When I was done I came out of the bathroom and, while I toweled myself dry, I watched Ziggy sleep.

I had so much to be thankful for. This guy had totally turned my life around. Oh, he would say it was me who did it, that he only pointed me in the right direction. Even if that was true, I still owed him my eternal thanks.

Life is a lot more complicated than just trucking down a highway following road signs. Truth is, I might not have ever found my way if it hadn't been for Ziggy. Ziggy seeing something in me that no one else had seen. And then, caring enough to help me see it, myself.

I hung up the towel and slipped back into bed, as gently as possible, lifting his arm and snuggling up against him into the same position we were in before, my back to his front.

He pulled me closer to him and sighed. At first I thought he was still asleep, but then he mumbled, "Where'd you go?"

"Nowhere, just the bathroom."

"Okay."

His cock was getting hard again, pressing against my butt. This time, though, he wasn't dreaming.

I had a hard on, too.

"You sure have learned how to make a guy happy, Josh."

"That's the best part," I said. "*I* made *you* happy."

"Dude, you've been making me happy ever since the day we met."

"Well, I'm glad I found another way to do it, then."

"I thought my days of getting fucked were over when George died."

"Don't ask *me* to make any sense of it," I said. "I'm totally clueless about this kind of stuff."

"What I mean is, um . . . ."

He paused, and I waited for him to finish.

"Hell, I don't know how to explain it. One thing I do know is, not only would he like you, Josh, he'd also be impressed with you.

It was a lot more than just technique, with him; George had this whole attitude. An outlook on life. It all worked together. I'm not saying you're like him, I don't mean that. But you have your own thing going, dude. You're different from him, but what you've got, it all works together. Perfectly."

"Uh, I'm not sure I understand all that, but anyway, I'm glad if you like it."

"You're a natural, Josh." He hugged me up close, and then I felt him kiss me on the back of my neck. He moved his hand gently over my chest, touching my nipples, and then he moved his hand lower. He found my hard cock, and gently put his fingers around it. "The mighty warrior's weapon," he said. He moved his fingers around on it, like he was examining its shape, getting to know it better.

"Careful, Zig, you'll make me come if you keep that up."

"Coming is a good thing, bro."

"Yeah, but there's something else I want you to do, first."

"What's that?"

"Um, well, you owe me an ass-lick. You promised, remember?"

"Calling in your I.O.U., huh?"

"That's right. But you said you like doing it, anyway, right?"

"With you? Sure."

"Well, I just took a shower, and I'm ready for it."

"You want me to do it *now*?"

"Yeah. Right now."

"Uh, okay. But give me half a minute. I gotta pee."

A minute or two later he got back into bed, grinning. "You shy guys are something else, you know that?"

I laughed. "How many shy guys do you know?"

"Just you."

"Okay." I turned around and got up on all fours, stuck my butt out a little bit, and waited.

First I felt his thumb; he pressed it right up against my asshole and started massaging the whole area, and squeezing my ass cheeks. Then I felt the wetness of his tongue. He didn't waste much time on preliminaries; he gave me one nice, long lick, starting at the base of my balls and going all the way up to where the crack of my ass ended and my lower back began. Then he did it again, and I shivered.

"You had enough? Or do you want more?"

"Oh, definitely, more. The whole rest of the night, if you want."

He laughed. "Oh, no. It doesn't work like that. If you want it all night, we'll have to take turns."

"Sounds good to me," I said.

"Right now, it's my turn. And I'm not done yet, pal." With that he started licking me again.

He licked me all over, but spent most of the time licking behind my balls and up around my asshole. At first it tickled, but soon I was enjoying the most incredible sensations I'd ever felt. And the longer he licked, the more it felt like the tip of his tongue was actually going inside my hole.

"You're really relaxed."

"Yeah, I've been practicing like you told me to do, every time I take a shower."

"Well, it's working, dude. Looks like you can really let yourself relax down there when you want to. Hell, we should have bought a dildo when we were at that store earlier, so you could practice with that."

"A *dildo*?"

"Yeah."

"Did you use a dildo, before George started fucking you?"

"No, hell no. He just started in with the real thing."

"And you liked it, right? He didn't hurt you?"

"I loved it. No one else has ever made me feel that good. Not until last night with you, that is."

"Oh, jeez."

"Like I said, George would have been proud of you."

"You really think so?"

"I know so. We talked about it, the last time he came to see me in St. Louis, when he was on leave from the Army."

"Talked about what?"

"He told me if anything ever happened to him, he wanted me to go out and find another buddy, someone who would look out for me as good as he did. He made me promise, Josh. I told him nothing was gonna happen to him, but he said, 'You never know.'"

"Wow."

"He said life is lonely by nature, and the only way to remedy that is to have a buddy, so you can look out for each other."

"Pretty smart."

"Yeah, he was smart. And he had a heart of gold, he really did. Like you, Josh."

"Aw, hell."

Ziggy ducked his head down and started licking me again.

"I wish I could have met him."

He licked my ass and underneath my balls. Then he came up for air. "Yeah, I wish you could have, too."

"So, um, tell me, for real now, it didn't hurt at all, the first time he fucked you?"

"Well, maybe a little, for half a minute. He was very gentle, Josh. He went really slow. And he got me ready for it first."

"With his tongue?"

"Yeah, with his tongue, and his fingers. And I enjoyed it every step of the way, he made sure of that."

"Well, then why would you want me to use a dildo? Why don't you just do it like George did?"

"Well, I don't know. I guess I could."

"Sure you could."

"I don't like the idea of hurting you, though. Not even for half a minute."

343

"It's okay, Zig. I can handle it. Jeez, if it's gonna hurt anyway, I want the real thing, not some old piece of plastic."

"I don't know, Josh."

"Zig, tell me, what was it like, the pain?"

"Uh, I remember that it hurt, briefly, but I don't specifically remember." He grinned. "Only the pleasure."

"See? It couldn't have been too bad, if you don't even remember it."

"Well, I remember it hurt more than I expected. It surprised the fuck out of me when the head of his cock went inside my asshole."

"Did you want it?"

"What, the pain?"

"No. I guess what I mean is, um, did you really want him to do it?"

"Oh, yeah. Definitely. I had this hero-worship thing going on with him. Plus I was a horny little devil. Believe me; he didn't have to talk me into trying it."

"Not at all?"

"Josh, it was my idea. I talked *him* into it."

"No way!"

"Yeah. My idea. See, one time when we were talking about sex, George told me that fucking pussy wasn't the only option. He said you could fuck a person in the ass, too, and the good thing about that was, it could be a girl or a guy, since everybody has one. I asked him wouldn't that hurt, but he said no, not if the guy doing the fucking was gentle and went slow at first. He said if the guy did it right it felt really great to be fucked. He said lots of people like getting fucked better than anything else."

"Are you sure he wasn't just trying to talk you into trying it?"

"I don't think so, Josh. I mean, he didn't even mention it again. But *I* sure did think about it a lot, after that. And I kept hoping he *would* talk about it again, but he didn't. Not another word about fucking ass, not for weeks. So finally, I came right out and told him I wanted to try it. With him."

"What did he say?"

"Well, he seemed surprised, but he was willing. He told me I ought to think about it, though, for a while, first. I told him I'd already thought about it plenty and I was ready to try it."

"Wow."

"So he said okay, if that's what I wanted, he'd be honored."

"Really?"

"He told me it was going to be a gift that we would be giving to each other. He had me stand still while he slowly took off all of my clothes. And when he finally slipped my underwear off and my hard dick stood up free, he told me I had a great cock that would make a lot of people happy. Then he asked me to turn around, and when I did, he said my ass was a work of art."

"He was right," I said. "About both."

"He had me undress him the same way. He had a perfect body, Josh. A naturally trim and fit body. And his dick was big, like yours. He let me feel it. It was really stiff and hard. Just as hard as mine was."

"Zig, you're making me horny."

"He kissed me all over. He said that's what people do before they fuck. He kissed me in places I'd never even thought of kissing somebody. Then he licked me, in all the same places. One thing followed another. Before long, his tongue was up my ass, and I was loving it. He got me very relaxed. Pretty soon he had a few fingers up there, too, which also felt good. Then he said he thought I was ready."

"Wow."

"I thought I was ready, too. Then, when he actually got his cockhead inside me I thought, 'Holy shit, if it hurts this much now, it's gonna rip me apart when he puts the rest of it in.' I was scared, I guess. I wasn't expecting it to hurt at all. I don't know why."

"Did you tell him to stop?"

"Yeah, I did."

"Did he?"

"Yeah. He stopped. He didn't take it out, but he stopped where he was."

"Then what happened?"

"I relaxed."

"You relaxed?"

"Yeah. It took a few minutes, but I relaxed. He played with my cock and my balls, he kissed me some more, and then I relaxed. It didn't hurt anymore after that. It felt good. And he was so gentle, and he went so slow, and he made me feel so good, fucking me, that it never did hurt after that. Ever."

"Jeez."

"Yeah."

"I want to try it," I said.

He smiled. "I know you do. And we will, I promise. When you're ready."

"No, I want to try it now. I'm ready now."

Chapter 26
LIKE MAGIC

"Now?"

"Yeah."

"Jesus, bro, there's no need to hurry this."

"I'm not hurrying it. I'm ready."

"You sure?"

"Zig, fuck me, okay? Gentle. Like George did, your first time."

I was still on the bed on my hands and knees, with Ziggy behind me, in position to lick my asshole. We were both naked, of course.

"Jesus, Josh!" He looked at me, and I looked at him. Finally he said, "Okay. If that's what you want, I'll do it. And yes, I'll be gentle. Of course I'll be gentle."

"Alright!" I was so happy I was laughing. "Um, how should we do it?"

He had to think about that for a minute. "How about you sitting on my cock?"

"Uh, you think I can relax that way?"

"Yeah. You can. You'll be the one in control, Josh. You'll be able to relax better, knowing you're in control." I moved aside while he gathered up all the pillows and put them together behind his head, lying down on his back. "Okay. Now, get up on top of me, Josh, like you're gonna suck my cock, turned around backwards with your butt in my face. So I can eat your ass some more."

So that's what we did. He got my asshole relaxed again, using his fingers and his tongue. I played with his cock when he let me, but he made me stop when he started getting close. And my dick was stiff and hard as ever. Even after he got three fingers up my ass.

"Alright," he said. "You're nice and relaxed, bud. And turned on, for sure." He put on a condom, and then he reached for the lube. He spread plenty of it on and inside my butt, and on his cock, too. "Move forward a little, and then lean back on your hands, over top of me. You're gonna hold yourself above me, on all fours, with your ass pointed at my cock."

It was awkward at first, but I did it. "That's it," he said. "I'll help hold you up, so your arms don't get worn out." He put his hands on my hips. "But you're gonna call the shots. Lower yourself onto my cock at your own speed. And raise yourself up whenever you need to. I know you want me to fuck you, but don't forget this is all about making it feel good for *you*, okay? Good enough that your cock stays hard. That's important. Alright?"

"Okay." I slowly lowered myself down, and Zig directed me with his hands so I was right on target. Soon I felt the head of his dick pushing against my butthole.

"Now, my cock is slick and hard, dude, but it's still not gonna go inside you until your asshole lets it. That's a good thing. That's the way we want it. So, you take your time, and let your asshole relax. When it's ready, it'll open up. Don't try to hurry it. You'll know when you can lower yourself down on my cock."

It took time, but it worked. And my dick stayed hard the whole time, Ziggy made sure of that. It took at least ten minutes to get him halfway up inside me. And several more to let myself down completely. But I finally sat all the way down on his cock, and I loved it. My dick was still as stiff and hard as his was.

"Zig," I said, "this is so hot. I can't believe this! I've got your dick all the way up my ass, and it feels good."

"Damn right, dude. Feels great here, too. My cock up my buddy's ass."

"Let me try moving up and down on it, okay?"

"Go for it. Just make sure whatever you do, it feels good for you."

I slowly lifted myself up and down on his dick. Exquisite. "This is incredible, Zig. This is better than I ever thought it could be."

"Now you see why I like it, huh?"

"Oh, yes." I kept moving up and down on him. "I wish I could see your face, though."

"That's easy enough. Lower yourself down on my cock, and then turn around. Just do it slowly, carefully. And try not to kick me in the head," he said, laughing. "That's all I ask."

"Okay." I slowly rotated myself around, carefully lifting my foot over his head. "Is this what they mean by 'Sit and Spin'?"

Ziggy laughed. "Yeah. Damn, your cock is really hard, dude. You like this, huh?"

"Sure. Hell yes."

He was looking at my stiff dick. "I'd try to suck you, but I don't think I can reach it."

"That's okay. I couldn't ask for anything better than this." I was leaning back, facing him, with my feet up next to his head.

"Why don't you try bending your legs underneath mine," he said, "so you can lean forward a little?"

So that's what I did. And then I was sitting straight up, on top of him, facing him, and I could lean forward as far as I wanted, while keeping his cock up inside my ass. "This is even better," I said.

He touched my dick with his fingers. "Want me to jack you off?"

"No. Not right now, anyway. I don't want to shoot off yet."

"Okay," he said. I started moving up and down on his dick again. "Damn, Josh, that feels mighty good, bro."

"Same here, Zig. I'll bet I could come this way." I kept rising up and lowering myself back down, a little faster as it went.

"Mmmmm," he said. "Damn, look at that monster cock of yours. It's too stiff to even flop up and down much. You really like this."

We didn't say much after that. I went on fucking myself on his cock. He closed his eyes and started moaning. I leaned forward and gently kissed his forehead and his cheeks. He kept his eyes closed and moaned some more.

I leaned back again and moved faster, up and down on him. I was absolutely thrilled to have him inside me. Up and down. He moaned louder. I moaned, too. I felt almost like I was having an orgasm, but I wasn't coming, not yet. Maybe this was just the way it felt to be fucked, to have your prostate massaged by your favorite dick?

"Jesus, Josh." He let out another moan and opened his eyes. "You're gonna make me come if you don't stop."

"I want you to come."

He closed his eyes again and groaned with pleasure. Another minute or two of fucking, and then he opened his eyes. "Josh, I'm almost there. Dude, I'm so close. Are you close?"

"Yeah," I said. "It's crazy. It feels almost like I've been coming for the last five minutes already."

"Wait till you actually shoot your load."

We kept it up, with him watching me move up and down on his dick. Then all the incredible sensations took over every inch of my body. "Zig," I gasped, "I think this is it." I leaned forward, closer to him, and I kissed him on the forehead again.

He closed his eyes and tilted his head back, and his mouth was right there, so I kissed his mouth. He kissed me back, so I kissed him harder. My tongue went right in between his lips and touched his tongue. He groaned, loudly, and pressed his tongue against mine.

"Ahhhhhh!" he said, opening his eyes. "Coming, Josh, coming! Coming inside you! Ahhhh!"

I moved up and down on his cock, feeling my own orgasm take over, wondering how it could feel this good when I wasn't even shooting my cum yet.

Ziggy's hips jerked hard against my ass and then I knew he was shooting his load. His hips jerked again, and he pushed his cock up as deep into me as possible. Then he held himself there, up against my ass, groaning as his dick unloaded everything he had inside me. He reached out and grabbed my cock and pulled on it.

Oh, my god, that's all it took. I started shooting cum everywhere.

I stopped the up-and-down motion and sat there, overcome with pleasure. For a few moments I thought I was going to faint. I shivered and shook as cum kept flying and wave after wave of ecstatic pleasure ran through my whole body.

It was the strongest orgasm I'd ever felt, even stronger than when I fucked him. I don't know how long it lasted. It seemed like there was so much going on, more than just the physical. A different kind of consciousness. It wasn't that it seemed to last forever; rather the element of time just wasn't part of it.

The waves of pleasure gradually subsided, but I felt like I was still experiencing something amazing, something that wasn't over yet.

Zig and I just looked at each other for the longest time. Me still on top of him.

"If you wait long enough," he finally said, "I might be able to go again, but, hell, twice in one night is good enough for me."

"Me, too," I said.

"Okay. Lift up slowly, then, and let my cock slip out."

Once we were disconnected, I turned around and sat down next to him on the bed. "That was amazing. Totally amazing."

"I know." He had some cum on his face. He pulled the bedspread up to wipe himself off. "There's no way to describe it to somebody," he said. "You have to experience it to know how incredible it can be."

"But, Zig, it was totally out of this world. My god, it was almost a religious experience. I think I actually left my body for a few seconds. Is that what happens to *you* when you get fucked, or was it just me?"

"Yeah, it's usually like that for me, too. It varies. Each time is a little different. But it can really be awesome, when everything is right."

"Now I know."

"Well," he said, while slowly pulling the condom off his dick, "It's definitely better when you can do it with someone you love, or someone you're hot for."

"Um, yeah, that would be you."

He smiled. "Yeah, that's what I mean. Same here. Hot for you, I mean."

"Sometimes I have to pinch myself," I said, "to make sure I'm not dreaming. Who would have ever believed the guy I'm hot for would be hot for me, too?"

"That's why we we're so lucky, Josh. I thank my lucky stars every night and every morning." He sighed, and leaned back on the bed.

"Uh, are you gonna toss that condom, or did you have something special planned for it?"

"Gonna toss it, you wise ass. Unless you wanna drink my cum out of it or something kinky like that." He got out of bed and walked toward the bathroom.

"I guess I'll pass on that," I told him. "I like it better when it's straight from the source."

He came back to bed, turning out the light on the way. "Well," he said, "that can be arranged."

We pulled the covers over us and scooted up against each other, him with his arm holding me close again. I don't know who fell asleep first. Me, I guess.

Chapter 27
GOOD BYE MR. PEABODY

Monday

ZIGGY WOKE UP before I did. I was still half-asleep when I heard him peeing, and then the toilet flushing. He came back and sat down on the bed next to me. I looked up at him and smiled. He said, "Hi."

"Good morning," I said. "What time is it?"

"Ten fifteen. I guess we better get going, huh?"

"Yeah. Did you shower yet?"

"Nah. I'm gonna get in there right now. Want to join me?"

"Sure!" I got up and followed him into the bathroom.

He got the temperature right, and we stepped into the tub. He stood under the water and drenched himself thoroughly, and then we switched places.

Zig lathered up his arms and chest, and then, like we do at home, he handed me the soap so I could wash his back. Then I moved down to his legs, and his feet.

He lifted each one so I could take my time and get all around and between his toes. Then I moved upward and gently lathered the soft globes of his ass, and the crevice in between them.

I reached underneath and stroked his balls. That woke him up a little. He turned around to give me better access. I lathered up his cock and he started getting hard, like I was.

"Look at this," he said. "You'd think this old pecker would be satisfied after last night, but he never does seem to get enough." We watched Ziggy's dick grow in length and rise up. "He came twice in one night, but he still wants more."

I laughed. "Greedy prick."

"No harm in asking for an extra helping, I guess."

"Are you ready to rinse off?"

We slipped past each other and I started lathering myself up.

"Here, give me the soap," he said. "I'll do that."

He took his time and lathered me up all over. When he got down to my hard dick I said, "While you're down there, tell the little guy he's had enough for one day."

"I think he already knows it. He's big, but he's not quite as stiff as he usually is."

"Keep playing with him like that and he might change his mind."

"We're two horny bastards, aren't we?" He grinned and let go of my dick, reaching underneath to soap up my balls and my ass. "Oops. Is your ass sore?"

"A little bit. But it's a good kind of sore."

"I hear you. Same here." He put the soap down and rinsed himself off. We switched places again, and while I rinsed, he stepped out of the tub.

We took our towels into the other room to dry off.

"Dude, all in all, I would say we've had an excellent weekend." He sat down on the bed to dry his feet.

"For sure."

"Most importantly, you got your novel back. Along with the rest of your stuff."

"Yeah, and I got to tell Fred face to face that he's out of my life."

Zig got some fresh briefs out of his pack and pulled them on. "Also," he said, "we both experienced something new, in the way of sex."

"I know I sure as hell did," I said. "Two things. Fucking, and getting fucked. Both were awesome. I couldn't tell you which I liked better."

"Yeah." He grinned. "Me neither. And I really didn't think I'd get to do either one of them again. Not in this life, not with my best buddy. But I did two new things, too."

"You're talking about me sucking your dick, right?" I put on my briefs.

"Right, that's one of them. I could really get accustomed to that, bro."

"Anytime you want, Zig, just say the word."

"And me sucking you, that was wild, too. I'd never done that before either. Never thought I would."

"That's something I'll never forget, Zig. Even if it doesn't happen again."

"Oh, it'll happen again, dude. Count on it."

Still wearing only our underwear, we started packing.

"So, Zig, how did you like your first convention?"

He laughed. "It was great. Seriously, Josh, we ought to do something like this again next year. Make it a tradition. Except next time, we'll go some place where you've never been to before."

"Sounds like a plan," I said.

"Like, maybe some place you've always dreamed of going to, but never thought you would. You got any places like that?"

"Aw, hell, Zig, any place is fine with me. I chose the place this time. You choose the next one."

"No way. I'm the one who got to visit a brand new place this time. The only thing special about Memphis for you is that you're leaving it. So, you get to choose next time."

"No, Zig, you ought to be the one to choose. You deserve it."

"Listen here, pal, *you* are gonna choose the next place. That's just the way it's gonna be," he said, grinning. "I'll *make* you do it, if I have to."

"You'll make me?"

"That's right." He nodded his head.

"And how the heck are you gonna do that?"

He put his pack down and turned toward me, smiling. "You really wanna know?"

"Yeah. How are you gonna make me do something like that?"

"I have my ways," he said, dramatically. He took a step closer, then another, still smiling, with his hands open and ready for mischief. I backed up a step or two, but then I was stopped by the bed. He said, "My methods start with . . . *tickle torture!*" And he grabbed me.

He started tickling me everywhere, pushing me onto the bed in the process. I was laughing like crazy. And he wouldn't stop! I couldn't quit laughing. "No, no, anything but tickling!" But he wouldn't stop, and I really didn't want him to. I tried my best to tickle him, too.

Pretty soon we were wrestling on the bed, wearing nothing but our underwear, each of us trying to find the most ticklish places on the other, moving our hands all over each other everywhere, both of us laughing so hard anybody who heard us would have thought we were crazy.

We were still laughing, even after we both had stiff boners. We moved our hands all over each other's squirming bodies, with constant feels of each other's hard dicks. Suddenly I realized I'd gone over the edge. "Zig," I gasped, "I'm gonna come! Oh my god!"

"Yeah, Josh! Yeah! Do it!" He was right on top of me, and quickly he pushed his hard cock down on mine and rubbed them together, up and down, and then he was coming, too. "Ahhhh! Ahh! Ahhhhhhh!"

We held ourselves together while our balls emptied and our hips jerked and our loads spurt out into the cotton fabric of our briefs. I don't think I'd ever before experienced an orgasm quite like that one. It was wonderful. Unexpected, unpremeditated ecstasy.

Minutes later we were still lying there, pressed together, as our heartbeats slowed down and we got our breath back.

"Wow."

We slowly let loose of each other, and lay side by side on the bed.

"Now you know my secret method of torture, dude."

"You haven't changed my mind, though," I said.

"You dare risk more of the same?"

"I'm pretty stubborn. Really, there's no telling how many more times you'll have to torture me like that before I give in."

"I'm stubborn, too," he said, grinning. "And I don't give up easy."

"God, I hope not."

Ziggy pulled out the band of his underwear and looked inside at the sticky mess. "Jesus. Good thing I still have another fresh pair left."

"Yeah, same here. I guess we better change and get going, huh?"

"Let's take another shower. We've got time for a quick one." We shed our sticky briefs, and it didn't take us long to soap up in the shower and rinse off.

Then we finished packing. When we were finally ready, we looked around the room. Ziggy said, "I guess that's it, then." We put on our backpacks and we left our room behind.

—

WE GOT A BIG SURPRISE when we reached the lobby. The elevator door opened onto a red carpet and there was a huge crowd of people, every last one of them looking directly at *us* with eager, smiling faces. Which instantly changed to disappointment, when they saw who we were. Or, rather, who we weren't.

I heard a kid say, "Them ain't no ducks, mamma."

We wormed our way to the front desk and joined the other people waiting in line to check out. I told Ziggy, "Man. It'll be good to get back to St. Louis."

"Yeah, no kidding," he said. "Hey, did I tell you what's coming up in a couple of weeks? The Balloon Race!"

"In St. Louis?"

"Yeah! In Forest Park."

"Hot-air balloons?"

"Yeah, dude."

"Oh, man, I love hot-air balloons!"

"Me, too. I want to ride in one someday."

"I tried following one in my car last year. I nearly wrecked."

"Josh, you nut, you can't follow a balloon in a car!"

"Yeah, I found that out. But it was so cool. They passed right above me. They were so close I could see their faces. I'd love to go up in one."

"We'll have to do that sometime," he said.

"Yeah, that would be fantastic."

"Another cool thing is, the night before the race, all the balloons are on the ground getting filled up with air, and they're all lit up inside. It's really beautiful. Eerie. I love it. And they're so huge."

"Man, I have to see that," I said.

"We will, don't worry. I never miss it."

We eventually got checked out and made our way down to the garage.

Ziggy rode shotgun. I checked the trunk to make sure all my stuff was still there—it was. Then I slid into the driver's seat and started the engine. "Here we go," I said.

"Is your novel still back there?"

"Yeah, safe and sound. Rescued from the clutches of the beastmaster. Now on its way to St. Louis to be completed."

"Excellent. Are you gonna let me read it?"

"Of course." We exited the gloomy garage into bright daylight. "Just don't expect it to be professional. After all, it's my first novel."

"Yeah, but it won't be your last. I'll bet it'll be super."

"Maybe. It still needs a lot of work." We drove west on Union Avenue.

"Have you written any other stuff before this?"

"Yeah, a few short stories. For school and stuff."

We drove through downtown Memphis, crossed over the Mid-America Mall, and then we turned north on Riverside Drive. Zig said, "There's Old Man River."

"Yep. Just keeps rolling along. Hey, remember that truck stop we saw on the way in? I was thinking we could eat breakfast there."

"Dude! Great idea."

"Unless you're not hungry yet."

"I'm definitely hungry."

"Okay. It might be our last chance to have a Southern breakfast. Have you ever eaten grits?"

"Nope. I've heard of them. What are they, pig intestines?"

I laughed. "No, you're thinking of chitterlings. That's completely different. Grits is like a hot cereal. It comes with your breakfast."

"Like oatmeal?"

"Kind of like that. It's made from ground corn. It's pretty standard in the South. So is iced tea, for that matter."

"People really like it, huh?"

"Oh, sure. Me included. You order it with your ham and eggs. Along with toast and jelly, or better yet, cornbread."

"Ham and eggs sounds excellent. And I'll try the grits, too. You know me, I'll try anything twice."

"That's what I like about you, Zig."

We followed the ramp onto I-40, which put us on the bridge over the Mississippi River. Zig looked out the window. "Josh, I think I see some guys on a raft down there. Hey! It's Huck Finn and Tom Sawyer!" He looked at me and grinned, and then he looked back out on the water.

"Did they come this far down the river?"

"If they did, they were braver than I am. That river is huge."

"Yeah, and the current is huge, too. It'll pull you down if you try to swim in it."

"I know Mark Twain came by here, though. More than once. He was a riverboat captain for a while."

"Really?"

"I wouldn't lie, bro."

"I guess it figures. As much as he was into the river and all."

"Hell, yes. He loved that river."

"Mark Twain was from Missouri, right?"

"Yeah. He grew up in Hannibal. We can drive up there and check it out sometime; it's not that far from St. Louis."

In another few minutes we were pulling into the truck stop. Ziggy said, "You've got me thinking about cornbread, now. I haven't had cornbread since I left the orphanage."

"I love cornbread."

"Me, too," he said.

"As a matter of fact, I've got my own recipe for cornbread." I parked the car in front of the building. "Learned it from watching an old lady I used to work with. She used to have us over for lunch."

"Damn, bro, you've been holding out on me. Fresh cornbread in the morning, before I go to work? That would be incredible."

"Well, say no more. You got it."

"Alright!"

We locked up the car and went inside the restaurant. The place was busy, but we were seated right away. Somebody came out of nowhere with water and silverware and disappeared again.

Then our waitress appeared with menus. "Mornin', boys," she said. "Coffee?" We both said yes. While she poured she said, "I don't think I've seen you two here before. Just passin' through?"

"Yeah," I said, "we're on our way back to St. Louis."

"Where you coming from?"

"Memphis. That's where I used to live, but not anymore."

She looked at Ziggy. "Are you from Memphis, too, darlin'?"

"No, not me. Born and raised in St. Louis. This was my first time here."

"Well," she said, "I hope you had a good time while you was here."

"Oh, I did. I definitely did."

"You boys ready to order?"

"I know what I want," he said. He looked at me.

"Sure, me, too. Go ahead, Zig."

"Ham and eggs, cornbread and grits. And some orange juice."

"Alright, hon. Two eggs, or three? And how do you want them?"

"Uh, three. Scrambled."

"Got it," she said. Then she looked at me. "How about you, hon?"

"I'll have the same, but make mine two eggs, over easy."

"Orange juice?"

"Yes, please."

"Back in a few," she said, smiling. "You need anything, holler."

We watched her walk away. Ziggy said, "I love truck stops. The waitresses are so friendly and down-to-earth."

"She's pretty, too," I said.

"Yeah, you're right, she is."

"You know what? She reminds me a little of Eleanor."

"Uh . . . okay, yeah, I can see that. Eleanor when she's in her thirties or forties, maybe."

"Yeah."

Ziggy sipped his coffee.

"You and Eleanor have anything planned for when you get back home?"

"Yeah, we were talking about getting together again this week, like on Thursday, maybe."

"Another hot date, huh?"

"You bet. Hey, I forgot to tell you what she said this Friday at work."

"Yeah?"

"She liked you, bro. She enjoyed talking with you. And she thought you were cute, too."

"Oh. Okay. Well, I liked her, too."

"That's not all. She thought it was kinky, fucking right there in front you while you were sleeping. Got her extra hot, she said, thinking you might wake up in the middle of everything."

"You didn't tell her I was already awake, did you?"

"Naw. But listen to this, dude! When we were talking about it? She said next time, we *should* wake you up."

"You mean, like, so I can leave and give you two some privacy?"

"No, dude, no! So you can *join* us."

"No way!"

"I'm not lying, that's what she was saying."

"Oh, hell, Zig. She was probably just kidding."

"Nope. She was serious. She was getting off on thinking about it, I could tell."

"Oh, jeez."

"Yeah, for real. Hey, and I think she knows what's up between you and me, too. And she likes it."

"You and her actually talked about all this?"

"Not about you and me. About the three of us. But she knows you're gay, or bi, and she knows we sleep together. In that bed. And, hell, she knows how much I like you."

"Okay, so . . . ."

Our conversation was interrupted when our waitress approached carrying a big tray. Zig said, "Alright! Food."

She set down everything we ordered in front of us. "Need anything else? Ketchup or hot sauce?"

I said, "No thanks, this is perfect."

Ziggy said, "I'm fine."

"Alright," she said, smiling. "Enjoy." She walked off, and we dug in like we were starving.

I don't know if it was my imagination or what, but that was the best breakfast I'd had in a long time. The food was great. Everything was perfect. And the best friend I'd ever had was sitting right there with me. I couldn't have asked for any better.

We polished off most of the meal, and then we sat there, sipping coffee.

Zig said, "I can't believe we only met ten days ago, Josh. I feel like I've known you for years."

"Yeah, same here. You read my mind."

"Remember what we said, a week ago? You'd live with me for a week, we'd try it out, and then we could call it off if it wasn't working out?"

"Right, I remember. I just couldn't believe you'd want somebody like me living with you."

"Somebody like you?"

"Yeah. A gay man. A very shy gay man, who thought you were about the sexiest thing on earth. I was so sure you wouldn't want me around after you figured out how horny I was for you."

He laughed. "I wasn't worried about that. I was afraid *you* wouldn't want to have anything to do with *me* anymore, once you realized I wasn't gonna be your gay husband."

"Oh, god, Zig. I knew that right from the beginning."

"You did?" He seemed surprised.

"Of course."

Now he almost seemed a little hurt. "Well, stranger things have happened, you know. Didn't you *want* me to be?"

"Well, of course I did. That would have been like an answer to my prayers. It's just that I didn't think it was even possible."

"Oh. Because you thought I was straight? Is that what you mean?"

"Yeah."

"But I told you I wasn't."

"I know. Maybe I thought you were just saying that to be nice. In any case, I couldn't picture you giving up being exactly who you are. Not for anybody."

"Well, you're right about that. I never will try to be anybody but myself. But that doesn't stop us from being, you know, partners."

"Really?"

"Really." He looked at me, grinning. "Partners."

"Cool!"

I don't know who was blushing more, him or me.

"Anyway," he said, "I didn't know what would happen. After all, we'd only just met. I figured we'd at least be friends, but beyond that, who knew? And sure, I knew you thought you could handle just being friends, but I didn't know if it would be enough for you."

"Being friends was what I wanted most of all, Zig. Real friends, I mean. Close friends. Lifelong friends. Being partners doesn't amount to much unless you can be friends, too."

"What I *did* know was that if you needed more than whatever I could give you, you'd end up looking for it somewhere else. That's just the way that works. And there wasn't anything I could do about it but hang in there and hope."

"Well," I said, "you don't have to worry anymore."

"No?"

"I've got everything I could want, Zig. Even if I could find the perfect 'gay husband' he wouldn't love me any more than you do."

Ziggy smiled.

"I mean it, Zig. You're all I need."

"Josh, you're the best partner a guy could ever ask for. I don't think anything is ever gonna come between us. I don't see how it could."

We sat there for a few more minutes, drinking our coffee. Our waitress brought our bill and topped off our coffee one more time.

We left a tip and headed out to the car. I tossed the keys to Ziggy as we walked.

"Zig," I said, "you really talked to Eleanor about the three of us having sex together?"

"She's the one who brought it up. But I think she knew I'd like the idea." He unlocked the car and we got in, him driving and me riding shotgun.

"She knew you'd like it? How's that?"

"I told her about the two guys and the girl in *Dhalgren*, sleeping and fucking together, and she said it sounded sweet. And sexy. Get this: she said she's always wanted to see two guys doing each other. And then she asked me if I would ever do something like that. I told her, yeah, I probably would, if the right opportunity came up."

"Was that before you two fucked, or after?"

"After. And then, later, when she was talking about getting your ass out of bed next time, she asked me again what I thought about it."

"What did you say?"

"I told her, hell yes, if that's what she wanted, and you were willing, then who was I to spoil the fun?" He grinned. "I told her, Sure! Listen, Josh, this is exactly what we hoped for, remember? Last week? We both wanted to do this, dude, and lo and behold. She wants it, too. I know she does."

"Yeah, I remember. Okay."

"Okay?"

"Yeah. Okay. I'm willing. I'll try it, Zig. I don't know if it'll work, but I'll try it."

"Dude!"

He held his palm up, and I slapped it with mine. He was grinning so hard he was almost laughing.

"I gotta warn you," I said, "I'm kind of nervous about it. I'm not used to being with a woman."

365

Josh Jango

"Now, see? I told you, you're one of the bravest guys I know. It takes balls to do something like that. Don't worry, dude, it'll work out okay. One way or another."

"I hope so."

"Sure it will. Listen; if nothing else, you can fuck me while I'm fucking her. Wouldn't that be awesome? You could do that, couldn't you?"

"Oh, yeah." I smiled. Then I pictured it, plain as day. "Hell yes. *That* would be incredible. My god, Zig! That would be like a dream. A fantasy come true."

"Yeah! Same here! I'd love it. Cool. Then it's settled. Damn, bro, this is gonna be so hot."

"It's gonna be wild," I said. "It's kind of scary, but I'm looking forward to it."

"Well, Thursday is a long way off. I'm sure you and I can figure out something to do in the meantime."

He started up the engine, and we headed for the highway.

Minutes later, we were tooling up Highway 55.

He sighed. "Five hours to St. Louis."

"Yeah, it's a long drive," I said. "Let me know when you get tired of driving. You can take a nap while I drive; I won't mind."

"I might take you up on that. Especially if I get drowsy."

"Sure. Listen, I appreciate you coming along with me on this trip."

"No problem, dude. I've enjoyed every minute of it. And we'll be back home before you know it. But you know what? I'm not in a hurry. I'm already right where I want to be. With my buddy." He looked at me and smiled.

"Same here, Zig. I like being with you."

We drove on in silence for a few minutes.

Then he said, "It's still early, you know. We could take that side trip we talked about before."

"Crowley's Ridge?"

366

"Yeah. You still want to? It sounded pretty interesting. And scenic. Hell, we might as well see something besides asphalt and concrete on the way back."

"Okay, sure. I'm definitely up for it if you are, Zig. You're the one who has to work tomorrow."

"I'll be okay, no problem. Crowley's Ridge it is, then. Cool, Josh. You be the navigator, alright?"

"Okay."

So, that's how it went. Sure, we had our destination in mind, but better than that, we had each other. We weren't in a big hurry to get where we were going because, really, we were perfectly happy right where we were.

Josh Jango grew up in the Maryland suburbs of Washington, D.C. He moved to Memphis, spent some time in St. Louis, and continued westward to the Pacific Northwest, where he still lives.

About the Northwest, Josh says, "It does rain often here, from fall to spring, but it's not the downpours people in other parts of the country get. It's a lighter rain, one that doesn't keep you inside.

"The winter nights are long, but Puget Sound, the North Cascades, the Olympics, the San Juan Islands—they're hard to beat. We have short days in winter, but they're more than balanced out by the long days in summer, when the sun does shine."

Josh Jango
jj@joshjango.com

CPSIA information can be obtained at www.ICGtesting.com
Printed in the USA
LVOW060157100713

342173LV00001B/71/P